Forest

and

Portrait of a Girl

Mary Williams lived in Cornwall since 1947, at one time writing a column for the *St Ives Times*. She always had an affinity with Celtic lands, especially as a lover of sea and mountains. She wrote and illustrated children's programmes for BBC Wales for six years and has subsequently concentrated on writing, interspersed with occasional art exhibitions. She wrote plays for theatre and television and historical fiction under the name of Marianne Harvey.

Forest Heritage
and
Portrait of a Girl

Mary Lewis

PAN BOOKS

Forest Heritage first published 1986 by William Kimber & Co Limited
Portrait of a Girl first published 1986 by William Kimber & Co Limited

This omnibus edition published 2002 by Pan Books
an imprint of Pan Macmillan Ltd
Pan Macmillan, 20 New Wharf Road, London N1 9RR
Basingstoke and Oxford
Associated companies throughout the world
www.panmacmillan.com

ISBN 1 330 40050 9

1 3 5 7 9 8 6 4 2

A CIP catalogue record for this book is available from the British Library.

Printed and bound in Great Britain by
Mackays of Chatham plc, Chatham, Kent

Forest Heritage

For friends
of long ago

Author's Note

Readers of this book who know the forest area of central England well may identify fictitious hamlets, towns and landmarks with real places. Bradgate Park exists. Other names and places have been altered and contrived to suit the story. All the characters are entirely fictitious.

M.W.

1

She couldn't rest. Watchful and tense, her nerves were stretched almost to breaking point. The ominous approach of thunder looming over the Burnwood hills didn't help. Storms there were violent, as though the ancient heart of the range was erupting to vengeful life again, after countless millions of centuries.

Emma Fairley, born in the vicinity and now in her twentieth year, had become sensitized to every mood of that particular north-western corner of Leyfordshire. Something of its lush sweetness, veiled mystery of its valleys and rugged freedom of rocky summits was in her very blood. A haunted area – one of volcanic origin, which at times could stir the imagination from dreamy peacefulness to a primitive awareness of a far-off bygone age. Apprehension then shuddered through Feyland Woods from the lonely tip of Hawkswycke Hill. The forest wilderness of larch, silver birch, and ancient oaks became a place of shadowed mystery; in the creeping mists of early summer and autumn, twisted branches of sloe and elder were grasping arms – the deep green tarns of Feyland, waiting graves for the unwary.

Emma, on that far off autumn evening, was keyed-up to face not only nature's elemental challenge, but a personal crisis which involved the whole of her future and that of her father, William Fairley –especially the latter. So much was at stake; on his meeting that day with Jonathan Bradley – business tycoon and owner of the new *Leyford Comet*, a daily newspaper intended to oust the well-established *Leyford Courier* – depended the survival of *The Charwood Echo*, her father's own newspaper and particular baby. Bradley was determined to acquire it by fair means or foul. He had the wealth and the power. Already the *Echo* had been hit by the new sensational publication *Comet* which was cheap in price, flashy perhaps, but sufficiently colourful to woo a considerable public!

At the expense of the *Echo*.

And this was only the beginning.

Ultimately?

Emma, who'd been her father's trusted confidante since her mother's death two years previously, shuddered to think. The only real hope, she well knew, was that Bradley might be induced to take up certain shares for a minimum of power on the *Echo*, leaving William and his co-director, Frank Page, in major control.

It was for this that Fairley had gone to Eastwood Hall that day for his meeting with Bradley. Although she hoped desperately for his success, she doubted it; and as the sullen sky darkened towards evening, bringing the first clap of thunder from the hills, her body stiffened, and despondency intensified.

William should have been back an hour – even two hours – ago. Had he called at the office in Charbrook before fortifying himself to bring news to her? Or could there have been an accident? The forest lanes were twisting and narrow, and could be dangerous to transport in the damp fading light, especially in the new-fangled motor car, which her father had insisted on purchasing for daily, quicker transport from home to his newspaper offices at Charbrook. The trap he'd used before was still retained in the stables at Oaklands, with their beloved mare, Lady, and so far the motor car, a Mercedes-Simplex, had not proved worth its cost. Emma herself had already learned to drive it. It could be fun, but not half so much enjoyment as a ride on Lady, and the mechanics worried her. It was the mechanics she feared every time her father set off at the wheel, making such a grinding noisy start to any journey.

She'd wanted him to go on horseback or take the trap that day. Eastwood Hall, as the crow flies, was only fifteen miles away, and on Lady he could have taken short cuts across the country. But William on this occasion had been determined to appear modern and as affluent as possible, setting out at the wheel wearing a sporting check cap and tweed jacket over knickerbockers of the same tone.

'The millionaire look,' he'd told his daughter whimsically, with a little tug of his carefully trimmed Imperial beard. 'I've met the man only twice, but he's a climber. The type always appreciative of style.'

'And money. Mean, I expect,' Emma had retorted shrewdly.

He'd smiled, trying to hide underlying anxiety.

'Don't be cynical, Emma, that's not your type.'

'What do you mean – *my* type?'

He flung her a shrewd glance.

'You know very well. Feminine. Womanly.'

'You sound so stuffy.'

'I am, my dear, over those I care about.'

This was true. But in Emma he recognised very well, there was a quality of excitement and adventure that put her apart– ahead of her time. Not traditionally a beauty, perhaps, but arresting and unpredictable, unlike her mother Claire, whose gentle serenity and fair classical features had provided always a refuge of peace when he needed assurance to steer him through financial and other problems of the *Echo*.

There was nothing really serene about Emma. Beneath her fine-boned, rather delicate exterior, was a quick-silver mind, forever darting this way and that to meet any challenge that might arise. The innocence of her widely-set luminous grey eyes was belied by a provocative tilted mouth in a heart-shaped face; her pert nose was slightly upturned, denoting what he termed a rare capacity for delving and digging into other people's affairs. The small determined chin had a cleft in it, and her head was proudly set on a slender neck.

Yes. Emma was indeed quite a force in his life.

Claire's death in giving birth to Rosalind, a younger daughter, following a dangerous lapse of fifteen years had eventually turned William's affections all the more fiercely on his elder child. He hadn't particularly wanted the new baby, and when she was proved to be backward and incapable of learning to speak or communicate properly, loss of Claire had turned to an inner resentment that could only be overcome by a quiet, almost fanatical determination to keep the family newspaper going – run in the traditional decent way first established by his grandfather.

The *Echo* and Emma.

Being a dedicated clear-sighted man, he recognised that a certain modernisation might be necessary. With moderate expenditure this could be done. But the policy of fair comment must remain. The *Echo* had never been a political publication, and he was determined at this time, following the ending of the Boer War, that he'd restrain it from being influenced too obviously by right or left. All the same – the tempo of life was changing. Liberalism was gaining steadily, and he had a shrewd idea that in a couple of years' time Campbell Bannerman might emerge as Prime Minister. The voice of radicalism was stirring among the minds of the people. Women, too, were showing a desire to play a part in the country's affairs other than mere domesticity. He couldn't see they'd have much success. But the future was chancy and unknowable. Meanwhile let the feminine appeal of the *Echo* have full play. Emma had been a great asset during the past twelve months contributing a weekly column dealing with dress, cooking, and social and gardening observations that for a time had sent the circulation up – a swing of the pendulum that might have continued, but for the sudden appearance on the scene of the *Leyford Comet*. Racy, witty, a little cheap and Americanised, it had gained immediate response.

And Bradley was certainly not going to allow it to decline.

William did not fear for the future of the *Weekly Echo* but the daily publication was a different matter. It was the *Daily* he feared for.

And so did Emma.

Why could life be so unfair and complicated, she wondered, as she wandered time after time to the gate of their garden overlooking the forest? Why must that rich stranger from up country have arrived at such a crucial time to upset things? Why had he to fling his wealth about so vulgarly, just to destroy the even tempo of the *Echo*'s progress, with his power? Her own column week by week had been gathering the interest of new readers. In time (though she hadn't yet broached the suggestion to William) she might even be a regular contributor to the *Daily*. Women journalists were few and far between. But there was no reason on earth why she shouldn't be among the first. Fame didn't particularly appeal to her. But proving herself did – proving that she could be an important factor in helping retain the standards of the respected newspaper established by her forbears so many years ago.

Oh dear! *Why* was he so late?

The housekeeper who'd been with them through and since her mother's illness came down the path, saying irritably, 'Can't you come in now? It's getting damp. And you with nothing on your shoulders.'

Emma smoothed a strand of russet hair from her brow.

'I'm not cold. I like the air.'

'Well, I don't. And it's already spitting with rain. You can't do any good standing about getting wet.'

Emma sighed. 'No. That's true. Very well – go along, Mrs Cox. I'll be there in a moment.'

She was turning to follow the receding figure when the familiar rattling sound of an engine chugged in fits and starts from a bend in the lane. Emma felt a surge of relief, and ignoring the heavy spatter of increasing rain, ran towards the blurred shape of the approaching vehicle. The gates below the house leading to the shed where the car was kept were already open. William turned in awkwardly.

'You're so *late*,' Emma exclaimed. 'I was wondering if you'd overturned into a ditch or something.'

Clambering out, William answered, pulling his cap off and wiping his forehead free of damp, 'You should control that imagination of yours better. There was a puncture about five miles back and I had to change a wheel.'

'Oh. Poor you. What a nuisance. Are you wet?'

'Yes.'

'And what happened? Did he – did you have any success with Bradley?'

'I'll tell you when we get into the house,' William said rather abruptly. '*Please*, my dear. I've had a long day.'

Emma's heart sank. Obviously he had nothing good to report.

Her deductions were correct.

When William had changed and gone into his study for a drink before the meal, he said heavily, 'It's no good, Emma. He won't co-operate. The *Echo* – yes. He wants it, and will invest a tidy sum provided he has an overall majority in the shareholdings. This would mean giving him complete power to alter the character of the paper in any way he chose – so—' he shrugged and gave an expressive gesture of the hands, 'it's no go.'

'But – didn't you *explain* properly? Couldn't he see that although his type of publication might draw in a new public, the present readers like it as it is—'

'Of course I did. But he's a hard thinker, looking ahead to the future. He even has a plan eventually to contain the whole lot – the *Courier*, *Echo* and *Comet* into one paper – *The Midlander*. Oh, he's got his head screwed on pretty firmly, but for once he won't get his way that easily. I'll spike his guns, by God.'

Emma shook her head slowly. How could he? When their annual income was only just sufficient to keep them and the *Echo*, out of debt? 'What plan have you?' she asked. 'If you haven't the money—'

'I *could* have,' he interrupted. 'There's a way. You won't like it. But – I've decided.'

The strained lines of his face – the hard look of hopeless defiance and determination about his mouth and eyes frightened her.

'Tell me.'

'I can sell Oaklands,' he stated, not looking at her. 'It's a unique place and would fetch a good sum. Whoever bought it *might* allow us to remain on a rental basis. It's the only way, Emma.'

'You can't *mean* it. *Oaklands!* It's been in the family for – for *generations*. My great-grandfather designed it. It's a heritage – a duty; an obligation.'

'The *Echo* comes first.'

'But why? *Why?*'

'Tradition – it's the only decent newspaper Charbook's ever had. And there are other places where we could live.'

Emma could feel her nails biting into the palms of both hands.

'Not like this,' she said fiercely. 'There's nowhere in Burnwood to compare. You've said yourself it's unique. Where else could anyone find a house built from the rock face? It's listed in books – a feature of the forest—' Emotion half choked her, bringing the flood of words to a halt.

'I know, my dear. I know—' he slumped forward suddenly, with his head in his hands. When he glanced up again the strange greyness of his face temporarily drove all other thoughts but anxiety from her mind. 'Are you all right, father?' she queried sharply.

He forced a smile. 'I will be. Pour me another brandy, child. Oh—' A hand suddenly went to the left side of his chest.

'What is it? What's the matter?'

'Nothing. A touch of indigestion. I get it occasionally when I'm tired. It'll soon pass.'

'Then you must see a doctor,' she said firmly. 'You've been working too hard for too long. And all this worry—'

He waved a hand in negation. 'I want no doctor. Fussy old pessimists all of them. Now, Emma—' He got up, straightened himself, thumped his chest, and with forced energy said, 'There's life in the old dog yet. So stop worrying. Things will work out. Just drop the talking now, and in the morning, maybe we'll both feel differently about things. The pendulum could swing either way.'

But Emma knew that business pendulums didn't swing that easily in her father's direction. Especially concerning the *Echo*.

For a moment she almost hated the paper. Hated it for sapping her father's energy, and endangering what were the roots of their very existence – Oaklands.

That evening, when William had retired to bed, she went downstairs and out into the steamy autumn night.

The thunder had cleared, leaving a freshness of the air, with a pale watery moon filtering through the haze of dying cloud.

Like sentinels of the past, the massed trees of the forest stood dimly shadowed beyond the garden. On one side the tip of Hawkshill was visible momentarily, then faded again. The distant glimmer of Marten Pool shone silver for a second beyond Feyland. An owl called softly from the woods. All was mystery – a threadwork of winding lanes and small lost hamlets. Yet she knew them, had walked them all, climbed every tumpy rock-tipped hill, since childhood. It was her birthright. They couldn't lose it now – neither she nor her father. Somehow both Oaklands and the *Echo* had to be saved.

But how?

Had her father been sufficiently tactful during the meeting with Bradley? When reason failed had he thrown his cards too bluntly on the table? William Fairley, though inherently and by practice diplomatic, could be amazingly defiant when pressed. Perhaps in the end when he'd found the other man so unco-operative he'd let his temper get the better of him and he'd issued a challenge he could not possibly win.

There was, then, only one course left. Without telling her father she'd herself visit Eastwood Hall that Thursday, which was publishing day for the *Echo*, knowing William would be fully occupied at Charbrook and would not miss her. She'd ride Lady cross-country, and deal with the hateful stranger in her own way. What that way would be, she hadn't a clue. Until they met face to face, she'd no way of assessing their instinctive reactions to each other. But she'd dress carefully and suitably, and while keeping her business senses alert, would make the most of her feminine attributes.

When the day arrived, luckily it was fine. She set off early before the silver mist had lifted from the short turf and undergrowth. Many of the trees were bare now of foliage, but a few leaves still hung from lean black branches, diamonded with glittering cobwebbed filaments of dew. Much of the forest appeared half-dream, half-reality. As Lady sniffed the air appreciatively passing the old Priory of Uldene, Emma recalled days of her childhood when she'd imagined herself a lost princess in a fairy tale. So much of her was bound up in this area of ancient territory – so evocative a sense of history and days gone by. The lake surrounded by the grouped tall trees, Hawkwycke Hill with its rugged peak and broken prehistoric circle, the deep green slate pits lurking mysteriously between shadowed trunks of oak and birch, and in springtime the acres of bluebells more softly bright than a cloudless summer sky. The ruined priory itself, and the monastery Coldale way where the silent brotherhood worked and had their being. This was enchanted country. Hers and William's. In its way a lost land, because few tourists came there unless it was to visit Bradgate Park and the ruin which had once been the home of Lady Jane Grey, the ill-fated nine-day queen – oh she'd never let Bradley force them away. Never, *never*.

Bringing herself harshly back to reality again she'd kicked Lady to a swift canter, and moments later Uldene had faded into a spectral shape soon completely lost in the shadows of the woods.

She avoided the outskirts of Charbrook, taking footpaths and bridle ways to the opposite side of the county where foxhunting was the chief sport on which the rich spent winter months during the season.

Here the land was more flat and verdant, dotted at intervals with picturesque villages and small market towns. To Emma the landscape, though pleasant, was ordinary. And any appreciation she had for it was marred by her hatred of a sport she considered as barbaric as cock-fighting. Although William, of a necessity, had to show impartiality towards differing sections of the Leyfordshire community, Emma, except for rare social occasions, had kept herself aloof from the snob set – her private term.

Now she had to face that however distasteful it was, she must play the odious 'pretend game' of being appreciative of the wealth, social status, and power of the formidable Bradleys.

Not that the rich Northerner could yet have been genuinely accepted by the county aristocracy. He had lived only two years at Eastwood, and had amassed his fortune from *Trade*. But in time a wily millionaire of his calibre might wheedle a baronetcy from the 'powers-that-be' – provided he paid enough. This would eventually woo him an avowed place in the Burnwood circle.

The whole situation filled Emma with contempt. But the day was fresh and invigorating; the keen sweet wind – redolent with the scents of damp earth, tumbled leaves and blackberries – brought a challenging glow to her cheeks. She rode side-saddle, wearing an olive green velvet habit, with her gleaming dark hair pinned up in a chignon under her tilted boat-shaped hat. A stray curl brushed one cheek, giving extra allure to her feminine elegance. It would have been more fun riding astride, as she frequently did, through the forest, but of course quite outrageous on this occasion. As the silver sun rose higher in the pale sky she felt resentful for a brief moment or two that she hadn't been free to look for mushrooms instead of gallivanting across lush parklands to Eastwood. A quantity of silvered umbrella shaped pale heads had appeared in Starvecrow field on the edge of the Woods when she passed. Tomorrow they would probably be gone, and her father liked them fried on toast. But there was no point in brooding. She kicked Lady to a smart gallop, and reached Eastwood shortly before eleven, wondering how she'd be greeted, and if Bradley's wife ruled there, as some chatelaine or queen.

Well, she'd soon find out.

She dismounted and was about to lead Lady by the bridle down a drive at the side of the mansion, when a man, obviously a groom, wearing gaiters and a leather jerkin over a woollen jersey, appeared from the opposite direction. He was a burly figure, shrewd-eyed, with a crop of ginger hair above a broad pink face. 'Can I help you, ma'am?' he asked. 'Wanting anyone, are you?'

'Mr Bradley,' Emma answered. 'Perhaps you can inform a servant of my arrival.'

'I can take thy horse for a while, but the master isn't in. Is he expecting you?'

The direct question took her aback, but only for a moment.

'He may well be,' she answered coolly. 'My name is Fairley, Miss Emma Fairley. My father was here yesterday.'

'Oh. You mean the newspaper man?'

She nodded.

'Well ma'am – miss, he isn't in. I'm sorry but there it is. Went off ridin' 'bout an hour ago. Whether it's worth thee waitin' a bit—' His Yorkshire voice broke off as a younger, taller man walked smartly through a gate in the drive leading from a field. He must have been well over six feet, and as he drew near Emma felt a stab of surprise – almost shock – seeing how very handsome he was – fair hair licked to brightest gold in the early sunlight, fine-featured, and with eyes so blue they startled her. He was attired fashionably in fawn twill knee breeches and a smartly cut velvet jacket. A silk scarf was knotted loosely, in the manner of a cravat, at his neck. He had a winning smile, slightly tilted to one side, which added to his charm. Obviously a lady-killer, Emma decided after the first impact was over, and one used to getting his way.

She drew herself up an inch or two higher whilst formal introductions were made. Then, when her business was made clear, he said, still with his magnetic gaze fixed upon her, 'Father's out, as you've just heard – unfortunate for you perhaps, but damned lucky for me.'

She flushed faintly.

'I ought to have made an appointment, of course, but—'

'Nonsense. I'm glad you didn't. He shouldn't be long. You can wait, I suppose? This business you have with him is important?'

She nodded decisively. 'Very.'

'Concerning the local rags. Am I right?'

'Yes. Mr – Bradley. You did say "father", didn't you?'

He grinned. 'Oh indisputably. I'm Arthur – the one-and-only. Except for Jessie, of course, my sister. But I'm afraid my rich tycoon of a sire *does* rather concentrate on the importance of having a male heir – however unsatisfactory a one I may be.'

Unable to decide how much of the statement was made in jest, how much in truth, Emma ignored it, and after a brief look round an ornamental garden at the side of the house, which included a pool overhung by willows and a Japanese maple, they went inside.

The interior was as massive as the outward facade of the Hall suggested; the corridors were wide, the rooms large with high encrusted ceilings. The furnishing was rich but unimaginative, comprising a good deal of red plush, gilt, and crystal. Ornate glass-faced clocks, probably French, ticked from marble mantel shelves and alcoves. The drapes were heavy, and the air was over-heated. From a reception room on the left into which Emma was shown, a conservatory led through a glass door to a path bordering a shrubbery. The smell of ferns was strong and heady. Emma had an urge to rush round pushing every possible window open; she felt smothered, sensing that she had come on a fool's errand. Anyone living in such a cloying overpowering atmosphere of ostentatious wealth could not possibly appreciate the wild sweet freshness of Burnwood, or her mission to save Oaklands. The rigidity of her pose, her air of bewildered distaste, didn't escape the young man's attention.

'A bit stuffy,' he commented, 'I agree. But my mother likes warmth, and the pater's not here often. Sit down, though. The chairs are comfortable. Like a drink?'

Emma took the nearest chair which was divided into three back to back, forming a circular design. The seats were low, of rich maroon shaded velvet, and surprisingly comfortable.

'No thank you,' she said primly, refusing the Madeira.

His fine arched brows shot up. 'No? Ah. I forgot. You're here on business.' The mocking note had returned to his voice.

Emma stiffened again.

'Do you mind telling me – I mean, have you any idea how long Mr Bradley will be?'

He shook his head. 'No, I'm afraid not. But I hope it will be a considerable time. Long enough for us to get to know each other.' Her grey eyes met his squarely, and once more she was impressed by their brilliance. He really was astonishingly good-looking; charming too, in his way, although something about him, a secret assessing quality, mildly intimidated her. Quite obviously he found her fascinating. At odd moments his gaze slid appreciatively over the slender lines in her figure, then back to the provocative features under the perky boat-shaped hat, and dark rich gleam of russet hair. A beauty, begad, he was thinking, and quite a character – one well worthy of adding to his retinue of female admirers. Could one have fun with her? Possibly. But it might be a dangerous game, and if Arthur Bradley considered any woman worth dallying with, he expected his own brand of response. Pride alone demanded it. Could he win this one? After a few speculative moments he decided to take up the challenge, and by the time Jonathan Bradley appeared an hour later, he'd succeeded in at least warming her interest.

Jonathan was shorter in height than his son – broader, of burly build, with a square high-coloured face, and determined chin. His eyes were shrewd and fiery below thick brows, lit by sparks of vitality suggesting a hot temper and considerable physical strength. Beneath his well-cultivated voice the north country accent was still strong. In age Emma judged him to be somewhere in the late forties. He was, actually, forty-seven, and Arthur, his son, twenty-five.

Introductions were cordial but brief. During his first few words, following Arthur's departure, Emma sensed she had no more chance than her father of success in her mission, although his appraising glance at the exotic spirited young creature confronting him was appreciative, even a little warm.

'I'm glad to meet you, young lady,' he said, 'relax now and be at ease. Maybe a Madeira would help, eh?' He fetched a decanter and glasses from the cupboard.

'Oh no, thank you,' Emma protested, 'your son *did* ask me, but—'

'Arthur?' Jonathan laughed shortly. 'This is *my* house, Miss Fairley, and if I've a mind for you and me to get down to business in a cosy way, I don't think you'll object. Come now.' He was pouring the wine. 'You've already mentioned business, so shall we start?' As she mutely accepted the glass, he added, 'I can guess what it's about; of course. The *Echo*.'

'Yes.' Her voice and manner were defiant. She had meant to be so tactful and subtle in her approach, but his bluntness, air of command and obvious assumption that he held all the cards before any discussion was begun, stirred her to reckless honesty.

'I don't expect concessions from you,' she said, 'I haven't come to beg or plead with you—'

'Good.'

'I just think if you could see another's – my father's – point of view, without prejudice,' she continued quickly, 'it could be to the advantage of both.'

He regarded her thoughtfully during a short pause, while a tinge of amusement touched his hard mouth. 'And what makes you think that?'

Her colour deepened to a becoming rose. 'Because I've lived all my life near Charbrook. I've grown up knowing of the newspaper's problems, I know what the public want. It's a – well, in a way, a *family* publication. People look for personal tit-bits and gossip as well as more general news. It could have a wider circulation of course, but with money invested this could be easy. Don't you *see*, Mr Bradley, to change its character could be a great mistake? Almost a disaster—' Her voice had changed, softened. The luminous brilliance of her grey eyes affected him in a way he was quite unprepared for.

'Miss Fairley,' he said more quietly, 'I understand your reasons for coming here. You're echoing very much what your father said. *He* knows, as you must, that I'm quite willing to sink a good deal into what is after all – a very minor provincial daily. But it must be on my terms, girl. I'm a businessman. D'you think for one moment I made all the brass I've got from old-fashioned dreams?'

'I—'

He raised a hand. 'No. Hear me out. I can understand your loyalty to Fairley. He's been a good man in his day, but—'

'What do you mean *in his day*? My father's still an active, intelligent editor. And popular—'

'Maybe, maybe. But he needs help, new ideas to face the challenge of the future. And I can give it. Another thing – you could brighten your own little ladies' columns up a bit – get around more, mix with the right set. Your job's safe if you go along with me. You c'n write. I could make you into something – something better than a scribbler on birds and trees. Now think about it. I've given a time limit to all of us. Use it and get facts square.'

'Meaning give you the over-all power? Fifty-one per cent of the shares in the *Echo*?'

'That's right. And believe me you'll find it'll not be half as bad as you think. Fairley will still hold the reins in the office. I shan't interfere except to expand a bit when necessary.'

'But it won't be *his* paper.' Her manner was mutinous.

'Not entirely. He can't afford it, can he?'

She winced, then got up and walking towards the door, said coldly, 'I can see I've wasted my time.'

'Not at all. Best for all of us to have things straight. We'll be meeting again, I've no doubt.'

She was passing through into the hall when a plump yellow-haired woman appeared from a room on the opposite side. She was made up rather badly, with over-rouged cheeks, and was attired fussily in pink; her smile was forced, a little tremulous. A distinct odour of perfume and alcohol tinged the air as she approached.

'Oh!' she gasped, with one small plump beringed hand at her breast, 'I'm sorry, I really am. I didn't know thee had company, Jonathan.' She teetered slightly on her feet.

Bradley frowned. 'My wife, Miss Fairley,' he said.

'Really? I'm delighted.' The broad face smiled, and Emma realised in one quick moment that when young she must have been pretty. Her eyes, half hidden now by puffed lids, gleamed china-blue. Obviously the son, Arthur, had inherited her colouring and one-time good looks. She was trying hard – painfully almost – to be welcoming and lady-like. Her feigned mimicry of the well-bred county accent was not only farcical, but pathetic. It was quite clear to Emma that she was in awe and a little frightened of her husband who was doubtless a bully in his domestic as well as business life.

Emma smiled encouragingly. 'I'm pleased to meet you,' she said.

'You must come over for tea one day,' the older woman said, more naturally. 'Our cook, Mrs Maggs, is a dab hand at cream cakes. Well – in Yorkshire we pride ourselves on our cooking, thee knows – *you* know,' she corrected herself quickly.

'Now, Amelia,' Bradley interrupted warningly, looking for an instant quite furious, 'Miss Fairley didn't come for a lecture on cookery.'

His wife's brief spell of vitality died out of her suddenly, like air from a pricked balloon.

'No, no, Jonathan. Well then – bye bye, luv – Miss Fairley.'

She turned, and with a rustle of silks disappeared like an immense ruffled pouter pigeon into the rosy glow of what was obviously a drawing room.

Minutes later Emma had extricated herself from the unsuccessful encounter with Jonathan, and was cantering on Lady down the drive to the lane. She had just turned the corner when another rider, Arthur Bradley, approached her at a smart pace. He reined alongside, showing fine teeth in a wide smile. His eyes caught the glint of sun, emphasising their blue brilliance. Her heart quickened, not entirely pleasurably; although it was clear to her he had been waiting for her, which was flattering, there was something – an indefinable quality about him – intimidating – that she found disturbing. Yet his manners were impeccable. He attempted no undue familiarity, expressing only the pleasure it had given him to meet her and the hope that she would pay another visit soon or allow him to call on her at Oaklands.

Her reply was ambiguous.

'Perhaps. But at the moment I think it's better to keep things on a business footing. It's my father, you see—' The lovely eyes raised to his were suddenly alight with warmth and emotion. 'For his sake I need desperately to get the paper's affairs settled.'

'I understand. And if there's anything I can do,' he assured her, 'let me know. Promise?'

She smiled. 'Very well, of course – and thank you.'

As she kicked Lady to a canter she didn't notice the sudden, almost imperceptible tightening of the lips, or the cold ice-blue quality of his stare. Blue – yes, but remote and chilling as the shadows of snow peaks in brilliant sunshine.

He wanted her; to have her under his control as neatly scheduled as the butterflies, pinned in his special collection under glass. A proud young madam, he thought, but he'd have and tame her.

That same evening he surprised his father by announcing calmly, 'The girl you had here – Miss Fairley—'

'Yes?'

'I want to marry her.'

'You – *what*?' Like a bullet from a gun the last word shattered the air.

'I want her for my wife.'

'Then you can damn well want,' Jonathan said roughly. 'When you take a wife it'll be someone of class, and with a good dowry. I'm having no cheeky little nobody in the Bradley family. It wasn't for that you went to Public School and Oxford, so just get that idea out of your head once and for all, lad. It won't be long before the right girl appears, to eat out of your hand when she knows how lucky she is.'

'This one will,' Arthur stated calmly, 'and she's the one I want.'

Eventually Bradley was forced to the conclusion that his heir – a stubborn and odd character, if ever there was one – really meant it.

Well if that was the case, he could do worse, he supposed. He didn't need a woman with cash, and marrying Emma might solve a number of problems.

So the matter was left in abeyance, and as it happened something occurred the following week which tragically solved everything.

2

'I'm drawing out,' Frank Page said bleakly, averting his eyes from William's face as he delivered the blunt statement. 'It's no good, Fairley. Unless we go in with Bradley we've had it. Profit from the *Echo*'s practically nil; in a few months we'll be in debt. Without compromising, that is.'

He raised his eyes slowly to William's face which in those few seconds had paled to ashen grey.

'You mean you want to sell? Every one of them? Every share?'

'I'm afraid so. I'm damned sorry. It's a blow to me, as much to you. Well – you've more to lose – I know that. But facts have to be faced. Without the capital we haven't a chance in a million of winning against Bradley. I'm willing to go along with him – up to a certain point, if you are. But then you're not, obviously.' He paused before adding, 'I take it there's nothing in your kitty to draw on? No personal assets to risk?'

'My property,' William answered honestly. 'That's about all. Oaklands.'

Page looked away again. 'In that case – why don't you call it a day? The *Courier* wants good men – you could get in there any time; I was chatting to Martin Drake the other day, and he as good as told me you'd not be wanting a decent post if you decided to fold up. A good salary, no worries, and the challenge of joining forces against Bradley and his *Comet*. You're respected in the newspaper world, and whatever that jumped-up northern Johnny thinks, his newfangled notions aren't going to affect the *Courier*.'

'Are you sure?'

'To no great extent anyway. He may have power, but it's the new kind. The Wilton family's got generations of traditions and trust – *and* solid currency behind it. If they have to, they'll fight, and win. Mark my words, in another ten years the *Comet* will be wiped out, and Bradley's new-fangled idea of *The Midlander* will be a second-rate memory, no more. You have a future there, old man, if you want it. And maybe a place on the Board. Mind you, I don't *know* but it's well worth following up. I do happen to have eyes and ears in my head, and Tom Wilton's always been a friend of mine.'

'Yes.'

There was a long embarrassed pause until Fairley said dully, 'You mean it, about selling?'

'Sorry. Yes. Unless you care to give Bradley what he wants.'

With sudden force, William, whose temper was generally controlled, jumped up from his chair, knocking the glass of whisky over, so it spilled in a stream across the office table, staining papers of copy waiting to be edited.

'Then go to hell with it,' he said. 'I thought you were a friend, Page; I never thought that in a bad patch you would just let me down. But that's just what you're doing, isn't it? *Isn't* it?'

All colour had left his face again. The knuckles of his clenched fist were very white on the crumpled papers.

'Here, steady on, old man,' Page remonstrated. 'You're not well. Sit down.'

'No thanks. I'm all right.' William reached for his coat from a peg, stiffened and remarked coldly, 'The meeting's over, I think. I'll lock up now, and call it a day. Ready?'

'If you're sure—'

'I'm sure. I know where I stand now. Alone – except for Emma.'

'I was thinking about her as well,' Page said as they went to the door. 'And the other one – Rosalind.'

'They'll be all right. My family's my own concern,' William stated decisively. 'They'll not starve.'

But what *would* they do?

As he drove erratically five minutes later from Charbrook towards the forest road leading to Oaklands, his mind, though whirling, felt empty and dead of ideas or the capacity to make plans.

On impulse, before reaching his home, he made a detour of three miles or so, taking a winding route past Feyland Woods towards Bradgate. Before he faced Emma he felt an urgent necessity to bring his emotions under control so they could discuss the issue together – assess a problem that at the moment appeared not only *un*discussable, but unsolvable.

He must have peace for a brief time, allow the rugged slopes and ancient history of the park to encompass him with the tranquillity and atmosphere of things by-gone. From his earliest youth Bradgate had been his sanctuary during periods of doubt and trouble – soothing over-sensitive nerves to rest and awareness of the illusion of Time.

On countless mornings he'd wandered there to hear birdsong as the first streaks of dawn lit the sky. At the knobbly roots of the ancient stunted oaks, where the ill-fated Lady Jane Grey had wandered before the proclamation of being proclaimed queen centuries ago, countless rabbits now had their burrows. At the time of her death, it was said, the trees also had been lopped. But sad events had not robbed the park of its beauty. The stream still trickled gently down the valley past the tumbled ruin; bracken grew thick at the base of the hills – fresh green in the spring, changing with autumn to russet, gold and brown. Deer moved gracefully and unmolested by thickets and up the slopes. Even in rutting time the great antlered stags showed no animosity. It was as though, in solitary hours, Nature's gentle hand had erased all conflict of past history, leaving only a dreaming quiet that had generally eased William's problems and reinforced his inherent energy.

That day, though, seemed a little different. He was more tired than usual; after parking the car and climbing the tricky ladder-like entrance to the domain, he walked only a few hundred yards or so, before the old nagging pain across the chest returned, forcing him to rest. He found a granite boulder, seated himself on it, and gradually the discomfiture passed. How quiet it was – not a breath of wind – only the damp sweet odours of earth and air, and occasional rustle of undergrowth where a rabbit's white tail showed momentarily then disappeared. On his left the shape of 'Old John' depicted by a miniature folly, a castle-like ruin, rose golden-brown, showing darker patches of bog, against the fading sky. He lit his pipe, smiling slightly, as he noted a landmark of a twisted dead tree halfway up the slope; it had been there ever since he was a boy. Emma called it the 'Witch', and as a child had woven fairy tales about it. 'P'raps she put a spell on poor Lady Jane,' his young daughter had suggested once when she was a little girl, 'and that's why she had her head cut off. Oh Papa – d'you think she's a ghost now, like the people say? D'you think she's happy?'

William had squeezed the small hand comfortingly.

'Wherever she is, she's all right,' he'd said. 'And you mustn't think of ghosts and witches. Look at that baby fawn over there—'

Diverted, Emma's attention had been drawn to the graceful animal shapes moving by a cluster of silver birch. But a curious sadness had stirred William's thoughts, and it was the same this evening, as he stared reflectively over the landscape. It wasn't difficult, in the fitful light, to imagine the frail ethereal shape of a young girl drifting soundlessly from her ruined home down the curving drive; perhaps, indeed, something of her spirit did remain there, imbuing the area with mystery and regret.

He pulled himself together with a jerk.

What was the matter with him? Soliloquising with himself like any sentimental woman. He must be leaving and return to Oaklands. Even at his home there was business for him to tackle, and Rosalind would be wanting to say goodnight before she went to bed.

As usual, his heart lurched when he thought of her. So beautiful to look at – fair like her mother, but incapable of a normal existence. He'd tried to love her, but it was difficult; his emotions were too complicated, and the thought of her future a constant worry. He sighed, tapped the bowl of his pipe on the granite, and forced the uncharacteristic vague mood from him.

The *Echo*!

Oaklands? – What to do?

His name was good at the bank, of course; he could get a mortgage on his old home. There *were* ways of keeping the *Echo* and its *Weekly* going. But ultimate survival was a different matter. And William had a fierce objection to shouldering loans which eventually might force him to bankruptcy. He had a little over two weeks left to solve the challenge, and with Bradley as opponent, he couldn't see a hope of winning.

Oh well! be damned to them! he'd soldier on to the last, and after that? Who could tell? How could any human being in the world really count on what the next week or even day would bring? Life was chancy anyway. Emma would have her mother's small capital when he went, and he had sufficient faith in his daughter's stubborn courage to know she'd somehow manage to look after Rosalind. So there was no point in worrying; none at all.

He got up, feeling suddenly better and released from strain. As he turned to take the steep path past a fenced spinney to the summit of the hill, he drew a deep breath. A rush of vigour stirred his blood. He lifted his chin to the sky, noted a last streak of dying daylight catch the tip of the folly; then – unpredictably, the earth seemed to sway beneath his feet. All round him trees, rocks, and the startled movements of a deer wheeled into a vortex of whirling darkness. There was a return of the cutting pain across his chest. He clutched his tweed jacket along the heart, gulped vainly for more air. It was no use.

As he tottered and fell a bird rose, squawking from the bracken nearby, and took flight towards the stretch of moor where the twisted form of the blackened old tree stood stark against its boggy pool.

Hours later a gamekeeper found him. He was lying on his back with his lifeless eyes staring at the sky.

When Emma heard, her first wild grief gradually turned to a cold deadly determination for vindication and resolve to avenge her father's death.

By whatever means, she swore to herself, the *Echo* and Oaklands would both survive. Somehow she'd beat the hateful

Bradleys and see that Fairley traditions were upheld, and endured. Never, *never* would the northern upstart get his fists on Fairley territory.

Just how her end would be achieved she couldn't visualise. Neither, at that point, did she try. Her emotions were too poignantly involved, finding, after the first tormented reactions, relief only in solitude and tears.

3

Both Jonathan Bradley and his son, Arthur, made a point of attending William's funeral which took place at the nearest church standing only half a mile from Oaklands in the centre of a small hamlet, Woodley.

Arthur's brilliant cold eyes strayed briefly once or twice to Emma's rigid form. She was wearing grey, knowing that William would have fiercely resented his daughter appearing as some dreary crow dressed all in black. She appeared tearless and completely composed during the sad ceremony; no trace of emotion belied her inner distress. She could have been an ice-maiden, Arthur thought, noting the set, exquisite profile. Even the rich fire of her hair was hidden under her hat. Her remoteness did not disturb him in the least. He didn't care for emotional over-wrought women; their vapours, moods, vagaries, everlasting demands and cravings for attention filled him with distaste. At one period, when he was young, he recalled how his mother had fretted and yearned for romance and affection from his father, and the ironic way in which he'd thwarted her. She'd been pretty then, in a rather plump, over-luscious way, which had been, Arthur discovered, the only reason for the union – well, at the base of it.

Jonathan had been foolish enough to fall for her charms when she worked at his father's mill – an affair ending in an unwanted pregnancy leading to a completely unsuitable marriage. Still, Amelia had done her best to fill the dutiful role of wife to the ambitious Jonathan. What she wanted he'd seen that she had, in reason, and in return she'd learned to keep out of the way when he wished, occupying his bed only when he crudely demanded it, which had become almost nil these days. For appearances' sake she appeared with him when necessary at social functions, and had learned to keep her Yorkshire brogue at a low ebb. She had been a good mother, and ran the house efficiently. Any brief 'affairs' he indulged in in no way interfered with her status, and were very rare. She might be hurt on such occasions, but she didn't show it. Her husband had her firmly trained in what was expected of her. She feared his temper, though it was always cold, and he'd never harmed or touched her. As a woman she had become a mere useful necessity in the running of Eastwood, and her son further despised her as much as his father did.

He knew he would never despise Emma; that was one reason why he was determined to possess her, to have her, like some exotic yet cool jewel in his possession, for gazing at, touching, and exhibiting when it suited him.

A week following William's funeral, he rode over to Oaklands to pay, presumably, a social visit, and one expressing his concern and sympathy.

Emma happened to be in the garden when he arrived, cutting a few last autumn leaves for the house. She was wearing green, of a dark olive shade that suited the rusty gleam of her molten hair. Her form was outlined elegantly against the winter foliage, her face pale and rather ethereal in the transient light.

Arthur doffed his bowler and swung himself from his saddle. With his hand at the gelding's bridle, he gave a little bow, came towards her, and said, 'Miss Fairley – Emma – I do hope I'm not precipitate in making a call to ask how you are? And of course once again offer my sympathy.' He came towards her, his hand extended. Reluctantly she let him take hers.

'I'm as well as can be expected, Mr Bradley,' she told him

with no trace of a smile. 'My father's death is a great loss. But—' her voice quivered slightly, '—his work has to go on.'

'You mean the *Echo*?'

She sighed. A spray of copper beech dropped from her grasp and fell to the damp earth. He bent down quickly, retrieved it and handed it to her.

'Of course.' Her voice was low, determined, and bitter. 'It's the only thing I can do for him now. Carry on.'

She glanced away. He touched her shoulder lightly. 'Emma—'

'*Please!* Don't.' With a sharp motion she jerked herself free.

'Very well. But there's something I'd like to talk over with you – if you can spare the time.'

She whirled round, facing him with rising colour, and a widening of her clear grey eyes. The brilliant blue flame of his own never faltered. 'I don't see what there *can* be between you and me to discuss,' she said coldly. 'The position of the *Echo* with you and Mr Bradley has already been made brutally clear. It's what killed my father.'

'A very cruel thing to say. But you naturally feel resentment. However, you're wrong, quite wrong about *one* thing. It wasn't my wish not to support William Fairley on his own terms. On the contrary I'd have been co-operative. It's been quite an achievement of his keeping the paper's character alive for so many years. I respect his will and determination, although if I'd been a member of the board I might have suggested a few alterations.'

Her astonishment was so great she didn't speak for some seconds, then she asked quietly, 'What, Mr Bradley?'

'Arthur,' he corrected her.

'Arthur then.'

'May we go into the house?' he suggested. 'Or would you rather walk a short way down the lane? That would be better perhaps, as I have Kismet, and it will cause less gossip than in the house.' He smiled faintly and patted his mount's neck.

She hesitated, but only for a moment. 'Very well. Although I really don't see the point. Any suggestion you had concerning the *Echo* is useless now. And I can't understand—'

'Of course you can't,' he interrupted. 'But my idea would have involved you very much, Emma. My father doesn't agree with me I know, but I believe the feminine viewpoint of your own column; and the space could be considerably extended. You have the will, the style, and knowledge of the locality that could make a talking point of the publication given a fair chance.'

She was astounded.

'If you could have got *your* father to see it when mine was alive, things might have worked out,' she reminded him. 'It seems so futile even talking about it now, when – when – oh I really do think we're wasting time, don't you?'

'No.' The short word silenced her. 'Come, please – just a few yards. I beg of you—'

'*You* beg me – how *very* ridiculous!'

All the same, with the hem of her skirt lifted in one hand, she found herself a moment or two later following him through the gate down the lane.

By a gate in a recess leading to a farm, he stopped, took her arm gently, and together, with the gelding on one side they moved towards the field.

She didn't glance at him. Her face was turned resolutely on the rutted track and dip in pasture land on either side before it dipped towards the woods, but his blue eyes were keen and covertly on her intriguing profile, the gentle swelling of breasts above the tiny waist, and proud, inaccessible lift of chin.

'Emma,' he said, after a short pause.

'Yes?'

'I want to marry you.'

'*Marry?*' Her mind for a moment was stupefied.

'I said so.'

She frowned, staring at him in astonishment. 'But you don't know me. We've hardly met. We've nothing in common. Nothing at all.'

'Haven't we?'

'Well—' Quick as lightning, after the first hesitation her thoughts leaped ahead, forming some kind of wild out-of-the-world plan that suddenly made cold clear sense. If he meant it – if his reckless proposal was genuine – couldn't it provide the answer to her problem? She didn't love him, no; but he was madly attractive and handsome, and if she was clever could be brought round probably with giving the support financially, for the *Echo*'s survival. In time possibly, her emotions would respond naturally to his. Many women made success of unions founded on convenience, and this one wouldn't be *entirely* that. From their first meeting she'd been fascinated, against her will by the enigmatic spectacular son of the greedy tycoon from the North. Arthur himself was cultured and educated, with sensitivity under his elegant facade which she had not suspected. He was entranced by her, he must be, or he would not have made this very reckless declaration.

'Well, Emma?' she heard him saying in slightly husky undertones.

Her cheeks, when she faced him, were faintly tinged with pink, holding the quality of sunlight shining through the texture of some delicate pale shell.

'I'll have to think,' she said quietly, though her heart was beating fiercely.

'Why?'

Staring into the ice-blue pools of his cold brilliant eyes, reason died into sudden abandoned acceptance. What had she to lose after all? Only gain could come from such a marriage, and vindication of her father's death – proof of his faith in her. Little by little she'd learn how to wind Arthur Bradley round her little finger. Then the *Echo* and Oaklands would be safe.

'Very well,' she managed to say in controlled even tones. 'All right, I'll marry you, Arthur.'

He attempted to kiss her, but she pushed him away.

'Later,' she said. 'You must give me the chance to face what I'm doing, and—'

'Yes?'

'There are things we have to discuss, aren't there? About the paper I mean, and—'

He was slightly chagrined, but did his best not to show it. 'Just as you say, business woman,' he remarked, with an odd smile on his mouth belying inward irritation. Let her plot and plan in any way she liked, he thought, about her ineffectual little newspaper rag. What she wanted there, she could have, in reason. And he, in his turn, would take what he wanted of her when the time came.

So the matter was settled.

In January of the following year Emma Fairley and Arthur Bradley were married. The *Echo*, reimbursed, flourished under the Fairley name still, and Oaklands was made permanently financially secure as Emma's private property to be used and lived in whenever she liked, for holiday periods or when Arthur was away on business.

Those were her conditions.

His proved to be very different.

*

Their bridal night was spent at a luxurious Bournemouth hotel prior to the couple's fortnight's visit to the Continent the next day. Their special suite was magnificent, commanding a wide view of the coast, the furnishings lavish, even exotic, subtly contrived to induce an air of romance. Deep rose-pink velvet, crystal and gold, with all the embellishments of a mediaeval fairy tale provided an extravagant background for the new young wife. The hotel service, if obsequious, was flatteringly conscious of the desire for complete privacy and immediate attention at the tinkle of a bell. Royalty could not have wished for more. They retired early. There were two separate dressing-rooms. Emma at last emerged from hers, clad in a cream satin gown patterned with small hand-embroidered roses. No princess could have looked lovelier. Lace swathed her shoulders, and bordered her negligée. Her hair was loose, and in the light from the crystal wall chandeliers glimmered burnished rich auburn. The lines of her breasts and thighs were clearly definable under the soft material – the cream of her skin only a shade warmer than the cream of her attire.

A glance in the cheval mirror had told her she looked lovely, so she had no lack of confidence when she pushed the door open and stepped on to the thick pile of the pink bedroom carpet.

She was a virgin, having no knowledge of sex at all, except what her instincts told her, and her innate innocence somehow gave her additional fey beauty. Her trousseau had cost her more than she could afford as Emma Fairley, but at Aden's – Feyland's most select costumiers – she had bowed to the wisdom of Madam Elana who ran the establishment, and who had cunningly implied the great importance of a young wife's first intimate impact on a husband.

Besides – a *Bradley*! A future Bradley had no need to spare expense.

The knowledge, to Emma, had had a heady, slightly unreal feeling about it. But now she was thankful for her extravagance, and when she saw Arthur in his blue robe come towards her, doubly so. Her heart quickened, not with love, but expectancy. She knew the rules of marriage, through having dealt with and reviewed so much literature on behalf of the *Echo*. One must appear willing, but not too obviously so. The woman *always* must be pursued. Shyness, a slight trepidation was acceptable, and in this case would be genuine. Already, though, her body, from tension, was relaxing. Arthur and she might not be exactly soul-mates, but oh! how very handsome he was.

She waited, with a queer mixture of alternating emotions in her, for him to take her in his arms. His blue eyes were so very bright, so concentrated, and – desirous was it? Or merely admiring?

She said nothing. Beneath the satin the quick thudding of her heart was visible. He took a swift stride towards her, drew her hand to his lips, then bent down and kissed the hem of her gown.

When he got up his face was blazing, not with affection, but with pride of possession.

'You are beautiful,' he said, 'gorgeous, my Emma.'

She stared as he touched her waist and let his fingers slide up her arm gently. 'You are more perfect even than my shepherdess – my exquisite little French piece—' he broke off. His smile was a little twisted, his eyes colder than coldest glass. 'So when you see my collection – my china masterpiece—'

She pulled her hand away abruptly, drawing her lacy wrap closer against her neck.

'What do you mean? Your collection? Aren't you going to – aren't we—?'

'Man and wife, darling? Of course we are. We shall sleep together, dance – ride; anything you wish to do and have you can – in reason. But—' he paused.

'Yes?' Her voice was suddenly shrill, unnatural.

He sighed.

'I do hope you're not going to be old-fashioned, Emma. Old-fashioned people are so deadly *boring*.' He moved away to the dressing table, took a cigarette from a gold case and lit it, theatrically. Then he turned and blew a smoke ring into the air.

'Do you understand, darling?'

'No. I don't think so.'

'Ah. A pity.'

She lifted her head challengingly. 'What is it you're trying to imply, Arthur?'

The smile on his thin lips died. 'Do I have to spell it out? Are you so naive?'

'I think I am, in certain ways,' she told him bluntly. 'And I think you *do* have to spell it out. I suppose—' her voice faltered slightly, '—I suppose the gist of it is that you *don't* really want me at all – physically. You're not interested in *me*, in having children, and a normal married life. You're just—'

'Well? Go on.' His command was steel cold, like his eyes.

She paused before daring to say at last, 'Abnormal in some way.'

He gave a little bow. 'Thank you. You've hit it, exactly. But in one way you're wrong. I do want you, Emma, because I prize beauty, with the same zest as I detest the conventional dull-as-ditchwater business of a man and woman doomed to the rules and regulations – of cohabitation. A messy business, I always think. All right for morons and the animals, but for an exquisite creature such as you – somehow offensive. Don't mistake me—' He touched her cheek lightly for a second, then pressed his lips against her shoulder fleetingly, 'You are lovely – you smell sweet and are quite bewitching, I love, adore you very much, in my own fashion. I'm sure we shall get along very well. You will be the elegant Mrs Arthur Bradley and the envy of society—'

'I shall also be owner of Oaklands, and of the *Echo*,' she cut in tartly and very clearly, pulling herself away firmly, dazed and humiliated still, but clinging to the one card she still held.

'Partly, I think.'

'More than partly,' she flashed, 'I shall hold you to it, and you'll see there's no interference from your father or I'll make you the laughing stock and scorn of Leyfordshire—'

'In which case—' he smiled cruelly, 'I might have to take a switch to your back, madam. I'm no weakling, you know.'

She shivered. He put an arm round her and said more gently, 'Emma, I didn't want a scene, and there's no reason, really, for such melodrama. I may be an odd – unique – kind of fellow, but you're not – sexually in love with me, are you? In marrying me there was quite a good deal of self-interest on your part. Then why can't you allow me the pleasure of admiring you and making you the pride of the county? – And mine?'

She shook her head slowly, and went to the bed flinging herself face down on the satin spread. He went over to the window, parted the curtain and stared out to sea. A moon was rising, lighting the quivering surface of the water to rippling gold.

'It's going to be fine in the morning,' she heard him saying matter-of-factly. 'Come to bed, Emma. You must feel rested for the Channel crossing.'

Presently she moved reluctantly and obeyed. They lay side by side; the bed was warm, the firelight played intriguingly round walls and ceiling. But without realising it her teeth chattered. She was cold. From time to time during the night she felt him touch her, and she moved involuntarily closer. There was no response. He gave a grunt, and turned away. For all he cared, she realised bitterly, she could have been a piece of marble, or stone.

And for that, she hated him.

In the morning early tea and breakfast were brought up to them. There was a knowing glint in the waitress's eye when she'd drawn the curtains and deposited the trays on the side tables.

'I hope you were comfortable, madam? Sir?' she said, envisaging amorous events of a rich honeymoon.

'Very comfortable, thank you,' Emma heard herself replying coolly.

'Good. If there is anything more you require—'

'There's nothing,' Arthur answered shortly.

The maid withdrew discreetly.

Arthur smiled down at his wife.

'You look very young,' he said, 'with your hair loose like that. Today perhaps you should wear a chignon under the sailor hat, the one in your box. There may be a breeze over the Channel.'

A sailor hat? It seemed somehow ludicrous. Recalling the fresh cold winds rustling through the woods of Burnwood on her face and through her tumbled locks, Emma felt a wild, almost overwhelming, longing to be back at her old home in the forest – free to wade barefoot through the cool streams, or wander up Hawkshill to the iron age settlement where she'd played and pretended as a child. But those days were gone now. She was Mrs Arthur Bradley. What irony. Thank heaven she hadn't really been in love with him. Supposing though – before the question really formulated in her mind, she smothered it resolutely. No one could have everything. A husband's natural love might be denied her, but Oaklands and the paper remained. She had saved them, for her father's sake. Did he guess? Was there such a thing, really, as immortality?

Oh yes, she told herself resolutely, there must be, somehow, in some way, however frail the spark might be. In no other way, now, could her life be justified.

The day went as planned, and the fortnight following they visited Holland, Italy, France, and Switzerland. Arthur proved himself a courteous companion, attentive in public, in private mostly remote and reflective. Once she was tempted to say bitterly, 'You must show me your shepherdess when we return to Eastwood, Arthur. Your prize-piece. I hope I'll be able to bear the comparison.'

After a brief glance at her tight expression he answered coldly, 'There's no need to be nasty, Emma, or jealous. You must learn to prize beauty for its own sake. As I do.'

She had a quick impulse to slap his face, but restrained herself.

'I already do, or I should not have married you, should I?'

'For your *Echo* you would,' he told her. 'Your conscience is a very flexible one, darling.'

She didn't reply. Such arguments after all were not only ineffectual, but cheap.

So time passed, a period during which most of the sights and grand landscapes of Europe were absorbed.

On their eventual return to Leyfordshire, the newly married couple found a reception prepared for them having all the trappings and extravaganza considered suitable for the emotional culmination of young love's union.

There was a warily expectant gleam in Jonathan's eyes, expressing the hope a son might have been conceived. Obviously, Emma thought, he had very little practical knowledge of his own son's potentials, or lack of them.

And she considered how she was going to bear it.

4

Following the return of his son and young wife to Eastwood from the Continent, Jonathan found himself appreciating Emma more than he would have believed possible before their marriage. In her he soon recognised qualities that mildly astonished him. She was a stronger character than he'd imagined, more remote and dignified than was usual in one so young. He'd been aware, of course, of her natural impetuosity, at their first meeting, when she'd challenged him and fought for the *Echo* on her father's behalf. But this Emma Fairley – or rather Emma Bradley – was quite different. She had slipped into the role of mistress of the establishment as easily as slipping her slim hand into a glove. Of course, Amelia, as his wife, still reigned, nominally. She had indeed over-dressed herself absurdly to emphasise the fact. But to his discerning eye, she too was impressed, refraining for a time, even, from her secret tippling, in order to keep a clear head with the capacity to put the young madam in her place.

Jonathan was amused. The domestic situation brought diversion to the more dull moments when he was confined to the house. Jessie, on the other hand, his daughter, saw nothing to smile about. She was a rather plain girl who had unfortunately inherited the weaker points in appearance of both parents, having Jonathan's square, rather hard, jaw and solid build, and her mother's indifferent features without her pretty colouring.

She was just seventeen, and was going as a boarder to a select finishing school in France the following year.

Emma tried to be nice to her, but it was difficult. Jessie simply had no charm, and from the beginning had been jealous of her brother's wife. The fact tickled Arthur's cruel sense of humour.

'Don't give up, old girl,' he said playfully once. 'Dress yourself up more, get a new riding habit and swing a leg before Roly Plummer. Got his eye on you already. Some men are like that – have a penchant for a nice plump rump—' he laughed mockingly.

'You beast. You vulgar creature,' Jessie cried. 'If Papa heard you talk like that – or that simpering wife of yours—'

'Ah, but he won't, neither will she,' he said meaningfully. 'You know quite well, sister dear, I'm an adept at suiting my conversation to my company.'

Jessie snorted and turned away.

'I don't know how she sticks you.'

'She's a highly intelligent woman,' he replied adroitly, thinking at the same time, too intelligent by half sometimes for his own comfort. The way, after only a week, she'd wormed her way into his father's interest, baffled him. She'd already, with his – Arthur's help – got what she wanted – a percentage of decisive shareholdings in the *Echo*, and a whole page on the weekly edition for her women's feature. That old house of rock was hers for all time, and Rosalind, her half-baked young sister, was safely settled there with the housekeeper and a young woman acting as a governess-cum-nurse, who to his mind was a damned unnecessary expense. She should have been put in a home. But he had never suggested it, knowing Emma might have left him on the spot.

Emma! Frequently he smiled wrily when thinking of her. At the moment she seemed to have the upper hand of him. But she'd better not flaunt the fact too openly. He had a smart little buggy-whip in his cupboard which he'd certainly use if she went too far. She was his possession. He'd *bought* her. She knew it, he knew it, and so did his father. But as days passed and Emma's presence grew more potent at Eastwood he came to the conclusion they should move to a separate establishment. There was a Dower House on the estate which could be made exotically comfortable, where their private life would not be too pried on by his astute father.

Emma received the suggestion agreeably. 'Yes,' she said, 'I

quite agree. We *should* have our own house. Another thing, Arthur—'

'Yes?'

Her grey eyes were straight and clear on his face when she said, 'I think I should spend one day and two nights a week at Oaklands.'

He stared at her, his blue eyes narrowed and cold. 'For heaven's sake why? If you expect me to traipse every week to that godforsaken hole—'

'I don't expect you to, Arthur.' Her voice was cold and clipped. 'I happen to have a sister who needs a little of my company. Whereas you – you don't *really* need me at all, do you? – Except to stare at me and touch for your odious little abnormal games, and to show me off to your friends?'

Her voice had a sneer in it.

He flushed.

'You're my wife, madam.'

'*Am* I?' The implication of the question did not escape him.

'*Yes*. And you will do as I say.'

'I've had no chance not to, have I? Not yet,' she remarked icily. 'Whatever you've wanted of me – mostly – you've taken, however unpleasant or warped it might be—'

'Warped? Did you say *warped*?' His face had gone very red.

'Most people would think so.'

'Most people? If—'

She waved a hand contemptuously. 'Oh, don't worry, Arthur. I don't intend to reveal your secret. On the other hand, I expect you to respect my wish concerning Oaklands.'

Eventually, Arthur grudgingly agreed.

Jonathan was mildly perturbed.

'*Every* weekend seems rather demanding,' he said to his son, not adding, 'the thin end of the wedge,' which he thought.

'It needn't work out that way,' Arthur remarked casually, 'in any case I've planned something else for the future.'

'Oh? *What?*'

Arthur explained his idea for the Dower House, and although Jonathan didn't at first agree, he was brought round to accepting it, when his son pointed out how very eccentric Amelia was becoming since his marriage. 'You can't have two women queening it in a house,' he said. 'Mama's not only showing off and making herself look a fool to the servants and everyone else, she's getting irritable and snappy. And that evening when the Darnleys came, she looked *ludicrous*! Absolutely. Her make-up! Well, for heaven's sake! You must've noticed. Her accent too – she never stopped talking, and it was all just to be one up on Emma. You've got to stop that, Pater, or your chances of getting into Parliament for the next term are nil.'

Jonathan was shocked by the observation, but when he'd had time to think things over, he saw that his son was right. It was essential he became accepted by the 'gentry' – the aristocratic horsey crowd and their associates who had mansions and hunting boxes dotted about that particular area of Leyfordshire. In time, with tact, an acceptable display of wealth, and generous donations to various charities and good causes he felt certain he could do it, provided Amelia was kept on a low key. As a potential future MP he needed support from the local party. The constituency had always been conservative. Alfred Carstairs, who was now an old man and not fit had already declared openly that at the next election he would not put up again, therefore it was up to Jonathan to create an acceptable public image before the crucial date arrived. The new radical lot would have no chance at all. A liberal just *might* – providing he had a sufficiently impressive background and sponsorship. That mustn't happen. Neither, Jonathan decided, must any other conservative be allowed to put himself against him, provided he could be dissuaded. Studying the position from every angle, Bradley came to the conclusion that the odds of his own support were encouragingly favourable, especially with the backing of his press – the Leyford *Comet*, and with luck and a little co-operation from Emma, the Charbrook *Echo*. The latter, he knew, might be tricky, but provided he was clever enough to win his daughter-in-law's approval, quite possible. She was now one of the Bradley family, and would recognise with her characteristic honesty that this fact alone demanded a certain duty from her; loyalty. He'd have to be careful not to tread on her toes, as they put it, where her late father was concerned. She would have extra space if she wanted it for her highfalutin' feminine and women's talk. He wouldn't cross her at any forthcoming Board Meetings. It would be a battle of wits – subtle, very subtle. But in the end he'd have what mattered of the *Echo*'s circulation in his pocket. Yes, he must cultivate Emma; with the combined papers working on his behalf, his influence would stretch across the county. He had also managed to be on friendly terms with Lord Wendle, which should be helpful.

He'd show them.

The old fashioned *Courier* wouldn't have a chance. Strictly non-political, over-rational when anything sensational rocked society, its influence would sink to a minimum. In time the *Midlander* would emerge, as he'd envisaged during the past two years. He, Jonathan Bradley, would be the one Newspaper Magnate of the area.

And after that? Wild dreams surged through his mind of a knighthood and eventually possible elevation to the peerage.

If only Amelia was equal to raising herself. If only he'd had more sense and less honour than to marry her following the disastrous affair of his youth. If it hadn't been for the warm night, honeysuckle scent, and the luscious white body half bursting from her bodice, she'd have been back at the Mill the next day, without a further thought from him. It was only by chance the thing had happened anyway. There'd been a dance and get-together at the village hall, celebrating his grandfather's birthday. Most of the employees had been there and in a weak moment afterwards, Jonathan had walked her home.

Home! A humble, but spotless cottage under the moor, where Amelia had been rigorously brought up by strict hard-working parents. At the time he'd been lusty and hot with life, and before taking her safely inside, the sweetness and scent of her had been too much for him. He'd had her in the bracken, with her hair spilled pale gold in the moonlight, her white thighs ripe and ready for his ravishing. He seldom remembered the occasion now, and when he did he was mildly ashamed – until he also thought of Arthur, who'd been the fruit of their union. A fine specimen he was now – to look at. But what was he *really* like, inside? Jonathan had never quite been able to fathom his son's mind or ways. He'd gone to public school and Oxford, yet still remained an enigma – sarcastic often, a little contemptuous of himself and others, though why, heaven alone knew. He had everything he wanted, with a clever, spectacular wife now, into the bargain.

Was the marriage all right?

At times Jonathan wondered. There seemed something – ambiguous, for want of a better word – between them, that he couldn't fathom. It could be purely imagination, of course; he hoped so, because Emma's co-operation could mean a good deal to him in the future.

Therefore he made no objection when, a month after the wedding, Emma left Eastwood for a weekend at Oaklands.

She drove herself in the Mercedes, which she'd insisted on retaining at her new home. Arthur had been mildly amused, Jonathan irritated, to see her sitting at the wheel of such a ramshackle uncertain thing. In fact, he didn't approve of any woman in control of transport unless it was a lady-like little governess cart pulled by a well-trained amiable mare on social visits or for charitable means in the district. However, he held his tongue, thinking, why the hell couldn't the girl have used his own chauffeur and the Rolls?

Certainly the journey would have been more comfortable and easier. Twice the engine of William's car stopped, and three miles down a lane from Feyland, Emma had to get the help of a farm labourer to crank it up and get it moving again.

It was midday when she reached Oaklands. Rosalind, wearing a pale blue woollen coat – Emma's first present to her following her marriage – was taken into the garden by the governess as the familiar grinding of the car sounded from the turn down the slope. That day in late February was chilly, but in sheltered spots close to the hedgerows aconites and the pale gold buds of celandines were already starring the lush pulsing brown earth. Certain trees of the forest were feathered by pale green, and as she walked down the path Emma's perceptive ears caught the faint tremor of bird song. Her heart lifted. How lovely to be back.

'Hullo, Rosalind,' she said, holding out her arms. The child didn't run to her in welcome. There was no response at all. She simply stood, looking incredibly lovely like some small princess from a fairy tale, fair hair loose about her shoulders, enormous violet eyes raised to Emma in curious, acquiescent bewilderment.

Emma knelt down and drew her close. The child allowed herself to be kissed, then pulled back, hiding her face against Helen Carly – the governess's – grey woollen dress.

Emma's heart smote her. Had she been recognised? Perhaps – vaguely; but it was impossible to know. Her young sister as always clung only to things of habit, and brief contacts that were forgotten the next moment, as she was diverted by the sight of a bird fluttering from a branch, or a leaf borne on the wind. There was no continuity of her mind. She would never grow up, and would always be a responsibility to others. No wonder William had despaired frequently and found it hard not to resent the presence of one so helpless who'd cost his beloved wife her life.

Emma released her sister, thinking philosophically, 'She hasn't missed me. I'm not really important to her any more.'

The thought faintly hurt at first, until she reminded herself that the fact would enable her to slip over on Sunday and see Will Clarke, acting business manager of the *Echo*. The News Editor had resigned recently, following Page's withdrawal, and Clarke at the moment had journalistic responsibilities on his own shoulders. There would have to be a new editor of the publication. A board meeting had already been arranged for the following week. Bradley would attend of course; he'd informed Emma he had a very likely man for the job in view. 'Go ahead, but pliable to reasonable suggestions,' he'd told Emma. 'I think we should consider his application carefully.'

'Of course,' Emma had agreed, although she was already

prepared to stand out against her father-in-law if there was the slightest sign of collusion or pre-united policy. She herself had insisted on being informed of any likely candidates hoping for the post. One interested her – a Welshman, Evan Lloyd, with wide experience as a reporter on a daily paper in Monmouthshire. He was not only a journalist, but a writer who'd had one book, a fiery commentary on current society, published, as well as a number of vigorously individual poems in minor but cultural magazines and periodicals. A man obviously of ideas and imagination, she'd thought, who might serve the *Echo* well. A naturalist too. She liked that. His Celtic ancestry – apart from a Welsh father, his mother had been Cornish – titillated the inherent romantic streak beneath her practical facade. Although they'd never met, his image was familiar to her from occasional press photographs. A fine head, with a wide brow, fly-away rebellious brown hair, a whimsical firm mouth above a cleft chin, and that hint of defiance in stance and expression suggesting he might very well eventually become a force in some sphere or the other.

Lively. Alert. A man after her father's own heart. Or *was* he? Was it more a matter of feminine instinct? She would never have admitted the latter possibility – even to herself. After all, when the crucial point arose personalities must be secondary to capacity and suitability for the post. She must be fair, and would be. So with her mind firmly set in this direction, she set off for Will Clarke's home, which was only four miles out of Feyland, near Marten Pool. If he chanced to be at Charbrook working overtime at the offices, she'd make a day of it, have a snack at the Windmill Inn on the way, and then take the main road to the town.

She did not have to. As she circled to the far side of the lake and reached the drive leading to the house, she spotted Clarke, fishing, only a hundred yards or so away. She stopped the car, jumped out, and hurried towards him. He was a short, quiet-looking middle-aged man, wearing tweeds and deerstalker.

'My dear Emma,' he said, getting up and coming to greet her. 'How nice to see you.'

She grinned mischievously, shaking her mane of russet hair back, looking suddenly very young indeed.

'Hullo, Mr Clarke. I hope I've not disturbed your fishing.'

He smiled, shaking his head. 'None to disturb. Not biting today. It's no matter though. A pleasure to see you, my dear. Had a meal yet? If not, you must come in and join us. Lucy would be pleased.'

'No thank you, ' she replied, 'really. I'm not hungry. This visit's a sort of spur-of-the-moment idea. The day was fine, and I wanted to see Rosalind. You too. And Oaklands of course.'

'*Ah*. Yes. You must miss it – or don't you? Being a young married lady now.'

'Oh yes I miss it,' she answered, more solemnly than he'd expected. '*Terribly*.'

'Hm!' He looked non-committal. 'Everything going well in your aristocratic establishment, I hope?'

She forced a bright smile. 'Naturally. I wish I was nearer Charbrook though. There's so much to discuss, and with the editor leaving, on top of Mr Page, you must be finding a lot to do.'

'True enough. But we get through. Burley's a great help, and Craddock, the sports editor's a good all-rounder, always willing to lend a hand. I took today off though, as you see. Nothing like a rod and line to ease the mind.' He paused before adding, 'You want to see me about something, don't you, Emma? What is it? The application?'

'Yes,' she said, and after learning from him that he'd as yet formulated no definite opinion concerning the possibility of names submitted for the *Echo*'s new editorship, managed subtly nevertheless to draw that of Evan Lloyd into the conversation.

Clarke was silent for a moment, then he remarked, 'A fiery customer – sharp-witted and clever, with a way about him. Call it charm, if you like. Oh yes, he's got that. Have you met him?'

'No.'

'Hm. I *have*, and was impressed. But for the *Echo*? I'm not sure, Emma; and I'm not at all certain he's the man your father would have backed. The *Echo*'s got to pull its socks up – we all know that. But to *jerk* them! – personally I'm not at all sure William would have approved.'

'No. Neither am I.'

Clarke's eyebrows shot up. 'Well then – why Lloyd?'

Emma's grey eyes lighted on Will's face directly. Something in their very clear straight gaze mildly disconcerted him.

'On most things my father and I thought alike,' she said after a short pause, 'but he was perhaps a little too conservative – even too honourable.' Again the mischievous look on the intriguing impish mouth. 'I think we have to explore new channels, Mr Clarke, and liven things up a bit.'

Will shrugged. 'You have the casting vote, to put it bluntly. And no doubt if you're determined for us to take on Lloyd, you'll succeed, in the end. You may be right at that. I wouldn't fight you.'

'Well, we shall see. After all, I'm only *one* voice. And truly I *will* be fair.'

He knew she'd try to be, but he also sensed that she'd get her way.

Which she did.

5

Jonathan's first reaction when Emma insisted on Evan Lloyd's name being put forward on the short list for the *Echo*, was to object. His instinct was to be wary of Celtic races, especially the Welsh, and the fellow already had a name for being a rebel and far too eager to seize the news of any project he was interested in. True, originality, and a go-ahead character were desirable for the paper's future, and incidentally his, Jonathan's. But not *too* original. He was surprised at Emma's stubborn support for

Lloyd. Arthur, he considered, had made a mistake in persuading him to allow her so much power. And he himself had been weak in giving in. But he'd never imagined any woman could be so pigheaded, or that she would risk bringing discord into the Bradley family now she was a member of it. It was her duty to support his wishes. In allowing her a ruling power of shareholdings he'd trusted her. They both had – he and his son. In a way he'd given in to bribery, because Arthur desired the little chit so much. Now see where it had got them both – a young woman setting her will against the judgement of the Board. Well – perhaps not *all*. Clarke seemed agreeable to taking on the Welshman, and maybe he'd have the support of the other two, Blake and Siddons, when it came to the vote.

There were too many with minor holdings for such a comparatively small newspaper, he thought irritably. Even so, Emma, by *one share* only, could defeat them all if she wanted.

The thought angered and shamed him. He'd been bought out. But then what man in his senses would have expected a twenty-year-old girl to take such an infernal interest in the running of an obscure county newspaper like the *Echo*? He'd expected her to be dutifully concerned with her new life at Eastwood, as Arthur's wife. Yet here she was, still fanatically dedicated to a dead man's ambitions – if they *could* have been William's, and this he doubted. William had been the conservative retiring type, not looking for trouble. But this girl was ready for trouble if it came her way. You could see it in the flash of her eyes and set of her chin when she argued. Well – in view of this he'd have to use subtler means, and apparently go along with her until a way was found to mould policy to his own ends.

It could be done.

If the Welshman came and appeared dangerous in any way – politically or socially, he'd find the means of getting him out!

Damn it all! It was *his* backing and money – Bradley brass – that was keeping the *Echo* going at all. Why didn't Arthur make the point clear to his wife? Remind her just where she stood? What sort of a husband was he? Sometimes Jonathan sensed uncomfortably that things weren't exactly as they should be between them. If so, whose fault was it? Emma's or Arthur's? He tried against his better judgement to blame the woman. She should have been *grateful* for family generosity. But there was something about his son – a streak of oddness he'd never understood, or even particularly tried to. His own passion had always been straightforward – simple, if sometimes crude. But Arthur was devious – the result, he supposed, of public school and Oxford. The suggestion of homosexuality didn't unduly trouble him. Young men went through the phase sometimes and emerged to become perfectly satisfactory husbands and fathers, and Arthur, he knew for a fact, had had, in the past, a good share of sultry affairs with women, mostly those of a lower order who could be dismissed after the pleasurable interludes, leaving no undue pangs of conscience behind. So he wasn't without passion, thank God. But what kind? And what had he done so soon to cause a rift between him and Emma?

Oh yes. The more he brooded on things when he had time, the more certain Jonathan was that there'd been a misunderstanding of some kind.

He tried probing Jessie's mind, subtly at first, then when she didn't respond, more bluntly.

'Do *you* think Arthur and Emma get on all right?' he asked one day. 'Is there something wrong between them?'

Jessie shrugged. 'How should I know? Emma's not my kind, she doesn't confide in me. She finds me boring, I suppose. I'm not interested in being glamorous, or charming businessmen, or having my name at the head of a newspaper column. Why don't you ask *her*? She might say. Or Arthur.' She looked away, knowing Arthur was the last person his father would tackle, simply because he wouldn't get an honest reply.

Jonathan grunted.

'You're not much help. And you should be. Women are supposed to have insight into these things.'

'Then why don't you speak to Mama?' Jessie's eyes held a momentary gleam of mischief that for a brief few seconds made her plain face almost attractive.

Jonathan turned and saying nothing more, strode down the

hall irritably and out of the front door. Speak to his wife! The very idea! – when her sole concern was to paint her ageing kittenish face, see that cook attended to the menus adequately, retiring later for a siesta with her glass of tonic or Madeira.

All the same, that same evening he made one of his rare visits to his wife's room. She was seated before her gilt-framed dressing-table mirror, patting her plump cheeks with cream. Her yellow hair, still thick for a woman of her age, fell about her spreading white shoulders. She was wearing a negligée over her nightdress of pale pink georgette.

She turned when the door opened, and to a man of finer sensibilities her look of pleasure and gratification would have aroused a touch of sympathy. He felt only irritation, knowing that he'd have to endure a tiresome session – however short – of lovemaking, before he got anything out of her that might cast aspersion on the character of her pampered beloved son.

'Hm!' he cleared his throat. 'You're looking very – fetching,' he lied, going towards her.

She got up, one hand pressed to a plump breast. Why on earth didn't she diet? he wondered. She was becoming almost gross in size, and though her flesh was white enough, and her skin good, there was far too much of it.

'Oh Jonathan,' she gushed, 'it's right good to have thee here.' She paused before adding, 'Is everything all right, love?'

He closed his eyes and let his lips touch her shoulder. It was fragrant and soft. Without looking at her he could almost imagine her as the girl he'd seduced so long ago.

After that, the passionate ritual was simple, and not half so distasteful as he'd imagined. When they lay afterwards side by side on the ornate bed, he started his subtle inquisition.

Amelia, though a simple woman in many ways, glanced at him warily. There were certain aspects of his character she knew well, and when Jonathan approached her over any subject in that devious particular way – over-casually, yet with subtle flattering innuendoes in his voice and manner, she recognised he was up to something. Something in which she could be useful. So that was it! He'd wanted her not for herself that night, as she'd foolishly imagined, but for what he could get out of her. Disillusion gripped her for a moment, then she smothered it with her usual commonsense. It was something, after all, that he depended on her for anything these days, coming to her bed whatever the reason might be.

'—As a mother and a woman—' he was saying, 'you've got a knowledge over certain matters I don't have. Maybe we've not seemed so close lately as we could've been. But I'm a busy man, and you've got enough on your hands taking care of this establishment without being burdened by my affairs.'

'I do what I can, Jonathan,' she said primly.

'Yes. Well—' He touched a stout forearm intimately and sensing the hidden response in her that she managed not to show, continued bluntly, 'It's Arthur.'

'*Arthur?*' She was surprised.

He attempted to explain his doubts of Bradley junior's relationship to Emma, and found it more difficult than he'd imagined, simply because he'd nothing tangible to go on.

Amelia shook her head slowly. 'They sleep together,' she said. 'They don't quarrel that I know of. What makes thee suspicious? I've noticed naught—'

'I know. That's part of it. There's nothing *to* notice, except that Emma's so restless and always poking her head into business affairs. She's a *damned* nuisance, and I thought you might be able to find out why. Get her talking; discover why she doesn't spend more time here, at Eastwood. Has she thought of starting a family? – That sort of thing.'

'I'll try,' Amelia answered doubtfully. 'But Emma and me – we're not exactly close. She avoids me as much as she can, thinks me a meddlesome old bore, I reckon.' A low chuckle escaped her, 'And she's probably right. If she was a bit interested in the home, love, it'd be different. But she's not. It's all the paper and getting to Oaklands to see that poor little sister of hers – Rosalind. Maybe if it wasn't for her she'd be thinking of a child of her own. But time's short yet. Don't worry. Young women these days like a bit of freedom afore startin' with nappies and sleepless nights. It'll all work out. And once the Dower House business is settled she'll find more'n enough to occupy her without treading on *your* toes. Anyway, Arthur wouldn't want her dangling round his neck all day. He's a bit of a loner, you know – a rum one in his way. And if it pleases Emma to bother about the *Echo* why should it worry *thee* so much?'

'It's important,' Jonathan answered abruptly. 'I've been a fool in allowing her so much power. I shouldn't have listened to Arthur. But he was so besotted – and apparently it was a condition—'

'A *condition*?'

'If she wed him, Oaklands and the paper had to remain independent – of me.'

'Of *you*? You mean you let her dictate?'

'To *him*? Yes. I thought marriage might steady him, bring him down to earth. So I gave in. But it hasn't affected him in the right way at all. He spends an hour or so a day at Feyland, with the *Comet* – studying accounts, throwing a few fine suggestions and orders about, then back again to the stables and horses. At board meetings he supports me, though I don't think he cares a bloody damn about business really.'

'With his background does he have to?'

'Don't be a fool, Amelia.' She winced. 'When election time comes round I shall need intelligent backing and help – especially from the press, and my family. At the moment it looks as though I'll have to fight for it. Especially with the young madam Arthur's married against me.'

'*Emma? Against* you?'

'And don't echo what I say, woman.' He got up, swung himself out of bed quickly and reached for his shirt. 'She's already started – by getting that fiery Welshman, Evan Lloyd, nominated as editor of the *Echo*.'

After a pause, Amelia dared to ask meekly, 'Is there anything against him being Welsh, Jonathan?'

He didn't reply, merely grabbed the rest of his clothes, dressed and left her, slamming the door sharply behind him.

She sighed, lay for a few moments in heavy disappointment, then reached for her own particular brand of tonic.

Jonathan meanwhile went to his study, perused documents, figures and studied recent editions of the rival Feyland *Courier*, after which he indulged himself with two glasses of vintage brandy before taking a short stroll about the grounds. The liquor dimmed his dark mood. It was a fine night, with a rising moon in the sky.

He'd get there, by God, he told himself, by the time the next election was over he'd have won his seat in the House, Emma or no Emma.

Aye! And somehow he'd find a way of bringing that son of his to heel. He'd be on to him like a leech from now on; and if he found his son and heir up to any little abnormal sexual games he'd have the hide off his back or disinherit him. Until then he hadn't frankly admitted his suspicions, even to himself. But the fact had to be faced sometime. Arthur, in some curious subtle way, was perverted, and had to be brought to a normal way of behaviour before the county knew.

His whole future could depend on this. There must be proof that besides the Bradley millions the family was capable of founding a strong and healthy dynasty. Therefore Emma and his son must produce an heir. Not for the first time he wished fervently that Arthur had only waited – held his horses until a more suitable match could be arranged. There were plenty of good-looking young women around, and Leyfordshire was noted for its pretty girls. In another couple of years, with luck, the Bradleys would have become accepted in the county – recognised as a power and asset to the community. Already he and his son were members of the Quayle Hunt; furthermore Jonathan was nibbling for an invitation to join a certain select club that would establish him firmly in the eyes of the majority of members. A few toffee-nosed snobs might cold-shoulder him – at the beginning. But Lord Wendle was on his side, and could be persuaded, through subtle means, Jonathan sensed, to back him as prospective Conservative candidate for East Leyfordshire. Wendle himself was a bit of an anachronism. But this was one of the strange things he had discovered, about the local aristocracy. True blue-bloods could afford to be democratic, whereas half-way socialities still had to keep a rigid eye on the climbers' ladder. And, of course, finance came into it. Wendle was always in need of cash. And there Jonathan Bradley held the whip hand.

Neither man had any illusions abut the other's aims or ambitions. This in itself held a camaraderie between them that was not only useful, but refreshing. Wendle was a good-humoured sporty old boy, Jonathan told himself frequently, and it was a pity his only daughter, Leila, hadn't been better-looking. A union between the two families could have been advantageous to both. But Leila Wendle was the large, hearty, fox-hunting type – good in the saddle, and with a gusty sense of humour. But there her assets ended. As a wife for Arthur her chances from the beginning had been nil.

Damn it all though, why on earth had Emma appeared on the scene just at the crucially wrong moment? And now she had, why couldn't she do her duty, keep Arthur more in tow, and produce the heir so desperately needed? A child was the only answer – someone to keep her chained to the home instead of interfering with the *Echo*.

The next day he made a point of following her when she went into the conservatory for flowers for the house. Since Amelia seemed so half-hearted about the subject, he'd decided on a direct approach.

She was snipping at a spray of scarlet blooms – some exotic foreign variety – as he strode in.

'Ah!' he said with forced cheer in his voice, 'warm in here, isn't it? And decorative. What are those things called, do you know? The late owner, Billington his name was, or something like it, had travelled a good deal. An authority on flowers and strange plants.'

To his surprise Emma knew the answer.

'Of course,' he said, recollecting her nature campaign in the *Echo*. 'I suppose you've had to do a good bit of reading up about these things to please your public. The sort of subject that goes down well with women.'

He waited for her reaction, but when she glanced at him

briefly, her face was expressionless yet discerning. Then she turned to give another snap of her scissors.

'Oh I don't deal with foreign flowers for the paper,' she said casually. 'It wouldn't be at all popular. Most women have a creative streak in them; it's a matter of how to draw it out – and for that you have to have an everyday basis – something that costs nothing preferably. I mean it's generally only rich people who have conservatories. So what would be the point of giving hints on flower arrangement if you use tropical blossoms and plants? Besides, autumn leaves, grasses – even certain twigs, can look lovely, and don't cost a penny.'

'I see,' Jonathan said stiffly, with the uncomfortable feeling of having been subtly put in his place. 'But once you've said that, it's done with, isn't it? You can't keep on repeating how to arrange autumn leaves and berries.'

A hint of mischief lit Emma's eyes. 'Oh, but I don't, Mr Bradley. Which you'd know, if you read my articles.' She laid the scissors down and rubbed her hands on the dainty apron she was wearing. Then she pulled the frilly thing off and laid it on a seat. There was a smile on her face when she asked, 'But you didn't follow me here to talk of botany, did you?'

'No,' he said bluntly, 'and I wish you wouldn't call me "Mr Bradley". Say "Jonathan" if you like – I don't care. Or else "pater". I'm "pater" or "the old man" to Arthur, and I prefer the first. Infernally snobbish, but that's what Oxford does, and as his wife you'd better follow suit.'

'All right – Pater.'

'You know what it means, of course – father of the house – I realise I don't have to tell you, being the intellectual young woman you are.'

'No,' she still looked slightly roguish. 'I *have* heard of it.'

'Well, then!' Jonathan gave a sigh before resuming. 'When you two have children of your own it'll be "grandfather" I suppose, or else "grandaddy". I'm looking forward to that day, Emma. Do you and Arthur ever discuss it?'

There was quite a pause before Emma answered. 'We haven't been married very long, and Arthur has had horses very much on his mind. As you know he pops off to Newmarket quite a lot these days, and when we *do* discuss the future it's mostly about the Dower House.'

'Yes, I suppose so. You'll have a lot to think about there. And that's natural. The right thing to do; I'm sure of it now. A newly married couple need an independent starting-home. A nest for the future you could say. There'll not be so much time for you to be running off to Oaklands.'

'Oaklands seems to worry you,' Emma said. 'You resent it, don't you?'

'My dear girl, the place doesn't affect me one way or the other,' Jonathan bluffed. 'Except—'

'Yes?'

'It can be an excuse for going to Charbrook,' he told her. 'When I – or rather when Arthur made it possible to have the *Echo* still under your pretty little thumb – neither of us realised quite how powerfully you meant to use it.'

She laughed.

'You exaggerate. I've missed one or two board meetings already. I only want to – to keep *certain* characteristics of the paper as they've always been. I suppose out of respect – memory of my father.'

'The true naive little sentimentalist.' His voice was wry.

She gave him a very direct look, and at that moment, before she said, 'You could call me that I suppose in some ways—' he was aware that his statement was indeed true. 'Naive' might have been the wrong word to use, but the clarity of her very clear grey eyes indicated an innocence and purity of purpose quite astonishing to his acute business sense. It was this quality in her that defeated his understanding. Whatever problem Arthur Bradley might present, his devious off-course attitude to life was of the worldly order. Beneath his brilliant handsome facade, a twisted streak glimmered unpleasantly at odd moments. Jonathan so far had managed mostly to disregard it. But he knew now, uncomfortably, that this girl never would. Her integrity – to whatever cause, however mistakenly – would endure to the bitter conclusion of any conflict. She was as stubborn in her own way as that Welsh rebel, Evan Lloyd, whom she'd successully wheedled or forced into the *Echo*'s orbit.

Remembering Evan temporarily swept other matters aside. The man had been accepted and was taking over the editorship the following week. There'd be a whole introductory article from him, he supposed irritably; he only hoped Lloyd would keep it on as low and practical a key as possible. No doubt his photograph would be displayed. The fellow had a good head, and impudent swaggering profile.

'Quite – powerful looking,' Emma had observed regarding the portrait at the last office meeting. 'I think he'll go down well.'

Jonathan had grunted. He wasn't so sure, but he'd a shrewd idea the women would be impressed, and that when Evan set his mind to a project he'd be justly dogged about it.

Well, the point now was that somehow he had to be brought round to presenting and supporting certain of Jonathan's own views. Politically especially. The *Echo* might be a small paper, but its influence could disrupt the power of the *Comet* to a certain extent, and be a cog in the wheel of the founding of *The Midlander*. This mustn't happen. Somehow or other he'd win Evan round. If he didn't, the man would go, and so would the paper itself, he'd see to that. Emma might hold the ruling shares, but without the other half, the *Echo* could never endure; it was within his – Jonathan's – capacity to close down, should the absolute necessity arise.

As though sensing his travel of thought, Emma said, 'You didn't *really* want to talk about newspapers just now, did you? It was to tell me how you wanted Arthur and me to have a baby.'

'Both. As I've only one son to inherit all I've worked for – and damned hard, let me tell you – I naturally want the family line to endure. In the normal way there'd have been no question of it, but—'

'As he's married an abnormal woman you're worried,' Emma interrupted sharply.

He paused before he spoke. She could feel his eyes burning into hers, searching through every curve of her enticing young body to the hidden impulses and motivations that made her what she was – exciting and damned attractive to the male libido, but at the same time inaccessible and remote, a contradiction with subleties in her which could be exceedingly irritating.

No wonder Arthur had wanted her. She was a challenge; all the same some wealthy young brood mare would have fitted far better into the scheme of things. She could feel her colour deepening, as he said, 'There's nothing abnormal about *you*, Emma. But as we're speaking plainly, I'll be frank. I didn't approve the marriage. Arthur had far better chances socially, and you're too intellectual to fit easily into our way of life. I can understand him being intrigued though – you too. You didn't marry a nobody, did you? He had damn good looks that'd sweep most girls off their feet, and loaded into the bargain.'

'With money you mean.' Her voice was faintly contemptuous.

'Yes. Money. The money that saved your precious *Echo*. Well—' his jaw took a pugnacious thrust '—I'm not grudging it, providing you play fair, keep to your proper place, and see my son gives you a child. Understand?'

Her cheeks had paled.

'Perfectly. But remember two are concerned in such a project.'

'Now what the devil—' He didn't finish. Emma had turned her back on him and was arranging the sprays of blooms in a small basket on her arm. He sighed, and walked heavily to the inner door, only pausing to say, before leaving, 'Think over what I've said. It's important.'

She knew it was, and in a desperate moment of clarity recognised also how badly she'd failed in assessing Arthur's character. What was it he wanted of her? Not love, certainly. Submission? Yes, probably. An heir? She doubted it. He wasn't interested in children and during the first weeks of marriage had effectively put her off wishing for any of his. Yet at the beginning he'd charmed her by being flattering and courteous. She'd believed that, emotionally, beneath his elegant facade he was a normal man, with the underlying instincts to make an enduring relationship of their marriage.

Well, she'd been wrong.

He wasn't.

Her only hope was in some way to salvage a basic friendship from the union. The thought was sterile, bitter, and it didn't help knowing how disappointed her father-in-law was going to be in the future.

That evening, Arthur, sensing an extra quietness and withdrawal in her, was sufficiently intrigued to ask curiously, 'What are you milling over, gorgeous?'

She was sitting at her dressing table, brushing the thick shining masses of chestnut-dark hair. No – not chestnut, he thought critically, copper-beech, that was it – a colour that changed subtly every time a beam of light caught it. He had an impulse to run his hand through it, twist it round her lovely neck gently, then draw it to his lips.

At the first mere touch of his hand she stiffened, 'Oh don't, Arthur. You'll tangle it.'

She shook it free, and his fingers enclosed her shoulder. They were very strong, and hurt. She looked up at him; his blue eyes blazed down on her as though lit by white fire.

'Aren't I allowed to touch my own wife?'

'*Wife?*' she echoed. 'Did you say "wife", Arthur?'

'What the devil do you mean?'

'You know very well.' She paused before adding, 'Or perhaps you don't. Perhaps you just wanted me as a – a kind of curiosity, because I'm different and didn't run after you. *A specimen*.'

He laughed, released her, and pushed her on to the bed. She fell back but recovered herself swiftly and sat up.

'Stay there,' he remarked, taking out his handkerchief and wiping his brow. 'You do as I say and we'll be all right. A specimen, possession – call it what you like. It's not an insult. If you hadn't been so intriguing I wouldn't have looked at you. I'm – a connoisseur, shall we say? I don't care for ordinary human beings or situations. It's the unusual I go for. The unique; and you're certainly that, Emma.' His voice trembled slightly, but his eyes remained hard and shining. His expression disturbed her. She edged back; he caught her by the neck of her nightdress and pulled her forward. 'Frightened, darling? You needn't be. Provided you behave. If you don't, I have that handy little whip of mine. Some women like being thrashed. Do you, Emma?'

She jerked herself free and rushed to the other side of the bed. Breathing heavily, she gasped, '—If you touch me, Arthur Bradley, I'll – I'll—'

He smiled. 'Well? What will you do? Run away? Tell my esteemed Papa? Divorce me? But you can't, my love, as I said – a man's *allowed* to touch his wife. So—' his voice hardened, 'come here instantly. You needn't be afraid. There'll be no whipping – yet; no scenes, no crying or shrieking for help. Just a little – tuition, sweetheart. In the methods of loving. You want to be loved, don't you? Then let me teach you.'

She didn't move.

'No.'

'Very well.' He strode towards her, and pulled the nightdress from her body letting it fall and lie in a crumpled heap at her feet. Rigid, but inwardly trembling, she stood pale and naked before him, yet with her swift mind already concentrating on a nearby heavy candlestick which she meant to spring for, if he attacked her.

But there was no need; with his blue eyes half closed, he touched first one soft breast, before his hand travelled insidiously, half consciously down her side to the gentle swelling of thigh and buttocks. Then he knelt down and kissed her bare toes. Involuntarily she shivered. He looked up, and she was astonished to see the glint of tears in his blue eyes.

'So beautiful,' he murmured thickly, 'so innocent and pure – pure as a young boy, as David—'

'David?'

'My friend.' The simple statement stunned her temporarily, until she said, 'I don't understand.' But somewhere, dark at the back of her mind, she did.

'Forgive me,' he said, reaching for her hand. 'Forgive me for being different and for wanting – the impossible. I *do* want you, you know, Emma – but not in *your* way. No children. No scheming sentimental preliminaries. In time, when you've become adjusted—'

She made a sudden violent movement, reached for her wrap, and pulled it round her fiercely. 'You're mad, Arthur,' she said coldly and very clearly, 'and don't ever dare to approach me again, or I'll tell your father – everything. Yes, I will, and he'll disinherit you.'

Rage rose in him again with a violence that drove her to the door.

'If you do that,' he said, 'I'll kill you, and I mean it. Or—' his lips twisted wrily into a mad semblance of a smile as he forced himself to be more calm, 'maybe I'd just inform him what a cheat and liar you are. There are ways you know – the countryside's not short of some stupid little whore in the family way – isn't that what they call it? – who could be easily paid, and proud to name *me* as their bastard's wicked papa – where would you be then, Emma, my love? Out in the cold, a frigid wife drawing him to another woman, and therefore no longer a member of the Bradley family. *I'd* see you soon lost your Oaklands and your precious *Echo* – I was cunning enough to have a clause inserted in the agreement which *does* give me a certain power.'

'I don't believe you.'

'You'd better. And now—' astonishingly he held out a conciliatory hand, 'let us be friends, shall we? Possibly, in time, you may learn to co-operate concerning our connubial existence. We could have fun, you know—'

'*Fun!*' Her voice was vituperative with contempt. 'I *hate* you.'

He shrugged. 'Oh well – that's a beginning.'

'Do you mind going.'

'Not at all.'

He left. And when the latch had clicked a wave of dizziness swept over her. She stood for a moment, until her head had cleared, then staggered to the window, pushed it open, and let the cool spring wind brush the darkness from her eyes.

The following week she had an interview with Evan Lloyd.

6

They sat facing each other at a small table where two cups of coffee were placed, with a conglomeration of files, newspaper cuttings, and other papers pushed to one side. The larger table across the window appeared in worse confusion; documents and letters everywhere – rather similar to an illustration from *Alice-in-Wonderland*, Emma thought, wondering how on earth any human being would manage to get it into order. She had been there once or twice before during her father's day. It had been a bit of a jumble then – but discreetly so, with glory holes, as William had called them, giving a facade of normality and order.

'There aren't proper places to keep the things in,' he'd explained. 'And if a sub-editor's off, or on calls, I have the whole lot to deal with myself. Now, Emma—' and he'd wagged a finger at her, 'don't tell me you're all tidy yourself—' and she'd laughed, remembering her wardrobe and chest-of-drawers at Oaklands where so many feminine fripperies, blouses, and underwear were often to be found, after a search, in the one place where they shouldn't be.

Still – *this*!

Her eyes, after wandering briefly round the littered floor and desk, came back to Evan who was watching her expectantly, with a whimsical lop-sided smile on his mouth.

'Pretty awful, isn't it,' he said. 'I shall get things sorted out in time, and the quicker the better, so I can start making my own muddles.'

'Oh. I see.' Although she didn't.

He watched her intently. The pause between them was electric, filled with an astonishment, a magic that was new to her, and profoundly disturbing. Lloyd was not handsome in the conventional style of Arthur – his features had a rebellious yet Puckish quality expressing a man capable of many moods, wayward perhaps, and with an impudent sense of humour, yet strong and purposeful. He had a slightly tilted nose above well-sculpted lips and a dogged cleft chin. His eyes were light and sparkling, varying between green and grey; his hair brown, curling rebelliously from a wide intellectual forehead. Yes. There was certainly something magnetic about him that set Emma's spine tingling. For this reason she appeared aloof, a little chilly.

When she said no more he continued, in casual, almost offhand tones, 'Newspapers aren't produced in ladies' drawing rooms, as you should know, Miss Fairley—' he corrected himself quickly, '—sorry. Mrs Bradley. The end product has to be in order, but getting the order means sometimes a darn lot of searching, sorting and puzzling out. Journalists – including editors – have all their own individual systems and aims. Mine may be very different to your father's. We shall see.'

'I hope not *too* different,' she said sharply.

His eyes once more flung her a quick quizzical glance. The next question was blunt and sudden, taking her unawares.

'*Why* have you come to see me today, Emma? Yes, if you don't mind I shall call you Emma right away, because if you continue with your column – which I hope you will – you'll be a member of my staff, and formalities won't be necessary.'

'All right.' An involuntary smile puckered her pretty lips. 'In that case you'll be Evan to me. Correct?'

He shook his head. '*No*. Most *in*correct. At Board meetings and in public you can address me as Mr Lloyd, but in private it should certainly be "Sir". Don't you agree?'

She frowned, wondering if he was joking, and suddenly he laughed; he *was*. 'For goodness sake,' he said, and his voice held a Welsh lilt in it, 'don't look like that—' The humour in his eyes faded, as he noted – with a rush of deepening interest tinged with something else, something more personal than admiration, more restrained than physical desire – the glowing colour mount her beautifully modelled cheeks, the proud set of her small head on the slim neck, exquisite features and russet curls straying below the brim of her absurd little velvet hat.

'Like what?' she asked, with her heart pumping at her throat.

He looked at a paper. 'I think I know. Being Welsh – a bit of scribbler-poet, I'm apt to let my imagination stray. I could say, I suppose, "a wild deer in a cool green forest – an elusive creature as swift and intrinsically gentle as the wayward winds of spring". On the other hand it could just as well be – "an attractive inquisitive girl wanting to poke her nose into other people's business".'

'Thank you *very* much.'

'Don't mention it. So long as we know where we stand, maybe it's time we got down to brass tacks, meaning, of course, our little business tête-a-tête.'

Although her mind and senses were still reeling, she managed to say, while fiddling with a froth of white lace edging the high neck of her waisted green velvet jacket, 'Yes, high time.'

Their following discussion, concerning the layout of the *Echo*, was surprisingly easy. Lloyd's ideas she discovered were flexible and mostly in harmony with her own. He wanted very little change, but suggested she should have a whole page, temporarily anyway, for social and feminine affairs, with space allotted also for any serious article she wished to deal with.

Of course she wished it. It was what she'd argued over with her father constantly.

'You'd have to talk over any – revolutionary idea with me first, of course,' he said over-casually, 'and I take it you'd be free of domestic ties to do it.'

Her back stiffened, giving her chin a higher tilt.

'Of course,' she said very clearly. 'My duties at Eastwood aren't many. In fact, I'm not needed in that way at all, really.'

He tore his eyes away from hers with difficulty. She'd appeared in that flash of time so vulnerable, and almost hurt, beneath the bravado and facade of independence.

'Then that's fine. It's settled. I'd suggest, though, we hold our horses temporarily over the additional stuff – the articles. You''l have to do me a specimen copy, anyway.'

'Naturally.' She got up, and he was inwardly amused to note the touch of defiance in her very erect pose, the almost discernible upthrust of young breasts beneath the fitted velvet jacket. 'My father never complained about my writing,' she added, 'and he was a good critic. His reviews went quite far afield, you know; even *The Stage* asked for them when any important show came to the Charbrook Olympia. He wrote up Ellen Terry in—'

'I know, I know,' Evan interrupted, waving a hand. 'I don't need reminding of William Fairley's prowess, and I'm sure I shan't have to complain about yours. But dramatic reviewing's very different from driving a strong point home in as few words as possible. That needs punch, fire, and enthusiasm. Also ability. The art of coming to the point quickly and firing the public conscience. Dash! drive! – so that controversy's roused. Do you understand?'

The light in his eyes had swept away hurt pride in her by a rush of enthusiasm.

'Yes. Of course I do.'

He took her hand then; its warm pressure thrilled her whole being. As their eyes met once more, expectancy, excitement, and a sense of overwhelming delight flowered between them.

In a dazed moment she heard him say, 'What a pity you're married, Emma Fairley, I should like to kiss you.'

The tips of two pearly teeth glimmered between her parted lips, as she said, half whispering, 'You can, if you like.'

His mouth was firm but gentle as it came down briefly upon hers. The contact was soon over, but she felt joyous, revitalised, when a moment later he showed her to the door.

Outside the Charbrook streets were patterned by the transient light and shade of the spring afternoon; ordinary streets of ordinary houes, with pedestrians, shoppers mostly, about their daily routine. Yet to her, the whole world seemed suddenly to be singing. In the last hour life had become different, completely changed for her.

That was how it began

*

During the next few days following the revealing and unpredictable emotional impact of her meeting with Lloyd, Emma was careful at Eastwood to control her suddenly awakened delight under a veneer of pleasant calm which did not entirely deceive Arthur. Where, before, she had frequently responded to his annoying manner of teasing, by quick-tempered rejoinders which he delighted in quelling, she now accepted with apparent unruffled calm. She tried not to betray dislike when his hand touched her body possessively. But he sensed that any hope or longing in her for a consummated relationship between them, had now faded into acquiescence of a completely sterile role. She would not accept his pleasurable indulgencies. She desired him to be *ordinary* – behave like any other conventional, normally sexed husband. Before, this wouldn't have troubled him, but he was puzzled by the secret glow about her which at times brought a meditative smile to her lips, and a shining translucent light to her eyes. He was annoyed too, because he knew very well it did not concern him. There was nothing he could put his finger on; but the fact that she had in any way the capacity to elude him irritated him to deepening sullen anger. She was his after all. He'd married her – she belonged. And by God if he caught her out in any funny business he'd take the whip to her back.

In the meantime he took it out on his dogs and horses – all except Thunder, his chestnut stallion whose blazing tawny eyes, magnificent frame, waving mane and pounding hooves were a match any day for his own wild thwarted spirit. There was affinity between them; they were, in a sense, counterparts of different species in all but one thing. Thunder could sire strong specimens of his kind. He, Arthur Bradley, could not. Neither did he wish to – only to possess – in any warped erratic way he fancied. And so far he hadn't abused his rights over Emma, merely deprived her.

Where had it all begun? Wherein was the origin of his

abnormality? What twisted gene had driven him, in early youth, to find active pleasure only through his own sex or in sadistic lust? Did his father know? Was he even aware of it? He doubted it, although occasionally he'd caught an assessing, half-bewildered glance in Jonathan's eyes. Arthur then, had felt more than ever irritated; why hadn't Bradley senior given his mother more sons? It was as though, having bred one outwardly perfect physical specimen, and following the birth of Jessie a boring, plain daughter, he'd given up, to concentrate all his hopes and future plans on Arthur.

Well, if that was so – if it was expected of him and Emma to found a dynasty, the old man was going to be disappointed.

The one redeeming fact, to Arthur, about the situation, was that the intriguing and lovely Emma was no longer free to produce others in her image. She was his alone, and he'd see she remained so.

7

Young summer came to the forest, sprinkling the valleys with carpets of bluebells glimmering in massed patches between the trees. Through pale trunks of silver birch and tender green leaves of oak and sycamore, the deep shining tarns of Feyland Woods shone deeply mysterious, broodingly dark one moment, the next dappled in transient sunlight to ever-changing ripples of purple and jade blue, lit to gold. There was a magical, almost legendary quality about the area that was nevertheless dangerous to strangers and the unwary. At points attempts had been made to fence certain places, but of the four pools only one was properly protected. The largest, nick-named locally as Green Harry, had been the scene in the past of several fatal accidents – including a horse and cart that had blundered off the track one misty night, and taken a farmer to his death. Also more than one suicide of which only a single body had been recovered. So alongside beauty lingered a sinister quality, giving the woods a reputation for being haunted.

Emma, however, from being a child had always loved the vicinity, which was only a mile or two from Bradgate and not far, as the crow flies, from Oaklands. She knew every secret path winding through thick tall bracken, past lush pale green dells, hoping, but not really believing, that one day she might catch a glimpse of the ill-fated Lady Jane Grey's ghost gliding through shadowed branches, damp with rising mist. To most people the story was merely imagination, but many locals stressed its truth.

Emma did not actually believe in visual ghosts but having lived so close to nature she was aware of strange influences and sometimes unexplainable happenings that could not be described in material terms. The sensitivity that had responded so immediately to Evan Lloyd had an instinctive affinity with moods of the unseen. Rosalind, too, though deprived of normal reasoning, had a deep, or as Emma termed, 'other knowledge' in her, which felt the same intuitive fascination. Places affected her more than people. Often, during her short life, she had beguiled Emma into taking her to the tarns, where she'd stand entranced, like some beautiful changeling creature, staring into the brooding azure depths.

Emma had watched her, saddened by the pathetic loveliness which would never know the normal fulfilment of a woman, wondering what thoughts, if any, haunted the little girl's bewildered hidden mind. Rosalind seldom gave indication that she had any, although she could say a few words indicating when she was hungry or wanted the toilet. Animals and birds seemed to have unconscious affinity with her. They were never afraid when she approached, and the child would smile then, an elfin far-away smile, holding out a pale hand so a tit, sparrow, or robin would perch there. Even a nearby farmer's dog that had been taught to be surly and bark shrilly, was quiet and gentle with her, wagging its tail and pushing its shaggy face up to be patted when it saw her. Emma's affection for her she simply accepted as a right – but was quite happy without it, and although generally docile, she had occasional tempers when thwarted, which died as quickly as a current of wind gone suddenly quiet.

Following Emma's departure to Eastwood, the housekeeper had developed quite a fierce pride in the little girl's beauty, and although the governess-nurse was nominally in charge of her, the older woman saw to it that she had prior command and kept a watchful eye on daily life at Oaklands.

'She misses you though,' she told Emma one summer day when she called. 'Oh yes. She has more depths in her than you think.'

Emma shook her head, smiling sadly. 'No, Mrs Cox, I'm sure that's not true. And I wouldn't want it to be. How could I be happy at all away from here, if I thought Rosalind was suffering for it?'

'Young women in love can be happy anywhere if the lover's there too,' came the answer a trifle sharply, and Emma for a quick second or two felt a guilty wave of joy surge through her. Was her potential happiness so obvious? So obvious that anyone could remotely guess the completely unexpected development her emotional life had taken? Evan? But no. They had met only once since that first interview alone together at Charbrook, and members of the board, including Arthur who was seldom present, had been there. Both Evan and Emma had been careful to give no indication of their inner feelings, had each even managed to avoid direct conversation with the other. But the electrical awareness had been there. Once when she'd caught a fleeting glance of his eyes upon her, her whole body had thrilled and stiffened, leaving, as she'd managed to look away, a swooning sense of delight in her.

Nobody could have noticed, she was sure. But later Arthur had said, 'That fellow, Lloyd. I don't like him.'

'Oh?' Her tone was impersonal, disinterested.

'He's a revolutionary.'

'Don't be ridiculous.'

'I know the type.'

'And I'm quite sure he knows yours,' she'd thought, but mercifully had controlled herself sufficiently to make no response.

Now, on this particular afternoon, with Eastwood miles away, and the sweetly-sad nostalgic sighing of the woods about her, Emma felt an irresistible desire to have a glimpse, face to face, of the man who'd awakened such wild emotions in her. Under the genuine pretext of making a visit to Rosalind there'd been a secret hope that she might come across him by chance, either down one of the lanes, in his car, or perhaps on foot. The latter was unlikely, of course. During the week Lloyd was mostly confined to his office, working hectically, as the following morning was publishing day for the weekly. Thinking briefly about her own column, she realised it wasn't quite up to standard, the reason being her own emotional involvement with personal matters. She'd have to pull herself together or he might not want her work at all. The prospect of special articles would fade, and with it many chances of meeting him.

That mustn't happen.

And with her decision came another. She *must* see him that very day and explain. He'd understand. He felt the same way about her, as she of him, only in his case, of course, being a man made him more capable of keeping business matters completely apart from the romantic.

Still – a fleeting smile touched her lips; just for a few precious moments she could surely penetrate officialdom.

Because of the sudden urgency in her, her walk with Rosalind was short that day. They wandered hand-in-hand, picking a few wild flowers and ferns, while Emma hummed an old tune from childhood days that somehow captured the atmosphere of place. Occasionally Rosalind's light voice joined in. Looking down into the lovely upturned young face, Emma was filled with regret because the luminous dark-fringed eyes, though momentarily happy, were completely devoid of understanding, reflecting only an awareness of elemental instinctive forces. The sun on her flaxen hair felt good. It was nice to hear the chortle of birds and feel the soft grass brush her legs. Otherwise the world was empty of meaning, and would be, Emma sensed, for always. Rosalind would never know how to reason, never savour the ache and longing for a home, lover and husband. When she was older, being so beautiful, men might desire her, and through that she would be in danger. It would be hers – Emma's duty – to see she was protected from assault and despoilment.

However, that problem was for the future, and mustn't destroy any joy of the present.

When the time came to return to Oaklands, Rosalind was acquiescient, though her pretty underlip pouted.

'Tarn?' she murmured questioningly. 'Emma – tarn?'

'Not today, darling. Emma has work to do.'

'Work,' she thought as the little girl reluctantly accompanied her back. 'What a liar you are, Emma Fairley.' In her own mind she had already replaced the newly acquired 'Bradley' for her father's name. Life at Eastwood was becoming increasingly more distasteful to her.

By four o'clock she had joined the main road to Charbrook, and in another twenty minutes was there.

8

The *Echo* offices stood in a side road of the town, near the canal, and a railway yard adjoining a dye-works. As she approached the steamy smell of water mingling faintly with that of newsprint rose in a wave of nostalgia to greet her – a familiarity based on former days during her father's lifetime. Any wind there'd been that afternoon had died, intensifying the damp rising heat. The clip clop of horses' hooves and jingling of harness came from the yard where the great shire horses ended their day's toil. There was occasional shouting from a coal barge drifting on the dark water towards the bridge.

All so familiar somehow, yet charged with a new magic to Emma whose pulses had already quickened alarmingly as she pushed the door to the *Echo*'s premises and stepped inside. She had a short flight of stairs to take before reaching a rather dark corridor leading to the editorial departments and Lloyd's room.

Before rapping sharply, she adjusted her hat and smoothed a curl from her cheek. Was he in, she wondered? Oh, she did hope so. If he wasn't – or was too rushed by the hectic business of seeing the daily and weekly editions brought out to bother about her, she'd feel not only disappointed but somehow painfully humiliated. She'd leave immediately, pretend she'd been merely passing and had called by chance to discuss a light matter of no immediate importance, and a second later be gone. If that happened she'd have to wait – perhaps for ages – until *he* contacted *her*, which would be almost unbearable.

Lloyd was in, however, and after a brief pause called, 'Yes? Come in.' His voice sounded on edge, irritable.

Emma turned the door knob and entered. Had she been aware how very striking she looked – young and entrancing in a new gold and russet outfit, complete with bustle and small hat tilted intriguingly forward, she'd have recognised his gasp of astonishment as one, also, of admiration. The pause between them was only momentary. His warm eyes lit up. He got up from his stool and came towards her.

'Emma,' he said, 'oh – Emma.'

'Hullo,' her voice was soft, shy. She wondered if he'd kiss her, and if he did, how she'd react – pull away conventionally, or respond. The latter, she knew. And then – but her thoughts were racing too far ahead. She mustn't anticipate – not here, in her dead father's sanctum. He wouldn't judge her, but neither would he approve. However much she desired Evan – however unhappy she might be in her abnormal marriage it was too soon yet to break faith. She could amost sense William's presence in that dusty darkish interior – hear him saying, 'Take care, Emma, love. Don't jump your fences. Go steadily – you've a reputation to keep up, and Oaklands—' All imagination of course, but in essence true. So in a way she was relieved when after only a warm hand-clasp he pulled a rickety chair from under the table, and told her to sit down. She did. 'I hope I've not come at too busy a time,' she began with a rush. 'I've been to see Rosalind at Oaklands, and I thought I'd call – perhaps I shouldn't have, though. Perhaps—'

'No, you shouldn't.' His voice was serious, his expression blank. But as she got to her feet preparing to do her vanishing act, he laughed, and panic in her subsided. 'My dear girl, don't be ridiculous. Sit down again at once or I'll – now what will I do? I really don't know; you appear such an elegant untouchable young lady. I'd really hate to ruffle a hair of your pretty head.'

She relaxed. 'It wouldn't be easy. This hat has so many pins in it, it's stuck on like glue.'

They both grinned. Then he asked, 'How long can you stay? As you know, it's publishing day, and I won't be free for a couple of hours. But—'

'I can't stay at all, Evan,' she told him. 'And—' with a rush of honesty confessed '—I wasn't just passing. I – I wanted to see you, that's all.'

'And my God, I've wanted to see you,' he told her. 'You've been torture to me – on my mind ever since the last meeting. Emma—'

'Yes?'

'We'll have to talk some time. I take it you realise that?'

'Of course.'

'Not here, though, not now.'

'When?'

He laughed, but his eyes were serious, warm and compelling.

'Give me a chance. We'll puzzle it out – settle it somehow – somewhere. Not in this poky hole, but where I can see you as you really are, without the hatpins and frills and furbelows.'

'Oh. Don't you like this dress?'

'No. As a fashion-plate, yes. But it's not you, Emma Fairley.'

'Bradley,' she corrected him.

'Oh yes, more's the pity; especially as I've heard the fellow's quite a bounder.'

She turned her head away, and walked to the door hoping he couldn't see the deepening rose colour of shame in her cheeks.

He was after her in a second and pulled her round to face him. 'Tell me,' he said, with his jaw thrust out aggressively, 'does he ill-treat you?'

Her answer was a question, ambiguous.

'Do you think I'd allow *that*?'

'You might, for the sake of the *Echo* and Oaklands. But if it's true, and I find out, I'll wring his blasted neck, and that's a promise.'

Regaining composure, and knowing he meant it, she said,

'Don't worry, I'm not stupid, Evan, and Arthur's not really a forceful character. Just—'

'Bent, twisted.'

She shrugged. 'I really don't know what you'd call it. Anyway—' she forced a smile, 'we don't see much of each other. He's too concerned with his horses, and—'

'Other unspeakable pursuits. I know.'

She was silent for a moment, then with a veneer of calm, said, 'Please don't worry about me, there's no need. I can take care of myself, and Jonathan, my father-in-law, is quite considerate to me. Generous in a way.'

The meeting ended there, inconclusively.

Minutes later Emma was making her way to the point where she'd left her car. A passing youth had to help her to crank it up, and after several grunts and heaves it started off and was taking her by the shortest possible route back to Eastwood. Pedestrians stared as she passed, and only then did it occur to her, with a wave of humour, that she must appear rather ludicrous at the wheel of one of 'them new-fangled things', wearing her smart outfit in her new hat with its shred of veiling floating behind!

9

During the first months of the *Comet*'s appearance, the circulation of the *Courier* had declined slightly, but by the late summer of 1904 it had regained most of its lost readership. In the beginning the new paper's brightness, including a page devoted to humour, including cartoons on aspects of ordinary life, had offset its extreme conservatism which had been cunningly kept at a low level. *Apparently*. Gradually, however, the man-in-the-street – beguiled also by an additional sheet of excellent photography and sensational headlines – had sensed political undercurrents, which eventually had driven him back to take up again the more dependable long-established *Courier*. The fact had registered almost immediately with the newly formed board of Bradley's *Comet*, and the price was instantly dropped by a halfpenny a copy, which had again stimulated the battle between the two newspapers.

Jonathan's resolve somehow to acquire the rival daily by fair means or foul – preferably the former – once more made an offer to Hardy Wilton, whose family had started and owned the paper for generations. It was quite an excessive sum, and Jonathan had high hopes it would be accepted. But Wilton took only a week to decline it politely. The fact was that had Wilton needed, or even wished for financial aid for the *Courier*, he had only to contact a certain well-known national press to get all the necessary backing. The firm had been as anxious as Jonathan, at one time, to amalgamate the *Courier* into its own particular group. Leyford was a thriving place, already rich through its boot and shoe trade and hosiery. Population was increasing rapidly; in the future any successful newspaper was going to more than double or treble its circulation.

The tycoons knew it; so did Wilton. Therefore he stuck to his guns, and the *Courier* remained the most affluent and widely read privately owned paper in the county. An independent – free of political party.

Jonathan was chagrined by the refusal of his offer and concentrated all the more on using the *Echo* as a vehicle of newsprint publicity to gain his own ends.

So far it hadn't worked, and this fact he put down sourly to the presence of Evan Lloyd being at the editorial helm – and Emma.

One day, losing patience, he confronted her when she returned from Oaklands.

After calling her into the library he waved the latest edition of the weekly at her, and said, 'What do you think you're doing, girl? What's all this? Eh? Explain if you can.'

Emma's brows rose slightly above her grey eyes.

'What do you mean? I don't understand.'

He flung the edition on the table angrily, pointing to the front page. She noticed that his hand was shaking.

'I think you do. And so does he. You're in collusion, aren't you – you two?'

'Collusion?' Her voice held exasperation tinged with contempt. 'Why? *How?* – for goodness sake—'

'And don't "goodness sake" me, girl. You know the rules – you made enough show after your father died of wanting to keep the paper the way he liked it. I trusted you, so did Arthur. We made it possible to survive. But there were terms too, weren't there? Conditions. No politics, no changes offensive to the board and smaller shareholders. Well then – what do you think *that* is?' He waited for a second, breathing heavily before continuing, 'Breach of contract, pure and simple. I can sue that fellow Lloyd for this. Now – have you got facts into your head? Well think sharp and tell me what you're going to do about it.'

Emma studied the sheet before her. Its headlines below *Charbrook Echo* were – 'Challenge to Leyford Authorities'. And underneath, covering three columns – an outspoken article condemning the County Council for its political bigotry, and lack of feeling to the underprivileged and needy, especially where housing was concerned. After a tart outspoken beginning, the lead continued:

> In certain country districts natives are forced to live under shockingly insanitary conditions, without amenities essential to human life. No proper lighting or heating facilities, cesspools all too often having to fulfil the need of even an outside lavatory. There are areas where the families on rich men's land, men, women and children, are forced to exist without the privacy a cow would have in its own shed. These flea-ridden hovels should be condemned. Instead of certain publicity hunting personalities seeking popularity by donating sums of money publicly to charitable causes – however deserving – concern should first be given to having their own homes in order. Wealthy men come down from the North and elsewhere to buy up lands for exploitation and their own benefit. This should be stopped immediately until this County Council has first inspected and been assured that human beings have protection for a decent way of life. In the forthcoming local elections it is to be hoped that the public conscience will not be influenced – or bribed by pretty speeches and false promises – to cast its vote in favour of some greedy Lord Tom Noddy, masquerading as a saintly beneficiary to mankind. In outlying districts beyond our lovely Burnwood, there are . . .

Emma stopped reading, and put the paper down, before facing her father-in-law. Her cheeks had paled, though his were fiery red.

'Well?' he demanded again, 'what about it? *He* knew, didn't he – that wise-cracking Welshman, so did you? – that I was putting up for a seat? *You* knew as well it would be a starting point for Westminster when the time came? Yet you allowed *this* to go through—' he was waving the paper again, shaking visibly. 'Clear as daylight it is – "from the North – some greedy Lord Tom Noddy". What the devil's your game?'

He broke off, for want of breath.

For a second or two Emma was frightened, afraid he'd have a fit. But gradually his colour ebbed to a more natural, mottled shade.

'I knew nothing about it,' she said, shocked, but managing to sound calm and firm. 'Why should I? I'm only concerned with my own column. And anyway—'

'Yes?'

'You can't be sure Evan wrote it, and your name isn't mentioned.'

'It doesn't *have* to be, does it?' Sarcasm had replaced the momentory abuse in his voice. 'It's libel just the same. The snobs will love it, mop it up and snigger over their whiskies in their select clubs – I could be a laughing stock. I've a good mind to take it up – fight a case. That would stir things up all right. Your Welshman would be done for; because take my word on it, I'd win, and break him.'

'You can't be sure.' Her quick mind took a fighting turn. 'Wouldn't it be safer, and far cleverer of you to *use* this – this article?'

He looked momentarily nonplussed.

'Use it? How?'

'By taking it up. Agreeing. Make yourself a real power to do good. Visit these – these hovels. Contact the people, especially round Coldale. Speak the truth of your findings to the press, and get yourself talked about that way.' There was a pause in which his astonishment turned to grudging acknowledgement of her perspicacity. Then she continued, 'Once you've made an impact you can surely be subtle enough to win the other side. After all – they *are* rather a smug lot, aren't they?'

'Smug? Maybe. But—'

'Really,' she interrupted, 'it's your chance – if you've the guts and will to tackle it. Taking a case against Evan wouldn't solve anything, not to your advantage. It would just give him an opportunity to flaunt his ego and personality.'

He studied her with slowly awakening respect. 'By God,' he thought, 'she's of my own kind, a real clever one.'

'You may be right at that,' he said at last.

'I'm sure I am.'

Subdued and still amazed that anyone so feminine and in some ways fragile-looking as this young woman Arthur had married could have such businesslike astuteness, Jonathan, after a few cursory remarks, left Emma to her own thoughts.

Lloyd's explosive attack had surprised her as much as it had angered Jonathan, and at first she had been dismayed. The conclusion, however, had been satisfactory, up to a point. She might even take up the matter herself, presumably on Jonathan's side. Then he couldn't fight her at meetings. One thing she must keep clear to herself, however, and this was Jonathan's fierce ambition to get to Westminster. He musn't defy the existing hierarchy of the aristocracy too openly.

Which meant Evan must be a little more subtle in the immediate future.

*

It was the first week in September before Emma and Lloyd met again, on a Saturday about a mile from Oaklands. He was cycling round a bend bordering Feyland Woods, casually dressed, wearing knickerbockers and a loose jacket, with a camera slung over his shoulder. As her car approached up a slope in the lane, he jumped from his machine, grinning; with a grinding of brakes she drew the motor to a halt, and holding her skirt up in one hand, extricated herself through the door. When she'd started off from Eastwood early that afternoon she'd worn a hat tied under the chin with a gauzy scarf, but once away from the district she'd taken it off – flung it on the seat leaving her hair free in the breeze. Its dark rich russet shades gleamed copper-bright in the afternoon sunlight. Her short-caped lilac coat, loose at the neck, blended with the artistry of an Impressionist's painting against the background of early autumnal foliage. Shadows danced across the thread of roadway, dappling tree trunks and richly coloured leaves. Through net-worked branches the glimmer of a reservoir flashed momentarily, then faded behind a belt of slowly moving misted cloud. The smell of air – of damp earth already redolent with the first fallen leaves sent a wave of nostalgia through her whole body – a sensation of emotional hunger that quickly mounted to heady excitement, as she hurried towards Lloyd. It seemed, for that brief time, that they were the only two human beings in the world. No sign, no sound of anyone else. Just themselves together.

'Well, well,' he said, grasping her hand, and pulling her towards him. 'Who would have thought it?'

'What?'

'*You!* That we should meet like this. Or did you plan it, you loose woman?' The tones were jocular, but his eyes were not, holding a wealth of wonder and desire.

She laughed falsely. 'Don't be silly.'

'Is that all you can say?'

She shook her head. 'I've not anything to say at all really, except that I'll get on with that article, you know, the one about the poor living conditions – next week – if you'll print it. I think—' She swallowed, striving to keep matters on a normal level, but speaking mechanically, quickly, and with the words tumbling out. 'I think—'

He drew her close suddenly, so the warmth of his body, and steamy smell of his jacket overcame her with such longing, she did not for a few precious moments resist.

'Don't think, darling,' he whispered, with his lips hot against her cheek and ear. 'Emma, my love – please, this isn't just chance – it's inevitable. We've both known it, from the beginning. Let me love you, Emma—'

With a terrible effort she pulled herself away.

'We mustn't. Not here. Not – not *ever*.' Before he knew her intention she'd turned and rushed back to the car. He caught her hand again before she got in, and twisted her round once more to face him.

'What's the matter with you? Frightened?'

She nodded. 'Perhaps – I don't know.'

'What of? – *Him?* Bradley?'

'Maybe. Or – there are other things.'

'The paper? Your reputation?'

'In a way. It has to be, hasn't it? My father would expect it.'

'For you to be unhappy? Embittered and thwarted?'

'Oh, Evan, no. Please try and understand.'

He dropped her hand suddenly.

'I can't; I'm sorry – life's too short. Understanding doesn't come into it.' His eyes had become steely, his jaw was a hard line, though a small muscle throbbed at one side.

She was suddenly frightened, bewildered by herself, her own feelings, his, and the issue which in so short a time had assumed terrifying reality. Lloyd would never be satisfied by dreams only; neither would she. They wanted everything, both of them. And so much was at stake. But if she lost him – the idea was unbearable. Desperately she fought for self-control, to be logical. It was impossible.

'Evan—'

'Yes?'

'Don't be like this. It's not fair. You know how I feel, but give me time; *please*—'

'What for? To think?'

'Yes. *Yes*.' Her voice and manner were sharp, fierce, 'I'm not just a – just a—'

'Farmer's wench all set for a roll in the hay? Right. If that's the way you see things, Mrs Bradley—'

'It's *not*. You know it's not!' She caught his sleeve impulsively, and when he forced himself to look down again into the clear grey of her shining limpid eyes, the anger and hot desire in him relaxed suddenly into something gentler and more compassionate. She wasn't playing with him. Just for a second or two he'd doubted her. But the sincerity of her gaze, the half-opened lips, and trembling form held no guile or sophistry. She was all longing, all woman – a virgin nymph lost in the labyrinth of wild instinct, and conventional conscience. As the muscles of his body eased and the hammering of his heart quietened, the truth of the situation registered with a certainty that annoyed him. Her virginity! he'd hit on it. It was true. No man had as yet bespoiled or claimed her pristine innocence. Not even that twisted swine Arthur she'd married. Then what *had* Bradley wanted of her?

'Emma—' He heard himself saying hesitantly.

'Yes?'

'I'm sorry for upsetting you.'

She shook her head. 'You haven't. Not really. I should have known. I'm as responsible as you. And I'm not a defenceless child. If you must know – I *wanted* you to go all wild and passionate and like you are – *exactly* like you are. I'm not a prig, and—' Gold flecks flew to her grey eyes challengingly. 'If you really love me – nothing else matters, not a damn!' Her stubborn little cleft chin and pert nose were set at a luminous angle. 'So if you like—'

Such longing rose in him his voice was husky, thick.

'Are you sure? Certain you won't regret—'

'Yes. Arthur doesn't count at all. If he'd been different – but he isn't; he's awful. Oh Evan – Evan—' Her arms reached to his neck. Shaking himself, he lifted her up, with his lips against her throat, carried her down a short path into the wood. After laying her down, he forced himself to leave her, remembering his bicycle and wheeled it swiftly through the undergrowth into the shadows of the trees.

When he returned to her, she was lying in the grass, with her hair unpinned, its copper lights rippling through crushed and springing bluebells; her eyes were wide, staring upwards through a tangle of silver birch and larch. Her pale elfin face was patterned by a tracery cast from quivering young leaves above. Her bodice was loose at the neck, showing the creamy whiteness of her slender neck. Yet there was nothing of the seductress about her – only a magical aura of undefiled passion and innocence awaiting fulfilment.

He knelt down, trembling, and took her hands, one by one, raising them to his lips; she smiled, and deliberately unbuttoned her gown, while desire mounted and hardened in him.

'Emma—' he whispered, '—oh God, it's so beautiful you are, *cariad*.' Unconsciously the lilting Welsh endearment blended with the hushed murmurs of the forest, of rustling undergrowth, distant faint trickle of a brook over stones, and her answering low-voiced 'Darling, darling,' until words were stilled between them, crushed into small cries and responses as his hands sought and ravished every secret curve and recess of her body. Beauty was everywhere. With limbs entwined, male and female were united not merely through physical need, but by the deepest ties and longings of humanity to be built of one entity, spirit and flesh.

For some time, when all was over, and they were at peace again, they lay side by side, watching the glimmer of sky fading behind the trees. He sat up presently, bent once more to kiss each breast, then took a lock of her hair and put it to his lips.

She stirred and reached for her bodice.

'It's getting late, isn't it?' she said. 'And I'm supposed to be at Oaklands.'

'And I'm supposed to be back at the office with photographs of some old ruin that's going to be restored. Now see what you've done – you witch!'

She laughed as he helped her to her feet.

'If anyone's seen my motor-car down the lane they may – think things,' she said, and then with genuine alarm, 'Oh Evan – suppose someone passed, and thought there'd been an accident or something – they'd recognise the car and go to the house. Do you think—?'

'No I don't,' he told her firmly. 'This lane's one of the loneliest in Burnwood, as you well know.'

'Yes, but some walker or a farm labourer—' A little frown creased her brow.

He drew her to him. 'My dear love, when *that* bridge comes we'll cross it. Anyway some day we've got to face the future, and I'm not one to cower in corners forever. Secret meetings may be necessary for a time, but only until we've found the guts to say "damn all" to society.'

She shivered faintly.

'What's the matter? Cold, love?'

'No. Just—'

'Frightened?'

'Of course not. Why should I be? Well, maybe I am – a bit. Not of us, or because of loving. For you, I think, mostly.'

'Me?'

She nodded. 'It may alter things for you rather badly, Evan, when they know. We *must* wait a bit; for both our sakes. Your career's important. Don't deny it!'

'Temporarily, maybe. Only that.' He paused, then continued, 'I won't deliver the bomb-shell yet. Just remember one thing though—'

'Yes?'

'We belong. And there's nothing in the world can change it.'

*

By a freak of chance, Emma met Arthur returning from the paddock as she drove the motor-car down a side drive to its allotted shed. She called it her garage; her husband referred to it contemptuously as 'a stye' in contrast to the smart building specifically erected for Jonathan's Rolls.

The delight in her heart ebbed to discomfited irritation. The last person in the world she wished to see just then was Arthur. But he waited until she'd parked 'the jalopy' – another of her husband's disparaging nicknames, and walked with her up the main side drive leading to Eastwood's front door.

'Oaklands again, I presume?' he said in an offhand manner.

'And other places,' she answered quickly. 'Why?'

He gave her an alert, sidelong look. 'You look radiant,' he answered. 'Different. What have you been up to, Emma?'

Unable to help the hot flush rising to her cheeks, she forced annoyance into her voice, hoping to divert his attention by a show of anger.

'Oh don't be ridiculous. Driving. Just *driving* – I do sometimes, you know, merely for the pleasure of it. Anything wrong in that?'

His handsome face darkened. 'Only *you* know. But there are times when it might be advisable for you to have a bit of a gallop with me. That new gelding the pater presented you with needs exercise, and we should be seen together sometimes, don't you think?'

'Aren't we? If ever we're invited out I join you. At the dances – that horrible aristocratic charity ball affair you managed to get involved in—'

'There's no reason to rub it in. I *got* there, that's the important point. The Bradley name registered.'

'And did you enjoy it? The dance? The toasting and back-slapping – the noise and fuss?'

'Of course. What the devil are you getting at?'

'*I* didn't,' she answered recklessly, 'enjoy it, if you must know. It was all so beastly snobbisly *obvious*. And you! – the way you flattered and fawned over Bettina Carnley – *Lady* Bettina,' she added meaningfully. 'Do you imagine people didn't notice?'

His underlip took a sullen thrust. 'She's a very attractive woman. And influential. If anyone noticed, all the better. I'm going along with my father for once, distributing my charms where they're appreciated by all concerned.'

'Oh I'm sure she must have been positively *thrilled* by your male attributes.' The sting in her words did not escape him. He gripped her arm hard, making her wince.

'You just wait, madam,' he said in a threatening undertone, close against her ear. 'I've taken a hell of a lot from you, but any more jibes and you'll need *two* bustles on your charming posterior for a week or more.'

'Don't be so vulgar,' she said, shaking herself free. 'I hate your – your threats and bullying, Arthur Bradley. Leave me alone, or I'll—'

'You'll do nothing but what you're told to,' he said. 'And now—' as they neared the terrace, '—pull yourself together. Remember your place, and who you are.' The hard glitter in his eyes melted slightly. 'It's a pity you can't accept things, Emma. You still intrigue me. Can't you try and make a go of our life? You've got everything you want except—'

'Normality,' she interrupted. 'Yes, I know.'

'Is normality so important? Anyway – is anyone completely normal? Are *you*? Always tripping off to newspaper gatherings and business meetings? And that Welsh fellow – Lloyd? Is *he*? To my mind he's an excessive phoney braggart with a dangerous tongue. *Now* I hear you're going to collaborate with him on some challenging social problem of housing; presumably with my father's blessing, in the belief it will give him a leg up in local government.' He paused. 'You must be crazy, both of you.'

'Thank you.' Her voice had become ice.

Before they went into the house he touched her hand tentatively.

'Emma—' he drew her to a halt. Her body went rigid. 'Tonight I'll try and show you I do care for you in my way. You never know – tonight perhaps—'

Recalling past experiences she shuddered inwardly, thinking 'Oh no, not that, dear God. Not that.'

'It's all right, Arthur,' she forced herself to say brightly. 'I believe you. And don't worry, I'll try to behave more as you wish me to. And certainly we'll go riding. You're quite right about the gelding. He needs exercise. I've been very remiss.'

He was mollified. 'That's all right. We could go for a canter tomorrow perhaps – call en route on that old fellow Lord Wendle. The pater's well in with him and hoping the friendship will pay off.'

She felt a brief stirring of pity for him. He was like his father, so naive – so completely ignorant of the tightly-knit, inherent perspicacity and loyalty of society's élite, one to the other. Wendle of course was something of an eccentric and oddity to his kind. But beneath the genial facade was a patronising quick-wittedness which would have surprised Jonathan had he guessed the extent of it. They had each other's measure, up to a point; each one was using the other to mutual advantage. Beyond that, familiarity ceased. The class bridge remained, and would be erased only by the passing of generations.

Still, so long as her father-in-law achieved superficial acceptance and his eventual seat in Parliament, Emma supposed that Bradley wouldn't care about deeper values. Money could do so much, and would probably, even in the end manipulate an advantageous marriage socially for Jessie. But happiness?

Poor Jessie.

Even her mother feared for her future. Her blunt personality and earthy rustic looks were hardly likely to stir romance in any young man's heart – especially some aristocratic snob out only for her dowry and money. Although Amelia herself was comparatively content and could no longer envisage living the humble life of her origins, she sensed Jessie's lack of confidence and incapacity to live up to the standards Jonathan expected of her. She had been taught to be well-mannered and dress tastefully. But the fact was that no clothes, however expensive, looked right on her. She simply had no outward charm, and Amelia knew that finishing school could never change, or supply the lack. In a more simple society – on the wild moors of her ancestry, she would probably have settled down easily with some steady young fellow who'd appreciate sound qualities of honesty, strength and physical health – Jessie's only attributes necessary for the making of a good wife and mother.

More than once Amelia had heard her husband refer to their daughter as a throw-back. On one occasion her blood had boiled in a flood of resentment.

'And if she is, what of it?' Amelia had asked bluntly. 'It's healthy stock she comes from, Jonathan Bradley, and don't you forget it. One day that sturdy girl of ours may make thee proud. There's other things in the world than silks an' satins an'—'

'All the liquor you consume in secret,' Jonathan had interrupted sharply.

There'd been a sullen, quiet pause, then, 'There's no secret about it. I hide nothing, and I'm not ungrateful for what you've done for me, Jonathan. It's not myself I'm grumbling about. But Jessie's my own. I bore her. I don't want her hurt.'

'She won't be. I'll see her secure. As secure as Arthur, though he doesn't appear to need any help from me. A handsome young ram if ever there was one.'

With a flash of insight Amelia had retorted unconsciously resorting to her North County brogue, 'Mebbe it would have been better for him if he'd had less of it.'

'Of what?'

'*Charm*. Looks. They're not allus an advantage. There's other things; such as—' She paused, struggling for the right word.

'Yes? Well, go on; have your say.'

'I will an' all; just to give you something to think about, Jonathan Bradley. I've allus kept quiet about Arthur's failings, for your sake, and because I'm so proud of him – mostly. But there's a sly side to him that puzzles me – specially with that grand, haughty look on him. And he can be cold. Heartless. I don't like that. He's got no kindness in him unless it suits his purpose. And that's what I meant about "those other things" – warmth, respect for others – to be able to give sometimes with naught in return. I reckon we've both failed in teaching the lad proper values.'

As she stopped speaking the rich colour in her face had faded visibly. For a moment or two her husband was speechless. It was the first time he remembered, since their marriage, Amelia being so forthright or having the courage to criticise him. He'd stared at her with a rare unexpected respect.

'That's quite a speech for you. Amelia. *Values!* So you think we've failed, eh?'

She'd shaken her head slowly. 'Sometimes I don't know what to think, and that's the truth. You asked me some time back, to sound him about him and Emma. Their marriage. But it's no good. Any mention of her name and he shuts up like a clam. And she's the same. Mind you, *I* can get on with her, she's a nice enough girl beneath all that intellectual talk. But there's no real *contact* between us. Well, there couldn't be, could there? – me coming from where I did, and *her* a *Fairley*.'

'I wish you'd stop harping on your background,' Jonathan snapped. 'You're my wife. That should be enough. Apparently it isn't though—' His gaze and voice had become resentful, moody. 'You have to have your liquor too, as well as fine clothes and rich food.'

'Aye,' she'd admitted, as she had, countless times before, sounding sad, resigned. 'Bucks me up when I'm down. There's many others like me, I reckon, with nothing much else in their lives but money.'

'If you took a bit of exercise now and then you'd probably feel fitter and certainly look better.'

'A bit late now,' she'd said.

Following the revealing conversation Jonathan had tried to dismiss his wife's criticism of their son from his mind, diverting his attention almost fanatically to business affairs, wheedling or blundering his way – some would have said, buying – into any important Leyford organisation available – donating gifts throughout the county to charitable concerns, with the satisfaction, later, of seeing his name printed as a member of worthy and respected committees. The Bradley name became synonymous with wealth and power. Despite innuendos and sly comments behind newspapers and brandies in select clubs, it could not be denied that with his guts and wherewithal Jonathan was steadily becoming a force to be reckoned with.

The old adage was true.

Money counted.

Gradually members of the élite bearing handles to their names – deigned to visit social functions at Eastwood – including a garden party on behalf of a certain charity attended by forefront personalities including a wealthy Maharajah and a fox-hunting Duchess who, following her recent divorce, had her eye on an eccentric minor member of Royalty. On a more intellectual level, the gardens of Eastwood were thrown open for a week's performance of Shakespeare, the proceeds of which were to be donated to a Welfare Fund for the unemployed and disabled. In the autumn of 1904 a masked ball was given in which servants of the house and two neighbouring large establishments were invited to join. Jonathan, while ploughing his way up the social ladder, never lost sight of the fact that when election time came the man-in-the-street would have a powerful part to play. Therefore, a little ploy to go ahead would pay off.

Before these events, however, his newspaper the *Comet* had a set-back, originating, he was doggedly certain, through Emma's article on the housing question.

She wrote it with fire and zeal in pungent terms which she'd not entirely realised until then that she possessed. Her sensitivity indeed, had been shocked when she visited the area of the benighted dwelling. It stood on the outskirts of Coldale, and in two rooms with a shanty outhouse, housed three generations of human beings, men, women and children; it was damp, with a leaking roof, a cess-pit not far from the door, and flea ridden. The inmates were belligerent, with a hopeless air of fatigue about them. The son and father were unemployed miners – the former through a pit closing, the second through silicosis.

There was no political reference to any party in Emma's comments; her attack was on governing authorities whom she accused of turning a blind eye on the distressful circumstances in which a certain sector of the population was condemned to live.

The effect when printed under bold headlines on the front page of a Friday edition of the *Echo*, followed by an extended version in the weekly, was electric. Letters followed immediately, demanding action, and condemning landowners who came from other parts to increase their wealth through Leyford industry which had made it the richest town in England.

Jonathan was furious – especially as Emma had used her maiden name of Emma Fairley instead of Bradley for the write-up. He blamed his daughter-in-law irately for this.

'And what did you think you were doing?' he demanded, waving the sheet at her. 'Putting me back a bit? Old prejudices, eh? Destroying all I've achieved during these last months? And Fairley! Why the devil did you have to call yourself that?'

'I'm known by it. It was my name.'

'Was – *was*. Aye!' he thumped his chest. 'But that's all over, by God. You're a Bradley now, and the idea of this – this writing business was to pull it up a bit. Help *me*. Me – d'you understand? Oh yes, you do all right. You're a deep one. You must've calculated in your mind for quite some time how to get the *Echo* on your side and poke fun at the *Comet*.'

Emma's lips went tight. Her voice was cold when she said, 'I didn't calculate at all. I spoke the truth. What I saw *shocked* me. You didn't come into it at all.'

'And who put you up to it? Who told you about that slum

place at all? – It was him, wasn't it? – The Welsh fellow Lloyd?'

Evading a direct answer Emma said, 'Evan's the editor of the newspaper. I have to consult him about any story.'

'Oh! so it's Evan now, is it?' The question was a bitter sneer. 'Well, my girl, it won't be much longer. There are political aims behind this drivel I don't like at all. You may think you've got the upper hand on the *Echo* at the moment, but you're mistaken. Fifty-one per cent of the shares! Eh? Well – with forty-nine of them gone, or near enough, that rag of your father's will be defunct. Nil. Worth nothing but for the waste-paper basket. I'll break Lloyd, by God I will. This business may have broken any chance I had of getting on to the Council.'

Whether the article was partly responsible for Jonathan's forecast, which proved weeks later to be true, was doubtful. The fact was he failed, by a minority, to be elected. That the authorities moved quickly to have the unfortunate families decently housed weighed nothing at all with him. No human factor counted. The damage was done. And to him it was all Emma's fault. In public, however, he put on a brave front, an air of bonhomie and almost genial acceptance which deceived most, hence the parties and social occasions at Eastwood. At such a crucial point in his life he recognised the importance of being judged as nothing but an honest fair-minded man. The great challenge lay ahead when the country gave its vote. For that day all potential obstacles must be effectively squashed, and the priority was to see that Evan Lloyd was got out of the way for good.

Emma did her best to appease Jonathan's disappointment by keeping her column, following the argument, on a lower key, and even in assuming a friendlier facade to Arthur. In public they represented a devoted young couple, to the majority of people. Arthur, fiercely jealous if he thought she appeared too interested in any other man, took fanatical pride in showing her off as his wife and therefore his unique possession. In private, life to her, was hell. She no longer fought him as she had at the beginning of their marriage; once in the past when she'd defied him, he'd flung her on the bed and abused her by not only slapping her soundly, but in other ways that had made her want to die. He had never used the whip – yet. And she had determined he never should. Having to bear his warped endearments was odious to her, but her apparent acquiescence reduced these eventually to a minimum. In fact he was beginning to tire of trying to goad her, and boredom led him to drink.

Jonathan noticed, and was worried.

'For God's sake take a good look at yourself,' he said one day. 'Pull yourself together. What's the matter with you? You've got all you want, haven't you? Wealth, looks, a handsome wife – and the time's approaching when you can be a help to me – to us all, the whole family, if you put your mind to it. Wendle's got it all fixed for me as candidate in the election, and it won't be long, lad, after that – a knighthood maybe, hereditary. Think where that puts you—'

'Me?' Arthur sneered derisively.

'Yes, you. My *son*.' There was a pause during which Jonathan's mind took another direction. 'Emma,' he said, 'your wife. She's not – cold is she, frigid? If that's it there *are* other women. Don't think I'd blame you—'

Arthur flung back his handsome head, gave a laugh as harsh and cold, despite the liquor he'd consumed, as the ice-flame of his eyes. 'Women! when the day comes I depend on any one of them I may as well be dead.'

He turned abruptly and marched, tall, arrogant, Nature's perfection in physical form, down the drive to the stables, where his stallion waited, eager for a gallop.

Such rides generally ended at a remote cottage on the edge of a lonely copse. The humble dwelling was inhabited by a farm labourer's widow and her twelve-year-old son, David. The woman, Cora, eked out a living by making brooms, and during the summer months selling daffodils and bunches of posies in Leyford. The boy, not too bright in the head, occasionally accompanied her. He was black-haired, unusually good-looking, and accepted gleefully the present taken to him by Arthur. In the privacy of the woods favours were equally bestowed. Their understanding was mutual, a secret carefully guarded, even from Cora, who conveniently left them alone together when necessary. She asked no questions; silence on the situation was golden in every sense.

Had Jonathan remotely suspected the depths of his son's depravity he'd doubtless 'have kicked him out' in his own terminology.

But he hadn't.

10

By the end of September Lloyd found himself in the unhappy position of editing a newspaper that was certainly on the downgrade financially. This was not due to any withdrawal of local support, but by pressure put on its production by Bradley. Although a completely united board could ensure continuance – through Emma's support – of its policy, she had neither the means nor devious knowledge required to thwart Bradley's aim. His mind so fanatically set in getting rid of Evan, conceived a number of subtle ways of achieving it. Firstly, he managed to get the two largest shareholders next to Emma and himself on to his side, then began manipulating advertisers against the *Echo*'s increasing 'new look'. Much of the revenue from sales depended on two pages devoted almost entirely to advertising – sometimes a full sheet was used by one business firm. Without income from this quarter the paper would indeed have a struggle to survive. Closure eventually would be inevitable. Jonathan's methods were brilliantly cunning; the cost to his own pocket was considerable – at the beginning. On the other hand, reimbursement soon followed by once more achieving rising circulation of the *Comet*.

Evan gradually found his hands tied from several angles. His chief reporter was lured to join the staff of the new paper, with a high rise in salary, and the promise of further advancement money-wise and in status when the *Echo* was eventually amalgamated into the proposed *Midlander*. New machinery was needed for printing and better transport for distribution. Emma, seeing how things were going, was desperate, no longer so much on her late father's behalf – he was dead and could no more be here – but for Lloyd, whom she so passionately loved and admired. During recent weeks they had managed to meet secretly, and as time passed had realised an inevitable crisis must soon be faced.

'It can't go on like this,' he told Emma, when they met one late afternoon in his office for discussion, presumably, of her column. 'Neither can the paper. I'll have to quit, and that's the truth of it.'

Dismay filled her as though a dark cloud had descended, sucking her into a dark well of misery. Until that moment she'd not accepted the possibility of life without Lloyd. Their moments of real intimacy, physical and mental, it was true, were few. But his image – the memory of his sudden, elfin smile, the clear eyes that could be so bright and piercing one moment, the next warm with desire and longing filled her days. His touch, the feel of his arms round her, of his body, close against hers, made her a new person, revitalised her will so that she could endure – without displaying how hateful it was – her life at Eastwood with Arthur. Pain gnawed her as she asked, 'Leave the *Echo*, you mean? But what will you do? Perhaps the *Courier*—'

Evan shook his head.

'No thank you, darling. If I quit the *Echo* I quit the problems of financial journalism. Freedom! I've got to have it, Emma. Bradley means to get his hand on the whole group of Midland newspapers, and in my opinion he may do it. The *Courier* will fight, and it may, it just *may* endure. But the tycoon warfare sickens me. Money – grab all – possessions? What does it all amount to? You tell me.'

'It can advertise you. Make your name known as a poet,' she said stubbornly. 'Don't you want *that*? You've got such a gift—'

She broke off as he walked to a window overlooking the street. Outside it was a perfect early autumn evening. The last rays of gold sunlight dappled streets and the few trees, touching the forms of passing pedestrians and colourful glory of leaves and herbage. A faint drift of woodsmoke crept into the room through the open window. All was still; a few lights glimmered from a factory on the opposite side of the canal, giving the impression of square eyes watching. A moment in time that could have been magical to both of them – *was* magical but filled for Emma with aching, nostalgic despair.

'Of course I want recognition,' she heard him say. 'Not because I'm dubbing myself a genius or pioneer, but because of *this*—' He turned suddenly, thumping his chest. 'Something *inside* me I want to say – something that's *real* and important and will perhaps give impetus to others. It may sound phoney – the kind of cant loafers use when they damn well shy away from a day's decent hard work. But I'm not that kind. I'm *hungry*, Emma. Hungry to express myself, to get to the heart of things in the way I choose – travel perhaps, adventure – share with them all, young and old, sick, healthy, black or white, discover what I was born for—' He broke off, smiled in the whimsical way that so touched her, and confessed '—Well, maybe I've done that already.'

He crossed the floor quickly, and took her in his arms. She closed her eyes, feeling suddenly so glowing and comforted, nothing else for a few seconds registered. Then she remembered.

'You're trying to say – telling me – you're going away?' she asked.

'I don't know. If I do it won't be for ever. It will be because I have to plan for us both, *cariad*.' The old endearment slipped out instinctively.

'But *where*? Wales?'

He drew her to the window. They both stood there, watching the first frail cloud of mist shimmer the water, taking figures and slowly moving traffic into blurred silhouette.

'Perhaps,' he answered after a pause. 'I'm known there, and

it's my home. I have my degree – I'm qualified – there are many clubs – where lecturers are needed. I've connections that would earn a week's keep by travelling about. It might even be possible to come to Leyford officially from time to time. The university and working men's college are both getting quite go-ahead. We wouldn't be *parted*, darling.'

'Wouldn't we?' Her voice was full and filled with doubt. 'How often would we see each other?'

'As often as I could damn well make it. You know that.'

'How do I know?'

The arm round her waist tightened. With eyes blazing down into hers, his lips came full and firm on her mouth, driving for that sad-sweet interval all emotion and passion from her.

She loved him; oh God – so much, so much. Not only his potent sexuality, his vitality and fire, but his brilliant quick mind, combined with a certain ruthless honesty that would inevitably lead him into dangerous confrontation with any placid status quo of society. His poetry too. Beneath the man of action was ever the dreamer, the romantic Celt in whose genes flowed still the fanatical love of his own land, who could bring lost legendry to life again in words, and make music of common everyday things: the miner eking out his days and energy underground in the pit; a hard working farmer's wife, baking bread in her small kitchen; the tramp of pedestrians' feet plodding to their homes down grey Welsh streets through the rain; and, beyond, the mountains, grim and bleak with their peaks inky black against a winter sky. The swirl of rivers coursing through narrow dark valleys past hamlets and towns towards the coast; and singing – forever the singing, not only of men's voices from taverns and clubs, but of an emotional longing and hunger bred in the very blood and genes of the Welsh: the inheritors.

Therein lay Evan's background and his gift. Through his senses he conveyed the unique richness of his ancestry, which was a curious blend of the worker and the scholar. His father had been a humble but dedicated mining engineer, his mother the fiery beautiful daughter of a well-educated schoolmaster of stern religious views. Their marriage had been against the wishes of both families, and had proved, later, to be a stormy one. But it had survived. Iestyn Lloyd had died in a mining accident when Evan, his son, was eleven years old, and Angharrad, his daughter, seven. Marged, the widow, refusing help from her parents had taken a post as village schoolmistress at a remote hamlet in the valleys, bringing up her children with a strictness against which Evan had rebelled. Fiercely, independently, he had worked his way through College, obtaining a literary degree. It was during that period his mother had been killed, also his sister, when a mountainous tip of coal refuse slid one tragic wet day, claiming many victims.

Evan had regretted her death, but not mourned her from the heart. She had been too stern, too violent. But the loss of little Angharrad and his father had sewn seeds of defiant pain in him which remained with him, at the root of his being, and always would.

He never spoke of such things, not even to Emma. But in his verse the dormant anguish surfaced occasionally with a poignancy that was almost discomforting. Emma was curious. If only he would open up to her, she'd thought more than once. It seemed to her they should share everything. Nothing should be withheld from two people in love as they were. She'd probed, and all he'd said was, 'Let the dead rest. Yours and mine. It's the future we have to plan for. That's what I mean to do.'

This was true, of course, and when she'd reviewed the situation objectively, she'd realised that she, also over certain matters, was as secretive as he was, in withholding the painful intimacies of her life with Arthur. So they were quits, in a way – but with a difference. Lloyd, now, was twenty-eight, and had admitted, without giving any specific details, that he'd had more than one love affair, omitting to reveal a certain interim that might, at that time, have changed Emma's whole attitude to him. As it was, one painful question gnawed her. Supposing, if he returned to Wales for an interim, there was some girl or woman waiting for him, to whom he once again was drawn and fell for?

What would she do?

How could she bear it?

It mustn't happen. It *mustn't*.

Suddenly, on that aching, nostalgic Autumn afternoon, she pulled away from him, and said.

'No, you can't. You *can't*.' Her small chin was set, her grey eyes tortured.

Dismay filled him. He was hurt – for both of them, but at that moment mostly for her. He was experienced and could be hard when necessary, but her innocence made her specially vulnerable. During past weeks he'd toyed with the idea of their taking off together immediately. But male practicality told him that in doing so they would both be so chained by circumstances the foundation of their union might suffer and wither into a grey dutiful struggle to exist. This mustn't happen, for her sake more than his.

'I've told you – I may *have* to,' he said gently. 'I shall be seeing you – never doubt that – oh, my darling, you must have faith. Once I've the wherewithal – a responsible post, or proper means of supporting you, I shall be down to carry you off with me on some fine steed, like knights in the *Mabinogian*.'

'The *Mabinogian*?'

'A Welsh book of legends,' he told her – 'a very ancient one. Traditional.'

His effort at humour brought a slight travesty of a smile to her lips.

'And suppose—' She broke off hesitantly.

'Suppose what?'

'If Arthur—'

'If the swine maltreats you,' he asserted, 'I've told you – that's different. I'll come immediately from wherever I am, and kill him.'

The touch of melodrama restored a vein of common sense in her.

'I wouldn't want that. And you wouldn't do it anyway. You're no potential murderer. And – you needn't worry – Arthur's never harmed me – physically.' The half-lie stuck in her throat, but her statement, combined with a return of rose colour to her cheeks, deceived him. He breathed a sigh of relief.

'Is there anything else?' he asked. 'Anything I can do, to make things easier? Be honest now. You understand?'

She nodded.

'I'm trying.' Then forcing a light tone into her voice, 'Just so long as you haven't another girl tucked away somewhere I'll survive, I suppose. Is there?'

His look was whimsical – full of mischief when he answered, 'Plenty. Black-haired, blondes, and redheads.' The banter died. 'Oh Emma,' he said, 'you shouldn't ask such a thing – even in fun.'

'No. I suppose not.'

'One day,' he continued, looking away from her at some paper on his desk, 'when everything's sorted out, I'll reveal the extent of my murky past, if you insist. It's not important anyway. The present, and the future's our problem.'

'Yes, yes, I know.' With an effort she dispelled a sense of hopelessness rising in her. 'And if you're really determined to go, that's it. I can understand, see your point. The paper isn't all *that* important.' Her voice trembled slightly.

'It's very important,' he asserted, 'or *was*. To you, especially. But against Jonathan Bradley, Emma, its chances of survival now are nil. And I don't intend being kicked out. I'm going.'

'When?' Her voice was firm, hard, but her throat ached.

'As soon as possible. We may see each other again first – or not. I don't know. But we shall be in contact, and one day there'll be no more goodbyes between us. You must trust me.'

'Evan—' She stepped towards him again, her grey eyes bright. 'Evan—'

'No tears,' he said. 'I couldn't stand it. And you're not the crying sort.'

'No.'

She picked up her scarf and went to the door.

'All right, it's goodbye then – or au revoir—'

'I'll write. To Oaklands.'

'Yes.'

Little more was said, and a moment or two later Emma was in the street walking mechanically towards her car. Twilight was already a veil of fading blue-green over the town, evoking an eerie sense of melancholy and bygone long-dead things; roofs and chimney-pots loomed blurred and grey through a rising mist. Thin chords of sadness tugged at her chest, like the taut strings of some ancient violin about to break on an old nostalgic tune. Nothing seemed real. The pale squares of factory windows glared with the haunting quality of empty eyes over pavements and the canal. As she neared the car an old man shuffled by, head bent, as though unseeing, to the ground. A woman stood at the corner waiting – for what? Her lips even in the deepening light were brilliantly red. Her eyes slanting and pointed like those of a creature in a dream. So many lives! So many ways, differing destinies bred of human demands, despairs, and ambitions. Fulfilment and frustration; the pattern of existence.

Shivering slightly, Emma tore herself from such uncharacteristic melancholy, cranked up the car, and was presently on her way from the town to the more wooded area of Burnwood.

The country was beautiful, even in the half light. A number of russet and amber leaves still clung to the tracery of dark branched trees. Once, near the old ruin of the ancient Priory, she drew to a halt and sniffed the damp air and woodsmoke deep into her lungs. Old emotions were reborn, old memories from her childhood when the ancient spirit of 'place' had impelled her to write fairy-tales, and act them within the ivied walls. She smiled gently, though she didn't realise it. A certain bitterness in her was healed – temporarily. Always, she told herself, there was the forest, and Oaklands. The sanctuary that held something and always would, of her most secret self.

Presently she drove on again, not calling at her old home because it was too late.

When next she went that way, a week later, Evan Lloyd had left the *Echo* and it was to be a considerable time before she saw him again.

*

Once Evan had gone, Jonathan's attitude to Emma became more conciliatory – even a trifle benevolent.

'Don't think I'm going to try and wipe your family newspaper out,' he said, after delivering the news that Clarke was taking over until a new editor for the *Echo* was found. 'That's what you've been told, I suppose, by Lloyd and others like him. At the moment they're quite wrong. Eventually – it's possible; but we've a long way to go to get *The Midlander* established, and during that time there'll be plenty of opportunity to test the *Echo*'s value – financially, and to the public. In fact, there's no reason on earth why a revised weekly shouldn't continue indefinitely. Natives and country people look forward to hearing tasty bits and pieces, and any sensational event in their area—'

'Such as Births and Deaths,' Emma interrupted tartly. 'Round Burnwood especially the people are a closely knit group. It isn't only the extraordinary that appeals to them. They appreciate sound facts.'

'Exactly,' drily. 'Thanks for pointing it out.' The vein of sarcasm didn't make any impact on Emma's point of view regarding the Bradleys or the *Echo*. She had to accept that the end of an era had come with Lloyd's departure. Although he'd been editor for so comparatively short a time, he'd made his mark which had been resented by Jonathan. Whoever next filled the post would be less colourful and more of a 'yes man'. Yes to the Bradleys. Her father even might have given in – she didn't know. She wasn't certain at that point of anything very much at all. Her sense of drive, with Evan's departure, had temporarily died in her. While Lloyd was in the vicinity the knowledge had given excitement and hope to her life. Now, though she still hoped, all manner of doubts and possibilities clouded her spirits.

Jonathan was puzzled. He'd expected opposition and arguments from her, but not the bitterness, almost dull disinterest that gave him no challenge or pride in his achievement. He'd won. But victory was in a curious way tasteless – flat.

To Arthur Emma was more acquiescent. For the first time she felt mildly sorry for him, recognising that in spite of his extraordinary good looks and capacity to charm when he wished, he was actually no more than a tool under his father's thumb and had been since his birth, a product fashioned to further Bradley ambitions, a course that had driven him to his own furtive other life, and to alcohol. Beneath the air of arrogant sangfroid there lurked a childish sense of impotence and failure.

Once she had discovered the crumbling foundation beneath the ice-cold veneer, Emma found that dealing with Arthur's twisted personality became easier. She used subtle means of flattery when dangerous signs of temper showed, and in this way a sense of balance was restored.

'It isn't so bad for you after all, is it, Emma?' he enquired one night as she prepared for bed. She was wearing a silk wrap of a becoming peach shade that enhanced her glowing skin and the gleaming of her rich hair.

'What?' she asked, drawing a brush through the copper mane. Although she had a maid, she'd insisted from the first in dealing with her own toilette at nights.

'Us. You and I. Our marriage.'

'If you're contented, that's all that matters,' she answered, ambiguously.

'*You* matter,' he asserted, touching her neck with a caressing finger. He had slim hands, elegant and tapering, unlike either of his parents. The finger stroked the base of her skull, travelling downwards lightly over each delicate vertebra of her spine. The brush fell from her hand. Automatically she stiffened.

He noticed, laughed a little self-consciously, and said, 'Don't worry, I'm not up to anything, as you've put it more than once. I was merely pointing out that I still – care for and admire you. You're very beautiful.'

'Thank you.'

'And lately you've been so much more cooperative.' Through the mirror she saw his face peering questioningly at her reflection, waiting for a reply. 'I wonder *why*?' he added ruminatively in a way that discomfited her.

'Must there be a reason?' she forced a smile. 'I suppose I know you better, and have learned not to expect certain things most women do. Ordinary women.'

'Ah.' With both hands, he pulled the hair from her face and rolled it in a tight knot at the back of her head. 'There!' he continued, when the fine bones were quite clear and freed of any silken curl or shadowed tendril on her forehead. 'You could be a boy now – or a golden statue of some young Greek god. Greek gods were never ordinary, neither are you. You could be – magnificent, Emma.'

His tone was so abnormally rapturous, his bright blue eyes so filled with cold fire, she made a quick movement, jerked his hands away, and stood up, sending the dressing table stool to the floor, facing him. Inadvertently, the wrap fell away from one breast revealing its subtle sensuous curve and rosy nipple beneath the fragile nightdress. Hurriedly she pulled the wrap close to her neck as her hair fell loose again over her shoulders.

He stepped back, stood quite still for a moment regarding her with shocked disgust. Then he said contemptuously, 'Go to bed, cover yourself. You *disgust* me.'

'But—'

The cold lines of his lips turned into an ugly sneer.

'You heard what I said.'

'Yes, I heard, and I'm not staying. You get to your bed. *You* with your dreams of Greek gods and eunuchs. You're not sane, Arthur. And you know it. But does *he*? Your father?'

The question hit him. He wiped his brow with a shred of cambric, and sat on the bed, with his head in his hands. When he looked up, the glittering eyes had quietened to blue pools softened by unshed tears.

He pulled himself together with astonishing speed, assuming even a shred of dignity.

'Please stay,' he said, 'I'm sorry, *I'll* sleep in the dressing room. But—' the lips tightened again, 'I rely on you to say nothing of this to my father; you understand? – Anyway, he wouldn't believe you.'

'No.'

Feeling unutterably weary, she went towards the bed, and

stood there with her back to him, waiting for him to go. Only when she heard the dressing room door open and close, did she make a move. Then she flung herself on the quilt and lay there for some time staring unseeingly at the ornate encrusted ceiling.

'Evan,' she thought helplessly. 'Oh Evan – why did you have to go away?'

She knew the answer, Lloyd's answer, but somehow it made no sense. He should have been near at hand to comfort and prove his reality by fulfilment of their love. She didn't yet know that fulfilment had already been achieved, giving life to the flowering tiny seed in her womb; the fruit of their love – hers and Evan's.

11

Emma, on edge, restlessly waited for news from Evan for over a week, making an excuse each day for either riding by horse or car to Oaklands, on the pretext, when necessary, that she had business to attend to concerning renovations at the Dower House which meant visits to Leyford, and sometimes a certain furnishers in Charbrook dealing with fabrics in new Liberty designs. She had legitimate reasons also for concerning herself with the *Echo* column following editorial changes. There was at that time therefore no reason for suspecting her motives and absences at Eastwood. Jonathan congratulated himself that the purpose of getting rid of Lloyd had been so effectively achieved with the minimum of trouble. Emma appeared during those first days comparatively docile and ready to accept his interim plan for the newspaper. The truth was that she was so dulled with disappointment by Evan's apparent neglect that for a brief time she didn't care about much else. When, after ten days, there was no word – no note from him waiting at Oaklands, she managed to pull herself together and turned once more to business matters, becoming efficiently involved in the *Echo*'s future. It was obvious to her that there would now be no chance of revitalising it into anything but a rather dull, middle-of-the-road local news-sheet – a publication that would just manage to pay its way until the time came for its extinction through amalgamation into the future *Midlander*. There would be no controversy in its columns during its waning life, no fire or spark of individuality. Therefore – the sooner it went the better. But not the weekly. Her quick mind, searching for creative interest to fill the aching loss of contact with Evan, found, at last, a solution. Having so pleased Jonathan with her apparent acceptance of his recent policies, she had no difficulty in interesting him by her new and sudden brainwave.

'The weekly,' she said boldly one day, 'why shouldn't the weekly stand on its own feet? You say the *Echo* would cost a fortune in the new machinery required for its successful survival. Well then! You've not much faith in it, anyway, for the future, so let it go. But the weekly could continue on what equipment's already there. And extra sheets – a kind of supplement could be published with it, dealing exclusively with *women's* affairs. Do you understand?'

Jonathan regarded his daughter-in-law with bewilderment, but faint interest stirring.

'Go on,' he said, 'be more explicit. What do you mean? – *women's affairs?*'

'Yes, *yes*. Don't you see? Women are in need of some paper, some personal news-sheet or magazine of their own. They're quite uncatered for at the moment, especially in country districts. But tips on fashion, cookery, crafts, gossip of social affairs, perhaps a 'woman of the week' paragraph plus a photograph – competitions, even a question-and-answer on home affairs, and dressmaking – gardening—' She paused, watching interest quicken in his eyes, as potential possibilities of her idea took shape. 'Don't you *see*? It would pay off. Double the circulation of the weekly, and gather a whole lot of new readers. It could be a money-spinner, Jonathan.'

There was a pause, while his fingers drummed a sharp tattoo on the table. Then he said, 'You have an idea there, Emma, a constructive one, but whether it's practical or not's another question. Who'd run it, to begin with?'

'*I* could, within reason. I—'

'But you've the Dower House and family affairs to deal with, as well as your interest in Oaklands.'

She set her chin stubbornly. 'I'd have to have help, of course – but only a minimum of personal staff, two at the most, and—'

'And what would you propose to call it?' he asked. 'This new venture?'

'Oh, yes. The name would be important. We'd have to

think—' he appreciated the 'we' '—perhaps something like *Woman's View*, or – or *Women at Home* – no, not that, too suburban. *Woman's Post*, perhaps, *that* would bring in letters. I just don't know yet. We'd hit on the right thing in the end. Honestly, the whole thing *is* practical.'

The short discussion ended by Bradley saying he'd give her idea consideration, and with that she had to be satisfied.

Privately he'd half accepted the idea, marvelling at the girl's perspicacity. A woman's paper. Why not? Especially starting with Emma at the helm. There was no knowing – with proper handling and advertisement it might expand in public appeal and circulation far further than the boundaries of Leyfordshire.

The more he viewed the suggestion the more enticing it became, although he kept any growing enthusiasm he had to himself. When he mentioned the matter to Arthur, his son appeared at first superciliously amused, then faintly resentful. 'Don't say dear Emma has got under your skin that much,' he remarked. 'A *woman's* paper. You must be crazy.'

'Watch your tongue,' Jonathan snapped, 'and put that glass down.' Arthur was half leaning against the table with a whisky in one hand, and the decanter in front of him. His cold eyes flamed angrily; he was about to defy the command when Jonathan's expression made him think again. He obeyed, with a short laugh. 'Now,' Bradley continued, 'pull yourself together and try to take an intelligent interest in something other than horses and drink for a change. I don't know what's happened to you lately, or why. If you're unable to sire a son by that wife of yours, at least you can give a thought to business expansion and consideration of my own ambitions, which should also be yours. If there's any problem I can help with—'

Concern momentarily quietened his manner, and his voice.

'Problem?' Arthur echoed brightly. 'What could there be?' He jerked himself to apparent attention. 'As far as I can see everything's going fine. The *Comet*'s on its way up again, you've effectively squashed The *Charbrook Echo*. You seem to be heading for a pretty safe seat in Parliament when the time comes. But a woman's paper – well, if you're attracted by such an off-beat proposal, go ahead with it, and good luck to you. No doubt it'll please Emma. I shan't try to do anything to oppose it.'

'If you'd try a little harder in the way I want and beget a son,' Jonathan said acerbically, 'it would please me much more.'

'Such things happen, or they don't,' Arthur pointed out curtly. 'Perhaps Emma's barren. Anyway—' he smiled brightly, 'there's always Jessie. Why don't you cut short the finishing school affair and find some poor aristocratic mug in need of cash. My sister may not be a beauty, but I'd gamble a bit on her breeding ability.'

Jonathan turned away, faintly disgusted. But before ending the unsatisfactory interview he said coldly, 'Watch your step; I expect more than sarcastic comments and doubtful habits from my heir. You may be my son, but you can't hold a candle to your sister in character. And remember—' he rounded on his heel savagely to regard Arthur from hot angry eyes under beetling brows '—if I want to I can strike you out of my will, leaving you not a penny.'

'I see. Threats.'

'No, no. Not yet,' Bradley answered heavily. 'Just try and show more interest in family affairs and interests, and less in – in that stuff. The bottle.'

Emma meanwhile, flung herself feverishly into the idea, driven mostly by the necessity somehow of shutting Evan Lloyd out of her mind.

It wasn't easy; every time she took certain lanes through the forest the beauty and magic of rare moments she'd spent with him was revived achingly on a tide of memory threatening to pierce her armour. So she steeled herself to a harsh attitude of condemnation, almost contempt, of past weakness, when she'd imagined even for a brief second he could be in love with her.

Had he cared at all, she told himself, he'd never have left so suddenly. He'd have stayed at least in the district for a while so they could plan in some way for the future. There was the workingmen's college in Leyford where he'd suggested he might find employment as lecturer for a period – and the *Courier* – whatever he'd said about prospects there, he hadn't seemed interested in finding out. No. Facts had to be faced. For a time their romantic interludes had given him pleasure, but the bitter truth was that their relationship had not been sufficiently important to him for full committal. At first she'd made excuses for his silence – there could have been an accident – he was ill – or his letters had gone astray. Each time she called at Oaklands she asked the housekeeper, was there any post? Once, Rosalind's governess produced a bill, another time an envelope containing advertisements. But nothing, ever, from Evan.

On the last occasion of her enquiries the housekeeper regarding her more intently than usual, asked meaningfully, 'Are you expecting something very important, then?'

Realising that agitation and concern must have shown on her face, Emma had replied with more force than was necessary, 'Certainly not. I was hoping to hear from a friend that's all. Someone I knew a long time ago.'

She'd shrugged her shoulders, and without another word left the woman staring after her, and went to look for Rosalind.

She never asked again.

In the following few weeks her outward business-like dedication to plans for the weekly supplement combined with her authoritative views on the redecoration of the Dower House, deceived everyone but Arthur, who sensed beneath her cold mature manner something of the wounded sensitive girl beneath. Her new role certainly made her, from his point of view, easier to get on with. She expected no emotional response from him any more, no gentleness, and little courtesy except in company when he still played the gallant surprisingly well. So long as he could still show her off as a prize possession in public, he was satisfied. But his cynical quick mind had told him for some time that her new attitude was due to something else, beyond his orbit. Since Lloyd's departure she'd changed, and he resented any male influences in her life beyond his own. In his sane moments he knew he couldn't blame her if she'd taken a lover. Faithlessness wouldn't have mattered if he'd condoned it first. But if she'd played any game with him behind his back, then he'd have revenge – *somehow*. Jonathan knew nothing of these dark suspicions that occasionally set Arthur's temper on edge.

By January of 1905 it became clear that the Conservative Government might be facing a crisis in the year ahead. Following the Boer War, despite sturdy support in certain quarters for the aristocracy, the party was slowly being forced into a defensive position. The possibility of a new election before its time created restlessness in the minds of those who were at all interested in political matters. Jonathan was one of them. He intensified what before had been a more or less sleeping campaign, into active public demonstration cunningly contrived to win support from both sectors of the community.

The *Echo*, as Lloyd had foreseen, very gradually displayed a subtle Tory policy, which was subtly offset by Emma's weekly, *Woman's Post* which had been launched at an amazing speed, creating an instant readership. A go-ahead girl journalist eager for country life out of London, had been bribed by Jonathan at a high salary, to help, under Emma's editorship, also a secretary. Emma's energy was fanatical. The local newspaper world was agog with shocks and surprises; Jonathan was elated; having won Lord Wendle's support and being named as local candidate for the party, it seemed to him that everything was going his way. When the time came there'd be a fight. But he'd win. And already, in Emma, he was finding the satisfaction he'd hoped for, through his son.

Arthur, amused, cynical, mildly contemptuous of his father's ambitions for fame, allowed his charm and spectacular front to be utilised on Jonathan's behalf at the right times and in right places. Otherwise he continued with his own indulgences, increasingly aware, which others were not, except Amelia, that there was something curiously changed about Emma.

Emma for some time had suspected her own condition, but had refused to face the truth, telling herself stoutly women frequently missed periods for no apparent reason at all, except perhaps, emotional conflict or upset of some kind, and God alone knew she'd had plenty of both.

A day came in February, however, when she was forced to

accept reality. The weather was mild, for the time of year, lush with the sense of pulsing new growth beneath the surface of brown earth. After a tiring afternoon at the *Echo* offices, she drove the car – still her father's old Mercedes – leisurely down the threadwork of lanes leading to Oaklands. Through the network of forest trees already feathered pale green with young buds, the sky was pale grey-blue predictive of rising mist. Beyond a clearing, as she passed, the tip of Hawkshill was visible, crowned by a thin belt of cloud. How often, when a child, she had climbed that particular hill, picking bluebells and pretending she was a character from the ancient past – some young princess who'd once had her castle where now only a few stones and rocks remained.

The natural rocky tip of the hill was itself castle-like in formation. 'Once a *great* mountain,' her father had told her, 'volcanic until the ice-age had covered it, and now millions of years later only nine hundred feet of it are left.'

The atmosphere though, could not have changed all that much, except that rabbits now hopped where once the great dinosaurs had roamed. That particular afternoon, the sense of elemental awareness in her seemed intensified. There was no wind; the chug of the car's engine was the only sound to break the utter stillness of the passing day; it was almost as though time died, imprinting the muted picture of trees against dusky blues and greens of fields, hedgerows and glint of water on her mind forever. Always she had felt a deep inexpressible familiarity with the scene, but on this occasion there was a subtle difference. Her heart, senses and whole being felt it. As she neared Oaklands, a wild deer and fawn emerged from a copse and stood watching while she drove by. Usually the animals, of which there were plenty in the district, ambled away peacefully at the approach of a human being or transport of any kind, but this time it was as though a strange kind of recognition was forged between them. Her stomach lurched then. A fleeting wave of dizziness overcame her, taking everything into blurred uncertainty. The experience was only momentary, but when it passed, she knew.

She stopped the car and sat for several minutes thinking back. The deer and its young turned and disappeared again into the copse. A farm labourer crossed the lane a hundred yards or so ahead, driving cattle down a track towards fields bordering the woods. Bit by bit memories made sense – small insignificant things at the time which she'd ignored as mere 'nothings', a touch of indigestion, over-tiredness, eating the wrong food, a feeling of faint nausea that she'd put down to her increasing resentment and disgust at Arthur's touch or one of his snide remarks. And giddiness! – yes, there'd been that too, at intervals following an over-enthusiastic day dealing with the first editions of the *Woman's Post*. Why hadn't she thought of the answer before? Put two and two together and reached the logical answer so that she could have planned along slightly different lines? The paper, of course, and agitation concerning Evan. If she hadn't been so desperately anxious, ill-at-ease, and over-enthusiastic concerning the weekly she'd have known earlier that she was with child.

The shock registered then, in a wave of sudden lonely longing. Evan's child, and he wasn't there – was nowhere around to contact or confide in. Oh God! what a mess. How beautiful, rich and rewarding everything could have been – however difficult, if he'd been at hand to share and steer her through this awesome period of her life.

But he wasn't. Some day they might meet again, by chance; such a possibility though, would then be too late. She would have faced the inevitable in her own way, and he would have no part in it.

Nostalgia passed quickly into renewed resentment; she restarted the car with a jerk, driving the vehicle at its full speed, in a direct line for Oaklands. At the gate bordering the path leading round the rocky side of the house she didn't brake quite soon enough, and banged the frame and front mudguard clumsily. She sat a moment, shocked, feeling sickness rising in her. It quickly passed. She pulled the car door with a sudden rattle to get out, and after a brief inspection of damage done, made her way to the entrance.

Mrs Cox was hurrying down the hall when Emma went in.

'My dear,' she exclaimed, 'whatever was it? A crash?'

Emma waved a hand in negation. 'No, no. Just a slight misjudgement. Nothing. I didn't brake properly. The gate will have to be repaired, but I'll see it's done as soon as possible. And my mudguard!' She gave a little moué of regret, meant to be humorous, but it didn't fool the housekeeper.

'You look pale – quite poorly,' she said with real concern. 'I know your father wouldn't agree with you driving that thing at all.'

'Oh yes, he would, he loved it,' Emma asserted sounding more confident. 'I *would* like a cup of tea though.'

When she was seated in the cosy lounge, with logs set ablaze in the grate, and a lamp shining comfortingly from a rosy shade by a side table, Mrs Cox brought in a silver tray covered by a clean embroidered traycloth bearing familiar family china, and a plate of new baked scones and cakes.

'Put plenty of sugar in,' she said, as she herself poured tea from the pot. 'You don't look well, whatever you say. What's the matter now? Is anything worrying you? If so – I know the master – your dear father would have wanted you to say.'

Not wishing to face the kindly questioning concern on the housekeeper's face, Emma avoided her gaze.

'No. Nothing; – I – I – *really* I'm just a bit tired,' there was a pause before she asked over-casually, 'That letter – the one I was expecting—' Her words trailed off.

'Yes, dear Mrs Bradley, you were saying—'

'Oh, it's nothing. I—'

'But I think it *is*.' The woman's voice assumed sudden firmness. 'And I've made up my mind now. You should *know*.'

'Know what?'

'Letters *did* come.' The statement was clear, deliberate, 'but *he* – Mr Arthur, your husband – was here one day, the first time, when the postman brought one. He took the envelope himself, looked at it and put it in his pocket. Then he told me it was someone worrying you – "a business concern" or – or – I don't exactly remember the words. Anyway, he showed it to me again – the writing was very bold, and said, "If you ever receive another of these, I *want* it. Keep it for me. I shall call every Monday and collect such offensive communications. They could be very upsetting", he said. I didn't know what to do, but in the end he was so insistent and almost threatened me. "If I find out you've not carried out my orders", he said, or something like it, "your employment here will end. I will *not* have Mrs Bradley worried—"'

The cold feeling of shock turned slowly to mounting joy and warmth, followed by rising anger.

So it had been Arthur after all, and *not* Evan's neglect. How dare he? Oh how dare he be so maliciously, deceitfully devious. Emma looked up then, her cheeks rose-pink from a conflict of emotions.

'If only you'd said,' she remarked reproachfully. 'If only – but no, I must not blame you, it wasn't your fault; you weren't to know.'

'What, my dear?'

'How very *very* important to me those notes were, and how very dear. Were there many?'

'Just two – until today. Mr Arthur had those. But another came this morning—'

Emma stood up quickly, jerking the tray, and knocking a cup over. Ignoring the stain of liquid down her bodice front, she held out a shaking hand. 'Give it to me, Mrs Cox, I promise you won't suffer for it. Just *give* it to me.'

The agony and frightened, imploring expectancy of the pale young face impelled Mrs Cox to hurry from the room and appear almost immediately with an envelope in her hand.

'This is the last one,' she said, almost pushing it into Emma's grasp. 'I don't know! – I may've been wrong in giving Mr Bradley the others, but the way he said it – that they'd upset you! I didn't want that. I was stupid not to know there must be something funny about the whole thing. I didn't like it; deep down I had doubts, but—' She broke off, shaking her head.

Emma, who'd hardly heard what was said, simply replied

mechnically, 'It's all right. I understand. Don't worry, just – just leave me, Mrs Cox; I want to be alone. This is important.'

'Very well, my dear. Only have your tea. You look quite exhausted to me, not yourself at all.' Her eyes – if Emma had seen and noticed, had a speculative look in them – a dawning knowledge slowing bringing recent past events into focus. The master's daughter was not merely concerned about an old friend, the housekeeper decided, she had all the signs on her of being what was known by fashionable circles as *enceinte*, or in 'an interesting condition'. And if that was so it might explain Mr Arthur's concern. Naturally, he wouldn't want his young wife worried at such a time. But why such secrecy? Hovering about the kitchen and hall, hoping she'd done no harm in producing the letter, Mrs Cox waited for the click of tea-cups or Emma's voice calling her back again. But quite ten minutes passed before she had a summons.

When she entered the lounge Emma was standing with the envelope clutched to one side of her bodice. Her grey eyes were brilliant now; a wild-rose colour flooded her cheeks. The mobile lips trembled slightly, verging between joy and a lingering anxiety. Inner excitement burned like the glow of a lamp about her. For a second or two Mrs Cox was taken aback and slightly afraid. She was a practical woman, not given to excessive moods or imaginings. But there seemed something suddenly *too* intense about the slender figure in dove-grey, confronting her. Why, she was even trembling, the poor child, and beneath a thin froth of lace at her neck, the quick jerking of a pulse betrayed the wild beating of her heart.

'Thank you. Oh, thank you, Mrs Cox,' she heard Emma's voice saying. 'You'll never understand what this means to me, and Arthur needn't know it's come. He *mustn't* – you do see that, don't you? No lies need to be told – there'll be no trouble, ever—' The colour suddenly drained from Emma's face; she swayed slightly and would have fallen if the other woman hadn't caught her and eased her gently back on to a chair.

'Now sit still,' Mrs Cox said. 'Just rest until I give you something—'

'It's all right, I—'

'You do as you're told,' came the short command, 'and don't dare move.' She hurried to the kitchen and quickly returned with something in a glass. Holding it to Emma's lips she said, 'Sal volatile. Better than brandy – in your condition.'

The words didn't register with Emma for quite a minute; then glancing up she asked, almost in a whisper, 'What's that? What did you say, about – about my *condition*?'

'You know very well, my dear. And it's nothing to be ashamed of. Forgive me if I'm wrong. But – you're going to have a baby aren't you?'

'I *think* so,' Emma agreed. 'That's why—'

'What?'

'I don't want people knowing until they have to. There's the paper, you see, and – other things. So please keep quiet, Mrs Cox, I'll be upset and really annoyed if you say anything.' Confidence and something of her old high-spirited manner were already reviving on a wave of optimism through her being. When she stood up after hastily swallowing the liquid, followed by a strong cup of sweet tea, her head had stopped whirling, and her feet were steady.

She looked radiant.

'Now,' she said, 'I'll have to hurry back. I'm late.'

'In that *car*? Is it safe? With you as you are?'

Emma laughed.

'I'm a healthy strong creature in full possession of my normal faculties,' she boasted, 'and I could drive that old thing blindfold.'

'I hope you won't try.' The remark was severe and meant to scold.

'As if I *would*. The only thing is—' There was a doubtful pause.

'Yes?'

'Rosalind – I haven't seen her.'

The housekeeper sighed.

'I wouldn't worry about that. She probably wouldn't notice you at all today. This morning she went into a temper over something, and if she'd been a normal child I'd have – I'd really have put her over my knee. But, of course, with Miss Rosalind, patience is the only thing, and leaving her alone. She's in her room now, sulking. That poor girl – the governess – takes endless trouble with her. Sometimes I think she's getting a little more approachable and reasonable. At others I just wonder what it will be like when she's older. Still, you've got to hope for the best; the future's unpredictable, as they say, and you never know.'

That was true, Emma thought, with a niggle of fear welling up again – no-one *ever* could tell, quite, what the days ahead would bring. In her own case, more than Rosalind's, a very large question mark had risen. What was it Evan wanted to talk to her about? And what would his reaction be when she told him about the coming child? Then Arthur! why had he taken such trouble to interfere with her correspondence? Did he suspect? But how could he? – she hadn't yet even consulted a doctor. She couldn't be absolutely *certain*. She *was*, though. Deep down she was as sure as she'd been of anything in her life, that she was carrying Evan Lloyd's baby.

In spite of her assertion of lateness, and having to get back to Eastwood as quickly as possible, she drove by a roundabout route through the forest, and stopped the car by the ruined priory, to take out the letter and read it again:

> Emma, where the devil are you? and why don't you reply? Is it some game you're playing with me? If so be honest with me and say so, so that I can call it a day and push off to the far east or somewhere. If it hadn't been for a spot of lecturing I got here that kept me tied every day I'd have been down like a shot and – what would I have done? – carried you off by the hair of your head to some benighted place where we could live off berries? God knows. The point is I need you, I'm mad about you, you're my obsession, and my dream, if a hard-boiled, practically penniless adventurer can be said to have a dream. Anyway that's the way it is. And I hope you feel the same. We've got to *talk*. I've news it's important for you to

know. Can you meet me in London – St Pancras Station, 12.30 p.m. a week today? You'd better. I'll be there, and if you don't turn up I shall know that either the Bradley odds are stacked too heavily against me, or you've changed your mind and decided after all that Evan Lloyd, Welshman and maybe a bit of an opportunist, isn't a good enough bet to squander your favours on. However, if you *don't* appear, my darling, I shall quite probably arrive on the doorstep of Oaklands or Eastwood unexpectedly, and make one hell of a fuss. So think up a plausible excuse if you have to for getting an early train – I'm sure your nimble mind can manage it. Understand?

Till we meet again then,
Evan.

He gave no address, which was annoying. She'd have liked to scribble an answer and get it into the post straightaway, saying 'I'll be there. However tricky it is, I'll come; Emma.'

But he hadn't given her the chance to refuse. Instead he'd bossily made a statement, which contained also a threat if she didn't comply.

She smiled secretly to herself, knowing she had no alternative but to go along with his plan. A meeting with him at Oaklands would be too dangerous. London was different. From St Pancras they could take a cab or go by underground to some tucked-away little cafe in Chelsea or Soho where they'd be free to talk, safe from prying eyes or malicious conjecturing. She'd drive from Eastwood to Leyford on the pretext of a shopping expedition, catching the early nine-thirty train for the City, which would allow her a brief time to visit the cloakroom, adjust her hat and veil, and see she was looking her best as she walked along the platform for her assignation with Lloyd. Of course, he might be there before her, waiting, as the train puffed in. It didn't matter; she would have comb, powder, rose-balm, and perfume in her reticule, and would see through the mirror of the first class ladies' toilette on the train, that her headgear was tilted at just the right angle, allowing the suspicion of silky fringe to show with one tendril of a curl over her cheek. The night before the exciting event, she'd take a pill containing laudanum, that the doctor had prescribed for her during a period of sleepless nights following her father's death. This would ensure she'd wake refreshed, with her eyes at their very best. Oh, she wanted to be beautiful for Lloyd. After the weeks of waiting he mustn't be disillusioned by his first glimpse of her again.

When the time arrived, everything went to plan and was even easier than she'd anticipated. Arthur had gone out unusually early on some project concerning a new foal. Jonathan was perusing a letter from Lord Wendle in the library when she set off in the car after making a casual statement to her maid about a shopping expedition. She left the vehicle at the nearest country train junction of Winkley from where she caught the train to the City.

It was in her own terms – 'a black and yellow day'. Trees and fields were misty grey under yellowing skies, the windows of her first class carriage damp with steam. Emma was alone in her compartment, with her reticule and a magazine on her lap. She appeared composed, but wasn't. Beneath a new golden-brown cape her heart beat riotously. Though her back was erect, and her perfect profile turned in a steady gaze to the passing landscape, her slim fingers in their soft brown gloves tapped restlessly on the paper. Every few minutes or so a hand strayed automatically to her temple, making sure that except for the single curl, no wanton tendrils of hair spoiled her elegant appearance. It was silly to be so particular, she thought – Evan had once told her she must never try to be sophisticated – he liked her wild and elusive looking as a woodland nymph.

But today was different. The expensive rust and gold outfit – the shining pointed-toed boots peeping beneath the braid trimmed hem of the silk gown, her provocatively tilted hat with its veiling and suggestion of osprey, the tiny gold buttons of her bodice glinting beneath the cape – and the bustle, not too large, but sufficiently so to lend a touch of audacity – all, somehow, made her feel mistress of the situation. She would at first be just a *trifle* aloof when she met Lloyd, then – suddenly, her hands would be in his, and they would be staring with wonder into each other's eyes. They wouldn't kiss, of course, not in public – but later? A smile twitched her mouth as she contemplated the precious time they'd have together.

Once or twice, lost in her wild imaginings, she was aware of figures passing down the corridor, and was careful to appear haughtily aloof, with not the quiver of an eyelash. It was a little unusual even in 1905 for a young woman of 'class' to be travelling alone, and young men could get mistaken ideas and prove troublesome, given the slightest encouragement. No attempt was made, however, to invade her privacy, and when, amid a great deal of puffing, and snorting, and thick whirling coils of smoke, the train drew in to St Pancras, she was able to smooth her skirts and cape effectively, tilt her saucy hat a further half an inch forward, and lifting her gown by one hand, in the other holding her reticule under the cape, stepped down through the door into the bustling crowd.

It was almost impossible at first to distinguish one figure from another – there was so much scuffling, calls for porters, wheeling of trucks, whistles and lights appearing intermittently through the smoke. The air smelled thick, and damp, and foggy. A man in a tall hat bumped into her and asked if he could get her a cab.

'No, no thank you,' Emma answered. 'Someone is meeting me.' The man gave a polite bow, touched his hat and went on.

But where was Evan? Obviously apart from the smoke, London was in the grip of a fog. She could discern ahead in the distance, the blurred shapes of cabs and horses waiting. Supposing Evan had been delayed or was late? Or supposing there'd been a street accident?

With a tiny niggle of panic rising in her she searched the platform, moving towards the gates where the ticket collector stood. There was a restaurant on her left, thank goodness. If all else failed, if something was wrong, she could go in there, have something to eat and then take the first train back again.

But there was no need.

Just as she was wondering what to do, a familiar figure emerged through the yellow light – hatless, and casually dressed, with a muffler round his neck.

Evan!

In her excitement and relief she ran forward, moving too quickly and carelessly. A large man carrying a case banged into her, knocking her precious, carefully arranged hat over one eye, on to her shoulder. She tried to retrieve it, but with the collision all sophistry had vanished. Curls tumbled from their coils and pins. She swept them from her eyes, and forgetting about stupid elegance and fashion, broke into a bubble of laughter, as Evan swept her into his arms.

Convention was forgotten. Passionate and desirous, hungry with longing, they stood there for a few moments locked so tightly together she could hardly breathe.

After that short delicious pause she pulled herself together, and heard him saying, 'A good thing you made it. And stop fiddling with that thing—' He pulled the hat from her hand, and by its ribbons, slung it over his shoulder.

'Evan, you *mustn't*. You can't—'

'Can't I?' She sensed rather than saw the mischievous tilt of his lips. 'Reserve telling me what I can or can't do until later. At the moment you must be hungry. So am I. I know a nice little place in Soho. Come on, we'll go there. I'll get a cab.'

Just as she'd imagined until then, although later things were to turn out very differently.

12

The tricky journey through London streets in the thickening fog was too uncertain – too confused by muffled sounds of rattling wheels, car horns, horses' hooves and shouting, for talk of plans or intimate conversation; but the warm strength of Evan's hand, his other tightly encasing her waist, was sufficient assurance to her that the bond between them had increased rather than waned.

The restaurant, L'Oiseau d'Or, was tucked away in a discreet Soho corner frequented mostly by artists and writers. Lace and gauze curtains obscured daylight to a mere glimmer, but inside rose-shaded lamps cast intriguing shadow-play over pannelled walls. Waiters moved soundlessly on thick-carpeted floors, treading their ways past small intimate tables – in and out of alcoves, carrying trays or gilt-embossed menu cards. Prices were comparatively reasonable, yet an air of luxury and secret excitement pervaded the atmosphere, intensified by the aroma of wines, tobacco smoke, mostly of Turkish origin, and feminine perfume suggesting intrigue and glamour.

The clientele was of a varied character, including one or two extravagantly clad elderly women hoping beneath their painted exteriors for a harmless touch of youth's lost romance – couples on the brink of amorous adventure, and the merely bored and sophisticated, savouring the best brandy and liqueurs, with watchful sardonic amusement; English, French, Italian – colourful continentals – all were there; but there was no ribaldry; no sound above muted conversation and laughter on a low key, except for the faint strains of a violin being played in a recess at the far end of the room.

Evan and Emma were conducted to a small table cunningly

shielded from public view by a bead curtain and wine was ordered, followed by a choice of entrées.

There was a pause until glasses were deposited before them, then, with their eyes riveted magnetically on each other's, Evan said, 'Now, I suppose, the story must be told.'

'Story?' she echoed, ineffectually.

'Or stories,' he added quickly, 'yours and mine; and how we – how we're going to deal with it all.' This wasn't quite what she'd expected. Actually she'd thought of nothing concisely – only joy of meeting him, of them being together again, and of the important news about the baby. But, of course, there was much more to explain, and tearing her gaze from his, she said in soft hurried tones, 'I never had your letters, Evan, until the last one. They – *he* – stopped them. So you see it wasn't my fault you had no answer.'

'Bradley you mean? That rotten—?' The flame of indignation burned his face.

She nodded. 'He intercepted them. But don't let's talk about him – I've something—'

He leaned forward, and stretching one arm, clasped her nearby hand in a tight grip, at the same moment interrupting what she'd so wanted to say. 'Listen, Emma darling, let me make things clear first then we can go on from there. There's a lot you know about me already – that I want you and care for you more than I have for any other woman in my life. That's the one thing that will never change, *cariad*. So for God's – no, not for God's – for both of us, you and me – try and understand the rest.'

Her heart sank a little.

'Go on, tell me then.'

'I've got to leave you for a time,' he continued, watching her intently, noting a little of the colour leave her face, and her eyes narrow under their fringes of dark lashes.

'*Leave* me? Again? For how long?'

'A year.'

'A year? But *why*? – when—?'

'Circumstance,' he told her. 'I've mentioned before that there was a good deal in my life you didn't know about. Well – for that matter we haven't known each other long, have we? Not comparatively, although I can't imagine now any worthwhile existence without you. But it has to be, Emma. If it was practical, I'd say come with me, fling your cap over the windmill and let's stay together. But it wouldn't work. This is a one-man job—'

'I see.' Even in her own ears her voice sounded shrill and high, a hard, mechanical squeak.

'No you damn well don't; why should you? Africa's only half the story.'

'*Africa?*'

'I've been offered a twelve-month teaching job in quite a go-ahead new college. Life will be pretty primitive, I suppose, and a woman wouldn't be welcome. I have to be free, without responsibilities of a domestic kind – and it'll be hard going. But I'll manage – on my own. I've *got* to. After that I shall be back with all I need to start our life together – that is – if you want to still.'

She was confounded. How *could* he sit there and so cold-bloodedly inform her that he wouldn't see her again for a whole year? In that one agonising moment of revelation all thought of telling him about the coming child was resolutely extinguished. He was *leaving* her – had *planned* to, while all the time she'd fretted and longed for a sight of him – just a word assuring her of his love and determination to guide her through the difficult months ahead.

Now, *Africa*.

Contempt of her own naiveté, her romantic stupid belief in him compelled her to say bitterly, 'I *quite* understand, Evan. And if that's what you wanted to tell me, I think we should finish the conversation, don't you?' She looked at her watch, while cold, unreal words left her lips. 'It's been nice seeing you, of course, but I *am* busy, and I'd like to catch the first train back—' She tried to get to her feet, but her dress caught, and a hand knocked a glass of wine over, spilling the remains of golden liquid down the white tablecloth.

'Sit *down*,' Lloyd told her, through his teeth. 'I've not finished yet, not by a long chalk. And there's no need to make a scene. Look, the waiter's coming.'

White-lipped, she adjusted her gown and once more seated herself rigidly on the chair.

When the waiter had mopped the wine up and taken the glass away, Evan said bluntly, 'You didn't know, of course, and you never asked, so I put off giving the information until I was sure of you – or thought so. The truth is, Emma, I'm married. I have a wife.'

'A *wife*?'

'Now don't look like that. Not in the way you think, not—'

'Then in what way? What other way is there? If you're married.'

In sarcastic tones he said drily, 'You should know.'

He flinched.

She waited. 'Well?'

'Do you want me to go on?'

'You may as well.' Shock had momentarily dimmed pain; all she felt was a wild kind of anger and shame.

'It all happened years ago. Eight, to be precise, when I was at College. I went over to Ireland during a vacation, on a walking tour. It was early summer. I found digs at a small place in the mountains that was all romantic, very Celtic, full of beauty and blarney – unreal somehow – like Wales in a way but with a difference. There were ruined castles and rivers, and cross-roads where they danced the Kerry Dance. There were black-shawled bent old women – very tiny, looking like pixies, and luscious black-eyed colleens with laughter that had music in it. Oh yes, it was an enchanted holiday, and one weekend there was a fair. It was then I met the girl – Shirin is her name, Shirin Kathleen O'Malley. She was the daughter of a schoolmaster – a grim hardworking underpaid disciplinarian who kept a watch on her as well as he could. But that night she managed to be free, and later – when the fun and games were over, we – the inevitable happened, as it sometimes does, between a lovely girl – and believe me, she was quite a beauty, curling black hair, rose-red lips and cheeks and the bluest eyes you ever saw – and a fellow like me. It wasn't planned, I was infatuated, briefly, but that was all. Unfortunately there were consequences. Some weeks after returning to Wales I heard from her that she was pregnant.'

'Oh.'

He didn't look at her, as he continued, 'I didn't doubt that I was the father. She'd been virgin till I came along. A second letter arrived from the father, censorious, vituperative, then more conciliatory when he informed me that he naturally expected and trusted me to do the honourable thing and return as soon as possible to Ireland and marry her. Which I did.'

Still no word came from Emma's lips.

'It was a fiasco from the start, of course,' Evan went on. 'I had no money, we had no interests in common. It was expected I would find something to do in the vicinity and make my way while we spent our days together with her father and his sister. She was a kindly but depressed kind of woman who'd done her best to bring up the little girl Shirin after her mother died when she was only two. I learned the reason for the woman's gloom – partially – only a month or two later following an unwarranted attack of temper from my young wife when she threatened me with a knife. There was a taint apparently in the family on her mother's side, and obviously Shirin had inherited it.'

'Is that all?'

'No. Shirin had a baby that died at birth – mercifully. I can see that now. But at the time things were worse; she, my wife, never recovered. I took various jobs in the meantime, and eventually left for Wales. All through the following years I've managed somehow, to contribute to her keep. But last month I heard the schoolmaster had died, leaving his sister practically nothing financially, with Shirin dependent on her. She's in a home now, completely mentally sick with no hope given for her recovery. The place is quite pleasant, but in future the cost for part of her board has to be paid. That's why I'm going to Africa. The post is a very rewarding one financially and whatever my faults, I *do* feel I've a certain duty to give what I can. If she'd no-one of her own to help. other sources or authorities would pay up I guess. But I'm her husband, by law, still. Divorce is out of the question so far. She's Catholic anyway. But soon, Emma, I'm seeing a solicitor about having proof of her insanity. In this country I believe a marriage *can* be annulled under certain circumstances. Until then—' His eyes searched her face intently, imploringly. 'Oh darling – can't you bear with me, and try, at least *try* to understand? A year apart, and then – oh hell! – if the legal business can't be gone through, we can at least be together. Isn't love the important thing?'

Recklessly Emma replied, 'I *thought* so. *Now* I'm wondering.'

'My God, you're a cold one,' he said bitterly.

She ignored his outburst. 'Why didn't you tell me before – about being married?'

'You mean I should have gone around wearing a placard saying, "I'm married, I've got a wife, so don't touch me"?'

'How ridiculous.'

'And how insensitive of you going on like this, determined not to understand.'

'Oh I *do*,' she snapped airily, hating herself for her facade of hardness, of sarcasm that was unlike her. 'Only too well. You've cared for me, yes – when it suited you. You've been—'

'Faithful to thee, Cynara, in my fashion,' he quoted. 'Oh well, that's it I suppose, if you're so dead set on putting the wrong interpretation on things. I know *one* thing though—' He paused, staring at her so fixedly she had to steel herself not to soften, or to blurt out the truth allowing the tears to flood her eyes, as she confessed all that was in her heart.

'Yes?' she said stonily. 'Go on.'

'We'll never be free of each other, Emma, not while we both live. *I* know it, and so do you. And I shall come back – one day when you discover what you've missed. I only hope it's not too late.'

She gave a light laugh meaning nothing. 'For what?'

He didn't reply.

The waiter, with tempting-looking omelettes with foreign names, smelling tastily savoury, came to the table. Both ate mechanically, Emma, only just contriving to swallow hers. It tasted like sawdust. Their conversation following was practical, dealing with trivialities that passed emptily like a scene in a play.

In another half hour the nightmare was over. They left, side by side, uncommunicative and miserable. In the cab taking Emma to the station, Lloyd made an effort to break the deadlock, but her mind was still too frozen to meet him halfway. The fog by then was a yellow blanket, and they only reached St Pancras in the nick of time to catch the early train back to Leyford. Evan helped her into the carriage. Thick coils of yellow smoke drifted past the window. Before he closed the door he grasped her hand suddenly, and pulled her tempestuously towards him. 'Don't go, Emma,' he said urgently. 'There's another train in two hours – don't – *please*—'

He tried to pull her out. It was no use.

There was a whistle; he stepped back on to the platform.

'I shall write,' he shouted, before the rhythm of the engine jerked the train forward, slowly at first, then with ever increasing speed. 'Leyford – post restante. Take care of yourself—'

The tears filled her eyes then, even his were bright. But neither saw. Her head under its absurd hat quickly became a mere intermittent shape receding into the distance, and his a vanishing blob through the uncertain blur of smoke and fog.

He stood watching until the serpent-like puffing form had finally disappeared, then turned and walked away on heavy feet.

Emma adjusted her cape and bustle in a corner seat of the carriage. An elderly man from the opposite side gave a brief glance over his paper then looked down again. He was mildly curious, sensing a lovers' tiff. Perhaps, during his scanning of the *Times* business columns a faint envy stirred him for the lost days of youth's vagaries. But presently only the train's steady rhythm registered.

Emma felt nothing at all but desolation and an emptiness worse at the time, than a forecast of death.

How could she get through the days ahead? She had no faith

in Evan's promise to write, or in any possibility of any mutual future. Most probably they would never meet again.

'Never – never—' the great mechanical wheels thudded as a changing vista of scenery passed by – fields, trees and grey villages huddled under a yellowing sky. It was all over.

Everything.

Then suddenly she felt sick, and remembered.

The child. The fruit of her love and Evan's – it would be born without his even knowing of its existence.

A Bradley.

Gradually the significance of the situation revolved into tormented reality. Arthur would have to know. Unless—.

For a second she toyed with the idea of an abortion, but as quickly abandoned it. She just couldn't resort to such bitter destruction.

Anyway – her mouth held a momentary sardonic twist – Jonathan would doubtless be pleased, and his pleasure would react on her husband very favourably. That Arthur's presumed son – and she felt strongly the baby would be a boy – was a bastard, wouldn't worry her husband at all. Perhaps he would not resent it, so long as no one ever knew about it. If they *did* – she shivered as she remembered his threats and the little horse whip in the cupboard.

Oh God! what had she gone into?

Panic for a few moments swamped all other emotions in her; but presently it subsided, leaving her curiously calm and bereft of all feeling.

It was evening when she reached Eastwood. No-one except a housemaid appeared to be about. She went upstairs immediately, changed, washed, and used more lip salve and makeup than usual.

When she went down to dinner later Arthur was already seated by the fire with the decanter and brandy and soda in front of him on the small table.

The firelight gave his fair hair a golden sheen. His blue eyes held a brilliance of sun on frozen water. No Greek god or legendary knight could have looked more handsome.

'Ah!' he said, half rising, then seating himself again. 'My wife. How very beautiful you look, my dear.'

Emma smiled.

'Thank you, Arthur.'

She'd taken pains with her appearance, because she knew now the best thing for her peace of mind, was to tell him about the baby, and get it over as quickly as possible, and that she must use a little flattery and beguilement, looking as ravishing as possible.

The silver-grey gown sprinkled with diamanté suited her fey, almost fairy-like appearance. The lip salve added both seduction and sophistry. In her hair a single white bloom from the conservatory glowed like a pale star against the molten coils of glistening hair. Round the pale column of her throat above the creamy shoulders, she wore a necklace of pearls given to her by Arthur as a wedding gift.

'A new dress?' he enquired. 'The result of your – shopping spree?' So he'd heard. They'd informed him at the stables, of course, before her maid did.

'No,' she replied. 'I didn't buy much after all. You've seen this before – at that important dance. Remember?'

'Ah, yes,' he agreed in a rather thick voice. He didn't, of course, he was already befuddled by too much liquor. But for once this only made matters easier, and later that night, when they'd retired to bed, he accepted her news of the pregnancy almost laconically, with far more tolerance than she'd believed possible.

'How very interesting,' he said, running a finger down her neck and one white breast. 'You have, then, been enjoying yourself quite a lot in your old-fashioned way, dearest?'

Steeling herself to an airy shows of light bravado, she bluffed, 'If you remember you suggested, or gave me permission first, to have a little life of my own. Otherwise, of course, I wouldn't have dared.' There was a pause in which she held her breath, then he said. 'That's true. Quite true. I take it, though, I'm entitled to know my – substitute's name? Though perhaps I can guess it—'

'I'm sure it's better not,' she said firmly. 'Unless you wish the child to be called by it, when he's born. But you wouldn't, would you? After all, it's what your father wants, isn't it? – Another Bradley in the family?'

'You're very clever, Emma. Yes, I agree.' After a further short silence, he continued reflectively, almost in a whisper, '—Bradley. Yes – a *Bradley*.'

Suddenly his hands were about her breasts, thighs and buttocks, his lips hot on her flesh, and he was ravishing her in a way she found particularly revolting.

'That seals it then,' he said at last, in smug satisfied tones, 'and I've never had to use the whip. You really *are* quite a gem of a wife, Emma. And tomorrow we'll tell my father.'

Exhausted, sick with humiliation, Emma lay rigidly beside him, sleepless until the morning.

After breakfast, Jonathan heard the news and was more than delighted – exuberant.

For a brief time, Emma wished she could die – until she remembered the living entity within her that was also Evan's, and later, the weekly *Woman's Post*.

Such things were *real*, and for the future.

She had to go on.

13

Emma had one short note from Evan before he sailed for Africa, and this was post-marked Ireland. It was waiting for her at Leyford General Post Office when she called, and the contents bore no address, just a brief communication saying:

Dearest stubborn Emma, I'm here, in this country of Kelpies and blue-eyed colleens. The air is balmy, mild, damp and empty. Empty without you; but I'm not going to dwell on romanticism and sentimental yearnings. That's for my verse-scribbling – such as it is. At heart I'm a realist able to face facts, as you are, though you don't admit it. If you weren't, we'd be no earthly use to each other. So don't fret and pine. A year isn't all that long, and though I detest the thought of your having to put up with A.B., I tell myself you've got all that it takes to keep him under control. Jonathan isn't a bad fellow beneath his bossy airs and ambitions. He may be devious, but there are no flies on him, he can see straight, and I'm sure would stick up for you in a crisis. So if anything worries you, turn to him. He'll see you through, and I mean that, however much I detest him.

Well, that's about all, I think. Words are just padding in a case like this. In the next week, after I've settled things here, I shall be sailing for Africa. Wish me luck.

As ever yours,
My love, Evan.

There was a postscript. 'Shirin is worse. It was a good thing I came. I'm more than ever certain it was the only thing for me to do.'

After a dull feeling of disappointment followed by a sense of frustration at the matter-of-fact tone of the letter, Emma tore it up, and put the pieces of paper into her reticule. She didn't want advice over her own life, or references to Shirin. That she existed at all as Evan's wife was still a shock to her. It wasn't the girl's fault, of course. If Evan had been more controlled, with any sense of discipline in him those years ago, his doomed marriage would never have taken place. In her loneliness she blamed him bitterly for the past. There were times when she felt acute resentment for his invasion into her life. He hadn't been free, even during their first passionate love-making. If he'd told her he had a wife she wouldn't have given him a second thought.

Or would she?

How could anyone say what *might* have been? Life could be so unpredictable and cruel. Her own marriage to Arthur had proved this. She'd married him believing their existence together would have glamour, security, and the power to further her father's ambition for the *Echo*.

But instead? At such a point she stifled her imagination, bringing facts ruthlessly into place. There were twelve long months ahead of her without Evan, a period in which anything might happen. What? No-one could tell, except for one thing. The birth of her baby – if all went well; and before that, endless days which she must see were not wasted. Oaklands still remained, and the newly launched *Woman's Post*. These were facets of her life peculiarly and individually her own. The knowledge fortified her. Sometimes it was as though she heard her loved father saying, 'You'll come through, Emma, hold on, love, everything will be all right in the end.' And it wasn't only imagination, she knew that. Something of him – of his genes – ran strong in her blood. She was a Fairley. This was her heritage, what she had to cling to.

*

Jonathan's elation concerning Emma's condition was so jubilant the whole household of Eastwood soon knew of it. There was a new feeling about the place. Good will and excitement combined with increasing optimism about his political future created a sense of bonhomie to which even Amelia responded, by refraining from her sessions of private tonic-taking, and evoking a load of kindly advice and tips to the expectant mother – old-fashioned many of them, but some of real help, for which Emma was grateful.

'You really *should* take a bit more rest now, love,' Amelia said one day, quite fondly. 'Not lie about all day like some do – but try to be a bit more placid. Stop driving that rickety old motor-car so much. I never liked those new-fangled things, and I reckon it's too late in life now to get used to them. But why don't we take a carriage trip together, you and me, and have a right good shopping spree? There's new clothes you'll be needing, and a French shop's opened for baby things in that Arcade place off High Street. We could have tea out, or a nip of sherry in Bartons. All the high-class folk go there. Jonathan'd like it. He's very fussy now about us appearing among the right people, and I'd be extra careful to talk right.'

She was so enthusiastic, so flushed at the prospect, that Emma couldn't help smiling, and agreeing.

'Yes. I'd like that. All right, we will.'

'Good. I allus say a change is as good as a – tonic – do they call it?' She laughed heartily. 'That's a joke. Anyway, my love, I can promise you you'll have no need to be ashamed of me. Not like that son of mine.' A shadow briefly crossed her face.

Emma felt a pang.

'I'm sure Arthur's not *ashamed*. Don't think such stupid things. You imagine too much.'

'No, my dear,' Amelia's voice sounded uncharacteristically firm. 'It's not imagination. I know where I stand. With Jonathan, too, though not so much. He treats me right, does what he can for me. Allus has. And at heart he's a good man. I hope he gets what he's aiming for, that's all.'

So did Emma.

The election so far didn't seem imminent, but at Westminster rivalry between the two chief parties was increasing, with the odds strengthening in Liberal favour. It was by then evident that women were becoming restive and wanting a share of management in the country's affairs. In 1870 a bill to give women the vote had successfully passed a second reading in the House, but in the years following had failed to become law. In 1903 Emmeline Pankhurst and her daughter had taken up the challenge and organised a group of women represented by all classes, to carry on the campaign. No major political party was in favour, but Jonathan, frequently one step ahead in foreseeing the trend of future events, was careful in currying favour with the feminine members of the constituency he was determined to represent. He worked untiringly, yet with a subtlety his daughter-in-law would not previously have thought him capable of. During the spring and summer months of the current year, he was helped unconsciously by Emma, who pushed *Woman's Post* into becoming, on its own account, a popular weekly.

Regarding herself one day through her mirror after returning to Eastwood from a particularly full and tiring day in Charbrook, she noted, with dismay that her face was thinner; emphasising the darkening rings under her eyes. She was wearing deep olive green that intensified her unusually pale skin and luxuriant copper-beech tones of her hair. But she looked older; no longer the radiant girl her father had known and loved. Something of her vivid tempestuous quality seemed to have been drained from her, replaced by a young matron of purpose who was already scheduled in certain circles as the 'new woman'.

Arthur, who came into the bedroom some minutes later must have noticed. After glancing at her, he said, 'Charbrook again, I suppose? Isn't it time you gave a little more thought to your appearance? These days you don't appear exactly ravishing, my dear.'

'I don't intend to,' she answered shortly. 'And I didn't ask you to come in here just at this moment before I've even taken off my hat, or washed and changed.'

'No indeed,' he said mockingly. 'A thousand apologies. I'd forgotten I had to have permission to enter the connubial bedchamber.'

'Oh, don't be so silly.'

With a sudden tug he jerked a pin from her hat, and pulled it off. She put a hand up as a rich coil of curls fell loose to her shoulder. 'What's the matter with you? Don't, Arthur—'

'Don't, *don't*!' he echoed in mincing high tones. 'It's always the same nowadays, isn't it? "Don't do this, Arthur, don't do that. Don't – don't – or I'll tell your papa". Oh I know you've got him under control, now his beloved heir-to-be is safely thriving in your plump little belly – pardon me, my love, I don't mean to be offensive.' He strolled over to her, put a hard arm round her shoulders, and pulled her round fiercely to face him. Her mouth was coldly set, her grey eyes – narrowed under their thick dark lashes as he jerked her chin upwards and said in the threatening way he used when he'd drunk too much '—But he isn't that by rights, is he? The bastard you're carrying? There's not a streak of Bradley blood in him. *I* know it, and you know it. So far the pater doesn't. But you should be careful, my dear. He'd take it badly – very badly indeed – to learn you'd delivered a by-blow into the family bosom.'

Her cheeks paled. She felt suddenly sick.

His manner changed quickly.

'Now sit down and behave.' He pushed her on to the bed. She was trembling, but forced herself to obey. With his cold eyes staring down on her, hard and brilliant as bright glass, he brought a hand sharp against her face, then jerked open her bodice and ripped it down the front. Following this he removed camisole, skirt and petticoats, and the rest of her undergarments, until she was quite naked. 'Now get up.'

Rigid, repulsed, with a slow creeping fear in her she didn't at first comply. It was only when she saw his glance stray to the cupboard where he kept the hated whip that she got to her feet.

He smiled maliciously. 'Ah! – that's better.' He touched a side of her stomach with the tips of two fingers almost caressingly. 'Poor little blighter,' he said in soft tones, almost a whisper. 'I hope he goes to hell. And you too,' he added after a short pause, 'bitch.'

She made a movement to rise. He bent down, picked up the

clothes and threw them across the room in a bundle. 'Now dress properly, wife dear – something ravishing that will tickle Wendle's fancy and make the old boy really envious. He's coming to dinner, remember? And the dear pater would be disappointed if you didn't appear your most beautiful whore-ish best. The scarlet silk, I think, showing too much bosom, with too many drapes at your intriguing behind. And for God's sake smile—'

No movement touched the hard lines of her lips. He came close again and took her once more by the bare shoulders. 'I said smile – *damn* you – or I'll give you the thrashing of your unholy sweet life—'

Mechanically her mouth stretched from side to side, revealing the white glint of pearly teeth.

With a sigh, he turned away. After a moment, when the crisis had passed, she reached for a wrap and pulled it round her body. He walked heavily to the door, paused there, and looked back before leaving. There was no pain on her face, except a lingering redness where his hard hand had struck her – only contempt and hatred.

Following his burst of temper his nerves quickened. 'Sorry if I was – rather heavy-handed,' he mumbled. 'It isn't easy – things being as they are, and *you*! – if it was *my* child it'd be different.'

'Don't make excuses,' she said, 'or try to explain. And don't ever behave or speak to me like that again, Arthur. If you do, I'll tell your father *everything* – not excusing you at all. I'll even go to a specialist or the Law; I'll expose you, I swear it. Maybe I ought to, anyway. Because you're mad – *mad*.' She paused breathlessly, while he put his hands to his forehead. When he glanced at her again, his handsome face was ravaged. 'Very well, madam. It's a bargain. Quits, if you like.'

He gave the semblance of a sardonic smile, and a second or two later the door slammed and he was gone.

It was only then, after he'd gone, that she relaxed weakly, and as the quick racing of her heart faded, fainted.

After this latest incident, Emma insisted in having the large bedroom that had been so sumptuously furnished for their marriage to herself. Arthur retired to his bachelor apartment; and no questions were asked. Emma was careful to admit in the presence of Amelia and Jonathan that she slept badly, and needed privacy both at night and in the daytime, to rest when she felt like it. Jonathan accepted the explanation for separate rooms. He supposed it was often a usual state of affairs during a woman's pregnancy. Amelia, simple in some ways, was more shrewd in others.

'I don't want to criticise, my dear,' she said one day to Emma, 'heaven knows I've no right. But don't you think the time's coming when you ought to give up going so much to Charbrook? Jolting about can't be all that good for you when you're expecting a baby, and then there's the Dower House. The renovations are almost done now. I don't want you to leave here, but if you and Arthur are going to settle down there before autumn and winter set in, I should have thought you'd want to have a go at making things pretty—' Her voice wavered off haltingly, her plump prettyish face had a frown on it.

'There's plenty of time yet,' Emma said, now hating the thought of moving anywhere with Arthur to be on their own. 'And I do often call on my way back from Oaklands. As for driving harming me—' she laughed, a rather brittle sound, 'I'm strong as an ox. Don't *worry*, Amelia. I couldn't stick being cooped up and cosseted here all the time, or measuring carpets and curtains at that place—'

'That place? What do you mean? Don't you like it any more?'

Emma sighed. 'I don't know. I mean, yes, I suppose so. Of course. Only don't *press* me about it. I'm not myself always these days. I have to get away to – to—' She broke off, wishing Amelia would leave. How could she explain? How could they even possibly talk together with such a secret between them? The great tormented gap of her passion for Evan which still lingered beneath the 'don't care' facade?

The truth would only seem treachery to Arthur's mother. She just had to go on as she was, living a lie until Evan returned to make things right.

If he *could*, and wanted to.

If he *did* return.

The conversation between the two women ended there, and Emma tried to put all thought of the future behind. Each day was lived by her energetically, with a sense of cold purpose for the *Echo*, and disregard for Amelia's fussing and Jonathan's intermittent fits of proprietary concern. His pride in her frequently made her feel traitorous. She wished wholeheartedly at times that the coming child could have been Arthur's. Not the Arthur she knew – the unpredictable warped character who delighted in taunting her whenever possible by snide remarks and sly looks, but the charming stranger she'd first met, the handsome character who'd appeared in the beginning so courteous and friendly. Yes; as a friend she might really have grown to love him in time – not with the devouring passion Evan had woken in her, but in an easy warm way that could have made of their union a successful and rewarding partnership. Now she had to recognise there could never be anything between them but dislike, and on her side contempt.

She did her best in public to hide the latter emotion and Jonathan was deceived, but not Arthur himself. He kept away from her as much as possible, making more frequent visits to David and his mother; but Emma's enmity rankled. Wounded pride and frustrated anger forced him into drinking more heavily as spring passed into summer. His father, away from the house so much, either visiting Lord Wendle or wooing popularity both in the countryside and Leyford itself, was unaware how rapidly a bad habit was quickly becoming a vice. Amelia knew, and tried to reason with him, to no avail.

'What a saint you're becoming at a late date, Mama,' Arthur remarked sarcastically once. 'The kettle calling the pot black, eh?' He laughed derisively, 'Or is it the other way round? – I don't care a bloody damn anyway. Mind your own business—'

He strode away to the stables, leaving Amelia shaken, with tears brimming in her eyes and spilling down her plump cheeks ineffectually.

Eventually Emma accepted that driving regularly to Charbrook had to be curtailed. She continued working on the editorial side of *Woman's Post* at Eastwood, and found slightly to her chagrin, that her presence at the offices was not missed unduly. The supplement had already been listed as a magazine in its own right, independent of the weekly *Echo*; a certain public was assured. In one way she had achieved her aim. The Fairley name still stood for something.

Her baby was born at the end of July – a healthy boy who gave the minimum of trouble coming into the world. At first he bore a striking resemblance to Emma, having small features, blue eyes quickly changing to grey, and a tuft of fair hair that was to become brown later.

Jonathan was delighted. 'A true Bradley,' he commented in admiring tones. 'Just like his father, by gum!' The North Country expression slipped out unknowingly.

Emma, smiling secretly to herself, didn't correct him – she knew so differently, and anyway it was pleasant that Jonathan should find so much gratification – however brief the illusion was to be – in the scrap of humanity lying in her arms.

He was named 'Jon Uldene Bradley' at her specific request – Jon to mollify Jonathan, who'd expected Arthur to be included, 'Uldene' because the vicinity of the ruined priory in the forest had been such a favourite place of hers when she was a child, and also of her father's. If she'd been free to do so her choice would have been William Evan, but as matters were, she realised that Arthur's suspicious mind would instantly seize on the truth, placing Lloyd in what could be a dangerous position. He tried hard to make her confirm the name of her lover, had even sneeringly mentioned Evan's name. But she'd admitted nothing; had been devious herself even – which was not a characteristic of hers – in diverting his attention to other possible sources. Deep down Arthur might know. But he would never hear it from her lips.

That summer was an achingly beautiful one, bringing lush thick carpets of bluebells to the forest, frothing clumps of white blossom foaming along hedgerows, and varying shades of green to trees where oak merged with silver birch, chestnut, and sycamore.

The Mercedes now was abandoned by Emma, but occasionally she got the man to drive her by carriage, to Oaklands, taking young Jon with her. Once there her spirits lifted. She felt relaxed, free, at home. The scents, sounds, and atmosphere of the forest revitalised and spread a warm glow of enchantment about her. During those rare hours, bitterness against Evan and blame for his departure, turned to a sad but understanding acceptance. She'd received no note from him since he'd sailed for Africa, but then travel by sea took a long time. Often, she knew, letters were lost. She made herself believe something of this had happened, and that one day, any time now, she'd have news.

Meanwhile Jonathan intensified his political campaign through the country, and in December that year of 1905, the Conservative administration resigned, and Campbell Bannerman formed an interim Liberal government.

Jonathan knew then that his subtle dual policies had been justified. Quite soon it was made known that a general election would be held in January 1906.

It was during the following weeks, therefore, before Christmas, that Bradley's first great challenge had to be faced both personally and politically.

But before the issue was resolved something extremely unpleasant and tragic happened at Eastwood.

*

Jessie had returned from boarding school in September. In appearance she had fined down a little, though she would never be a beauty, or what could honestly be termed as good-looking. Nevertheless, her directness, honesty, and straight clear gaze of her blue eyes under thick fair lashes, had an appeal for country folk. She had 'no side' as they said, and was always natural and the same with everyone she met, from lord to stable-boy. To his surprise, Jonathan found her quite an asset in his campaign. She displayed an astute knowledge of politics, which, though demonstrating a touch of a rebel in her, was useful in bridging misunderstandings that might have lost him a following in more radical quarters.

'I wish Arthur was more like you,' Jonathan told her one day, still wondering at the change in her during the last twelve months. 'You should have been a boy.'

Jessie shrugged. 'Perhaps. But because I'm a girl doesn't mean I'm an idiot. Women *ought* to have more of a share in the country's affairs.'

'Now you're talking like one of those "new women",' Jonathan told her a trifle censoriously. 'Don't think along lines like that. Woman's place first of all is in the home, making a happy life for a husband and children.'

'*All* women don't want to get married,' Jessie pointed out. 'They're as capable as men of having careers, given a chance.'

'Been reading about the cranky lot led by that woman Emmeline Pankhurst, have you?' Jonathan's voice was stern. 'Well, forget it, my girl. Nothing will come of it. All they'll get in the end is to fade out as a laughing stock, or land up in prison. So watch your step. And don't scoff at marriage. There'll be a chance coming along – and not too far off, I hope – for you to make a good match. I hope so. I want more grandchildren. The way Arthur and Emma are carrying on doesn't appear very satisfactory to me. Their boy's a fine child, but one isn't enough.'

'Be thankful you have him, anyway,' Jessie said cryptically. 'Jon Uldene!' she laughed. 'I bet Arthur wasn't pleased. *Uldene!* Just fancy.'

'Yes. I agree. But once Emma's made up her mind she won't budge. Like the Dower House – it's all ready, waiting. Yet she makes no move to go there. It's as though she's frightened or something.'

'Perhaps she is,' Jessie spoke laconically, but Jonathan glanced at her sharply, saying, 'What do you mean?'

Jessie shrugged. 'I'm not sure. But there's something about Arthur that would give me the willies if *I* were his wife. He's nearly always half-seas over anyway.'

After a pause, Jonathan said moodily, 'I think you're wrong.

I've pointed out already to him that he was getting too free with the bottle. Lately I thought he'd taken my advice. I hoped so.'

'I should watch him and find out for yourself,' Jessie remarked. 'For your own sake you don't want people talking at this point.'

Jonathan's brows lifted in mild surprise. 'You're becoming a very observant young woman,' he said. 'Practical, too. But don't overdo it. Remember young men like feminine girls.'

'Young men really don't interest me very much,' his daughter re-affirmed flatly, adding with one of her rare attempts at humour, 'Maybe *I* should put up for Parliament, too. Would you appreciate having a daughter appear in the House of Commons as the first female MP ever? It would be something, wouldn't it? A woman making laws instead of babies?'

Jonathan smiled, pretending to be amused; but he wasn't. Banter on such an unlikely topic didn't interest him, although Jessie's reference to Arthur did. Without admitting it, even to himself, concern over his son's increasing tendency to alcoholism already troubled him in his rare leisure moments, and a few evenings following the brief conversation his worst fears were proved.

*

Twilight was slowly deepening over the countryside when Arthur on his way from the Hungry Man, a somewhat bawdy inn on the outskirts of Market Hoe, a village only a few miles from Eastwood, rode the gelding tipsily along the side drive of the house towards the stables. He was seated lop-sided in the saddle, head slumped forward, and was obviously quite drunk. In his free hand he waved a bottle, putting it to his mouth at intervals, then breaking into unintelligible muttering, followed by a brief attempt at a song.

There was no-one at the stables, and as he passed the rear of the house all else was quiet; most of the servants had been given an evening off to go to the local fair. His mount, unsettled and restless at such unpredictable behaviour, reared once or twice. Arthur brought the whip sharply against flanks and neck, and on they went – past rose-gardens and an ornamental pool, lurching shadowed shapes throwing a macabre pattern over the lane from a watery rising moon.

From an upstairs window a square of light showed. It blinked once like a watchful eye, then all was blank and dimmed again. A moment later the horse neighed shrilly, startled by a sudden roar of sound from its rider. Arthur, swearing, dealt it a further savage blow with his crop. The animal reared, throwing its tormentor. For a second or two Arthur was dragged in a stirrup by one boot, then freed. The horse galloped ahead to the stables, leaving Arthur shocked but comparatively unhurt on the ground. Moments later he heaved himself up and stood swaying from side to side, one hand rubbing the back of his head. A trickle of blood oozed between his fingers, but the impact had steadied his senses, and restored an awareness of reality.

He was making his way along a side path past the pool, towards a door which led into the house through a conservatory, when Jonathan's figure suddenly appeared before him – a furious figure of condemnation taking shape from the shadows of a drooping willow tree.

'What the hell do you think you're doing?' he growled, grasping his son by the tumbled neckscarf, 'What are you playing at, eh? – *eh?*' He shook the startled figure mercilessly, until Arthur's face was crimson and gasping. 'Determined to make a scandal are you? – a mockery of all I've done for you? My ambitions – all my plans and hopes—'

'Oh damn your bloody ambitions,' Arthur managed to shout as the relentless hard hand released him. 'Leave me alone, blast you! What d'you care about *me*? Nothing – *nothing*!' he spat crudely, waved an arm and would have pushed past Jonathan, but his father was too quick and brought a fist hard against the younger man's face. Arthur reeled for a second, then recovered, and started laughing, a mocking jarring sound of undiluted contempt.

'Don't try your bullying ways on *me*, papa,' he said sneeringly. 'If it comes to a punch-up, I'm a better man anyway. Go on, get out of my way. Leave me in peace for God's sake, or you'll be the laughing stock of the neighbourhood.' He took a step backwards. Jonathan followed.

'Oh *no*. I'll never be that. I'm not having folk round here poke and sneer at me or my family, specially now when all I've aimed for is in sight, and I've a grandson into the bargain – an heir to carry on after me—'

'An *heir*? Ask that precious wife of mine. How could he be? I'm impotent, I tell you – *impotent*.'

Arthur threw back his head, gave another thick mocking laugh, then stopped suddenly and faced his father with such a look of hatred in his cold eyes and on his sneering mouth, that Jonathan was shocked into temporary rigidity. Through a wan beam of moonlight the younger man's raised upper lip showed the gleam of teeth bared. So might an animal have appeared, that had been captured and was fighting for life.

'Arthur—' involuntarily the name slipped out. 'Calm down now—'

But Arthur was beyond calming. From a side pocket of his coat he brought out a revolver, pointed it waveringly at his father and was about to press the trigger when his foot slipped, and he fell. He scrambled to his feet then tottered backwards, while Jonathan watched, rigid, and unmoving. There was a splash as the body hit the surface of the water. A hand clawed upwards, accompanied by a thin cry for help.

Arthur couldn't swim, and the pool was deep; circles of ripples – eerily black, lit by intermittent glimmers of pale light, widened and spread, showing briefly the greenish white countenance gasping for air.

Jonathan remained motionless, numbed of feeling, except for a curious detached sense of relief. He made no attempt to save his son's life, for the first time, perhaps, accepting the grim truth that there was little, after all, worth saving.

Presently, when the last vestige of what had been Arthur Bradley had disappeared, and the surface of the pool had settled, Jonathan automatically picked up the revolver which had fallen on the ground, slipped it into his pocket, turned, and made his way, on heavy feet, to the house.

No-one appeared to have heard anything. Amelia was in her bedroom at the front, with her tonic, and Emma, already asleep.

It was only the next day that Arthur's body was located – a body not only sodden with water, but with drink. The state of the horse, and other clues gave ample evidence of the manner of his end, and at the inquest later, a verdict of accidental death was reached, with due sympathy for the young widow and bereaved parents.

So Jonathan, publicly, was not involved at all.

The event in no way tarred his rising popularity, but rather evoked sympathy and respect for his fortitude in carrying on with his campaign.

Only one thing worried him. 'Impotent', Arthur had said. If that really was so . . . for days he daren't face the challenge, the terrible implication of what such a state of affairs could mean.

There was only one possible course to take.

He must ask Emma.

She wouldn't lie to him. However unsavoury her answer was, he had to know.

14

Jonathan kept silent concerning his son's last terrible taunt discrediting Emma and her baby until after the funeral. He endured the trappings of the burial service, the genuine sympathy of the countryside including many people he hardly knew, with a strong stoical set to his face, taken by all who noticed, as grief. No-one knew what he was feeling, the shocked shame mingling with a hurt so acute he could hardly accept the reality. Truth still did not completely register. At times he sensed a queer kind of Nemesis in the last disgraceful episode that had resulted in Arthur's death. He, his father, hadn't pushed him – the fates, some mysterious sense of justice, had interfered with the warped debauchery that in the end would inevitably have destroyed the bitter fruit of his, Jonathan's, union with Amelia. At other rare moments he accepted with brutal honesty that he could have saved his son, and hadn't. He'd let him die, cold-bloodedly without any attempt or wish to save him, thus sparing further disgrace – and perhaps far worse tragedy in the future. Whichever trend Jonathan's thoughts took, there was no point in debating what might or might not have been. Arthur was gone, leaving no-one really to regret him maybe, except Amelia. But the child! Emma's child – whom he'd been so fanatically proud to accept as his heir and grandson! Bitterness that could amount to hatred if Arthur's last jibe was proved to be true, gnawed to the roots of his being causing at times anguished physical pain.

At the graveside he glanced fleetingly once or twice at Emma. She appeared rigid and aloof in her black gown, her face pale, almost white behind the shroud of her veil. As far as he could tell she'd shed no tears, which was honest of her – he'd known for a considerable time that things weren't right between her and Arthur. But some slight display of emotion, he thought, might have brought a little softness to the scene. She acted befittingly in throwing a last handful of earth and a single white rose on to the coffin as it was lowered, but her actions were jerky, like those of a marionette.

She didn't preside over refreshments later in the hall and drawing room of Eastwood, but retired to her room with the plausible excuse of having a headache. None remotely guessed what she was feeling – a confused sensation of escape from a long tyranny combined with unexpected sadness over the passing of someone who'd first appeared to her as a gallant young knight come to relieve her of her many problems. She had no thought or plans for the future; her mind had become, mostly, a blank void of imagination; but beneath the cold despair a small spark of hope, of survival, lingered. One day it must break into flame again, whether for Evan or some other purpose there was no knowing. The conventional answer from most people would have been 'you have your child – your son'. This was true. At the present time, however, the baby seemed curiously unimportant, perhaps because of the very fact that he was bound to bring complications to her existence ahead.

She slept heavily from exhaustion that night, and when morning came she woke late, and had breakfast in bed before going downstairs.

She found Jonathan waiting for her, hovering in the hall by the library. Defying the conventional rule of wearing dead black for a certain period following the death of a husband, she was attired in deep purple trimmed by dark velvet braid that emphasised subtly her delicate complexion and lustrous rich shades of her piled up hair.

'If you'll come into the library for a moment or two, Emma,' Jonathan said, 'I think there is a matter we must discuss. You feel up to it, I hope?'

The directness of his question combined with the set expression and unswerving hard gleam of his eyes put her on her guard. She drew herself up proudly and answered, 'Yes, I'm quite all right, thank you.'

He nodded, opened the door for her, and when she'd gone through followed her. Although the weather wasn't cold, a fire was burning in the grate at the far end of the book-lined room. Emma wondered, for no specific reason at all, if her father-in-law had spent the night there. Perhaps so. Perhaps after all he'd gone through he'd felt unable completely to relax. There was an empty whisky bottle on a table, with a glass beside it, and a half smoked cigar was still smouldering in a small dish among the ash of others.

'Do sit down,' he said non-committally, and as she did so, continued heavily, 'What I have to say isn't pleasant. If I'm mistaken in having any doubts about – the subject, you must accept my apologies. But—' He paused, eyeing her reflectively.

'Yes?'

He came to the point abruptly.

'Before the tragedy my son, your husband, Arthur, dropped a very nasty bombshell. He told me bluntly that he was not the father of your son. That he was impotent. Is that true, Emma?'

Her heart quickened, the tinge of colour in her cheeks drained swiftly from her face, leaving it deadly white. Her fingers tore at the shred of handkerchief in her hand as she said in faint but steady tones, 'Yes, I'm afraid so. We never – Arthur and I – never actually made love. Perhaps—'

'Then why the devil didn't you tell me?' she heard him saying harshly, so loudly that anyone listening outside must have heard. 'What do you mean by keeping a thing like that to yourself? Do you understand what you've done? Not only betrayed the family by bedding with some lusting fornicator – but withholding information I should have had so matters could have been righted. There was nothing wrong with Arthur physically. He was an athlete, a strapping man with a fine constitution. The state of affairs between you could have been *your* fault? Do you realise it – if you'd gone together to see some specialist – some – some—'

Frustration mingled with pity for the man who was so desperately trying to exonerate his son's shortcomings, at least in part, by putting the blame elsewhere caused Emma to say with more calm than she felt, 'I kept the worst things in our marriage hidden because it seemed fairer to everyone. You didn't want a scandal, did you? And that's what would have happened if I'd even tried to explain. In the end I'd have left him, because there was nothing you could have done – or I, or anyone else. Arthur was born as he was—'

'No.' Jonathan's fist was clenched. 'He was a normal baby like any other – like the one you bore, the bastard I took such pride in at first.' He was aware of a further blanching of her colour, of her lips parting, but no answering sound coming from them. 'Somewhere along the line,' he resumed heavily, 'someone – his mother, myself, you – perhaps all of us – went wrong. I notice you've not defended his statement, made no effort to excuse yourself; that being so—'

'Yes?' The word was a whisper.

'Would you mind informing me the name of the father?'

She stared at him for a moment before answering, 'I'd rather not.'

'Could it be that Welshman, Lloyd?'

She didn't reply.

The silence between them, following the last direct question was itself significant.

'I see.'

'No, you can't possibly,' Emma managed to say then. 'I've told you nothing. And I shan't – ever. For Uldene's sake. Jon's I mean.'

'Uldene. Yes. It always came first, didn't it? Your precious forest, your father, Oaklands – your – heritage.'

Her head drooped. She looked suddenly tired, drained of all energy and desire to justify herself.

He poured her a brandy and handed it to her.

'Drink it up. Now the inquisition's over I'll tell you what I mean to do.'

'*You?*'

'The boy was born a Bradley. And a Bradley he'll remain. Concerning his background you'll hold your tongue, for the sake of us all, especially his. To the outside world he'll be my grandson and heir, and by God his bringing up will be different from Arthur's. No molly-coddling by that stupid wife of mine, no public school where drink and sodomy get a grip before a lad's character's properly formed. He'll have an understanding but strict tutor here – or perhaps Rugby. I've heard there are no twisted goings on there. Whatever I choose for him he'll get, and grin and bear it like a gentleman. Do you understand, Emma? I'll shape him somehow into the son I always wanted—?' He broke off, breathing heavily.

When Emma spoke it was drily, but with an undercurrent of temper rising in her. 'And what about me?'

'You? Things will go on here as they began. But the Dower House will be out. You won't need it now.'

'And I may not need *you*.' Before she knew it the statement was out.

His complexion turned a deep red. 'What do you mean? What are you implying?'

'I'm his mother. He's *my* child, I bore him. No-one's going to say what he does and does not do, or what his education will be, but me – *me*. You understand?' Her eyes flashed, changing from grey to blue-green lit by flecks of dancing gold. Temper made her suddenly not only beautiful but irresistible. Determination mingled with a strange sense of defeat and desire rose in Jonathan's breast driving him towards her. A hand touched a soft shoulder, lingered there, then fell to his side with fingers digging into his palms. Both were breathing quickly – she, because she sensed the conflict in him, he through thwarted emotions. 'If thing's were otherwise,' she heard him say, 'if you were not my daughter-in-law, I'd sire a son by you myself.' He turned away. 'Arthur was not only a disgrace, but a fool.'

'He was mad, Jonathan.'

He turned to look at her again. 'Is that all you can say?'

'There's nothing more *to* say, is there? You've made your intentions perfectly clear, and you know mine.'

'No, I *don't*. I want confirmation – your promise, that you'll agree to my plans for the boy. You're a woman of your word, as much as any human being *can* be. I give you credit for that.' He paused, 'Well?'

Sympthy for him, a sudden awareness of how deep his hurt was, combined with an acceptance of her own position and the child's, that she was beginning to believe Evan might never see, softened her sufficiently to ambiguous agreement. 'I'll – keep things to myself,' she said, 'and stay here, as long as it seems right, and works out. I don't want to harm Arthur's image more than necessary—'

'He's done that himself already,' Jonathan interrupted harshly. 'Only the boy matters now. You understand?' He thumped his chest hard. 'In time maybe I'll manage to forget or lay aside just as a bad memory, the way he came into being. But you must stand by me, so the word bastard never fouls the Bradley name.'

She remained silent.

Before the interlude between them ended, he said, 'I rely on you never to divulge a word of this to my wife. Women like Amelia are inclined to let their tongues wag under certain – stimulus. And Jessie.'

'I shouldn't dream of confiding in either,' Emma remarked rather coldly, thinking wrily that it was quite conceivable both had a good idea of the truth.

'Hm.'

As Jonathan walked to the door opening it for her to leave, she noticed that he appeared to have aged ten years. The next day, however, his energy and spirits seemed to have revived. He had a heavy day of canvassing and returned late to Eastwood fanatically determined to win in the forthcoming election. 'With Wendle behind me, and the constituency well primed,' he said, 'I don't see I can lose.'

His prophecy proved to be correct. In January 1906, Jonathan Bradley was elected as MP to Westminster.

For his sake, Emma was pleased. She had to be, living at Eastwood, and with still no word of Evan.

Evan!

Every time his image unwillingly invaded her mind, she thrust it ruthlessly away, believing she would probably never see him again.

15

Almost from his earliest days, the tiny Jon Uldene displayed an increasing interest in Jonathan. Bradley, so busy most days either in his constituency, or on frequent visits to Westminster where he made an effective maiden speech, did not at first spend much time with the child. Emma and the nursemaid had full command in the nursery; besides, apart from his fresh resonsibilities, there were still board meetings of the *Comet* and proposed *Midlander* to attend to. However, during the first days of early spring, something about the small entity destined to play such a vital part in his life, stirred a gradually awakening response. He couldn't help being aware of the child's large greyish blue eyes following him solemnly when he left the room after a brief visit to the nursery, or of the clinging of tiny fingers to his hand whenever he gave a pat to a plump cheek or dig to the stomach. Such gestures were intended primarily as an indication to Emma that he bore Jon no resentment, only goodwill. But inevitably the baby's curiosity, and obvious pleasure in his company, woke a grudging affection which had nothing to do with the fact that Jon Uldene was merely a substitute for the real grandson he'd hoped for. What did genes matter, after all? They were important, of course; nothing could alter the fact that his heir hadn't been sired a Bradley by blood. But there was something else – closeness, an affinity of spirit, which could, given a chance, mean more. And miraculously this quality had been inbued somehow between man and infant from the very beginning of the little boy's birth.

On Jon, beyond all Jonathan's aspirations for the future, both politically and in business, his hopes became more firmly fixed. A latent sense of humour developed between them. A comical face or wiggling of a finger, a strange attitude when Bradley pretended to be a dog begging and barking – brought gurgles of delight from the baby. On such occasions the man himself felt gratified and amused, though such antics only happend in Emma's absence – he'd already sensed a rising unacknowledged jealousy in her which he didn't wish to provoke.

Once, when the nursemaid was in the bathroom, and the baby alone in his cot cooing softly, Amelia came to the door quietly and heard her husband say as he bent down, 'Eh, well, son, you're one of us all right. Jonathan *Bradley*, and don't you forget it.' There was a pause before he added, 'My *grandson*,' with a kind of wonder in his voice.

An inadvertent slight cough from Amelia jerked him up abruptly. Turning, he saw her standing there, appearing mildly embarrassed and ashamed.

'Sorry,' she muttered apologetically. 'I wasn't prying, Jonathan, I was coming along to see the little one myself.'

After his first stab of annoyance her husband cleared his throat, covered his irritation, and said, 'Eh, well! come along in then. You've as much right as anyone, I reckon, to have a peep now and then. But don't go spoiling him, Amelia, not like you did – Arthur. No sweetmeats out of mealtimes or mollycoddling and cuddling when you get the chance. This one's going to be a real man when he grows up. One to do us credit.'

'Aye, you're right,' Amelia said, glowing with pleasure to hear once more the warm North Country accent in her husband's voice.

It was perhaps unfortunate that at such a moment Emma should appear upon the scene. She was looking particularly lovely in a dress of primrose yellow that gave a golden glow to her skin, enriching the piled-up copper glint of her rich hair.

A stab of jealousy seized her. Although she smiled, her voice was brittle when she asked, 'Where's Lily, his nurse?'

'Getting a fresh nappy, I wouldn't wonder,' Amelia answered quickly, sniffing comically. 'You need it, don't you, ducks?' she reached down and took the baby up into her plump arms. Emma instantly pulled Jon from her.

Jonathan gave a grunt. 'We're not wanted here obviously,' he said. 'Come along, Amelia, leave him to his mother.'

They had turned to leave when the baby started to wail, kicking his tiny knees at Emma's stomach. Amelia went out, but Jonathan stood briefly at the door before returning to the cot where mother and child were standing.

At the sight of his face the little boy's temper died. He quietened, staring at Bradley for a full few seconds before a slow smile spread from ear to ear.

'Now then, you just be good,' Jonathan said. 'No fireworks, understand. Be nice to your mama now and behave—'

His eyes sought Emma's, half pleadingly. 'It's always the same with babies.' His voice was gruff, placating. 'Never know what they want from one moment to the next. It was the same with—' he was about to say 'Arthur', but withheld it in time, and said, 'Jessie.'

'I know,' Emma retorted lightly. 'And I should be used to my own child's moods by now.' But she wasn't. There were occasions when she found herself completely bewildered, even irritated by her son's unpredictable behaviour. He was hers – hers and Evan's. Then why did he have to show such obvious preference for Jonathan's company? Perhaps he was becoming too much immersed in the atmosphere of Eastwood. After all, by blood he was a Fairley. The time had come, quite clearly, when he should have more contact with Burnwood and Oaklands.

In the April of that year 1906, she was once more able to take an active interest in the weekly publication of *Woman's Post*, and decided that in future she would take Jon with her on fine days, leaving him in the charge of Mrs Cox at Oaklands during her sessions at Charbrook for board meetings or on editorial business.

Mrs Cox was pleased to have him; with her he was good, although distinctly unresponsive. Rosalind tried, in her simple way, to be friendly, but it was as though Jon sensed something 'different' about her; he would stare at her from his huge eyes, with his thumb in his mouth, as though already assessing her personality. Being a forward child for his age, he could already say intelligible words, some of which he'd concocted himself. Animals delighted him.

Once, feeling particularly generous Rosalind offered him her favourite teddy bear to hold. He pushed it away contemptuously, and would not even have it in his push-cart. Rosalind had one of her tempers, ending in a fit of screaming. Emma, after comforting her with a gift – a box of candies she'd brought – carried the baby to one of her favourite spots from where the ruined priory could be seen swathed in a thin veil of silvery mist, and in the other direction the glint of deep blue-green through the trees. Far beyond the woods, the rocky tips of Hawkshill rose above the ancient granite hamlet of Eavesley.

'One day,' Emma said, lifting the child as high as she could, in her arms, 'I'll take you up there; the rocks are like tiny castles, and rabbits have their homes there. There are all kinds of things to find – and secret places where you can hide—' Her words trailed off dreamily. She knew he wasn't listening, and if he did, he wouldn't understand. But the quiet magic of the forest was all about her.

When the soft wind brushed a cheek it was as though whispers from the past stirred old memories to life again; she was a child, immersed in a world of ancient legendry in which every stirring of the grass, or a branch shaking its leaves, was indicative of some stranger's approach – a presence unseen – exciting and mysterious, who could be anyone or anything, gnarled witch, or handsome knight taking shape from the shadows. As puberty approached fairy-tales had somehow merged into reality, but the reality was no less magical, holding the wonder of growing things and murmur of brooks rippling over the stones; of the sweet damp earth pulsing with life in the spring – tips of bluebells and curling golden-green ferns, lush clearings and dells starred with celandines, violets, and golden heads of kingcups by marshy ground. And on the verge of the forest, fields and fields of buttercups!

So beautiful! So far removed from the pain that life could bring.

As she stared that day through the interlaced branches of the at the shimmering sky, the inevitable picture returned of the time she'd first lain with Evan in the grass.

Would she ever see him again? Would Jon ever know his father? Would he realise when he was older, one small fraction of what this place meant to her?

She put him down gently, to relieve her aching arms. He started to grumble instantly. Bending down and staring into his eyes, she said, 'Isn't it nice here, then? Don't you like it, Jon?'

Obviously he didn't. Disappointment filled her. He was still only a baby, of course, but surely something in the vicinity of Oaklands must strike a chord somewhere in his being – an inborn sense of familiarity bred through William and his forefathers.

No. She had to accept that he was wanting Eastwood, and probably Jonathan.

Jonathan!

A fit of irritation swept through her. 'Oh, come along then,' she said, 'We'll get back. I won't go to Charbrook today. You've tired me out already.'

Following this visit she made others with her young son. Sometimes he displayed an interest at the sight of some shy deer or lolloping rabbit, but mostly he appeared bored or fractious. Her will asserted itself then; she became firmer, even at times quick-tempered, having to accept that Jonathan was his idol, and would have to be stopped spoiling him and giving the little boy so much attention.

The idea occurred to her of moving for a time to Oaklands, in this way forcing the child to accept his true environment. She broached the suggestion tentatively to Amelia.

'Oh I wouldn't, love,' her mother-in-law advised, shaking her head. 'You know how it is – Jonathan's set his heart on thinking the boy's his own—'

'Yes. That's the trouble. He *isn't*. He's mine.'

'But after all he went through, with Arthur, wouldn't it be kind of – cruel – to separate them?'

'It would only be for periods.'

'Would it, love?' Amelia sounded unconvinced.

Emma didn't reply.

After this short conversation life went on for a time in its usual way, except that *Woman's Post* once more assumed greater importance in Emma's life. She started an advice column on social and domestic problems which at the beginning brought in only a few letters – occasionally from male readers of a sarcastic nature. One even ended by saying '. . . first let Lady Anne—' the name she wrote under 'learn her onions, and grow up a bit before trotting out clichés to wives and grandmothers. Or maybe she writes and answers those rubbishy notes herself?'.

Emma's face flamed when she read it, because for the first two issues she *had* had to resort to such devious means in three cases. Her first reaction was to end the new feature, then decided to battle on with it, and answered by writing:

> If the gentleman concerned, and I must assume he *is* a gentleman – refrained from interfering with two columns headed 'FOR WOMEN ONLY' he would not find himself in the humiliating position of professing such ignorance of feminine affairs. I notice he gives no address or legitimate name – only a non-de-plume. However, if he wishes further education concerning home-making and marriage, I can assure him Lady Anne will do her utmost to help.

Following this exchange, correspondence between readers and the editorial department, speeded up, and the recently appointed new managing editor of the combined *Echo* and *Woman's Post* congratulated Emma on her titillating brainchild.

Apart from this mainly light side of the paper, Emma still found time to write a monthly article on some serious topic such as housing and health. There was always a short space in the magazine for 'Gardening Tips', and one for 'Creative Crafts', dealt with by the girl journalist. Fashion – except for 'Home Dressmaking' was not included. The magazine did not attempt to present a glamorous image. In catering for the ordinary girl, wife, and mother, both in country and town districts, it earned an increasingly appreciative public.

And yet, Emma thought once or twice, as she drove back to Eastwood, what right, really, had *she* to give any hints on marriage-making, especially when her own had been so abnormal? Would her father have admired and congratulated her on her venture which had enabled the *Echo* to continue for considerably longer than Bradley otherwise would have allowed it to? Also the Fairley name was still known in the newspaper world, even though in a different sphere than William had anticipated. She had moved with the times, that was all. But there was nothing brash or garish about her contribution. *Woman's Post* was a healthy thriving shoot sprung from her father's dream. In this way she had justified her inheritance. Everyone 'in the know', of course, realised that the *Echo* was very gradually being faded out into The *Midlander*. Jonathan was chagrined that he had not also been able to acquire the *Courier*. But so far he was having to accept that the older well-established Leyford daily was far too firmly rooted in traditional appeal, and too well trusted to be shaken by any new company, however large and powerful. One thing, he discovered, somewhat to his surprise, money could *not* buy – and that was loyalty.

He meant to go on trying, but was doubtful by then of any fruitful outcome. The *Midlander* might prove a worthy rival, and more successful than the *Comet*, but the *Courier*, independent, non-political, sound and trustworthy in its views, had already proved unshakable through the county and elsewhere. Jonathan, having acquired his seat in Westminster, no longer fretted over losing this certain newspaper battle. The other papers were thriving, and he had an honest respect for any privately owned company that could squarely face a formidable challenge and win.

He had, as well, this further growing interest in his life – young Jon. Sometimes, in the rare leisure moments when he'd been playing with the child, a dull sense of dread filled him at the thought a day might come when Emma might want to marry again, and take him from the family to another home. Would she have the right to uproot him in such an event? Or could he, as legal grandfather, have a claim? Knowing the former was probably true, that he'd fight if he had to, but probably fail, he was careful to please his daughter-in-law by all means in his power, fanning and intensifying her interest and involvement with *Woman's Post* so she felt secure and unhampered in her life at Eastwood.

One day, in early September when Emma was feeling irritated by a fractious interlude with her young son, she drove herself, in a fit of nostalgia, towards Oaklands, not Charbrook or on any journalistic business, but solely to be alone in her own environment of the forest. Autumn, to her, was always a nostalgic period, and the woods at their most colourful. The morning was fine, clear and golden, faintly filmed by thin blueish mist hovering about hill, lanes and hedgerows. There was no wind, no stirring through foliage or undergrowth, although occasionally a brown leaf floated down from a tree as she passed. She took the drive leisurely, steering down any particular lane that took her fancy. Before reaching the more thickly wooded areas, she had a sudden urge to see the park, and made a detour to Bradgate. She stopped the car at the gates, parked it and entered the old historical territory.

Not far from the main drive the brook rippled between rocks and over stones shot with gold and silver light from the climbing sun. The white tails of rabbits bobbed in the tall bracken – russet and brown now – as she passed. A deer, soft-eyed, stood for a moment watching under an ancient oak, then moved gracefully up the slope towards a thicket of trees. Emma glanced upwards. Staring down, quite motionless, was the proud antlered shape of a red stag.

She'd been warned time after time when she was young, never to approach a male deer near the rutting season, but had taken little advice. Neither did she now. From being a young child she'd felt an affinity with all creatures of the forest, and that day was no exception. At one point the richly shaded satin-coated form came a few yards nearer, then leisurely turned and with arched neck, proud head raised magnificently, retreated into the shadowed copse.

Emma continued her walk, taking the turn by the ruined

mansion which had once been the home of the unfortunate Lady Jane Grey, and then, suddenly – coming towards her down a slope on her left, she saw him; a sturdy youngish figure, bare-headed, with the morning light touching his brown hair to gold.

Evan.

It was like a dream coming to life. So many times during the past year she'd envisioned him, in sleep, somehow, somewhere – appearing unexpectedly – round a corner of a road, at the top of a flight of stairs, or at the end of a long corridor – on a mountain side, or in a crowded thoroughfare or dance hall – but always out of reach. In her sleep she'd called to him and run struggling to catch him before he vanished. But he'd always gone – sometimes merely fading, as though forces beyond her control pulled him, at others he'd himself shaken his head and left her, becoming no more than a shadow in all the other shadows of that unseen twilight world.

When she'd woken there'd generally been tears on her lashes, with a terrible sense of loss in her heart.

But now! *now* – she stood for a second or two staring; he did the same. And then suddenly they were running towards each other, and she was locked in an embrace so hard, so wild and filled with joy they couldn't at first speak.

How long they remained silent they never knew. The world was hushed and filled with wonder about them.

Evan was back. He had come home – to her, and the forest.

16

After that first passionate reunion, they walked hand in hand through the golden afternoon to where Emma's car was parked. They got in, and Evan's arm once more went round her, drawing her closer. He had been to Eastwood apparently, and having been told 'Mrs Arthur' was out, by a maid, and that no-one knew when she'd be back, he'd guessed and hoped he might find her at Oaklands, and had driven there in his own small car.

The housekeeper had informed him when he arrived she wasn't expected that day. In a desultory way he'd wandered around for some time, wondering whether or not to go on to Charbrook, and then, suddenly he'd had the idea of walking through the park.

'Must have been a sixth sense – telepathy, if you like,' he told her. 'Oh Emma, my sweet, wild, wilful love – why didn't you answer my letters?'

'Letters? But I never had one – not from Africa,' she told him, only one from Ireland. Arthur must have—'

'That swine! If I could get my hands on him I'd—' Lloyd explained.

'You can't,' Emma stated in such flat dulled tones he glanced at her sharply. 'No-one can. Arthur's dead.'

'Oh. That means—?'

'Yes,' she said before he could finish, 'I'm free, and yet I'm not – in a way. I'm bound, just as much as you are, Evan – but differently.'

'What do you mean?'

Haltingly at first, then in a rush, the words came tumbling out. The whole story of her discovery that she was having a baby – *his* child – of the long endless months of waiting to hear from him, of longing, despair, Jon's birth and Arthur's tragic death, followed by her determination to survive and her fanatical dedication to *Woman's Post*.

'It was like being a machine,' she said at last. 'I just went on and on—'

'But why the devil didn't you let me know about the baby?' Evan demanded, 'It was my right, and presumably you knew the last time we met, in London?'

'Oh yes. But before I could say, you callously informed me you had a wife,' Emma retorted sharply. 'How do you think I felt then? But perhaps you *didn't* think at all. Perhaps you assumed I was just content to be an incident—' Renewed indignation flooded her voice and lovely eyes.

He took both her shoulders and forced her round to face him. 'Now look here, my love, none of that; don't you *dare* suggest such a thing. A bare-faced lie, and you know it. And if you go on in this way I'll – I'll—'

'Yes, Evan?' Her tones were suddenly meek.

'I'll put you over my knee and wallop you soundly in public. Damned if I won't.'

'How interesting for the birds and bees and baby rabbits,' she said, with no trace of expression on her face. He relaxed, smiling slightly, then said more quietly, 'Don't joke, Emma.'

'I'm not. It's just – oh so much has happened, and now you suddenly appear and I'm sort of lost and quite out of my depth. Because you see, nothing's solved really. There's still Shirin; and Jon, my little boy – he's like you, Evan, but it's his grandfather who matters to him. I don't really see any possibility of us being together.'

'Then you'd better start looking,' Evan replied brusquely. 'Because I'm not letting you off the chain any more, my love, and I want my son. You'd better get that into your head once and for all.'

'How can I? And what would I be to you? A sort of permanent mistress during the time you're not in Ireland?'

He gritted his teeth, and staring stonily ahead, through the wind-screen, said, 'I shall never go to Ireland again.'

'But, Shirin—'

'Shirin also is dead.'

'Oh.'

'It happened months ago. She had a kind of seizure, a fit. It wasn't pleasant. I happened to be there at the time, and I'm glad now. Her aunt needed someone, and even a womanising kind of adventurer like me can have feelings, a sense of duty if you like.'

There was a pause, followed by Emma saying, 'Oh Evan, I'm sorry.'

'No need to be. Poor Shirin's well out of it. You regretted your father's death – that was natural. He happened to be a normal human being. But I've no patience with anyone pretending to moan at the end of a crazy unhappy creature's suffering, whether a human being or animal. So please let us drop the subject.'

'Of course,' she agreed quietly, feeling rebuked for her own insensitivity. Of *course* Evan was hurt, and still remembered the past, as she did her own – with Arthur. However impossible and unfortunate both she and Evan's marriages had been, they'd *happened*, and helped make each of them the people they now were – able to understand better, and add a wider dimension to their own loving.

She let her fingers stray lightly over Evan's near hand. 'There's a lot we'll have to put aside now,' she said, 'and accept about each other.'

'Yes,' said Evan. 'It's the future we have to think about.'

Which they proceeded to do, without any further delay.

*

Emma at first was all in favour that she and Evan should be married before informing the Bradleys, Jonathan in particular. But Evan was determined to have everything in the open. 'There's been too much secrecy already,' he told her the next day when they met in Leyford, 'too many devious undercurrents and evasions. Bradley won't like it, of course, but he's got other fish to fry now, with all his Parliamentary commitments. When we're off the scene with young Jon he'll adapt and come round in the end and see sense. Jon's *my* son, after all. And anyway I suppose we'll keep in touch—'

'Oh Evan – *keep in touch*!' Emma shook her head. 'You don't understand one half of what the baby means to that man. They're *devoted*. It's as though—'

'What?'

'As though—' Emma broke off, searching for words, then continued hesitantly, '—as though it was *meant*.'

'What do you mean *meant*?'

'For Jon to take Arthur's place,' she said bluntly.

'But—'

'*No*. Wait. Just listen to me first and then say what you like. I know you've got a point in wanting to claim Jon. But he doesn't know you – he's never even *seen* you. All these months, more than a year, when I never had a line from you and made myself plan my future round the *Woman's Post*, *driving* myself, doing my damnedest to forget you, Jonathan and Jon have forged a bond—'

'Forged a *bond*! Come now, Emma. This is real life. How can a baby forge anything?'

'Wait until you see our son,' she said calmly, almost grimly, 'then you'll get a surprise.'

There was a long pause before Evan queried stiffly, 'Are you trying to suggest that we start our married life without the child?'

Her clear grey eyes stared directly into his. She shook her head slowly.

'No, darling. I'm not suggesting anything yet. But it's a possibility, isn't it? And would it be so bad, just you and I together?'

Gazing at her, entranced utterly once more by the pale heart-shaped face framed by its wayward wealth of dark russet curls – by the tilted trembling mouth and arch of slim neck, above all by her honesty and sincerity which still held so much of a child's innocence, he knew that indeed *with* her he would have everything, and without her nothing.

The well-remembered whimsical smile touched his mouth.

'You *are* a superb actress, Emma,' he murmured, before his lips enclosed hers.

'*Actress?* How dare you?'

'Oh I dare, my darling. Never doubt my courage. And you won't always win, you know, in any battle ahead of us.'

'I wouldn't want to, Evan Lloyd. Just so long as you promise one thing.'

'What?'

'Not to go jaunting off to foreign climes leaving me at Oaklands alone ever again.

'That's a bargain. But neither do I intend being tied to your apron strings. More likely you'll have a halter round your neck. And then Oaklands! – you seem to have arranged things pretty quickly in your nimble mind. Who said we were going to live there?'

'Me. For part of the time anyway.'

'I'm glad you added the last bit. Because there's another world beyond, you know, *my* land. Oh, *cariad*, my sweet wild Emma, one day I'll take you there. There's music in the valleys, and the mountains have a mystery and magic about them you find nowhere else. There's poverty too, and bigotry in parts, but hearts are warm and generous. Until we go there together, I can't properly explain. How can I?' He smiled again whimsically, 'A Welshman treading the soil of England!'

'Now you're Evan Lloyd the poet,' Emma remarked, 'and I know – I've *always* known – that the public will accept you one day.'

'Public be damned,' Evan said vigorously, 'haven't I got all I want right here in my arms?'

'Yes – oh yes,' she agreed, 'and so have I. But your work matters, your own particular kind of talent, your unique sort of Welshness, and that's going to be our aim – *mine* anyway – to spread it everywhere, around the world.'

They were both being ridiculously exultantly confident, and were well aware of it. But it didn't matter. Nothing was of any account at the moment beyond their coming together again.

Later, when the practical point arose of informing Jonathan

of their plants and intended marriage, Jonathan was at first assessingly doubtful, then grudgingly acquiescent.

'If you want to do such a mad-headed thing,' he told his daughter-in-law grimly, 'you'll do it. I should know you by now. But the boy!' He thrust his jaw out before enquiring bluntly, 'I take it you'll leave him here where he rightly belongs? Legally he was born my grandson, and I think I can give him greater security and personal contentment than you two ever will—'

Evan's temper flared.

'You've no right to say that. A son's place is with his parents. I happen to be his father, and I think the law would agree—'

'The law has nothing to do with it. If it came to a battle in court your own claim would be nullified immediately. As for Emma—' His voice softened slightly. 'I think if she's honest – which she generally is – she'll agree with me that the youngster's happier here than at Oaklands. Another thing – there'll most likely soon be other children coming along, once you're wed. Well – think about it. There's plenty of time. Get to know the boy a bit. When you see how things are, I reckon you'll agree what I've said is right.'

This proved to be true. Although Evan recognised and was proud of Jon's looks, healthy stamina, and bright mind – no true affinity registered between them. To all intents and purposes the toddler had been born and destined to become a Bradley.

So it was settled, not without certain heart-searching on Emma's part.

On a day in late October 1906, Mrs Arthur Bradley became Mrs Evan Lloyd, and the one true adventure of their joint life began.

A son was born the following year, followed by twins in 1910. By then King Edward VII had died, and a new monarch was on the throne. 'The *Echo* had successfully been amalgamated with the *Comet* into The *Midlander*, but *Woman's Post* thrived and at the time of the Coronation a special edition was published showing photographs of the event.

So began a dynasty of magazine enterprise first founded by

the Fairley family, which eventually had a counterpart in America.

But that is another story.

Emma and Evan had the normal difficulties, successes, arguments and makings up of any passionate couple deeply in love.

Meanwhile the life of the forest went on, unchanged except for a few tourists in summer time.

William's faith in Emma was justified.

Oaklands was safe, for all time.

EPILOGUE

1915

On a cold day in nineteen fifteen, Emma Lloyd and her three children stood on a platform at Leyford Station watching the train puff in that was to take Evan to the Front. It was wartime. Countless other women and their families waited with her as Evan, only one of the khaki-clad crowd, was jostled through a door into the maze of steamy corridors and compartments.

Thin sleet, mingled with smoke, half obscured the features of loved faces pressed against windows eagerly searching for a last glance of the ones to be left behind.

Emma, for the sake of the children, tried to appear controlled. But her eyes were half blinded with tears, as following a parting embrace, her husband shouted, 'Thumbs up, Emma *cariad*, I'll be back.'

The next moment the slow throbbing of the train's engine increased, taking the serpent-like shape gradually into a blurred distance of thickening nonentity. The desperate waving of handkerchiefs and disc-like watching faces finally disappeared.

It was over.

For many, the last farewells had been said, to leave a blankness and emptiness in hearts which could never completely be filled again.

Presently, one by one, and then in small groups, the families turned, and moved slowly from the platform. As Emma, grasping the hands of the twins, accompanied by her elder son, William, passed up the steps to the station entrance, she noticed a poster depicting Kitchener with a pointing finger, and a message printed bodly by it, saying 'Your Country Needs You'. Further on there was another – 'Make the Cap Fit. *WEAR IT*.'

As the four of them entered the sleet-blown street, she heard above the rattle of tram-cars the voices of girls singing from a nearby pub:

> Oh we don't want to lose you, but we think you ought
> to go –
> For your King and your Country, *do* need you so.
> We shall love you and miss you, but with all our
> might and main,
> We will hug you, thank you, kiss you –
> When you come back again –

Would Evan come back? *Would* he? But of course. He *must*. He'd promised. Clinging to the hope, she walked on courageously, while one tiny voice asked, 'Will it take Daddy long to win the war, Mummy?'

'No. Not long, darling,' Emma answered, hoping and praying desperately that it would be true, but that even if he didn't, the new world those thousands of young men were fighting and dying for, would be worthwhile.

Portrait of a Girl

To the memory of dear Mike,
my husband, whose courage and
enduring love enabled me to
carry on, and write this book.

I

1866

Whenever I think of Kerrysmoor, I see in memory the dark granite shapes of the Three Maidens standing stark against a fading cold sky. In the shadowed valley below, the mansion crouches square-faced beside a wind-driven copse of leafless trees. The vision is only momentary and quickly fades into a veil of drifting fog which finally resolves into something else – the cottage half a mile away that was to bring such beauty and tragedy into my life. Bushes wave in a thin breeze about its doors, swaying rhythmically to the haunted echo of singing.

For a few seconds I am a girl again, caught into the magic and mystery of the past. I see Rupert riding through the fitful light to meet me.

And the pool.

It is still there, but the cottage has become an empty shell, and Kerrysmoor is no more.

A wave of chill suddenly floods me; then just as quickly it is gone, and I am real again, in a present I thought at times could never be.

The beginning of it all was so different. I had my ambitions, from an early age but they were the glittering fantastic dreams of childhood only – of riding like a princess in a shining chaise drawn by white-plumed horses through cheering crowds. 'Princess' – that's what my father called me. He was a Breton seaman and each time he returned home to Falmouth from weeks – sometimes months – away, he brought gifts of silk and wonderful shawls and we'd have a 'dressing up' time while he pinned my hair high with fancy shining combs and ribbons and he would say, '*Ah! – c'est magnifique*! – a real princess.' In time, although my real name was Josephine, I was always Princess to him, which made his wife jealous. She was the daughter of a tavern keeper in Falmouth's docklands where we lived. Anna, who was good-looking in a fierce bold way, liked attention only for herself. There was little sympathy between us, which perhaps was understandable, as she was really only my stepmother. My own mother had died when I was three years old, and Pierre had married Anna twelve months later.

So when he was drowned at sea, I was left, by blood, an orphan, and felt very much alone. I think Anna did her best at first to care for me. But she was over-fond of men, and during my father's absence had been forever in the bar. Consequently I spent hours as a child wandering about the maze of fashionably cobbled streets round Falmouth's harbour, or hiding in corners and round the door of the taproom, listening to bawdy jokes and laughter, and strange chatter in foreign tongues. There was music and singing. Sometimes even I caught the echo of a Celtic melody heard in babyhood, and then I hummed it myself, softly at first, until a strange longing for something unknown and far away filled me. Forgetting caution, and as my voice swelled, I danced, impelled by instinct and a blurred memory of my mother's face – dark-eyed and pale, with her dusky hair blown wild and free as clouds over the Cornish sea. She had been Welsh and '*très belle*', Pierre often told me. Anna had hated him saying it, and once he'd set sail again on a long journey, she'd remarked cruelly; '*Belle*! that means "beauty". And "Princess". Forget it. A little Froggie *you* are – no more. So don't go getting fine ideas. There's only work ahead for you, my girl. And plenty of it.'

Six weeks later we learned that his ship had foundered off the African coast, taking all hands with it.

He was dead.

The next few years were sordid in many ways, holding, however, a strange colourful side that gradually absorbed me by its demimonde atmosphere of dark excitement. I could sing; and as time passed my voice sweetened and matured. While Anna sank further and further into debauchery and shame, I spent many of the night hours entertaining clients of the district's numerous hostelries and inns, by songs and ballads remembered from childhood. In this way I earned sufficient casual money to have occasional good meals and buy shoes, combs and other etceteras to wear with the silk shawls brought for me in the past from overseas by my Breton father.

My looks, also, caught men's attention. I was very pale-skinned, but with a wealth of black hair and eyes of deep dark blue, fringed by thick lashes. When I stared at myself through the mirror occasionally, chin up-tilted, with a little smile on my full lips, I knew why my father had called me 'Princess', and when I sang, I really became one. The dusty interiors of tap rooms and inns disappeared, taking the smell of spirits and bawdy laughter with them, and I was singing – singing – to far away regions of enchantment – of mountains and rivers and eternal springtime. There was sadness too, of dying and being born again! Oh, I never wanted my singing to end; it was as though only through my voice I could really be myself.

Pierre's Princess.

Feeling so made me proud. I allowed no liberties, no man to touch me. Their admiration flattered me, and one day I thought, perhaps someone with influence – some musician or opera producer – might be induced to launch me on the stage to a wider audience. The idea was just a wild dream of those early years, but it was sufficiently vivid and inspiring to keep my life apart from Anna's influence. Occasionally, when she was at her lowest ebb and I had had a particularly successful period singing at some respectable hostelry, I helped her a little financially; in a way I was sorry for her. The inn had become a place of ill-fame, and she had turned into nothing more than a slatternly promiscuous harridan available for any man who wanted her. Her father, who lived drunkenly in an upstairs room, died from a stroke, and soon afterwards Anna herself was found with her throat cut in a dark alley leading from the docks.

Her murderer was never found. The police didn't bother much. Her death was no loss. Only I attended her sordid funeral, and though I tried to feel grief, no tears came – merely a sense of gratitude that Pierre had never known her degradation.

I left that particular district soon after the event, and moved to a more respectable area, where the clientele of the various inns and eating houses had a more restrained and cultured character. My voice soon became appreciated, and my appearances in demand. It was wonderful knowing I could sing, and sing, without lascivious hands wishing to touch me or fondle me. Money too was good. I no longer had to accept what was thrown or meanly afforded.

At the Golden Bird, an establishment frequented by travellers and moneyed people, I was eventually given employment on the regular basis of two hour nightly sessions each evening, for which I was paid quite a handsome sum, and allowed sleeping quarters for myself. My looks and voice still blossomed. I became a symbol for the inn and was soon known as 'the Bird'. Oh, I was happy for those first few months; then gradually a deep longing flooded me for wider spheres and audiences. Singing had become my life. But there were other things too, an awakening emotional hunger of which my voice was only a part.

I was just sixteen when I first met Rupert Verne. It was his eyes that arrested my attention. They were long slits of smouldering deepest gold, unswerving in their gaze, under heavy brows and a wide forehead from which crisp, thick hair waved back. In that first moment of awareness between us I felt excitement flood my veins with a passionate desire that he should know the best of me – the wildest part perhaps – but sense the magic of my songs and share the far-away dreams born in me of my Welsh mother and her love for Pierre my father.

Written down this may sound naive and childish. To Rupert I suppose I could have *seemed* almost a child, with my flying hair and satin skirt swirling beneath the yellow shawl. But my throat had never before arched so joyously, or music trilled so sweetly from it as I lifted my arms above and towards the grouped heads before me. Faces had dimmed and become only blurred discs intermingled with smoke and the fragrance of perfumes and spirits; Rupert's eyes alone glowed, bright with vitality and fire – eyes that never left my face and that I knew must somehow have great significance in my life.

As my song ended he got up. I half believed that he'd make his way between the tables and come towards me. But he didn't. He stood quite still for a moment, watching me, and then turned and slowly, deliberately went away.

Others applauded, and would have crowded round me, but I was so heavy with disappointment. I rushed from the lounge past the taproom to my own humble apartment.

Why had he gone so quickly I wondered? Why had he left without a single word of appreciation? Perhaps after all my singing hadn't really pleased him. He was not exactly a young man – probably in the late thirties – with considerable experience of the Opera. Yet his eyes! – I couldn't forget them, or the way they'd seemed to drain my very spirit from me.

The next night he was there again, alone at a small table with a glass of wine in his hand. The glow of a lantern from an alcove gave the fawn velvet coat he wore the lustre of satin. Everything about him, though of quite good taste, marked him as a man of quality. Yet beneath the civilized facade I sensed emotional undercurrents as tumultuous as my own.

Still he didn't approach me, but as my singing session ended, moved quietly away into the dusk outside. I watched him through the window, place his tall beaver hat on his head, then without another glance at the inn mount the step of a waiting carriage.

Joe Burns, the landlord of the Golden Bird, must have noticed my concentration. He touched my arm in a friendly way and said, 'No use having a fancy for that one, girl – A real gentleman he is, an' with a fine lady wife into the bargain. Verne, his name is – Mr Rupert Verne. Got a large estate on the North Coast. So there's nothin' there for 'ee. Now young Harry Bolson – '

I shrugged, snapped my fingers, and said contemptuously, '*Bolson*! – he's not my kind, and your Mr Verne doesn't interest me. No man does.' I could hear my earrings tinkle as I tossed my head.

Joe Burns regarded me solemnly for a moment then turned away and said, 'That's all right by me, girl. There's always work for you here. As a matter of fact, I was thinking of raisin' your wage again.'

He kept to his word; I should have been content, but I wasn't, simply because for seven whole evenings Mr Rupert Verne didn't appear again. I supposed during the interim he'd become bored with my entertainment and had found something more stimulating – perhaps even returned to the vast estate I'd been told of in North Cornwall.

Oh well, I decided defiantly, so be it. There were other, more youthful, male faces to admire me. At the end of the week therefore, being in a coquettish mood, I donned a particularly gay attire of an orange-coloured swirling skirt over a peacock-blue silk shawl, and with a poppy behind one ear, above a jingling earring, broke into a medley of French songs, dancing to the rhythm of an Apache number. How my feet pirouetted, how my arms swayed and my thick dark curls flew to the melody, and oh! – how wonderful it was when the door at the far end of the taproom opened revealing the square-shouldered figure of Rupert Verne impressively silhouetted against the glow of the swinging oil lamp outside.

He was wearing a caped coat, and as he entered swung his stove hat from his head. The light's rays lit the chestnut hair and lean carved lines of his face to orange fire. Something electric in the atmosphere caused heads to turn. Movement ceased, mugs and bottles were momentarily stilled. No sound any more came from my throat. My slippers were motionless on the floor.

Then, suddenly, he strode forward, and said for all to hear, 'I beg no pardon for the intrusion, but ask your co-operation. This young lady and myself have matters of some importance to discuss, and I've had a hard ride, so for your deprivation of the night's pleasure – allow me – !'

He flung a fistful of coins into the gathering, quickened his approach to me and took the tips of my fingers for a second in his, then led me into the shadowed back portion of the inn.

I was bemused and exhilarated at the same time; it was as though a strange kind of enchantment had fallen upon me. The door of the back parlour opened slightly – through a chink of light I saw Joe Burns' face watching curiously. At a quick glance from Mr Verne the latch snapped, and we were alone in the fusty room. I stood with my head raised, fiddling with the fringe of shawl drawn close to my neck. There was a brief pause in which the monotonous sound of an ancient carved mahogony clock ticked the moments away. It was a drab brown room that badly needed dusting. An oleograph of the Battle of Trafalgar hung on the wall, a tired potted plant drooped on the sill, yellow and sick-looking in the wan lamplight. Embers in the fireplace were already dying, and remains of a meal had been left on the table. I was aware of these things, but they held no meaning for me. My heart was beating wildly. Every sense in me was heightened and expectant.

I waited.

Through the film of blurred air I watched the golden slits of eyes widen, and a faint smile pucker his lips. Then he spoke. 'Don't be afraid. I've no foul designs on you.'

Beneath the shawl I could feel my flesh burn, and felt a warm glow flood my cheeks. Words came from my lips mechanically. 'Of course not. Why should you?'

His whole body relaxed. 'Sit down,' he said. 'We may as well be comfortable. I have a proposition to put to you.'

I obeyed, waiting for him to take a seat, but he didn't, he just perched himself on the edge of the table and continued, 'Don't you want to know what it is?'

Already aware of the designs of most men, I managed to answer a little haughtily, 'I'm not sure, sir. I may be young but I've had propositions before.'

His voice hardened. 'Not of this kind. I'm not lusting after your luscious pretty body or any feminine favours. In other words, child, I'm a married man with no taste for affairs on the sly – '

'I – '

He raised a hand from which an emerald flashed its green fire. 'Now don't argue, if you please. You have a voice. Looks, too, of course, of a wild kind, but it is your voice I – covet.'

'Why? What for?'

'Ah. That's better. What for? To have trained – to bring it to its full potential. Do you understand?'

When I shook my head mutely, he resumed. 'You should have wider audiences than those in hostelries and taverns. I can make no promises of course – but I'm pretty certain that after a period of tuition you would be welcome on the best concert stages of Cornwall and the West – later perhaps through the whole land. You'd have to work hard and accept strict discipline, naturally, but luckily I happen to have friends in the theatre world – and the man I have in mind lives now not too far away – retired – near Truro. I'm quite sure he'd be delighted to undertake your tuition, if you're willing and agree to my plans – ' His voice broke off.

I simply stared. Although I'd long dreamed of the opportunity offered, I hadn't really expected it to materialise. I could feel my heart bumping wildly, then miss a beat or two as the blood rushed to my face before receding to leave me trembling. Damp curls clung to my forehead. This was all I had longed for, and more, much more – simply because Rupert Verne himself was concerned. That he was older than me – nearer forty than thirty, married, with a wife and owner of a large estate – that he had wealth and position, didn't in those first ecstatic moments register. A bond, a promise, had already been forged between us. Whatever happened in the future I knew that in some strange way we were already bound, for good or ill.

'Well?' I heard him say, through the dizzy whirl of excitement. 'Are you dumb, child? Or just not interested?'

'Of course I'm interested,' I heard myself reply, almost in a whisper. 'Of course. Of course – '

He smiled, and touched my shoulder lightly. It could have been a fatherly touch; but it wasn't – quite. For a second or two the years between us were dispelled. The whole world seemed to brighten and sing. We stood – woman and man facing each other on an enchanted shore while knowledge flowered and I knew life would never be quite the same again. Then, suddenly, it was over. Facts came into focus. I was merely Josephine Lebrun, a girl possessing a voice good enough to stir the interest of a would-be wealthy sponsor. So I steeled myself to appear dignified, even a little aloof, and continued, though still breathlessly, 'Who is he? This theatre person? And how do you know I'd please him?'

'I don't. We shall have to find out.'

The sudden abrupt tone of voice and manner chilled me. It was as though in a few short words he deliberately intended to cast me down.

Perhaps I'd been stupid and taken too much for granted. Perhaps after all, this idea of his was a mere whim – a rich man's passing game to provide stimulus and amusement for a time. Or perhaps he really was genuine, but cautious of disappointing me. The uncertainty must have shown in my expression. I felt my shoulders droop as I got up and turned towards the door. In a second he was there before me.

'Now don't you run away,' I heard him saying, as though talking to a child. 'You must learn not to show moods or tempers. And don't expect praise all the time. You have a nice voice, yes. But Signor Luigi will expect more than that – '

'Luigi?'

'My friend. He is half Italian, and was once a famous name in Opera – as a tenor in his prime, and later as producer. So of course, his contacts are valuable. If he thinks your talent worth troubling about I've no doubt I'll be able to persuade him to take you on. But you'll have to obey him and work hard. He can be a difficult tutor, because he is naturally a perfectionist. Do you understand? Have you the first idea of what I'm trying to din into you?'

The golden slits of his eyes gleamed brilliantly, unswervingly on mine.

With my chin lifted an inch higher I faced him very directly.

'I think so. I'm trying.'

'Very well. This then is what I propose. You will leave the Golden Bird in the next few days, and travel with me to my home on the North Coast. There is a cottage on the estate where you can live providing you keep an eye on certain things. I have a caretaker there, but she is getting old and not entirely capable of handling special *objets d'art.* Her eyes are no longer very good, and her hands are shaky, but she can cook still, and do a certain amount of cleaning. If you are willing you will assist her when necessary, for your board and lodging, and of course to help pay for your tuition. Luigi does not give his services for nothing.'

He paused; and after a moment I asked, 'Where, if I agree, shall I have my lessons? There? At your cottage?'

He gave a short laugh.

'My dear girl! no, of course not. Once or twice a week my chaise will take you to Truro. Your lessons can be arranged for suitable premises according to Luigi's choice. That is – if he agrees.'

If – *if*! again the doubt.

Although exhilarated still, I was bewildered, a little uneasy. Everything had happened so quickly, and I couldn't help wishing that the future could have been arranged without the necessity of having to be dictated to by the 'perfectionist' – the critical and, I was sure, fiery Italian Luigi.

Apart from that the condition that I'd be expected to help at the cottage in any caretaking business seemed a little strange. I didn't much like the idea of being confined in a small cottage with a shaky old woman whose faculties were failing. Did it mean that I'd hardly ever see Rupert Verne? I had no *right* to, of course. I must remember that always. He was married. His interest in me was supposedly because of my voice only. So, if I really co-operated with his plan I must severely control all emotional impulses. Only through my singing would my heart be free to express the hunger and joy of living.

Therefore, I forced myself to appear more calm and dignified, and the result of that propitious interview was that the following week I set off with Mr Rupert Verne in his chaise for Kerrysmoor.

We travelled cross-country over a high moorland route up and down brown hills, past grey farms and villages, and bleak hamlets of miners' cottages huddled along the coast. The wild horizon of earth and sky was dotted intermittently by dolmens, standing stones, and the rhythmic movement of tin-mine pumping rods smokily dark in the yellowing autumn evening. Occasionally the winding road curved close to giant cliffs bordering the sea. Through the clip clop of horses' hooves and rattle of wheels the thunderous pounding of waves could be heard menacingly crashing against jutting rocks hundreds of feet below.

Mr Verne was silent for most of the way. The coldness of the landscape began to oppress me. For the last few miles we passed no living creature but a few cows and sheep huddled in stone-walled fields, and a pedlar's cart pulled by a donkey driven by a hunched brown-skinned man. He wore a woollen cap with a feather in it, and touched it as the vehicle passed by. Rupert Verne gave a slight inclination of his head. I glanced at him enquiringly.

'Tammy Vicks the pedlar,' Rupert said casually, adding with a hint of humour in his voice though no smile touched his lips. 'A much respected man hereabouts – Tammy.'

'Oh.'

'Heard of pellars?'

'No,' I replied. 'Pedlars, yes. But pellar –'

'Almost the same thing. Both go about selling things. But a true pellar is also a conjurer said to possess magic powers and cures for healing.'

I stared at him. 'Do *you* believe that, sir?'

'What *I* believe is of no account,' he answered shortly.

'I see.' I felt snubbed and must have shown it, for he continued after a short pause, 'I accept what I know to be fact and take the rest with a pinch of salt. You'll hear many strange stories round here – myths and legends grown from ancient times. Take them as such. Remember the reason you've come to Kerrysmoor. Your voice.'

'I hope you won't be disappointed.'

'So do I, for your own sake.'

His stiff words sent a wave of resentment through me.

'I could always return to Falmouth. Mr Burns was satisfied. I brought him good custom,' I said sharply.

'Did you indeed?' Conscious that he had turned his head quickly to look at me, I kept my chin up, and eyes fixed straight ahead.

'Yes,' I heard him continue, still in the same abrupt stilted tones, 'I can well believe it. You have a piquant air.'

That was not what I'd wished him to say. Not the type of compliment I'd expected when I recalled the intense interest of those strange amber eyes as they'd first rested on me in the taproom of the Golden Bird. Sudden chill filled me; not only because of my deflated mood, but because freshened with the fading of daylight, drifts of cool air penetrated the interior of the chaise in damp waves of rising mist.

I pulled my cloak more tightly to my chin, and then, as the vehicle rounded a corner of the lane I saw the house hunched square and dark against the shape of a rising hill. Through the uncertain light no details of style or architecture were visible. To one side a copse of trees blew in a thin wind. The rest of the valley was in shadow, but the rim of moor above was starkly clear against the greenish glow of fading twilight, topped by three tall standing stones. My heart, for a second, seemed to miss a beat, because it seemed to me that as the chaise drew nearer to the drive, they appeared to lurch forward of their own volition.

Mr Verne must have noticed. He gave a short laugh. 'The Three Maidens,' he said. 'Quite dramatic at certain times of day. Not that you'll have time to go wandering that way. Tonight you'll stay at Kerrysmoor, but tomorrow you'll be driven to the cottage – Tregonnis, and quite soon I shall arrange a meeting for you with your tutor.'

Such was my introduction to a whole new phase of my life which was to hold such disaster, tragedy, and periods of overwhelming joy.

*

The interior of the house depressed me on that first evening. The lighting from various lamps was insufficient to penetrate the gloom of winding corridors and dark recesses where shadows flickered eerily over black-framed, ancient portraits, giving a curious impression of life.

An elderly woman wearing a mob cap and apron over a starched, dark dress greeted me grudgingly, and was introduced by Mr Verne as Mrs Treen, the housekeeper. She nodded curtly, saying, 'Follow me. Your room's this way.'

I glanced at Mr Verne; his face was expressionless. He was waiting obviously for me to obey, which I did. The hall was flagged, covered at intervals by rugs. Half way down we passed a wide staircase leading up from the right. It curved sharply in a bend beneath a Gothic-style stained-glass window, and for a moment a brilliant shaft of lighting from above threw a static figure into vivid clarity. The form was that of a woman – elegantly thin and wearing a purple wrap. Her face was deadly pale under the intensely black piled-up hair. She held a lamp in one hand, and stood so still and watchful I was discomforted, sensing no welcome or warmth from her – only critical resentment.

'Come along, girl,' I heard Mrs Treen say. 'We haven't all the time in the world.' Rupert Verne moved away, and at the same time the woman turned and retreated round the bend into the shadows. A faint soughing of wind and tree tapping against the window merged into the rustle of silk skirts and softly dying footsteps.

'Who was that?' I had the temerity to ask. 'On the stairs.'

'It isn't really your business,' came the reply tartly. 'But as you're leaving tomorrow, and there's no mystery about Madam's presence I'll tell you – for your own good. The lady on the stairs was Mr Rupert's wife, Lady Alicia. She's the daughter of a very noble house, and much respected. So if you happen to meet before your departure you'd better remember your manners.'

I wanted to retort indignantly that I did not come from the gutter, and knew how to behave in the presence of gentry, but was wise enough to keep the words back. After all, entertaining well-bred pleasure seekers in respectable hostelries like the Golden Bird had demanded quite a different code of behaviour than bowing to her ladyship. No curtseying or minding one's words – just smiling and dancing, and singing for the joy of it. Depression enfolded me in a grey cloud. For the first time I doubted the wisdom of having left Falmouth for the grim atmosphere of Kerrysmoor.

In the morning, though, optimism had returned. When I jumped out of bed and pulled the window curtains wide, pearly sunlight touched distant cliffs to gold. The sea beyond was calm under a lifting cloudless sky. Immediately below the wall of the house, terraced gardens sloped to an expanse of moor where gorse flamed between clumps of purple heather and burnished undergrowth. Any memory of the steep hill behind surmounted by the gloomy Three Maidens was dispelled.

'I shall like it here,' I thought, forgetting for a moment that in an hour or two, perhaps less, I should be leaving for the unknown destination of Tregonnis.

I had breakfast on my own in a small back parlour off the kitchen, consisting of gruel and a slice of thick ham. The master, I was told, had already eaten and her ladyship never rose until noon, taking little refreshment before the midday meal for which she was usually joined by Mr Verne in the dining room.

'The mistress isn't well today,' Mrs Treen told me, a little smugly, I thought, 'so 'tisn't likely you'll meet before you leave.'

I was slightly disappointed – not by missing any direct encounter with the haughty creature glimpsed on the stairs the previous night, but by the silence of the house and apparent shortage of staff. I had expected to see footmen and servants about, but except for a kitchen maid and a boy in shabby livery carrying boots from the scullery, no one appeared. In daylight the interior of Kerrysmoor had a dingy appearance. Walls needed re-decorating and there were gaps in tiled floors showing damp in places. The rugs in the back hall were partially threadbare.

From Joe Burns' description of a wealthy household I had expected spic and span elegance, even in servants' quarters. But sunlight streaming across floors and corners emphasised years of long neglect.

The housekeeper must have sensed my unspoken criticism. 'This place is old and takes a deal of keepin' in order,' she said. 'And large. You haven't seen anything of the proper dwelling quarters, or the West Wing where Lady Alicia has her apartments. Really elegant it is there. Every year sees it done up and something new added. But of course that's only right, seeing who she is.'

'I see,' I replied ineffectually.

She shook her head. 'No, my girl, you don't. 'Tisn't to be expected. Not with your background.'

'What do you mean? You don't know a thing about me.'

'Now, now, don't get all hoity toity! No harm meant. I was only going by your appearance.'

'And what's wrong with it?'

She smiled – not pleasantly – as her small eyes regarded me shrewdly.

'You've a bit of a wild look on you, to me. That black hair and those eyes! And the way you walk and swing your hips! Oh, attractive in a way I s'pose – enough to charm the master. Gipsyish. But – '

Discretion deserted me. 'Do you mind holding your tongue? My father was a sea-captain, Breton. And my mother was Welsh. That's why I'm here – I've inherited it – her voice. Mr Verne heard me perform and has offered to give me training.'

My sudden haughty tone had the effect of quietening her manner – or perhaps it was the unexpected appearance of Rupert Verne – quite unknown to me – in the doorway.

'I meant no offence,' she said. 'You took my words wrongly – '

'I should hope so,' Rupert's voice interrupted cuttingly.

Startled, both of us turned. He was standing motionless there, with the light from the window striking sideways across his lean face, emphasising the stern, tight-lipped set of his mouth and cold fire of his eyes.

'I didn't mean – ' Mrs Treen began, but was silenced by a wave of his hand. He came towards us and addressing the housekeeper continued, 'You should know by now that any guest in my household must be treated with respect, Mrs Treen. I'm most displeased; however, this time the incident will be overlooked providing nothing of the kind ever happens again. Josephine – Miss Lebrun – ' He glanced at me sharply –

'Yes, sir?'

'It *would* perhaps be more suitable to the occasion now if

you changed into quieter attire. In half an hour's time we're setting off for the cottage, and my caretaker there will probably expect her new companion to appear less flamboyant.'

I should have felt snubbed if it had not been for the unexpected glint of amusement in his glance.

'Very well,' I said. 'I'm sorry.'

He shrugged. 'No need to be. I'm sure Signor Luigi will appreciate a taste of colour providing your voice also charms his artistic heart.'

So I left him with Mrs Treen and went upstairs to the bedroom where I had a black shawl and skirt, and a dark cape to cover everything. I took the rings from my ears, and tied my hair back before pinning it to the top of my head. Over this I placed a small bonnet trimmed only by two flat velvet flowers. It had ribbons to tie under the chin, and the whole effect, when I was dressed, made me suddenly want to giggle. I could have been some young Breton housewife attired primly for a shopping expedition to market.

However, Mr Verne made no comment when I went down later carrying my small valise, ready for the journey. No glance from his eyes even denoted approval or the reverse. I was disappointed, but determined not to show it. If he wished now to have things on an entirely impersonal and business-like basis then I'd prove I was quite capable of obliging.

We spoke little during the journey. The lane curved round the base of a high moorland hill on one side, with a narrow thread of river on the other. The morning air was pungent with the damp smell of mist, fallen leaves and blackberries, and decaying vegetation. Far to the west silvered sunlight lit the distant sea. But the glimpse was soon lost as the chaise turned abruptly inland to the left. The trees bordering the lane thickened; dew diamonded their lean dark branches, giving an air of mystery and enchantment. Everything was very still – the hollow sound of hooves and wheels reverberated weirdly through the windless air. I lifted my hand once to clear the smudged glass of a window.

'There's not much to see yet,' Mr Verne said. 'By mid-day when the fog's lifted you'll find the view more hospitable. I must see some of these trees are cut down.'

'Are we still on your estate then, sir?' I asked.

'Not really. The cottage is on Kerrysmoor land. As the crow flies – if we had wings – ' he continued, 'we could be there in next to no time at all. This hill is Rosecarrion; we're bending back now towards the area from where we started.'

'Oh.' I tried to get an accurate picture in my mind of the locality. 'Then isn't it possible to go the other way, or over the hill?'

'There's no road fit for a carriage of any kind on the other side,' he answered, 'and crossing the hill would be not only difficult, but quite dangerous.'

'Dangerous?'

'Bog, and mine shafts – also adders,' I was told. 'I don't advise you to take any future rambles directly up Rosecarrion.' He glanced in the opposite direction where a humped bridge crossed the river. 'If you go that way you'll discover pleasant paths leading to Tharne. Tharne, though only a small village, is comparatively civilised, and even has a stores where I'm sure you'd find pleasing varieties and most things women want.'

I didn't answer. The mere fact that he'd done his best to put me off wandering about the wild hill had stimulated a wish in me to do so. I was used to going my own way; I suppose it was an instinct born in me through my Celtic and Breton ancestry. To be referred to in the category of 'most women' was mildly irritating. Freedom was in my very blood. I bit my lip momentarily, then relaxed, realising that in the future I would most certainly have to discipline myself to certain rules and regulations.

Round a sudden corner of the hill the lane branched off to the left into what was little more than a track. Long shadows now showed only a thread-like glimmer of light. The coach took the bend, carefully at a slow speed under drooping trees. Evening had deepened so swiftly it could have been almost night. Then as the trunks of oak, sycamore, larch and willow thinned, a shaft of light zig-zagged down the path, revealing a cottage tucked behind a square of garden, with a mellow glow streaming from a half open door.

The chaise drew up nearby; there was the whinnying of horses, and Rupert Verne's voice saying, 'Here we are. Tregonnis.'

He got up, and as he helped me from the vehicle the figure of an old lady appeared coming towards us down the path. She was thin, small, a little bent at the shoulders, but agile in movement, and strangely dressed in old-fashioned attire, wearing a frilled lace cap and apron, a hooped black silk dress spattered with sparkling jewels and brooches. Under the glow of an oil lamp already lighted in the hall I saw the tips of red satin slippers peeping beneath her skirts. She had red ribbons also at her wrists and decorating her hemline in tiny rosettes. Rings glittered from fingers of both hands. Her face was thin and pale with a pointed chin and high-bridged nose.

Mr Verne introduced her as Dame Jenny Trenoweth, 'keeper of Tregonnis', and I as his temporary ward who would be for the time being in her charge, and to give help when necessary. Obviously, she had been well primed concerning my stay at the cottage and the true purpose of it. She expressed no surprise, but nodded all the time he was speaking, her small bright eyes regarding me shrewdly and unblinkingly.

Having expected to find someone more of Mrs Treen's type, I was bewildered by this first glimpse of the quaint creature who appeared more suited to be a character in a play than in real life. Her voice, too, was light and high, but I guessed could be sharp if she felt like it.

Conversation between the three of us was short. Indeed after the first introduction and intimating of my expected behaviour and duties, Rupert Verne appeared anxious to leave.

'The horses will be getting restless,' he said. 'The light's bad, and my wife likes dinner to be punctual. First, though, I would like to show you my – collection. Dame Jenny has been its previous guardian for many years. In future you will share the duty. Dame Trenoweth – ' he indicated the parlour door with a wave of his hand, 'you first please, and we'll follow.'

The red slippers made a tapping noise, the necklaces and silk dress tinkled and rustled as the tiny figure led us through the hall to a door on the right, further down. The surround was arched, and the wood, of light oak, was panelled and carved in a symbolic and intricate design. From a pochette hanging at her wrist Dame Jenny took a bunch of keys, she inserted one in the lock, and we went into the room. It was larger than I'd expected, and at some time in the past, obviously, had been converted from perhaps two smaller ones of plain architecture into an interior of intriguing nooks and alcoves.

Candles had already been lighted, throwing fantastic shadows about the treasures stored there – French figurines, music boxes, ivory miniatures in velvet frames, and paintings of exquisite beauty; the walls were silver grey, the ceiling blue and one wall comprised entirely of a large white marble fireplace with settles round it for seating.

It was not possible at first glance to absorb details. The rosy glow of burning logs and candles emphasised the air of mystery and days long ago – countless years in which the treasures must have been collected. There were paintings – mostly water-colours of landscapes that seemed to quiver with life as transient shadows crossed their surface. The delicate poised figure of a glass dancing piper flashed with rainbow movement when I took a step forward, disturbing the quiet air. Then it was stilled again into shadow. I stared round wonderingly, then glanced back again to the fireplace because above it was the focal point of the whole room.

A portrait.

The painting of a girl with upswept silver-pale gold hair tied high with a green ribbon. Her face was heart-shaped from which hazel eyes stared with the translucent quality of moorland pools lit briefly by sunlight. The mouth appeared on the verge of laughter but the whole effect was of longing – the longing and sadness of beauty unfulfilled. I was fascinated, briefly magnetised, sensing that the surroundings were merely a background, perhaps a dedication, to her personality. Above a froth of lace her slim neck held an opalescent glow, ivory pale, yet changeful in the flickering candlelight with all the glowing radiance of waves breaking gently on a cool shore.

Who was she, I wondered? Envy stirred me for a moment, because I felt instinctively she must somehow, in some secret way, hold a place in Rupert Verne's life.

'What a lovely portrait,' I heard myself saying ineffectually.

'Yes.' The one word fell short and curtly from his lips. I glanced at him expectantly. 'Is it anyone – ?'

'You'll never meet her,' he interrupted. 'It's just a good painting, and the setting is right. That's why it's there.'

'I see.' But I was disappointed; I felt he could have told me so much more. His expression, I noticed, had tightened. There was a bleak guarded look in his eyes and in the set of his mouth that told me I trod dangerous ground and should stop questioning.

So I said no more on the subject. More practical matters were discussed in which I learned I would not be seeing Signor Luigi until the end of the following week, when the chaise would arrive to take me to Truro.

'Dame Jenny will have time to see that your clothes are in order and suitable for your introduction,' he added before leaving. 'She's an excellent needlewoman, and if anything is required word can be sent to Kerrysmoor. Jan Carne will bring a message.' I wondered who Jan was, but didn't ask.

'That's right,' the old lady said, nodding her head briskly several times. 'These old fingers of mine mayn't be as nimble as they once were, but I can still sew a seam or tuck, and put in a daisy or two when needed.'

Her cheeks had turned very pink; she reminded me of a bedecked robin inquisitively inspecting its domain. I noticed also that her thin ringed hands had a tremor. No wonder Mr Verne no longer considered her quite capable of safely dusting and moving the treasured figurines and curios in the room we'd just left. I had misgivings myself when I considered the responsibilities were in future to be partly mine.

Minutes later Rupert was at the door saying farewell. He held the tall beaver hat in his hand a second before replacing it on his head, turning, and walking briskly away down the path to the waiting chaise. During that brief second his eyes held mine again while excitement churned in me – an electrical awareness of communion binding all the nerves of my body into a hungry fire of desire.

Against my will I made a slight instinctive movement towards him. Did his left hand make a faint gesture of acknowledgement beneath the lace cuff? Just for that fleeting instant did the lines of his stern mouth soften? – the lids quiver over the long golden eyes? I shall never know. My head and senses were whirling so that imagination became confused out of focus with reality.

When my heart had steadied he was already at the gate. A minute afterwards he was ensconced in the chaise, and the vehicle, following a flick of the coachman's whip, was moving down the shadowed lane, throwing a zig-zag of fading light before it, from the swaying lamps.

Evening had faded into deep dusk. When we moved into the hall again Dame Jenny took me up a narrow staircase to my bedroom. The walls were all of white, the furnishings of light oak in an old world style. There was one window overlooking the garden at the back of the cottage. After the old lady had gone I pulled the curtains and looked out. The deep velvet blue sky was already pin-pointed by starlight, but the night was not yet dark enough to obscure the looming shape of the hill rising formidably against it. There was something else too – which I thought at first was probably my imagination. But in the morning I knew my conjecture to be true. Three gaunt shapes stood at a different angle from my first glimpse of them – silhouetted in the morning light.

The Three Maidens.

There was no practical reason why I should have sensed an omen in their presence. But I was filled with momentary, irrational depression. Why? A second later I'd dispelled it. I was, after all, half Welsh, half Breton, which could be the reason for my Celtic mood.

It was the only sensible answer and one I made myself accept.

II

During those first few days at Tregonnis, Dame Jenny was completely non-communicative about matters concerning Kerrysmoor or the Verne family, and when I questioned her about the history of the cottage and priceless valuables of the 'treasure room', she became stubbornly silent – almost hostile.

'None of your business, miss,' she said in her thin piping tones. 'All you have to do is help me, as the master said – take down anything that needs dusting so there's no danger of it falling, and polishing – those fancy chairs' legs need attention. 'Tisn't so easy any more for me to bend or get down on my old knees. I keep the key of the room myself. Every morning I take a look round, so see you're about between ten and eleven, an' I'll be able to let thee in.'

'Yes, Dame Jenny,' I agreed meekly.

She nodded, adding, 'You can help me with the baking too. There's an apron in the kitchen to cover all those fancy things you do wear. Then soon as possible we'll get to thinking 'bout what stitching's to be done to make thee presentable for meeting the music man.'

I smiled to myself at her reference to Signor Luigi as 'the music man'.

'Hope you know how to use the needle *properly*,' she added. 'I was always one with a liking for dainty flowers and tucks. But, of course, your cape must be quiet and moderate, I've a piece of brown velvet upstairs might do. No use worrying the master for gold to waste on material when it's there safely folded in my chest upstairs. Still, we'll see 'bout those things a bit later; maybe tomorrow. You take things easily today, girl, get used to the cottage an' garden. Done any prunin' or weedin', have thee?'

I shook my head. 'No. In Falmouth we didn't have a garden.'

'Hm. Well, there'll be bits to do here. But never touch my roses, mind. Roses is delicate things that need dainty handling. With care I have them bloomin' most all the year round. Even at Christmas I've known red buds openin' to cheer the winter.'

When I went out to the back later I discovered that she had in no way exaggerated. On one side of a path comprised of pebbles and small rocks of granite quartz reflecting different shades, in the early morning sunlight crimson roses blossomed, mingling colourfully with bronze and gold chrysanthemums.

On the other side, half shadowed by drooping willow, water-lily leaves dappled the surface of a motionless pool. It appeared deep, reflecting the shape of a poised white marble statue at the far end – that of a woman emerging from reeds and ferns, staring into the water. She had one arm over a breast, a bowl or kind of urn held in the other, from which delicate plants trailed. Much of the figure was lost in the verdant undergrowth, but the evasive light gave an uncanny impression of life and momentary movement. The whole effect emanated an emotional quality that affected me oddly.

I tore my eyes from the pool and glared up at the great hill behind. The morning light emphasised the rugged character of the rising moor – great boulders and tumps of heather and gorse, interspersed with the inky grassy darkness of bog and gaping shafts. A derelict mine stack stood halfway down below the Three Maidens. Not a pleasant vista exactly – primitive, intimidating almost, in its wild aloofness, yet challenging, and I knew, despite Rupert Verne's warning, a day would come when I would set out in exploration.

Meanwhile I determined to make every effort at pleasing

the quaint keeper of Tregonnis, and managed to acquire a certain amount of trust from her, though her old eyes had a watchful look whenever I strayed beyond the garden gate.

'Ye recall what the master told thee – ' she said one day. 'Keep away from the hill. There's plenty of interest in the garden since you like fresh air, and I can teach thee a deal 'bout herbs from my own small patch – it's at the side beyond the roses. There's some bunchings to do before drying – your hands look nimble enough. And what about your voice? I haven't heard any singing yet to speak of – just that humming when you're in the treasure room. There's my fiddle to accompany you when you feel like practising. I was good on the strings in my day.'

I didn't attempt to explain to her that all her fussy restrictions quelled any natural impulse to burst into song, or that her country style of fiddling would only put me off. However, she didn't press the point, but insisted on me putting certain hours of every day into stitching at my 'wardrobe'. The velvet material was used for a cloak-coat with velvet band trimmings. The material was sent to Truro to be cut by a costumier patronised by Lady Verne and sent back to Dame Jenny for making up. This was a tiring business for me, and my day-dress of green silk to be fixed over a moderate bustle, was more so. It had an apron front and white lace collar. There was a good deal of piping to do, and numerous tiny buttons to sew on. Dame Jenny was certainly nimble with her fingers. If she hadn't been I should have been working day and night, because in the past I'd worn mostly colourful shawls to cover hastily converted gowns. Inwardly I fumed and fretted; how much easier and more relaxing it would have been to have taken Rupert Verne's offer of buying clothes from a professional establishment.

I liked the headgear. It was re-styled, hardly a bonnet, hardly a hat – with small flowers and bows on it, and was a relic from the old lady's chest where she kept precious nick-nacks of her own stowed away. A single white plume curved neatly round the back of the crown, with a shred of veiling floating behind. Tilted precociously forward on my coiled upswept hair it looked quite intriguing. Dame Jenny nodded cautiously when I turned from the mirror to face her.

'It will do, I suppose,' she said one afternoon with a hint of criticism in her voice. 'A little saucy, but then you've that air about you. So long as you do keep your eyes fixed down modest-like we must hope it won't offend. I've heard tell those Italians, singers and such-like, go in for a bit of show. A little rice powder on your cheeks will help make you less – colourful.' Her lips closed primly on the last word.

I laughed; I couldn't help it. Everything – the whole situation, the future, the old lady's grudging admiration and the thought of extending a gloved hand to Signor Luigi like any duchess stirred pleasurable excitement in me. I felt my throat trembling, and without warning joyous notes of solfa rose from my lips, turning involuntarily into a song – a song of mountains and rivers, of far off places and unknown passion luring me to the sweet rich fulfilment of love. I was trilling in the only way I knew – naturally, with abandon. My voice was firm, and full and sweet, realising all the longing I'd felt during the last few weeks for Rupert Verne.

When the sound died and I waited hesitantly with my bosom rising and falling breathlessly under my bodice, there was a prolonged pause from the old lady. She stood simply staring before remarking: 'You certainly have a pair of good lungs, girl. But if you take my advice you'll remember to control them in a ladylike fashion when the time comes to meet the great man. No doubt in low class hostelries, sailors and drinking folk 'ppreciate a deal of show and noise – but any famous acquaintance of the master will expect a taste of refinement.'

'Oh, but I have to sing as I feel,' I told her bluntly. 'Refinement or – or coarseness doesn't come into it. If I had to be controlled and careful there'd be no song – ' I broke off with a tinge of doubt rising in me, and it was at that moment the door creaked, sending a wave of cooler air into the parlour.

Startled, I looked round. Mr Verne stood there, top hat in one hand, wearing a black broadcloth cut-away coat with a cape slung over the other arm. His watchful eyes had a concentrated enigmatic look in them, but I fancied there was a tilt of approval round his mouth, and I was once more conscious of his strange sense of power, of an awareness between us that set my pulses leaping with wild restrained joy.

'Practising already?' he said in level tones. 'Good. In two days' time we go to meet Signor Luigi.'

'Two days?' I echoed. 'I thought – '

'If you're ready, that is,' he added and turning to Dame Jenny remarked, 'providing the dress-making session permits. At the moment I must say you look – quite charming.'

Dame Jenny appeared slightly flustered.

'If I'd known you were calling today, master, I'd have had things more shipshape. This is only a try on. There be gloves and all manner of little things to 'tend to, and a few alterations. And – ' with quite a stern glance at me, 'no more interruptions of tra-la-ing.'

He allowed himself to smile then. 'Oh, I'd call what I heard at the gate more than tra-la-la-ing. Surely *you* with your knowledge of good music must appreciate that, Mrs Trenoweth?'

Mollified, she replied, 'Good music? I'm not all that well versed in such as opera, Master Verne. The fiddle's more to my taste, as it was to my father and his before him. But if you 'ppreciate my young lady's voice then good it must be, I'm sure.'

Shortly after that brief interim of conversation between us, Mr Verne left. There was a further flurry of the dressmaking session, during which I was content to keep silent in case I betrayed my secret feelings to Mrs Trenoweth. Excitement gradually calmed to a deep glowing happiness that held no thought of the past or morrow, or the strange circumstances that had brought me into contact with Rupert. No impossible plans for the future stirred me. He was married, and not the type of man to treat any woman lightly. If he had been I wouldn't have admired – longed for him so passionately. To have visioned any outcome could have been ridiculous. As it was, a few precious moments in his presence were sufficent to make the day glow – the sun more bright, the skies over the wild autumn landscape a clearer more translucent blue.

When the prodding, pinching and pinning were over and the bustle adjusted perfectly into place Dame Jenny, at last tired herself, suggested I might like a breath of fresh air. 'There's not much to do in the kitchen,' she said, 'the baking's over, and Jan comes tomorrow to clean the floors. Take a stroll if you want to, girl. Only don't thee go wanderin' 'bout that hill. Remember, or there'll be trouble. Understand?'

I nodded, and promised I'd take the valley lane towards the village.

It was a dazzling day, speckled with frail misty air that dappled trees and undergrowth with shimmering light. The damp earth smells were redolent with the odour of fallen leaves and tumbled ripe blackberries; there was no wind, and the extreme silence – broken only by the flap of a solitary bird's wings or scuttle of some small wild creature from the bushes, emphasised autumn's magic. It had been the same when I was a child – only then the salty tang of sea mingled with all the other odours of dockland – of malt, fish, and crowds swarming round newly berthed ships had filled my young nostrils nostalgically reminding me my father Pierre would appear any day, bringing some exciting gift for his Princess.

Lost briefly in reminiscences of the past I came to the curve at the base of the hill which led in one direction towards Kerrysmoor along the route I'd driven with Rupert in the chaise. I had turned the corner when the rattle of horses' hooves and wheels approached from the opposite direction. Quickly I stepped aside and stood motionless against a hedge of willow and thorn, waiting for it to pass.

As it went by a face stared at me from the window. In a shaft of pale sunlight the features were comparatively clear – hard and set, thin-lipped, with brilliant black eyes emphasised by the extreme deep-whiteness of her complexion. A regal figure, wearing something dark, either purple or black. For some reason I felt discomforted, but it was not until the carriage had passed that I realised why.

The countenance affecting me so unpleasantly was the same I had noticed watching me from the stairs on my arrival at Kerrysmoor.

She didn't like me. There had been resentment, even contempt and a kind of hatred in that concentrated gaze.

Rupert's wife. Yes, I knew intuitively without doubt it was she. Well, I had done nothing to deserve it, and if possible would avoid doing so.

But I recognised for the first time there could be dangerous obstacles confronting me in my new life.

III

The day was chill when Mr Verne and I set off in the chaise for Truro and my auspicious meeting with Signor Luigi. No sunlight swept the landscape; under the grey skies, the scattered grey hamlets appeared sombre as the smoky mine stacks standing back against the moorland hills. A thin wind blew through the almost naked branches of bushes and trees. A few gulls drifted overhead, and an occasional dead leaf brushed the window as we clattered along. I drew my cloak close under my chin, and tidied a stray, straggling curl from my cheek under the frivolous headgear, feeling suddenly out of place and uncharacteristically self-conscious.

Mr Verne was so quiet. Any slight movement from him, any contact at all would have lifted my spirits, but he gave no indication at all of any pleasure in my company, and I wondered if I could have offended him in some way the day before, or if the 'chatelaine' – that is how I now thought of his lady wife – 'the Chatelaine of Kerrysmoor' – had somehow contrived to put a barrier between us. I couldn't help remembering the cold contempt of that icy stare as she passed in the carriage the previous afternoon. It was probable, I thought, that she violently disagreed with her husband sponsoring me. She might even have some knowledge of the stage, and had made up her mind already I would be a failure and the venture a waste of money.

Well, I would have to show her how wrong she was. The challenge gradually lifted depression to determination and a burst of anger. After all, I wasn't just a nobody. Pierre, my father, had taught me from an early age how to have pride in myself, and when the occasion arose behave as his Princess. Because of this I'd gathered what education was possible during my colourful 'vagabondish' days in Falmouth, learning much from listening to conversation of all types of people, and secretly mastering the art of reading in both English and French.

So I had nothing to fear from her ladyship, I told myself stubbornly, and for the rest of the journey felt better and in a more courageous mood to meet Signor Luigi.

By the time we reached Truro the skies had slightly brightened, though no trace of sunlight caught rooftops or the imposing shape of the Cathedral. I was surprised when we left the town centre behind and travelled towards the outskirts.

'My friend owns a property that was once a small playhouse,' Rupert told me. 'It's now only used on rare occasions and for individual cultural performances. Mostly it's empty – but to Luigi it holds memories – his own dwelling is nearby – and the acoustics are good, especially for vocal requirements and rehearsing sometimes. You may find the interior somewhat gloomy and neglected, but I can assure you, you won't have time to be depressed.'

This proved to be true.

The granite building was square and bleak-looking, of no particular period, looking more like an abandoned chapel than an ex-theatre. Except for a house huddled in trees a short distance away, and a few cottages, the landscape appeared curiously without life or activity. The house I guessed was Luigi's home, and was probably more attractive from the other side because the glint of water showed through the interlaced branches of woodland, which could have been the river winding below.

'So here we are,' I heard Mr Verne saying, as the chaise came to a halt. He took my gloved hand and helped me from the vehicle, adding a second later, 'You're very quiet. Nervous?'

'No,' I told him, 'well, a little perhaps. I was just thinking how deserted everything seems – ' My voice trailed off vaguely.

'Oh, Luigi likes solitude, except for opera and good music.'

'Is there an organ inside?' I asked thoughtlessly.

'Good heavens, no. There might have been once of course. Before it was a theatre, in early Methodist times the place was a chapel.'

So I'd been right. 'I *thought* so.'

'Did you now?'

'Yes. I kind of felt it.'

'Well, bring your thoughts to what is important at the moment and think of how to make a good impression on my friend,' Mr Verne said almost sternly.

I could feel myself flush, resentful that he should address me like that, as though I was a child.

'I shall do my best,' I said stiffly. 'I'm not entirely an ignoramus.'

His hand involuntarily tightened on my arm.

'Calm yourself,' he said, as we mounted the few steps to the door. 'There's no need to snap. I'm more concerned for your welfare than my own. Just be your natural self and put on no airs then everything will be all right.' There was a pause before he touched the bell-pull. 'You look – quite adorable,' he added encouragingly after a hurried glance at my profile.

The compliment startled me, sending a rush of exhilaration through my veins. I raised my head proudly in anticipation of the meeting, and as the heavy bell clanged, reverberating with a hollow sound through the silence, I smoothed my gloves and then lifted my cloak a few inches so the hem was saved from dust or catching the toes of my pointed boots.

There was a rattle of a bolt being drawn, and we went in. My instant impression was of emptiness and tall narrow windows in recesses where lamps had been lighted. At the far end was a raised platform, presumably a one-time stage.

The whole effect was gloomy rather than inspiring. I could imagine in the past, before the building had been a theatre, dark-clad preachers issuing dire forebodings to congregations of sombre religious converts. The singing would be of doleful psalms and hymns.

I felt suddenly trapped, with a wild instinctive desire to turn and rush out into the fresh air. Just as quickly I came to myself again. The nerve-crisis was over, and I was aware of Mr Verne presenting another shorter figure – Signor Luigi. I lifted my right hand instinctively, and as dutifully the rather portly little man raised it to his lips brushing the tips of my fingers briefly, before straightening up to his full height so the light fell directly on his face.

His brow was wide under thick crisply curling white hair; his complexion, though olive, was flushed at the high cheek bones, and this somehow added to the intense piercing quality of curiously light grey eyes under beetling brows. A carefully clipped grey beard added to an air of almost regal distinction which was emphasised by a maroon-coloured waisted velvet jacket and carefully cut black fitting trousers. He wore a white silk neckcloth. In spite of his somewhat florid appearance, there was still an aura of theatre about him, and I guessed he had a temper and could be irascible.

My deduction proved to be correct.

Following the first introductions Rupert Verne left, saying he would return in an hour to collect me.

After that my testing period – more of an interrogation, I felt – began.

First of all, under his frightening gaze, and from the platform, he put me through my scales, not once but time after time. Then I was allowed to sing one of the faraway Celtic melodies taught to me by my father. He gave no word of criticism or encouragement – simply stared, looking, I thought, more contemptuously critical than pleased.

It's difficult now to recall exactly what further endless exercises I was put through, but at last he said flatly, 'Not too bad. You have a good range. Your voice has possibilities. But ignorant – no control – no instinctive knowledge *at all* of discipline or of what the opera demands. Have you ever heard of Wagner, Miss Lebrun? Or Offenbach? Verdi? – But no. Of course not.' He shrugged. 'You are simply raw and very doubtful material.'

My temper flared.

'You must have known that,' I said hotly. 'Rupert – Mr Verne – surely told you, or I wouldn't be here. But as a matter of fact, I *have* heard of your great composers and some singers – but I can assure you I never aspired to such – such great heights. I didn't even ask to meet you. It was *him*. Rupert – ' Unconsciously the Christian name slipped out. Before he could interrupt I continued. 'Obviously you have no use for me, so I'd rather you just said so, instead of scolding and deriding.'

I broke off breathlessly.

There was a pause, then the great man – or *once* great man – said, almost appeasingly, 'My dear child, you astonish me. Famous singers in the past would have been gratified to earn even a word of criticism from Arnoldo Luigi. If I thought you had no promise do you imagine I would trouble one jot about you – ' He snapped his fingers. 'Eh?'

I was confused, even a little ashamed.

'I – I'm sorry. I didn't mean. I – '

'Aha!' he smiled then, a gesture with a kind of mischief, even wickedness in it, ' – you have a temper, temperament. That is good. No one without the flame, the longing, the glory and despair in the blood would have a chance to stir the heart and bring audiences to joy and tears. I can give you no promise, of course. But in time perhaps, with hard work and many, many scoldings from me – well, perhaps – just *perhaps* – we may, together make something of you.'

So that was the beginning.

The following week my training in voice production and stage craft commenced under the strict tuition of Arnoldo Luigi for, hopefully, a successful debut as a possible future prima donna.

Twice weekly the Vernes' chaise drove me to Truro for long sessions that were frequently tiring, leaving me chafing at what appeared to be my own inadequacies. Luigi was an irate critic, and sparse in praise, although at points when I was in a sudden too-low an ebb or on the verge of flouncing away in a temper he would unexpectedly produce a compliment and smile to restore confidence. There were also occasions when he allowed me to revert to my own choice of Celtic ballads and give full expression to the sense of romantic drama inherited from my mother. This I discovered later was not merely for my pleasure but to provide a yardstick for judging voice control – of what I'd learned so far in giving subtle but full power to my vocal range.

'Yes,' he said once, 'you have learned something, not much, but a little. In six months' time maybe – only *maybe*, you hear me? – we will give you a real test on a real stage. For that you will have to learn to move properly.'

'But – '

'Aha!' he waved a hand disparagingly, 'do not interrupt. Sometimes you show a *minimum* of grace, yes; at others you are a calf – a young cow – or a colt galloping in. *Discipline*, Miss Lebrun. Only discipline can give the essential dignity to any singer of repute. You have yet *much* to learn in every way.'

Such admonishments frequently depressed me, at other times fired my temper. Surprisingly, he was amused then, and gradually understanding developed between us.

The months passed, bringing a winter of wild gales and high seas lashing the gaunt granite coast. Apart from sessions at Truro I spent most of my time helping Dame Jenny, or attending to my duties dusting the precious treasures and figurines in the locked room. Being there was like entering another world – mostly because the girl's portrait so dominated the atmosphere. I couldn't help wondering about her – why Rupert had replied so brusquely when I'd questioned him about it. I was sure the painting meant more to him in some way than that of a mere acquisition hung where it was because it fitted the place. Was the likeness of some dead relative that his wife objected to? Or was she still alive living perhaps in another country because of a family quarrel?

I brought the subject up more than once to the old lady. She dismissed my queries with a shake of the head and fierce look each time.

'I know nothing 'bout her,' she said, 'neither should you be digging and delving. Too curious you are by half 'bout things not your business. And remember what they say – "curiosity killed the cat".'

'But I'm not a cat,' I replied pertly, sensing she was withholding at least a shred of truth.

'No. Well – sometimes you do act like one,' she remarked meaningfully – 'The way you go prowling of an evening sometimes t'wards Rosecarrion. I saw you yesterday, staring up the path that's forbidden you. "If she takes one step up", I said to myself, "I'll give a shout, and have to tell the master too".'

I shrugged. 'It seems so stupid. It's only a hill, an ordinary moorland hill, and the afternoon was quiet yesterday, I'd have enjoyed a walk in a different direction for a time.'

'What you enjoy and what's allowed can be two separate things,' she told me sharply. 'You should watch yourself and take care not to anger Mr Verne. You've a deal to thank him for, and be grateful. Remember that, girl.'

I did. I remembered all the time, and wished I had more opportunity for telling him so. But I seldom saw him. After the first visit to Truro the chaise called for me and I was driven there alone, then picked up at a certain hour and taken back to Tregonnis in the same manner unaccompanied.

The festive season approached, and Dame Jenny and I were invited up to the big house for Christmas Day. This was the one occasion in the year I was told, when servants, tenants and family joined in a dinner at night, followed by dancing in the large hall.

'Because you are being trained for life in a larger world,' the old lady said, unable to check disapproval in her voice, 'you will be allowed to eat with her ladyship and the master at midday as well. At first the idea seemed odd to me – very odd – Lady Verne is usually so particular 'bout who's allowed such intimacy. But thinking it over I saw sense in it. After months of training with the music man you should've learned certain manners. You'll have to watch yourself and show fitting modesty so Master Verne won't be ashamed of thee.'

'You can rely on me,' I said shortly. 'Will you be there too?'

Colour rose in the old bird-like face. '*Me*? There's no need to ask that. Who do you think I am, girl? An ordinary servant?'

'Of course not. I'm sorry. I shouldn't have asked such a stupid question.'

'It's as I said – you've still a deal to learn 'bout what to say and what not. In my opinion the less you speak in the comp'ny of her ladyship the better. Then there'll be your dress to think of. The brown silk made from the material bought last time we visited Truro should be suitable, providing you wear the lace shoulder shawl to cover you decently.'

'*That* dark thing?' I exclaimed, 'but it's so drab – almost *black* – and black and brown don't go together. The yellow fringed one would look so much more attractive – and why should I wear the brown dress anyway? There's that violet velvet. I could – '

'Tut tut! hold your tongue,' Dame Jenny said sharply. 'In her ladyship's comp'ny taste counts above everything. Remember, too – ' she wagged a finger in admonishment – 'you've no fame yet; just a pupil to do the master's bidding, and *I'm* responsible for your behaviour.'

'I don't remember Mr Verne saying so,' I couldn't help

replying coldly.

'There's a lot you haven't heard or know anything about,' came the tart reply. 'So have done now and no more arguments, if you please.'

I let the matter drop, resigning myself to the fact I'd have to wear the brown silk to save unpleasantness, but determined to produce a few additions and alterations at the appointed time.

In my own chest of clothes used in the past for my appearances at the Golden Bird I had a number of artificial flowers and lengths of braid in striking colours of the shades that were fashionable at that period – royal blue, emerald green, magenta, plum and vivid cerise. Cerise, I thought, would be striking decoration for my hair which I should wear up-coiled for the festive occasion and could be fixed at the last minute so that it would not be noticed under the hood of my cape. I would be tactful in wearing the brown gown and shawl but would arrange it so it could easily slip down after arriving at Kerrysmoor, revealing my shoulders. The effect would be attractive but not immodest. At my breast a velvet blossom would be pinned, and providing I could get down to a stitching session unknown to Dame Jenny, I'd sew stripes of cerise braid at the dress hem, with also a brightening touch to the corsage.

The effect, after I'd removed my cloak at the big house might irritate and shock the guardian of Tregonnis, even bring a glance of distaste from Lady Verne's cold face. This didn't worry me at all; the thought of making any impression – whether good or ill, only added stimulus and a mischievous sense of excitement.

Rupert, I knew, wouldn't wish me to appear drab and dull as a humble sparrow among the Christmas throng. His eyes would be searching for me – hopefully – from the first moment of my arrival. How did I know, or guess this? Intuition, I suppose – that electrical awareness there had been between us when our eyes had first met at the Golden Bird those months ago. Although he'd not appeared at

Tregonnis for some time, I couldn't believe he didn't think of me. Deep emotion which could so easily become love was not merely a visual thing, but a joy and a pain retained in the mind, and the very air of hills, sea and driven clouds sweeping the winter skies.

There was no sense of guilt in what I felt for him, however excessive and impractical the reality might be. At the moment it would have been senseless to plan. A few hours in his company had to suffice. After all, that marble-cold barrier of a wife stood between us; he had married her, she must mean something, and he was obviously disciplined and a man of principle. If he hadn't been I wouldn't have cared for him. So trying to think things out was hopeless.

There was no answer, except that I knew without any doubt at all that no man – ever – could take his place in my heart, just as I recognised that however much he tried to deny it, he felt the same. Facing the truth released certain tensions and restraint placed on me during my weeks of tuition under Signor Luigi. As Christmas drew close, I sang about the cottage, and put more and more energy into helping Dame Jenny, running up and down stairs, lifting, cleaning, dusting, only properly containing myself when I was confined, under the enigmatic gaze of the girl in the portrait, in the treasure room.

'Don't know what's got into you,' the old lady said speculatively on one occasion. 'Like lightning you are these days – a real wild one. Still, you're a help I must say, even though your voice shakes these old walls sometimes.'

'Yes,' I thought, 'I *am* wild. Wild with happiness, and just because I'm going to spend a few hours in Rupert Verne's company.'

I sighed to myself, knowing I was stupid, but revelling in my stupidity.

The day came.

Fine sleet was blown on a wind from the sea on Christmas morning when the chaise arrived to take us to Kerrysmoor.

I had been successful in hiding the flower and ribbons in

my hair under the hood of the cape, and Dame Jenny was too concerned with her own fripperies of jewels – brooches, necklaces, bracelets and glittering embellishments placed at every possible angle, to take undue notice of me. However, then the time came to have my cape removed with the assistance of a servant in the hall of the great house she was at first speechless to see me standing there, shawl already half fallen, leaving my skin feeling deliciously cool and soft.

Then she said in shocked tones from almost under her breath:

'Cover theeself. 'Tisn't decent – '

One old hand came up to assist me in obeying, but she was defeated by the unexpected appearance of Rupert through a door on the left. He was elegantly attired in a dark olive green-coloured velvet suit, with a satin waistcoat and white frilled shirt. Such details registered only vaguely after the first startled impact of us seeing each other. For a second he was taken off his guard. His strange amber eyes glowed with a warmer fire – their narrow long lids widened and he actually smiled. In a daze, with my heart quickening painfully I allowed him to touch my hand, then heard him order the servant to show Dame Jenny and myself to the ladies' retiring room where my cloak was removed and hung on a peg.

The decor was pink and gold – unexpectedly bright and frivolous looking compared with the sombre hall we'd just left. Through a long mirror I adjusted the flower at my corsage, tidied my hair and saw the artificial bloom was still secure in my curls. Then I placed the lace shawl over my arm and turned to face an outraged Dame Jenny.

''Tisn' decent,' she said in a dark undertone, almost a whisper. 'Remember who you are – '

I smiled defiantly. 'That's just what I'm doing. I'm sorry if it offends you.' She said something else and attempted to push the lace to my neck, but she was too short, and I was too quick for her. The next moment I was at the door of the ante-room and out again in the big hall, followed by the old lady making clucking sounds like an ancient ruffled hen.

I shall never forget the midday meal, which was taken in the great dining room; Rupert sat at the head of the table, Lady Verne at the other end. Dame Jenny and myself faced each other on either side, and I was grateful for the large bowl of holly and greenery interlaced with scarlet satin ribbon and tiny silver bells which prevented her having a direct look at me. The fare was lavish and sumptuous, including roasted pig's head, turkey, numerous entrées and Christmas pudding heavily laced with brandy sauce.

In spite of my spinning head made dizzy with wine, I was aware at brief ecstatic moments of Mr Verne's eyes on me. I think his wife must have noticed. At one point when I glanced at her, her lips were tightly set, her black eyes smouldering with dislike. I knew very well how much she resented me.

If she'd shown one gesture of welcome or friendliness, the future might have been very different, although I don't think anything in the world could have changed my feelings for Rupert. As it was, an equal cold hostility rose in me. It was clear to me that there was little warmth between her and her husband. So I put any feelings of remorse or guilt behind me, knowing that if Rupert ever needed or wanted me I would go to him, oh so willingly.

The day passed, under a veneer of goodwill, including the usual revelry, dancing and wassailing.

When the time came to leave I said a polite farewell dutifully to her ladyship, with thanks for her hospitality. She did not smile or take my hand, merely bowed her proud head, features cold and enigmatic, under the jewels winking in her black piled hair, and remarked:

'The event is a traditional one which Mr Verne chooses to retain.'

I said nothing, but must have glanced briefly at Rupert who was standing at her side. He nodded slightly, and made a point of enclosing my gloved fingers in his palm. Through the fine material I could feel his warm blood pulsing rapidly, and as the pressure momentarily increased knew everything was well between us. During the whole evening no intimate word had been said; personal contact under the severe gaze of her ladyship and watchful beady eyes of Dame Jenny, had been impossible.

But one day, sometime, I told myself, as we walked down the terrace steps to the chaise, it would be different. Awareness of the developing emotional relationship between us could not be stilled forever. Just as snowdrops and primroses pierced the cold earth in their time, so must the strength and beauty of passion come to natural flowering.

I loved him. I was still very young, but what I felt was the oldest, richest human experience in the world. Something would happen eventually that would release tension and longing, bringing natural fulfilment. It must – it was inevitable. How, and when, was impossible even to imagine; but I was impatient, and hoped it would not be too long.

The fine sleet had turned to snow as the chaise left for Tregonnis. Quite large flakes feathered the windows in a ghostly ballet of blurred movement brought to life against the swaying light of the coach's lamps. Moors, undergrowth, and stunted trees were obscured into fitful nonentity. Dame Jenny was tense and nervous, too nervous to upbraid me then for my rebellious behaviour, though I guessed she would scold me later. One claw-like old hand was clenched on her knee. The rings flashed occasionally on the ivory knuckles when a sudden beam of light caught their brilliance. In the darkness, the jolting of wheels over the cobbles and rough ground seemed accentuated – merely imagination of course, but somehow exciting – an excitement intensified by my own heightened emotions.

Rupert – Rupert! the name was magic! The meaning of his last glance at me before we left – of my hand in his, made me want to sing and cry ridiculous lovely things to the soughing wind and snow-swept sky. He must know, I thought – he might not admit the truth yet, but soon he would, because our recognition had been mutual. In spirit we already belonged.

It was only after we entered Tregonnis and made the usual nightly inspection of the treasure room that my elation faded, subduing me to normality.

The glow of the oil lamp held by Dame Jenny suddenly brought the face of the girl in the portrait into full focus. The silver-gold hair and exquisite features seemed to assume uncanny life, and I remembered, against my will, Rupert Verne's reluctance to talk of her. Doubt clouded my happiness. I tried to dispel it, but it was no use. There was a mystery somewhere involved concerning his possession of the painting – a mystery from which I was completely excluded. My mind played this way and that in search of a possible explanation until tired from the events and activities of the day, I went to bed and fell soon into a deep sleep.

When I woke it was to find the frozen weather had turned into a thaw. Grey mist hugged the landscape through which only fading drifts of white still lingered. Enchantment had gone; Dame Jenny also seemed depressed and more uncommunicative than usual. She made no attempt to chide me, as I'd expected, but went about household tasks muttering to herself on a low key. I longed for the spring, and change in the weather, and found myself looking forward to visiting Signor Luigi again early in the New Year. He had gone to Italy for a brief respite before starting once more on my tuition.

During the first few days following my jaunt to Kerrysmoor I hope desperately for a sight of Rupert, wondering if he would make a call at the cottage. But he did not. I made excuses to myself for his absence. He had matters on the estate to attend to – duty calls to make on families working at the Verne coppermine still active, Wheal Glory, or perhaps his wife was making extra demands on his attention.

Somehow, though, no contrived explanations rang true. If he'd really wanted to see me surely he could have found a means to do so. There were several horses in the stables, and her ladyship could not have kept watch on him all the time. In any case he wasn't a weakling to be ordered about by any woman. No. Search as I would I could find no plausible reason for his apparent neglect unless it was that on thinking things over he'd decided any relationship or commitment to me would be completely impracticable and therefore to be avoided at any cost.

As usual, whenever I became too elated or distressed over any situation, my capacity to keep imagination under controlled suffered. I was so frustrated and tormented by longing, I took every opportunity during that short period, of slipping out of the house and taking short wanders in my thickest cloak, about the countryside, and it was in such a mood that I made my way one evening round the forbidden track curving to the left and upwards towards the wild slope of Rosecarrion, leaving Dame Jenny sleeping in her rocking chair over her needlework.

Twilight would soon fall, but when I set off, except for a thin veil of rising mist hugging the high ridge, everything was comparatively clear. The area held a brooding atmosphere of primeval menace, as though something of ancient history still lingered as guardian of the past. A narrow path wound intricately between furze and great boulders entangled by bramble and spiky gorse. In spite of my boots I kept my eyes alert for any snake-like shape slithering from a stone or root of stunted tree. Although the air was so still, hidden life seemed everywhere. I was fascinated – a little keyed-up and on edge, but through curiousity impelled to go on.

Not realising I had climbed quite so far, I paused a quarter of the way up the hill, and searched the land in every direction. Daylight had almost faded leaving a queer greenish glow behind the misted summit. It was when I turned to the west that I saw with surprise the ribbon of lane below cutting abruptly inwards above and around a gully filled by a gently lapping tide. I hadn't known how near the coast the path had led me. At times in rough weather the locality would be dangerous – a fall over the high cliffs only too easy for the unwary. Was that why Rupert had forbidden me to go that way?

For some moments I stood motionless watching, and as a frail belt of cloud lifted there was movement where the slope of land met sky; a man's shape emerged from the tumbled ruins of what could once have been the relics of a cottage or old mine workings, and made his way round a further bend away from me, until he was lost to sight. His figure had been humped at a curious angle, and I wondered if he'd been carrying something; a poacher perhaps?

If I'd not been away from Tregonnis for so long or afraid that Dame Jenny might already be angrily waiting for me I'd have cut round to the right to find out where the path led. There were so many bewildering tracks winding from the point where I was standing. One leading directly down towards the creek was wider and appeared to have been well-trodden recently. It was all very bewildering; a torn piece of material – probably from a neckscarf or kerchief hung on a jagged briar nearby. So *someone* had walked or ridden that area not long ago. Tinkers, or gypsies?

I was still ruminating when a bird rose screeching from behind a boulder on my left. I turned my head, then glanced upwards at the dark winged shape soaring to the sky. At that very moment a shaft of light zig-zagged down the hill, through the quickly fading half light, wavered, and circled round the moor, missing my form by only a few feet.

Just as suddenly as it had appeared, the light swung upwards and disappeared, but not before my startled eyes had recognised in a brief lifting of cloud, the stark shapes of the Three Maidens outlined for an instance on the horizon. Even seen at a different angle from my first glimpse of them, the gaunt stones held the same quality of menace and impending doom. Drawing my cloak close I turned quickly and made my way towards the valley. Unfortunately I chose the wrong path and had to make a detour guided only by the distant outline of the mine, Wheal Glory, against the moor.

By the time I reached the cottage it was quite dark. The old lady was standing at the gate huddled into her shawl with a lantern in one hand.

'You've had me frightened,' she exclaimed, almost in a high-pitched scream. 'Where've 'ee been? The Master called earlier, soon after thee'd gone out. There came a rap on th' door. I was dozin' and it set my heart all of a flutter. But that wasn't the point. The point was you should say when you're taking off for a stroll, and tell me where. He didn't like it when I couldn't say, and rode off very put out – ' She broke off breathlessly.

'I'm sorry,' I said lamely, and I was. Not only on account of Dame Jenny's distress, but because I'd missed Rupert.

I wondered what he wanted me for.

The next day I knew.

He'd heard from Signor Luigi that he was returning earlier than expected from Italy, having learned of an opportunity to launch me as Lucy Lockett in John Gay's *Beggars' Opera* scheduled to open at an Exeter theatre in three weeks' time. The actress Linda Dewhurst who had rehearsed for the role had been suddenly taken ill which had left the part open for anyone with the looks, and capacity to learn quickly, who also possessed the necessary vocal qualities and acting ability. There was no understudy, owing to the young lady have been dismissed two days previously through a serious quarrel with the manager.

Hence my chance.

All this was explained to me the next morning by Rupert seated opposite to me in the front parlour of Tregonnis. 'You're very lucky,' he said. 'If Signor Luigi had not been an intimate friend of Frederick Allen and able to contact him so quickly some other actress might have been found. As it is –' He smiled and for a few seconds the years fell away. His whole face changed, became younger, warm with pride, affection, and ambition for me. Then he continued more seriously, 'Aren't you pleased? Surely it's what you wanted – to appear on a real stage before an audience fully qualified to appreciate your voice and – you?'

In a whirl of conflicting emotions – delight, excitement, mingled with doubt, apprehension and awe, I answered, 'Oh, yes. Of course. But – ' I swallowed painfully ' – my voice isn't properly trained yet. After my last lesson Signor Luigi told me I bellowed like a barmaid, and moved like a – like a horse or something.' I shook my head 'I don't think I'd be right for this – this Lucy person *really*.'

'*You* may not think so,' I heard Rupert remarking, quite unperturbed, 'but I've complete faith in my friend's judgement. If he's willing to back you I'm sure I am. As for his criticism – ' he shrugged, displaying the palms of both hands in a dismissive gesture ' – Luigi wouldn't waste one breath on you if he didn't recognise your talent. He can be more than forthright – even offensive to some when he feels like it – but only when he considered the material is worthwhile. It's his way of getting the best out of a pupil.'

'A rather odd way,' I remarked pertly. 'Not usual, surely?'

'But then neither are you.'

He got up, came towards me, and drew me to my feet. I was wearing a violet-coloured daydress I remember, made by my own hand with the help of the old lady, from a piece of material Pierre had brought me on his last visit to Falmouth, and which I'd kept hoarded away in my small chest with a few other treasures. It had a white lace collar and cuffs, and fell in soft folds, drawn gently to the back from a nipped-in waist. Dame Jenny had told me when I came downstairs that day that it was too elegant for normal use. I had agreed with her and promised to change as soon as possible into something more suitable.

I was pleased now that I hadn't. Those passionate enigmatic eyes of the man who so desperately fascinated me, were for once alight in obvious fiery admiration. His hands released mine suddenly, and were on my shoulders.

Automatically I raised my head. A few curls fell from their combs and brushed my neck softly.

'You're very – beautiful, Josephine,' he said in low, slightly husky tones. 'And your eyes – you're a subtle creature to wear blue – '

'Violet,' I corrected him.

'Violet, then. Dammit what does it matter? You know well enough how lovely you are – '

Through my wild excitement a thought struck me. On impulse I spoke. 'Am I? Am I *really*? As lovely as – as that girl in the painting? The one hanging in the treasure room?'

I shouldn't have said it. It was a grave mistake, and in a moment I knew. He drew away from me abruptly. His gaze was hard when he faced me again. Dull with disappointment, because I'd known he'd been about to kiss me, furious with myself for the stupid blunder, I heard him remark in remote tones, 'Comparisons are odious. If I pay a compliment it should be taken for that and no more. I'm afraid you have still a few things to learn about tact and etiquette.'

'Of course I have,' I said hotly. 'I'm not gently bred like your lady wife, and – '

'Leave my wife out of it, if you please,' he said curtly, 'and curb that wild temper of yours. Do you understand?'

'Certainly,' I retorted, feeling the warm blood rush to my cheeks. 'In future I'll curtsey to you when you address me, if you choose, and remember to say "sir" on every occasion we speak.'

His mood suddenly changed. He laughed. 'You'll make an admirable Lucy Lockett, I'm sure. So enough of your moods, Miss Lebrun. On Thursday you'll be driven to Truro. I shall accompany you, and we'll see what arrangement Signor Luigi intends to make regarding the performance.'

'He may not think I'm good enough when he hears me singing again,' I pointed out, 'and if I move like a horse – '

'You won't,' he stated firmly. 'You'll be your natural

graceful self with your voice and fiery tongue under equal control.'

'And if I don't wish to appear at Exeter?' I persisted stubbornly.

He paused before saying significantly, 'I think you will, because *I* wish it.'

And in that he was right.

The interview ended shortly after arrangements for the following Thursday had been concluded. At the door Rupert took my hand briefly and raised it to his lips – a polite gentlemanly gesture of farewell, no more. It was as though he was determined to erase any former show of sentiment, subduing passion under a mask of wellbred formality. I waited hopefully for his eyes once more to rest on mine, but they did not.

Dame Jenny appeared in the hall, holding out his stove hat and cane. He took them murmuring a quiet thank you. The last I saw of him that day was his caped figure walking smartly down the path to the lane where the chaise waited.

Seconds later he had gone.

IV

On the evening vefore my visit to Signor Luigi, I received a note from Rupert delivered by a Kerrysmoor servant, saying that he would not after all be able to accompany me to Truro owing to an unexpected matter of business arising. He apologised, but sent his best wishes, adding that he was sure everything would go well, that 'the maestro' would confirm my suitability to play the role of Lucy, and that when next we met I should have good news for him. The brief epistle ended on a formal note – 'Yours with every encouragement, Rupert Verne.'

I stared blankly at the sheet for some moments, heavy with disappointment. What possible business could he have, I thought unreasonably, that should have to be dealt with just at the time I was depending on him for support? And why couldn't he have fixed whatever it was at another hour or day? I'd looked forward so much to sitting beside him in the chaise with no one to disturb our proximity, imagined the touch of his hand on mine, savoured in advance the exciting closeness of his body, the pressure of an arm as the coach jolted or lurched over a rough piece of roadway.

The warmth of his breath would mingle with mine – his lips brush my cheek; and when in delight and confusion I looked up into those strange golden eyes they would be hot with desire, and I would be close against him, my whole body alight with flowering love. However short the contact, he'd recognise the futility of denial. What happened in the future would be of his choice, which I would abide by, because he was the man, and considerably older than I. I was in no position to make plans. All I could do was to submit, given the chance.

The chance?

But apparently either other things came first, or he was not prepared to endanger one iota of his status and good name in society.

Utterly depressed I tore the piece of paper into shreds and threw them into the parlour fire, watching them gradually curl, blaze, then disintegrate into smoke.

After a time I forced myself to a more philosophical mood. Whether I was successful or not in persuading Signor Luigi that I was sufficiently competent for the role in *The Beggar's Opera* I was bound to come face to face with Rupert on some future occasion. So the important thing was to be a success, and make him proud of me.

Before retiring that evening I tried out my voice in my bedroom, choosing a song that had been one of my mother's favourites. There was no hoarseness or flaw in my vocal chords, no quiver of hesitancy or lack of control. I stood at the window giving full range to any talent I possessed, singing – singing – and realising at the same time how much I had learned under the strict tuition of the fierce little Italian.

When it was over I waited motionless for a short time, with my eyes fixed on the moonlit landscape. The window faced from the side of Tregonnis, overlooking Rosecarrion and part of the area where I'd wandered before Christmas. There was a wind, and the scene was one of purple and blue shadows lit by fleeting splashes of gold. The Three Maidens were nowhere in view, being cut off to the left, but if I strained my head and gazed to the other side a glimmer of sea could be glimpsed in the far distance.

I was staring in that direction when I saw something else – something not shadow or stunted tree waving in the wind – a crouched moving shape that I took at first to be that of some large animal on night prowl. Then as the form partly disintegrated, or rather split up, I realised it was a group. Small dots of figures took an upward course towards what I imagined must be the ruined building – cottage or mineworks – that I'd seen on my forbidden exploration weeks before.

In the constantly changing vista of light and sudden shadow it was difficult to be sure or even guess what they were about. Poachers probably I told myself, as I had before, or could they be fishermen plodding to their homes after a hard day at sea? Perhaps the track provided a short cut to outlying cottages over the ridge of moor.

Whatever the explanation, I had an uneasy feeling that something strange was going on, and determined to question Dame Jenny about it in the morning.

When daylight came, however, I was far too busy and excited to bother. I had only a light breakfast, and at eight o'clock as arranged the chaise arrived to take me to Truro. I wore my best attire and most frivolous headgear, and had even applied a touch of rose lipsalve to my mouth, purloined wickedly in a hasty moment from a tiny jar that Dame Jenny had left carelessly on a mantelshelf. My cheeks were already over-bright from excitement and for this I used a film of rice powder. The result gave me confidence and an elated sense of sophistication. There was a hint of suspicion in the old lady's eyes as she bid me farewell, with affection, yet admonishment as well in her voice.

'Good luck, child,' she said, 'and remember to be modest and careful how ye do address the great music-man. Talent you must have, or the master wouldn' be doin' all this for thee. But good manners count always, remember that.'

I glanced back, smiling at her over my shoulder. 'I'll do my best,' I said, and meant it.

The day was fine, and pale winter sunlight spread its gold over the city, and all around giving added enchantment to the occasion which wasn't however entirely without trepidation on my part. But I needn't have worried.

Signor Luigi instead of appearing fierce and over-critical that day as he usually was, acted in an entirely different manner, being quite flattering and warm in encouragement following my tryout of Lucy Lockett's first ditty in the opera.

'That is good,' he said. 'There are points here and there needing strict attention, and you still have much to study of stagecraft. We have three weeks of intensive training before us, during which, in your spare time you must learn – *learn*, until words come automatically without thought. I shall scold you maybe sometimes, perhaps very often, and you must expect my friend, the producer, will do more of it during the two days in Exeter before the opening performance. Well?' He cocked his head sideways like an inquisitive robin, 'do you wish to become Lucy Lockett for a time, Miss Josephine? And if so – can you promise solemnly to obey instructions without argument or show of your fiery temper? It is a great chance you have before you. Do not forget it.'

I agreed with alacrity. 'Oh yes – yes. If you think I'm good enough, of *course* – ' I cried.

'I do not think you are yet good,' he told me with a whimsical smile. 'But you have grace and talent. See that you apply both to the best of your ability and I'm sure no one will have cause to complain.'

So it was that I returned to Tregonnis that evening able to tell Dame Jenny of my success, wishing at the same time that Rupert was there to hear the news.

During the following weeks most of my time was spent in Truro. It was a period of conflicting moods – of expectancy, exhilaration, optimism and disappointments combined with physical exertion that left me too tired at the end of each day to brood on other matters. Luigi, anxious that I should not *over*-strain my voice, included hours of concentrated dramatic tuition that occasionally so irritated and frustrated me, I could have screamed. However, I miraculously managed to keep any nervous reaction under control – outwardly, though Dame Jenny commented frequently that I was touchy and on edge at Tregonnis.

'I must say you do speak over-sharp to me these days,' she commented once. 'I hope when the master calls you'll remember to be more polite.'

'I don't think the master's much interested in me or what I'm doing,' I replied shortly, and I had really begun to believe this was true, since he'd looked in at the cottage only once during the first fortnight of rehearsing, and had then appeared remote and withdrawn as though he had other more important affairs on his mind.

'That's a wicked thing to say,' the old lady retorted irately, ' 'specially when he's paying a little fortune to get you where you want to be.'

'I didn't expect or ask him to launch me,' I replied, 'or for his money either. This *Beggar's Opera* business and the lessons with Signor Luigi were forced on me – in a way.'

'Nonsense.' The one word came out explosively, like a pistol shot. 'I do recall very well the day at Christmas when you flaunted yourself before his eyes with your shoulders bare, and that wicked gypsy look in your eyes. Oh you were all out to make an impression, girl, so no trying to pull the wool over my eyes.'

I flushed, bit my lip, and was silent. It was true, I *had* wished Rupert to notice me, and contrived to make myself as spectacular as possible. And I had not entirely failed; the memory of his warm glances on me and the mutual interest between us – the understanding that had so fiercely flamed for those few revealing moments, returned painfully, stirring me with sudden longing.

When I didn't speak, Dame Jenny said in more conciliatory tones, 'Now, now! There's no need to be cast down. Just take heed of a bit of advice, that's all, and remember what the master've told you; if what you said was true, get as much fresh air in your spare time to relax thee and keep the breath sweet in your lungs. I won't be bothering asking so much where you've been so long as you're back to time. "Don't chain her too hard," Mr Verne said the other afternoon when he was passing, "she's a free spirit," he said, "let her roam a bit, t'will do her no harm." '

"I didn't know he'd called, you didn't tell me.'

'I don't report on every small happening of the day, girl. 'Tisn't my duty to do so. I'm only tellin' thee now for your own encouragement. You were a bit later back from Truro than usual or you'd have seen him for thyself.'

I recalled that on one occasion the signor had pressed me into staying at rehearsal for an extra half an hour to get my words better perfected. What a nuisance, I thought, that Rupert had chosen the very time to visit Tregonnis.

Still, I was slightly uplifted by the knowledge he'd taken the trouble to call at all, and decided his advice to Dame Jenny was right. I needed fresh air and exercise.

It was a fine afternoon. Clouds of the morning had cleared, leaving the countryside splashed with pale golden sunshine. Quite soon it would start to sink lower in the sky, sending long shadows snaking down the moors, but if I started immediately – it was only four o'clock – I would have almost an hour for an enjoyable stroll.

So I set off wearing boots and a loose grey cloak to cover my gown, taking the lane round the base of Rosecarrion. I didn't venture to climb the hill – the air was sweet enough in the valley, heady with the scents of early spring, and I had an urge to follow the roadway in the direction of the sea where the moor cut so sharply and surprisingly inwards to the gully. With my eyes averted from glancing upwards at the Three Maidens sloping slightly sideways at a peculiar angle, their menace for me had abated a little during the hectic period of intense rehearsals, and when a fleeting memory of them *had* occurred I'd told myself reasoningly that their unpleasant impact had only lingered because the rigid starkness of the ancient stones reminded me in a childish way of the rigid coldness of Rupert's lady wife.

It was pleasant walking. As I neared the gully – it was really a very narrow creek – the smell of brine mingled with that of heather, damp sweet earth, and all the other odours of thrusting young life and herbage. The narrow river on the opposite side of the lane had curved abruptly in another direction, away from the coast, but the gaunt cliffs loomed precipitously close to the road, and the shadowed cut in the lane appeared as though giants' teeth had taken a savage bite leaving a cruel void of darkness and death for the unwary.

I paused, held by the wild fascination of the scene. It was then that I glimpsed movement, and after a moment's astonishment was able to distinguish close against the far side of the inlet a vessel at anchor. Details or name of the ship were impossible to discern. In the slowly fading light and shadows of overhanging cliffs boat and rocks were almost blended into one.

At first I'd thought I could be mistaken, but I wasn't. When I moved forward a human shape appeared on deck, followed by another. Their appearance was only brief. In a few seconds they'd disappeared – moved below. But my heart jerked. In that fleeting space of time something about the first figure had been curiously familiar – the build and way of moving in the caped coat – his bold erect stance and sudden manner of turning and striding away bore an uncanny resemblance to Rupert. I was puzzled; what could Rupert Verne be doing at such at hour aboard a strange vessel in such an unlikely, dangerous, and remote harbour?

I managed presently to convince myself I'd been wrong, and had concocted unconsciously an image of the man who was always so deep in my mind. Even then doubts lingered. I waited a little longer wondering if the forms would return. But they did not. A single dot of light flickered for a moment then disappeared. All was dark. The sky, too, had quickly faded, merging the horizon of sea and land into one.

Hoping Dame Jenny would be unaware of my over-long absence from the house, I turned and took the thread of curving lane as quickly as possible back to Tregonnis.

*

The day for travelling to Exeter for the opening performance at the Regal Opera House at last arrived. I was given a sleeping potion the evening before to enable me to face the journey calmly, in the company of Mr Verne and his lady wife, who, unfortunately for me, insisted upon being present herself at my debut. We journeyed by luxury four horse omnibus from Truro to Plymouth, where we stayed the night. In the morning we set off by rail for Exeter, arriving at the city by four-thirty in the afternoon. Signor Luigi accompanied us for which I was grateful. He had a stabilising influence on my growing excitement and nervous tension, and although being quite tired conversation was intermittent, his presence kept me less conscious of Lady Verne's cold stare than otherwise I would have been.

She was looking quite regal in a plain-coloured wild crimson silk gown, under a silver grey paletot with a shoulder cape. Bands of velvet braid and plum covered buttons completed an elegant effect, and her bonnet of the same shades was worn at a fashionable angle, revealing glossy glimpses of shining black hair in contrast to the extreme magnolia pallor of her finely set features.

I wore a new cape which her ladyship had insisted on choosing herself. It was of good quality, but as usual, brown, and rather severe, giving no glamour to my looks. My bonnet-hat, too, was ordinary. However, I contrived to add a length of green ribbon and a spray of shining leaves to brighten the effect, and from the look on my lady's face when she noticed, I knew I'd succeeded in my objective.

When I think back now on the next few days, no words can express the conflict of emotions – confusion, excitement, and daze of events following one upon the other at such speed my head still whirls. It was like living in a dream. I was both bewildered and exhilarated by the luxury of the hotel overlooking gardens, the delicious meals, impeccable service, the rose and gold furnishings, rich carpeting and soundless approach of servants and footmen to fulfil our slightest wish. My bedroom was huge, ornately furnished with an elegance I'd imagined existed only for royalty or in fairy tales. If I had not been so physically tired I wouldn't have slept at all that night. But the great bed was so soft and comfortable, I drifted almost at once into dreamless slumber, waking up only when a maid servant arrived with morning tea.

After breakfast I was taken on a shopping expedition to equip me more suitably to meet the manager in the afternoon at the theatre. He was a tall, thin man with an eagle gaze and brusque manner. He wore an eye-glass and seldom stood still, but walked to and fro unsmilingly, taking, I thought, only cursory glances at me. He made me sing a scale, move, turn, bow and curtsey, all the time frowning a little, then nodding. Eventually he said:

'All right, all right. That's enough. I hope you know your words. There'll be a rehearsal in half an hour; Elise – ' He turned his head towards the wings from where a small woman in black silk appeared as though she'd been waiting for a cue ' – Take Miss – Miss – ?' He glanced at me enquiringly.

'Lebrun. Josephine Lebrun,' Signor Luigi interposed for me.

'Take Miss Lebrun to the dressing room,' the manager continued, 'and see she's attired appropriately as Lucy.' He scrutinised me closely then added, 'Green I think. The emerald green. Red is more usual for the role but would be atrocious with this girl's colouring.'

Trying not to feel mildly squashed, I did as I was bid and followed the little woman to the back of the stage, and along a maze of narrow dark passages and doors. The room we entered was small and stuffy, smelling mustily of dust, perspiration and makeup. There were several mirrors and tables placed about, and obviously I was not to be the only occupant. I had thought such places – anything to do with the stage – would be glamorous. But there was no glamour here, although gowns of different shades hung from pegs and an open wardrobe, and an array of gaudy glittering jewellery lay displayed giving an impression of brightness. Various pots of paint and cream cluttered shelves, and a young woman with brassy yellow hair was already seated at a dressing table cleaning her face with a cloth.

'Miss Annette Gold,' I was told by the dresser, 'she is the star of the production. A well-known actress – you must have heard of her – she plays Polly Peachum. It's a privilege for you to have a role opposite to her. If it hadn't been for –' she broke off suddenly, continuing after taking a deep breath, ' – but never mind. We can only hope that you come up to scratch. It's always a chancy business taking on an unknown player. Had any experience at all, have you?'

'Oh yes, some,' I answered not feeling it was a lie when I recollected the long arduous hours spent with Signor Luigi at Truro, and also my performances at the Golden Bird.

'Hm! that's as well.'

She bustled around telling me to disrobe as time was short for all to be punctual for the rehearsal. Clad only in bodice and pantalettes, I was then directed to sit on a stool to be pummelled, rubbed and slapped about the face by the make-up artist, until I was considered in adequate shape for being painted and powdered – garishly I thought – for the role of Lucy. When I saw myself through the mirror I was not only astonished but dismayed. The voluptuous-looking highly-coloured creature was a travesty of my real self – looking more like a successful prostitute from Dockland than Pierre's cherished 'princess'.

'But that can't be *me*!' I gasped.

'You're not supposed to be 'you'. You're Lucy Lockett,' came the quick reply.

'But my lips – so bright! And my *eyes*!'

'If you'd any knowledge of the stage, which you said you had, you'd know that under the lights and to the audience you'll look quite different. And Lucy, remember, is a bold character. Now just keep calm and we'll see if the dress is right.'

Whether right or wrong the brilliant emerald-green velvet was certainly spectacular, and with a little swift taking-in at the waist fitted perfectly. My dismay gave place to incredulity, holding a certain mischievous pleasure, when at last, with my dark curls pulled back in a sophisticated style, one lock left to fall on a bare shoulder, I surveyed my full length reflection through a long glass. I was trembling a little, and gasping from excitement. The bodice was cut so low at the bosom, the nipples of my breasts almost showed. I pulled one side of the material up – or tried to. It was no use. There was a short laugh from somewhere behind me. I turned. Polly Peachum was standing there looking more attractive than I'd expected in a pink period gown, with a white apron and pretty white mob-cap.

'Got the jitters, have you?' she asked. 'Nerves. Well, it's natural. I've been hearing things.'

'What things?'

'How it's your first real part in opera. Raw beginner, aren't you? But don't you fret. You'll do all right. Willie will be along presently. He'll tell you.'

'Who's Willie?'

'Willie Spark, stage manager and assistant director; an acquaintance of that fine lady something or other who brought you along – '

'Of Lady *Verne*?'

'Yes, that's it. Oh, I don't mean they're *friends* or anything like that, they just met once or twice in the past, when she was in London. Willie's quite a character – a bit talkative when he's under the influence – you know – ' she gave an imitation of lifting a glass to her lips ' – but comes of a good family, the reprobate, so to speak. A charmer though. Could charm the hind legs off a horse so to speak. Clever in his way.'

When I met him, during a break in the rehearsal, I agreed. He was quick and deft at organising scenic effects in the least possible time, and had as well a soothing effect on the players, never scolding or becoming irate; his good looks and amiable disposition in fact had the whole cast comparatively cheerful, and only too willing to follow his suggestions. Obviously he was a bit of a dandy – his attire was colourful, and reminiscent of an earlier decade – artistic rather than fashionable, including a gold velvet waistcoat, and silk cravat with a yellow bow-tie. I got little praise for my performance from the producer, but when the tiring session of the rehearsal was over, Willie – everyone called him that – congratulated me. 'You will make a most picturesque Lucy,' he said, 'and the range of your voice was most remarkable.'

Such compliments raised my spirits, and later, at the hotel I was able to face Rupert and his icy wife with confidence, even a hint of pride. I hadn't expected to have 'to run through the play' again – the producer's words – on Sunday. Lady Verne openly disapproved, and I knew if Dame Jenny had known, so would she. But it was held in the afternoon, following morning service at Exeter Cathedral where her ladyship had appeared extremely smart and devout in black silk relieved by a touch of crimson. I'd been forced once more to wear my sober brown cape. I'd hoped desperately that there would be a chance for Rupert to show me some of the sights, but there was no time, and even if there had been I guessed her odious ladyship would have insisted on accompanying us. On the Monday morning a further rehearsal followed, and in the afternoon I was ordered to rest before the great occasion of the opening night at the theatre.

Oh, how highly-wrought and on edge I felt. So much depended on the result of this debut. Waiting in the wings for my first appearance was sheer torture. My spine was rigid, alternate waves of icy cold and heat flooded me. At one moment my heart raced so wildly I thought I'd faint. But Willie, mercifully, sensing the ordeal, came to my aid speedily, smiling, and with a small glass containing a potion of clear liquid. In a moment, when no-one could observe me, he handed it to me, whispering, 'Drink that up, darling, it will revive and steady you. And have no fear. Without nerves you'd be no actress. You'll be splendid – ' he withdrew quickly, and automatically I obeyed and swallowed the potion.

For minutes afterwards I felt comforted and calm, eager, in fact, to make my entrance. The stimulant, combined with the knowledge that I looked well in the striking green velvet, and that Rupert had the best seat in the dress circle to watch, filled me with sudden overpowering joy. My head felt light, even my legs were a little unsteady, but I knew my voice was in good form. I would be a successful rival to Polly Peachum. Rupert would be proud of me – I would become a great singer, just for him.

At last my cue came.

Lifting my head I swept – almost tottering – on to the stage. The lights at first bewildered me, then, at a sign from the stage manager, as the accompaniment struck up, I opened my mouth for the first full-throated notes to emerge.

What exactly happened next I can't clearly recall – only that for a dreadful few seconds no sound came. My throat felt dry, parched. I took a deep breath and a harsh croak shattered the air. I paused and tried again. It was useless, terrifying. What had happened? Where had my voice gone? I couldn't sing. From shocked astonishment the audience gave vent to low 'boos' and muffled laughter that quickly changed to guffaws of derision. Rude comments were shouted as I struggled for composure, to refrain from swooning. My last conscious memory was of the curtain rattling down and white masks of faces crowding round as I was pulled and half-carried from the stage to the dressing room.

Then mercifully oblivion claimed me, and when I came to myself I was in a cab being taken back to the hotel, sick, faint, a failure, and wishing I could die.

V

For two days following the terrible episode leading to the disgrace and failure of what should have been my successful debut as a singer and actress, a depressing silence lay like a pall over Tregonnis. Dame Jenny said little, but I sensed she was not unsympathetic.

'Never mind,' she said. 'Showing off to a lot of folk isn't all that important. To my mind 'tis a far more honourable accomplishment knowing how to bake a good cake or stitch a tidy sampler. Cheer up, my maid. Thee'll discover all in good time that it was for the best. Life has a cunning pattern to it that's not always seen till later when it's clear as daylight.'

'I failed,' I answered. 'I was just no good, and Mr Verne there! – I'll never forget, *never*. And I can't *understand*. I hadn't my voice at all – my throat was dry, and when I opened my mouth it was as though all breath went, and – and my head ached so. I couldn't even *see* properly. There must have been a reason. But what? – *What?*'

'Now, now, don't work thyself into a tizzy,' the old lady remarked calmly. 'Probably it was nerves brought on a turn. Anyway the doctor will find out when he calls.'

'The doctor?'

'Her ladyship's specialist. I had word brought by Jan, farmer Carne's boy, about an hour ago, that he'd be calling this morning to give an examination.'

'On *me?*'

Dame Jenny nodded. 'And quite right, too.'

I was suddenly suspicious, and for no logical reason I suppose, but anything to do with Lady Verne was hateful to me.

'Did she write it?'

'No, the Master. I have it here. You can read it if you like.'

She went to her own small desk and handed me an envelope. I took the piece of paper out, and read:

> Just a word, ma'am, to say that Doctor Zane, my lady wife's medical adviser, will be calling this morning about twelve o'clock to make certain Miss Lebrun has fully recovered from her collapse and that she is suffering no signs of serious illness. His professional opinion will then be conveyed to me, and we will be in a position to decide her future.
>
> Yours faithfully,
> Rupert Verne.

I handed the note back to her.

'I see. Thank you.'

So formal, so cold; so detached as though I was some embarrassing commodity or horse from the stables, to be priced and sold, if necessary, to a convenient bidder.

A horse! I remembered vividly the occasion on which Signor Luigi had likened my movements to one of the species. Perhaps it was true, I thought, reviewing my status disparagingly. Perhaps the fire in Rupert's eyes for me had kindled merely because I'd appeared a worthwhile investment. If so, how shamefully I had been deceived.

Involuntarily the nails of both hands dug hard into my clenched palms.

'So we shall have to abide by the doctor's verdict,' I heard Dame Jenny saying fatuously. 'And if – '

'I don't think the doctor will find anything wrong with my health,' I interrupted sharply. 'And whether he does or not, I'm quite capable of deciding my own future.'

'Maybe. But you've got to remember all the Master's done for thee, which leaves you indebted to him, surely?'

'I shall be able to repay anything that's been spent on me,' I said, lifting my head proudly. 'I lived quite profitably before, and can do so again, if necessary.'

'Hoity-toity! Singing in cheap inns and houses of ill-fame do 'ee mean? An' suppose you do suffer another fit like the one at Exeter?'

'It wasn't a fit. It was – '

I broke off because I had no explanation to give, unless – I suddenly stiffened. My spine went rigid and my senses froze as I recalled the draught given to me by Willie, who had not only been stage manager at the theatre, but also an acquaintance of Lady Verne. Why had the connection not occurred to me before? Or could it have been coincidence? Whatever the answer I had no way of proving it. Neither would the doctor be of any use. I felt intuitively that he would do his best to prove me an unreliable character given to fits of hysteria which would make me therefore quite unsuitable for a serious stage career. Yes, the doctor was a friend of her ladyship and this was exactly what she would wish.

Perhaps I was being mean in attributing such unethical conduct to a man I'd never met; but half an hour later, when he walked into the parlour my instinctive suspicions were intensified.

He was a small portly figure, over-elegantly dressed for a professional man, with a smooth tongue, obsequious manners, and a way of smiling with his lips but not his eyes, that discomforted me.

In Dame Jenny's presence he made me unbutton my bodice, then with odious plump fingers started tapping here and there, lingering sensuously for a second or two about my breasts where I clutched my camisole tightly above the nipples.

At last, becoming irritated with such an unobliging patient, he released me, put his stethoscope away, and remarked in bored booming tones, 'Nothing I can find wrong with you at all – *physically*. That you should lose your voice and go into a swoon on such an important occasion denotes a certain nervous instability, no more. I will inform your master and her ladyship that there is no need for concern. That is all then, thank you!'

He gave a little bow, collected his bag, and with the old lady fluttering before him to open the door, left.

When she returned I remarked derisively, 'I *thought* so.'

'What do you mean, girl?'

'That he'd try to make me out a half-wit and hysteric,' I answered bluntly. 'Being Lady Verne's doctor, he *would*.'

'Now that's not at all a nice thing to say,' the old lady said, pursing her lips. 'It just shows you're not yourself. Her ladyship and the Master've done all they could to bring you fame and riches. But you weren't bred for it, girl, and – '

'What do you mean *bred* for it?' I flashed, before she could finish. 'My breeding – if you *must* use such an obnoxious word, is as good as any in the land. My mother was beautiful, of a respectable Welsh family, and my father was a fine Breton seaman. He died in a wreck, bringing food to this country, and both my parents had a love of music. He taught me early how to sing and to learn good language. They weren't rich or anything, but what does that matter? Money's nothing without happiness or talent. And they loved each other. *Really* loved.'

I broke off breathlessly, feeling suddenly so low and depressed I could have broken into sobs. But I didn't. What point was there in crying when the old lady would merely have taken it as proof of the doctor's opinion that I was indeed nervously unstable, and that my terrible stage debut had been the result of a fit of hysterics? It was important I controlled myself, giving a show of pride, whatever doubts her ladyship and Doctor Zane contrived to instill into Rupert's mind.

After a short pause I heard Dame Jenny say placatingly, 'No one suggested anything against your folk. You're fancying things, girl. Perhaps it's natural, after what you've been through. I was just pointing out to thee, that persons of high standing like the master and his lady wife are on a different level from us humbler kind, which you'd do well to remember.'

'Social levels mean nothing to me,' I stated, a little rudely perhaps.

'No. You've made that clear,' she said sharply. 'But it will be to the benefit of both of us if you behave in a proper manner when Master Verne calls.'

'He may not call at all.'

'Oh yes, indeed he will,' came the reply. 'Tomorrow sometime, after he's had the doctor's report.'

And he did.

Against Dame Jenny's specific instructions I wore the violet velvet, ignoring her fumings, which at one point almost rose to high-pitched screaming. She'd probably also noticed I'd applied a little lip salve which gave me confidence.

'I told thee 'twasn't seemly for the occasion,' she cried, thrusting her old chin forward aggressively. 'Why you've got to be so stubborn an' headstrong I don' know. Shameless, you are. *Shameful*. There's a devil in 'ee an' that's f'r sure. Just when it's right to show a little modesty you come downstairs lookin' like a strumpet from a bad-house – '

I strolled over to the mirror, lifted my chin, and loosened a stray dark curl from the lilac ribbons that held it, so it fell against one cheek softly. Then I shrugged, appearing more nonchalant that I felt.

'As you think of me in that way surely it's correct to be obvious.'

'And now, on top of it all – impudence,' she muttered raspingly.

'Perhaps,' I agreed. 'If so I've nothing to lose. Let Master Verne see me as *you* do, a strumpet, then maybe you'll be rid of me sooner than you expected.'

It was a cruel statement to make because I knew in many ways I was of great help to the old lady, and that she'd miss me sorely. But tart words just then seemed the only possible way to ease my tension during the waiting period for Rupert Verne's arrival.

He came in the afternoon looking tired and a little

worried, but so incredibly handsome my heart lurched in the old familiar way, but more intensely, more longingly, mingled with a dread feeling of hopelessness.

He dismissed Dame Jenny tactfully, bade me sit down, then walked to the window, staring towards the garden for a few seconds before turning again to me.

'I hope you've recovered,' he said before easing himself against the table, half sitting, half standing. 'I had the doctor's report yesterday evening.'

'Oh yes,' I murmured over-casually. 'I can guess what it was.'

'Indeed?' his voice was sceptical, but his eyes were so intent on my face I turned my gaze away, trying to quell the creeping flush up my spine which could so easily stain my cheeks to vivid rose. There was a pause until he continued, 'I've every faith in Doctor Zane's opinion which is that the stress of the occasion must have been too much for your highly-strung temperament – '

I gave a false short laugh. 'Of course. I knew it would be that.'

'And how did you know?'

'Because he'd made up his mind beforehand,' I answered recklessly. 'He'd been well primed.'

'Whatever are you talking about?' He jerked himself upright; a second later I too was standing, facing him. I was on the point of blurting out what I believed, but realising that to bring his wife into the affair at that point would be useless, and only turn him against me, I prevaricated clumsily, saying, 'A concoction – a draught of something was given to me to drink before I went on the stage. It was the stage-manager – it was supposed to steady me, the potion I mean. But it could have been something else, couldn't it? – And suppose he knew the doctor – ' I paused briefly then continued quickly, almost swallowing my words, ' – There's a lot of jealousy among the cast, and I kind of sensed that one or two didn't like me – ' Oh, what a mess I was making of everything, I thought, suddenly breaking off.

Rupert shook his head slowly, a look of disbelief and pity on his face.

'My dear girl, what you lack in stage-discipline, you certainly make up for in imagination. The whole idea is quite ridiculous. No, please don't try such absurd excuses on me – '

'*Excuses?*' I echoed hotly. 'I'm not trying to excuse myself. Why should I? I was a failure and that's all that matters. I'm sorry you should have wasted time and money on me, but I'll repay you somehow. There's no point in talking about it any more. I said you wouldn't believe me. So please – ' I swallowed painfully.

'Yes, Josephine? Please what?'

His voice had softened. He put both hands on my shoulders. I turned my face away, and tried to free myself before I weakened and flung myself into his arms. I longed to – God knows I did. But pride and fear he'd despise me, made me fight.

'Let me go,' I said brokenly. 'That's all. Let me go!'

He did so immediately.

'Certainly. I've no taste for your dramatics.'

I walked away from him, brushed a lock of hair from my forehead, make a pretence of tidying a ribbon at my bodice, then turned, cheeks flaming, and regarded him with what I hoped was a touch of dignity.

His expression was stony except for a small line of hurt bewilderment creasing from his forehead to the high bridge of his nose.

'I'm sorry,' I blurted out. 'I didn't mean – '

'No need to apologise. I should be the one to do that for daring to touch you.'

'But – '

'No buts, either, Miss Lebrun. You've made your position perfectly clear, it will take only a few minutes to explain mine. Do sit down again, it discomforts me seeing you stand so accusingly before me.'

Weakly I obeyed.

'Now! – ' He walked to the window, hands behind his back, then turned sharply, and continued in remote cool tones as though addressing a stranger or business acquaintance, 'I shall, of course, apologise to Signor Luigi on your behalf, and offer compensation to him for what may be taken by the public as a serious misjudgement of talent on his part. Whether he will accept it or not I can't say. In your favour, I shall point out how rushed arrangements were for you to play Lucy at such short notice, and that we all knowingly took the risk. Your youth and inexperience will be taken into account, I'm sure. He is a fair man, but under the circumstances I doubt he'll accept you as a protégée any longer. In fact, I'm sure of it, which means no more lessons are forthcoming – '

'I realise that,' I interrupted, 'of course. I shall return as soon as possible to Falmouth, and – '

'You will do nothing of the sort.'

The peremptory statement startled me. 'I don't – '

'You don't understand?' His brows lifted in mock astonishment, or was he merely play-acting? I couldn't tell. 'Then accept it as fact, Miss Lebrun. I think you'll agree when I point out that one of the conditions of my sponsorship and your tuition under Signor Luigi was that you also helped Dame Jenny in her duties at the cottage. I can't physically imprison you here, of course, but I hardly think under the circumstances you'd be so thoughtless as to walk out leaving her to shoulder all the responsibilities of Tregonnis. It was a bargain we made, and I expect you to keep to your side of it.'

I tried to speak, but he stopped me with a wave of his hand. 'No, wait until I've finished.'

Mortified, I pressed my lips firmly together and waited.

'You'd expect payment, naturally. I'm prepared to give it – and more I'm sure than you received at the various hostelries where you worked – '

I could stand no more. Ignoring his command to remain silent, I cried, 'I expect nothing. I don't want your money or your help. About Dame Jenny – yes! I see it wouldn't be fair to leave her in the lurch, and I'll be able to do more for her without those wretched singing lessons, but only until you find someone more suitable.'

'That may take quite a time,' he stated practically, 'in the meantime, whether you like it or not you'll receive a weekly sum to provide any feminine fal-als and frippery necessary.'

'I see. A servant.'

'Do you find the word offensive?'

'Of course not. But – '

'Shall we say "help"?' he suggested. 'Do you find that more agreeable?'

'Oh – !' Misery engulfed me because he was managing to put me in such a poor light. ' – I don't care, call me what you like.' I turned my back on him, took a few steps to the door, turned and remarked with forced politeness, 'Is that all, sir?'

'No.' His mood changed suddenly. He strode rapidly towards me, and before I could prevent him he'd swept me up into his arms and his lips were on mine – passionate, angry, desirous lips, that left me breathless and bewildered, dizzy with my own longing and reciprocation.

Then, suddenly, it was all over. He reached for his hat from a chair, made a mock bow and remarked ironically, 'My apologies. I can promise you there will be no repetition of such a distasteful incident for you in the future. However, dear Miss Lebrun, should you ever have the chance to play Lucy Lockett again I'm sure this little – rehearsal, shall we say – may prove to be a useful experience.'

The next moment he had gone.

VI

The days following my disastrous debut, though peaceful, were without inspiration or interest for me. I did my best to help Dame Jenny in her domestic routine, but she was obviously averse to my taking any initiative. Her routine was set, and she wished for no alteration. Jan, the farmer's boy, came twice a week to scrub out the floors and chop wood, and I found myself doing little more than I did when I was having lessons from Signor Luigi. As Rupert had stipulated, a weekly sum was paid to me and delivered by a servant from Kerrysmoor with Dame Jenny's salary. She counted mine out carefully and handed it to me always with the same words, 'Be grateful to have such an obliging master. It's good money for a maid such as thee.'

What exactly her statement implied I don't know, but I don't think she meant it in any derogatory sense. Once, when I was feeling particularly moody and depressed, she remarked with a touch of concern, 'I've not heard thee sing lately. Haven't you any voice left, or is it a fit of sulks? Sulks do nothing to raise the spirits. And maybe with a little practice you could start trillin' 'gain like a bird. It's the time for it – with all the spring flowers pushing through and the sweet air blowin'.'

Yes, no one knew that more than I. A sight of or one word from Rupert Verne might have brought a burst of music from my throat, but cast off as I felt myself to be, I hadn't the heart. So I answered, 'I don't feel like it. What's the use?'

'There's use in everything if you do the best you can with it,' she told me sharply, and the irritation in her voice caused a quick movement of her head which set the bright rings flashing from her ears, and a quivering glitter of all the jewellery she wore. 'You're getting dull, girl – stir yourself up. There's always a job waiting for useful hands. What about the garden? No touching my roses, of course – I've told thee that before. But weeds are springing up as quick as mushrooms. You could lend a hand there. Thee should know a weed from a flower by now.'

'All right,' I agreed, 'yes, I can do that.'

So on a day when no wind stirred the countryside and a faint bluish haze lifted gradually above the earth and rising moors, I took a trowel and fork from the tool shed at the back of the cottage, and set to work pulling and digging carefully where unwanted wild plants threatened to thrive and smother the old lady's cherished herbs and blooms. The air was sweet and faintly damp, and as the sun brightened, golden rays caught a froth of blossom on an ancient apple tree. Occasionally a bird's rich twitter broke the silence.

After a period of bending and kneeling I stood up to ease my back, shaking the soil from my apron, and pushing the tumbled curls from my forehead. I paused, staring across the pool to its far side, where daises starred a patch of lawn. The extreme quiet was almost uncanny. In the distance the Three Maidens – no longer quite so menacing in the morning light, were touched to transient gold flame, and I visualised Kerrysmoor in the dip below hidden by its curve of the hill where Rupert would be up and about, and his lady wife perhaps still lazing in her luxurious boudoir.

Rupert.

Something in me stirred and came to life painfully. If I'd thought he'd never really cared about me at all, the ache wouldn't have hurt so acutely, but in the beginning he had – I was sure of it. Not sufficiently though to want me as a failure, an embarrassment to his friendship with Luigi, and the theatrical world. I was perhaps exaggerating; Exeter was not London, and probably I hadn't been important enough to cause even a word of criticism or derision anywhere except perhaps in a limited local press. Very well. I had to accept it; I was no use to him, except as assistance to Dame Jenny, and for keeping an eye on his precious treasures, including the mysterious portrait of the lovely girl.

I glanced down into the pool where small silver and gold fish darted through the glossy leaves of water lilies and pale spreading fern-like plants. A frail breath of air shivered over the surface causing circles of light to ebb and flow in a myriad of reflected shapes including my own face, which for an instant appeared to be that of another – of the girl who could be alive or dead, but who still haunted my imagination every time I glimpsed her limpid eyes staring at me from the heavy frame.

Nothing, for the moment, seemed quite real. Everything around me held a secret other-world atmosphere that for the first time since the disastrous *Beggar's Opera* episode, took my mind from that wretched business to different channels. I recalled the day I'd climbed the area round Rosecarrion and seen the vessel in the shadows of the narrow creek, then the other occasion – twice – when dots of human forms in the far distance, had appeared momentarily and disappeared again. Perhaps I'd been mistaken in thinking I'd recognised Rupert on the boat. But if I'd been right, was the 'matter of business' he'd more than once referred to concerning his apparent avoidance of Tregonnis, something to do with contraband? And could the latter be the true cause for making the moor there forbidden territory?

During my time at Falmouth, contact with sailors and merchants had taught me much about smuggling. As a child I'd learned to accept it almost as a way of life for some – a trade frequently indulged in by the rich, and conveniently ignored by certain members of the Preventative. Agreements were often made in taverns, and taprooms of inns and kiddleywinks. Following my father's death I'd listened avidly to plots being hatched with knowing looks and snide remarks passed both in French and English. Tragedies –

stories of shootings resulting in death were not uncommon. Mostly the Preventative men were loyal to their calling, but bribery often played a large part in the success or failure of an illegal operation.

Swift as lightning the question flashed through my brain. Was Rupert Verne entirely the conventional well-bred gentleman he appeared to be? Or was that merely a daytime front, a facade to hide a more dangerous daring side of his character. This could be. If so it would explain much – the adventurous gleam in his strange amber eyes – the quick flash of desire and challenge roused unexpectedly through a chance word or incident. He could be a man to whom fresh challenge was the breath of life. And I had been a part of it. He'd thought to create a legend of me – through my voice and looks expand his own dream of self-expression. Likewise in outwitting the law, he would be proving master of circumstance and other men.

Freedom! Beneath the elegant front surely was a rebellious spirit, equal to my own – as wild as the gales and storm-swept granite shores – as live and unquenchable as the impulse in me that all my life until so very recently had stirred me to joy and tears and the sweet fulfilment of song.

'Oh Rupert, Rupert,' I thought, as I turned my gaze from the pool towards the moorland ridge, 'why did you have to marry that proud iceberg of a woman? Why couldn't I have lain in your arms at night feeling our bodies close in passion – abandoned and rich in love?'

With the tangy sweet air soft and sensuous against my cheeks, I could imagine the touch of his flesh against mine – the oneness of giving and taking – a throbbing unity bred from the very heart of Nature itself. Even as I stood there my senses thrilled in wild anticipation; I released my wealth of dark curls, and loosened my bodice at the neck. Just for a brief interim the whole world seemed to sing, and a treble of music broke briefly from my throat.

Then, suddenly, I remembered.

The moments of ecstasy passed. Sober commonsense

replaced the dream. I was Josephine Lebrun, servant to Dame Jenny, employed by the Master of Kerrysmoor who insisted on paying me for my services, although most of what he gave was put away in a drawer, so that when the appropriate time came and other help could be found for the old lady I would be able to return the money, either by messenger or in person, with the words, 'Thank you so much, sir, your ladyship, – for the charity so kindly offered. I'm glad to have been of use, but I really do not need your gold.'

Yes; the latter method of repayment would give me the greater satisfaction – to lift my chin arrogantly at Lady Verne's cold countenance, savour the amazed astonishment in her narrowed eyes and on her thin lips. During the brief occasions we'd met so far she'd used every subtle means to insult me, but one day, I told myself, my pride alone would defeat her.

'A princess,' Pierre had told me so often. 'You are my princess. Never forget that, *ma chère*.' Remembering now, urged me into a gentler mood. It was as though a soothing hand and voice from the past were resurrected momentarily lulling conflicting emotions to reason and renewed confidence.

Presently I went back into the cottage. The sky had darkened slightly, bringing a train of cloud from the west. A faint breeze stirred the stillness taking the frail hazed sunlight behind a veil of grey.

'Shouldn't be surprised if we had a storm later,' Dame Jenny said when I walked into the kitchen. 'There was the smell of rain about in the early hours.'

'That will be good for your garden, won't it?'

'S'long as it doesn't beat my roses down,' she replied guardedly.

She needn't have feared. When evening came only misted rain fell, clearing sufficiently to give at intervals a glimmer of blurred moonlight. A strange, nostalgic kind of night, reminding me again of times long ago, when as a child I'd waited by Falmouth harbour searching the waters for the sight of a ship emerging from a grey horizon with my father at the helm. Perhaps it was the atmosphere that made me restless, but I had an impulse to go wandering – to climb Rosecarrion and explore the territory above the creek – to find out for myself if the boat had left, or was still there. Commonsense told me that it would hardly have remained inactive since my first glimpse of it. Instinct, though, was stranger than commonsense. I just knew something was going on that concerned Rupert Verne; moreover the misty scene moon-washed one moment, the next darkened by cloud, was exactly right for a successful smuggling operation – yet could bewilder the Preventative men with its constantly changing shadowed shapes – of rocks, twisted trees and bushes crouching towards the water above jagged thrusting cliffs.

I took a close look at Dame Jenny, who was busy with her needle by the fire. Although springtime, the nights could still be chilly, and that morning Jan had brought logs, so a cheerful blaze enabled her to concentrate comfortably, with the aid of an oil lamp on the table. I knew though that she was getting sleepy, and was not surprised when she said, 'I'll be going to my bed early tonight, girl, and I advise you to do the same. There'll be baking to do tomorrow, and ironing of the aprons and caps.'

'Don't worry,' I said, 'I'm quite capable of baking bread and buns now, and the ironing's nothing. Still, I'll do as you say. There's the garden too.'

She scrutinised me sharply from her small bright eyes.

'Tired thee, did it? – The weedin' and diggin'?'

'Not really,' I said. 'I just feel comfortably lazy.'

I didn't like lying to her, but I knew very well that if she'd the least inkling of my plan when she was safely asleep, she'd put a stop to it, and it would be very difficult to get a second chance. So I put on an air of placidity which beguiled her into retiring early, while I made my way to my own bedroom.

I waited for over an hour before opening my door and tip-toeing along the short landing to her room which overlooked the lane. Pressing my ear to the keyhole I was reassured by the distinct rhythmical sound of her snoring, which indicated she had taken her dose of hot toddy, and would probably sleep innocently through the night.

The rest, though tricky, was not really difficult. Wearing a cape over my clothes, and with my boots in one hand I crept softly downstairs, unlatched the kitchen window which was down to the ground, and climbed cautiously out. I waited a moment, listening. There was no sound from above, no flicker of light or indication that the old lady had heard. I knew I was safe for an hour or two, and after a minute or so moved cautiously along the side of the cottage to the garden gate leading into the lane.

From there, with the hood covering my hair, head forward, I hurried, half-running, to the hill's curve where a track wound upwards, then to my right in the direction of the creek. I followed it. But finding the exact path I'd taken before was impossible in the shrouded shadows, drifting mist, and intermittent glimpses of rain-washed moonlight. Briar and thorn, twisted clumps of heather and gorse hunched by tumbled granite boulders made progress slow. But at last through a brief sudden clearance of cloud, a glimmer of sea glittered ahead, only to be taken the next moment into darkness again. I was more certain then of the exact locality, and decided to climb higher, and wend my way round the top end of the ravine – or creek, so a view – however blurred – might be possible of anything going on below.

Nearer the summit of the slope the land was more barren and free of tortuous obstructions. At a point above the ruin that I'd observed previously, I paused to look down on the gaunt cut in the rock face where the boat had been anchored. The mist and fine rain had thinned a little, leaving a grey desolate vista of land and sea. The creek was merely a gash of darkness. No ship was discernible, no sign of human life – the atmosphere was one of elemental desolation, and suddenly I felt chilled. I had been wrong then to sense adventure in which Rupert Verne might have been concerned.

Then, quite unexpectedly the moon's pale glare broke completely free of cloud and drizzle spreading luminous clarity over the landscape.

I was astonished. The boat *was* there, hunched close above the tide against the glassy black brilliance of the rock face. But it was obviously a wreck, and in the past sometime had floundered and been forsaken, which seemed odd, as vessels of that type were usually salvaged by owners or the authorities. There could be no other answer; but the question still remained concerning the male figures I'd seen on deck before, taking one to be Rupert. I had probably been mistaken, concocting an image of who I wished it to be, from an overwrought imagination.

Reluctantly, I turned and made my way back to Tregonnis, but on impulse took a route passing close to the ruin. The rain had ceased now, and the mist and cloud had lifted considerably. When I neared the tumbled granite relic I guessed that generations ago it had probably been a moorland chapel, built to serve worshippers of outlying mining hamlets and farms. Methodism, still a force in Cornwall, had flourished with wild fervour then. Even John Wesley himself could have preached there. Later as certain copper mines in the district failed and families took off to the Americas or left for the North Country and employment in the cotton industry, many such buildings would have lost their use except as shelter for cattle, tramping vagabonds, or occasional dumping for smuggled goods. Yes, the latter was possible, though hardly likely to be suspect by the military, being on Verne land. And there were so many such ruins dotted about the Cornish coast. The Preventative generally had far more important business on their hands than to go searching and keeping an eye on every forsaken relic left to decay.

All the same – due to my heightened imagination, the eerie night and my concern over Rupert – stimulated by impulse and my own wild thoughts, I pushed my way through brambles, over stones and rough patches of inky damp earth, until I reached the entrance half obscured by rocks and fallen stones.

I went in.

The roof was almost completely gone. Only three walls were left standing, and the far side facing the coast was a mere wreck of fallen granite allowing the weak moonlight to streak across the rough floor. Queer shadows lurked from corners filling the interior with creeping uneasy menace. The air had a fetid, musty smell, mingled with something else – something reminiscent of certain ancient kiddleywinks I'd once known in childhood. Whisky. Was it whisky I could smell? Had some drunken vagabond been spending an hour or two there with his bottle? I felt the skin tighten about the back of my neck and skull. Was that dark lump in the far corner that of a human being – dead perhaps? I wanted to turn and leave the sinister place, but curiosity forbade me.

I went forward cautiously, keeping my eyes on the ground, half feeling my way, and in a wanton beam of moonlight I discovered that the floor was flagged. Well, of course, it would be if the place had ever been a chapel or part of a mine house.

Then I had a surprise. My heart and pulses jerked. Near the open wall facing the coast, slabs had been moved, and it appeared to me, fairly recently. There was a gap of darkness – empty darkness – between two, that suggested an underground tunnel of some constructed foundation below. Earth had been dislodged and had not yet settled. Someone had been there.

I stood, puzzled, forgetful of how chilled I was becoming, of the passing of time, or that Dame Jenny might soon be stirring. It was very rarely in the night she did so, but there was always a slight chance; nothing registered in my thoughts though save the mounting excitement I'd *discovered* something.

I bent down to examine the dislodged flagstone, and then I heard it – the thud, thud of horses' hooves coming nearer – nearer – just as though the wild black horseman of the Cornish moors – of the legendary Devil's Carn – was riding to seize me. I'd read stories about him in my youth, most Cornish folk had; but until that moment I'd had no fear, had felt only a pleasurable stirring excitement.

Now I knew why the myth had arisen. Were the sounds *really* those of a rider of the night? Or due to some strange elemental manifestation that could be explained by a naturalist or geological expert? I waited with my ears strained, listening. Louder and louder. Thud, thud, thud. The hollow sound seemed to reverberate underfoot and through the air. There could be no mistake about it – whether demon or man, the rider – or could it be some wild stallion rampaging on its own? – was making for the ruin.

Tensely I pushed my spine rigidly against the damp granite wall. Seconds passed, and then suddenly the thudding ceased; there was a snorting and neighing, a murmuring of a male voice, and rattle of metal or reins; a moment later a dark form pushed through the ruined doorway, kicking and striking stones with his boots as he approached.

Then he paused.

Except for the drip of water trickling from between granite bricks, no sound penetrated the short silence that followed. The weird lemon light struck sideways on his face, accentuating the deep carved lines of it, dominant nose, thrusting jaw, and the glint of yellow eyes under heavy brows.

Rupert.

I waited for him to speak first; the seconds seemed interminable.

Then, as though from a dream, I heard him say in deadly calm tones, 'What are *you* doing here?'

Unable to concoct a satisfactory answer – well, what *could* be satisfactory under such conditions? – I blurted out, 'I was just poking round. I was curious.'

He still didn't attempt to touch me.

'Obviously. And what right do you think you have? On *my* land, on such a night, at such a time, and when you've expressly been forbidden to come this way at all?'

My nerve began to return, and with it a welling-up of my quick temper.

'None, of course. Since coming to Tregonnis, I seem to have given up all the rights I ever had. But for once I wanted to feel free and take a bit of a wander without being watched or told where to go. Oh I know you've been very kind to me – in a way – paying for my lessons with that fiery little Italian – forcing me into a – a – debut I wasn't ready for on that beastly Exeter stage – letting me make a fool of myself, and then turning me into some sort of servant to that funny old lady. Your wife, too! – she hates me – you can see it in her eyes, her manner, and the way she lifts her long nose every time we meet! – and why – *why*?' I broke off, breathless, but somehow relieved to get it all out.

'*You* know why,' he said, and his voice was meaningful, a little unsteady and harsh.

The moon had slipped behind cloud again. Everything was damp darkness, filled with lurking shadows, strange and exciting, pulsing with all the hidden secret forces of that Cornish night. The ground squelched underfoot as he took one stride towards me. A bramble caught his sleeve.

He tore his arm free, and suddenly it was round me, taking my body close to his; his lips were warm against my neck, mouth and damp shoulder and breast where the cloak had fallen away. I struggled a little, then let my head fall and lie against him. How heavily his heart beat, and how wonderful it was to hear its steady thumping – strong with the urge and longing of life.

'You know very well why,' he murmured again.

I could feel the hardening of him, and felt response rise in me. I wanted to cry, 'Love me. Rupert, oh, love me – ' but he forced me from him gently, firmly.

'Hardly an ideal place for such – indiscretions,' he said, with an attempt of lighthearted mockery. He sighed, folded his arms, and continued in more level tones, 'Now what the devil am I going to do with you? For you're a witch if ever there was one.'

'Not all witches are bad,' I answered, trying to match my mood to his. At that moment the moon must have slipped out from behind the clouds again. The dark walls lightened to eerie bluish green, giving a radiance and brief clarity to the scene which before had been a mere background of shadow, and in those first few seconds I happened to glance down and noticed once more the line between slab and dislodged earth. Quick as lightning his gaze followed mine.

'Your bright eyes are observant, I note.' The dry tone was back in his voice. 'I might have known you'd miss nothing.'

'Was it important I should?'

'Yes,' he answered. 'Knowing my business is hardly your affair – living as you are. And I have never made a habit of sharing any of my male interests with women – '

'I'm not just *women* I'm – '

'I know, I know. You're a deuced aggravating, inquisitive little baggage who's managed to steal a march on me in every way – first as a singer, then as an intriguing young woman, and now as a would-be pirate.'

'Pirate?' I gasped.

He laughed.

'What you suspect *me* of being – smuggler.'

'I – '

'Which I am,' he interrupted. 'Oh, I'm not going to deny it. What would be the use? You've already somehow got your pretty little nose on the scent. How? Why? – God knows. Maybe your training in bars and kiddleywinks. Or maybe just an uncanny sixth sense – something peculiarly special between the two of us.' His manner changed, softened. 'Is that it, Josephine?' Through the fitful light his eyes searched mine – narrow golden eyes warm with desire and tenderness.

'I think it must be,' I admitted, 'but I didn't *know*. You needn't have told me. You see – ' Words quickened from my lips ' – I'd seen things from my window at Tregonnis. Not as far as this, of course – but a man, walking – half crawling at times along the hill as though – as though – ' I broke off, continuing quickly, 'Well, I thought the first time it was a miner going home, but there isn't a mine just there, is there? And then once or twice I went for a walk – '

'*Ah.*'

' – Where you'd told me not to, and I found the creek where the boat was, the old wreck. I didn't connect you exactly, not then. But the next time I went further, and saw figures on the deck. They weren't very clear, it was some distance away; all the same – I was certain you were one of them. And it seemed funny; I wondered what you were doing – '

'As I thought. And tonight you decided to investigate.'

'Something like that.'

'Why? – Why tonight?'

'I've told you, I was bored by being kept on a string, and wanted to be free.'

He threw out his arms and let them fall to his sides in exasperation. 'Freedom. That's all you think of – freedom. And now look what you've got into – '

'I'd *like* to look,' I said impudently.

'Then you'll have to be disappointed,' he replied promptly. 'And I mean it. You'll do what you're told, and believe me when I inform you that even if I made the effort to remove that slab you'd find nothing in the dank dungeon below, but a load of rubbish and mud and snails – don't you realise, my love, that a clever villain like myself always has an alibi? For instance it's my right to hunt prowling poachers on a dark night? So don't go airing stupid ideas. No one would believe your word against Master Verne's.'

'The smell of spirits *is* very strong,' I pointed out, impertinently.

He shook his head, and grasped my arm. 'Come along, Miss Lebrun. Time for quizzing and play-acting is done. I'm taking you back to Tregonnis as quickly as Flash can make it, and I repeat, not a word of this, you understand? Then in the morning what's left of it – you'll tell yourself all your strange imaginings were just a dream.'

'You're saying – you didn't really mean it?'

'Mean what?'

'When you kissed me,' I said bluntly.

For answer he slipped his arm round me and said gently, 'Yes, I meant it. And one day – '

'One day?' I prompted.

'We'll have to see, won't we, how things work out?'

It wasn't the answer I'd wanted, but it sufficed.

The next moment, still with his hand on my arm he was leading me from the ruin to the stump of a tree where his stallion, Flash, was tethered.

So it was that we rode together that night under a belt of thin cloud – lovers not yet free to love openly, but with the rich secret of passion between us that I knew must one day be revealed.

Dame Jenny was still safely in her bedroom when I pushed the kitchen window open and climbed over the sill.

I removed my boots, crept up the stairs and into my room, not waiting to listen for any slight sound from the old lady's bedroom. It must have been one o'clock by then. For some time excitement and a sense of wild fulfilment kept me awake. But at last I slept, and when morning came it was fine, and a blackbird was trilling from somewhere near my window.

I wanted to sing too. For the first time since the Exeter disaster I thought it possible I would.

And all because Rupert had kissed me and in a careless moment called me his love.

VII

A week following my moorland adventure I went down to the kitchen one morning and found Dame Jenny lying on the floor. She was a pathetic sight, with her old face twisted to one side, and a broken cup shattered by one jewelled hand. An earring had been knocked off, and her mob cap fallen, taking her hair with it. I hadn't known she wore a wig, and the sight of her so defenceless and very ancient, moved me to pity.

I managed to lift her up somehow and ease her into her favourite chair. She made an effort to say something, but what I couldn't tell, the words were illegible. Luckily it was a day when Jan called with wood, and as soon as he arrived I sent him to Kerrysmoor with a message of what had happened.

Then I made her a hot drink and waited, holding her hand. I wasn't terribly surprised at her collapse; for some time I'd noticed that she was gradually failing. Her hands had shaken more under the slightest stress, and she'd been inclined to 'get in a tizzy' over nothing. Her walk had lost its lightness, and she'd been mislaying things in the house more and more frequently. It was clear to me she'd suffered a stroke, and I hoped her high-and-mighty ladyship wouldn't want the poor old thing to be carted away to an institution.

I needn't have worried.

When the doctor had been, and delivered his verdict, which was the same as mine, Rupert told me to pack Dame Jenny's valise with all that was necessary, while he carried the old lady outside.

'And you'd better include her reticule and jewel box,' he

said. 'Her stay at Kerrysmoor may be a prolonged one, but obviously it's the best place for her.'

I did what he said and in a matter of less than half an hour the frail old lady was being carefully deposited in the waiting chaise with the help of the doctor. Rupert came back for a moment before leaving.

'You're not afraid to remain here alone, I hope? At least for a day or two. After that possibly it can be arranged for a servant from the house to be installed here as company. Here's a pistol – ' he handed me one carefully, ' – in case any unwelcome visitors should appear. It's loaded, but the safety catch is on. You know how to use it, I presume?' His voice had a questioning note, the narrowed eyes were anxious.

I lifted my head boldly. 'I'm afraid of no intruder, sir, and yes, I *do* know how to handle it, if necessary. There's no need to worry about me at all, or to send a servant down. I shall be quite all right.'

His lips closed in a tight line. 'That's for me to say.'

I flushed. The look he gave me was dark, a little forbidding and commanding. 'You may be very courageous,' he continued after a brief pause, 'but you are somewhat – unpredictable – and a great deal of wealth is stored here. For some time I thought added protection was advisable, so in the meantime, until we make more permanent arrangements, I shall insist on you having a dog – Brutus – who is a trained guard, but a faithful affectionate hound and friend to those in his charge. He's well-known to Jan who'll be given instructions to bring food over once every day, and to give the animal regular exercise. Tomorrow Jan will collect him from Kerrysmoor and bring him along. In a very short time, I can assure you, you'll be firm friends.'

'I hope so,' I said rather primly.

His mood changed in the unexpected way I was becoming accustomed to.

'Josephine – ' the tentative flicker of a smile touched his lips, 'don't entirely neglect your singing. I have faith in your voice, and still believe that one day, perhaps, its quality will be recognised.'

'Oh!' I laughed artificially. 'What does my *voice* matter?'

'To me it does. And when I look in one day to see how things are with you and Brutus, I hope I shall have the privilege of hearing it.'

So polite and formal; yet my heart leaped through hearing that he would be visiting Tregonnis.

'Well – ' he stood uncertainly for a moment, while I wondered wildly if he'd kiss me. But he didn't. He merely touched my hand, gave a slight bow, and was gone.

Of course, I told myself, as the chaise started off down the road, he'd been afraid lest the doctor's shrewd eyes should notice any slight intimacy between us.

Etiquette!

How stupid that feelings had to be disguised under a mask of manners. But *were* his rare passionate lapses deep and true as mine were? – or was he playing a little side-game with me? Keeping me on a string for his own ends? How did I *know*? Men, my stepmother used to tell me, were false feckless creatures, and the more highly born, the more deviously cunning their motives could be. But then she'd had no standing and put no value on herself or her body; perhaps if Pierre had lived – the question didn't arise though. I knew deep down she would have eventually betrayed him. And I was sad remembering how my father had trusted her.

Looking back too intensely can bring its worries, and at that moment, as I recalled Pierre, I wondered what his advice would have been at this exact point in my life – to follow love where I knew it lay, and grasp it with both hands and all the will and strength I had? – Or to cut adrift and seek fulfilment somewhere else in some other fashion? I still had my voice. There was nothing in the world now to stop me walking out, and wandering the wild sweet lanes of summer where blossom foamed about the hedges and lush bluebells grew.

Rupert, after all, was a married man with a stately home and a noble wife. He was bound by ties which would not easily be broken. I was an intruder into his heart – as he was in mine. But I was mistress of my own destiny, whereas he was not of his, and unless his love was as strong and all-consuming as mine, any future between us would be ignoble and wrong. Yes, I knew I was right in my judgement there, and that Pierre would have said the same. Of this I was certain, and with the certainty something in me that had been reckless and immature grew up and brought me to a calmer mood.

I would stay at Tregonnis for the time being, I decided; this was only fair considering the arrangements that were being made concerning the dog, and there being no one else to guard Rupert's treasure room. But later – I sighed. How futile it was to make plans when I'd no idea *exactly* of what others were being made for me. Already my thoughts were becoming too involved to view rationally. So I cleared my mind of all problems, and decided to have a breath of air in the garden. As I passed down the short hall I noticed that the door of the treasure room was slightly ajar; Dame Jenny must have been looking round before she collapsed.

I fetched the key and was about to close and lock it, when I thought I heard a sound. I stepped inside and had a glance round. No one was there; the faint creaking could have been of old wood, a floor board, or draught of air playing about the figurines. A slanting beam of sunlight quivered over glass, giving life to the delicate miniatures in their black velvet mounts and gold frames. Shadows made a fine tracery over rugs and up walls; the slightest movement of cloud or drifting light from outside lit the crystal and glass to momentary shivering brilliance. It was as though for a few brief moments the interior came alive and I stood in a world of fantasy and bygone luxury.

I glanced towards the fireplace. The girl in the portrait stared down at me with a serene sweet-sad half-smile on her lips.

'I wish I knew all about you,' I thought, 'I wish I knew who you were, and what part you played in Rupert's life.'

It did not occur to me as strange just then, that I should think of her in the past tense, or connect her so personally with Rupert. Was I jealous? Perhaps. Jealous because her place there was obviously of great importance, and cherished above all the other contents of that secret domain. I had sensed it from my first day at Tregonnis, a feeling that had been endorsed by Rupert's refusal to talk of her, and Dame Jenny's irate snub when I'd asked for information.

As I turned and went out, locking the door behind me, I realised fully, for the first time, what a world of mystery and adventure, I'd become involved in since leaving Falmouth. Rupert! – the smuggling – Signor Luigi – the terrible theatrical experience – even Lady Verne's peculiar animosity towards me, and the secret room dominated by the picture of the beautiful unknown girl.

The pistol also. I hadn't been quite honest with Rupert when I'd told him I knew how to use it. It was just that during my life at the inn I'd seen firearms threateningly wielded and had once even witnessed a duel, unknown to my stepmother. I was a little surprised that Mr Verne should have trusted me with such a weapon – I'd no idea that the dangerous looking object was loaded with blank bullets only and was merely for a means of frightening off any offender, and ensuring my own self-confidence.

Still, burglaries, shootings, and smuggling, seemed remote and very far away that day, as I wandered round the garden, thinking sadly of Dame Jenny. She would be cared for, yes, at Kerrysmoor, but I doubted that even if she recovered sufficiently to walk about again on her own two feet, she would ever be happy living as a dependent without her own small precious domain to reign over. And why had she been left on her own for so long, considering the responsibilities entailed as 'keeper of Tregonnis'? – Perhaps because in the eyes of many country folk and natives of Tharne she had the reputation of being some sort of a witch – a *white* witch, it was emphasised, although in the tiny village post office one day I'd heard two local women agreeing in an undertone that there was no such thing as the white kind. '*Any* witch is bound to have a bit o' dark power in her.'

So her quaint eccentricities – jewels, fineries, diminutive stature and her herbs had probably been her protection. Even her roses might have added to the superstition; they were certainly extremely lush, over-large, and beautiful, and that morning their scent hung sweetly and particularly powerfully in the summer air. Their velvet petalled colour – flame, yellow, and deep dark crimson filled the whole of one wide border at the side of the pool; a few petals drifted on the shining water. It was indeed as though a magical hand had brushed the terrain. Or were such thoughts merely crowding my mind because I was so completely alone, and shocked by the niggling thought that the old lady might never see her beloved blossoms again?

I was looking forward to meeting Brutus, and hoped very much that the following day when Jan called for him at Kerrysmoor Rupert also might decide to come along. I spent a little time in the garden, reluctant somehow to go immediately back into the cottage which would be an empty place without the old lady. In a strange way I'd grown fond of her – the thought of the quaint interior – silent except for the ticking of the old clock and occasional tinkle from the treasure room when a waft of air drifted against mobile crystal, was melancholy. So I wandered first to the very end of Tregonnis land, which looked over a small buttercup field before rising to the rough patch of moor.

'You needn't bother trying to weed over there,' Dame Jenny had told me more than once. 'No proper flowers grow in that thick scrub. All brambles and holes and stones it is. A real rubbish dump of its kind. One day I'll have Jan clear it and cut some of the thorns down. You could get all kinds of wild animal critters sneakin' there. Once there was a fox had its hole nearby. Things used to disappear from the pantry – cheese, eggs – anything eatable there was and I just couldn't understand how – until one mornin' I saw the fox streakin' across the field. Then I knew. Must get rid of *that*, I said to myself. And I did. That very evening.'

'Do you mean you had it shot or something?' I'd questioned her.

She'd looked shocked.

'My dear life, I wouldn't do such a thing to a livin' critter however wicked it might be. Oh *no*, my dear.' She'd paused and added, 'I have other means of getting rid of unwelcome visitors.'

'How?'

'That's *my* secret,' she'd said smugly, with a little nod of the head that had sent the bright earbobs shaking beneath her mob cap. I'd known then why the natives were suspicious of the old lady.

I was recalling the incident, when I pushed the briars away that morning following her collapse and departure. The smothering undergrowth, indeed, could provide effective coverage for many small wild creatures. I found a sturdy stick – part of a branch torn from a tree – and started beating the thorny barrier down. It wasn't easy, and perhaps I was stupid to bother; my hand and wrist got badly scratched, and an end of my pinafore was ripped. However, as I neared what remained of a half-tumbled fence, my curiosity was roused by a roundish dark patch covered by trailing weeds and thorn indicating there might be a hole or vacuum below.

I bent forward for a closer look, and poked the stick through the tangle of smothering intertwined branches. The ground beneath was hollow. It took me sometime to manipulate sufficient space to peer down, and what I saw sent a shiver of excitement through me. At first glimpse I thought it was a shaft of an old mine, then I realised it was not quite wide enough. It could only have been a well then, at some time. But if so – why was there no water in it now? All I could see was blackness vanishing into the dark earth, and obviously it had been originally man-made. On one side near the surface, granite bricks jutted out almost like steps.

I screwed my eyes up trying to get a more accurate view, but it was impossible. So presently I straightened up, dusted small twigs and leaves from my hair, shook my skirt and damaged apron, and after lightly replacing some of the weedy tendrils and branches, turned to go back into the cottage. Why I'd bothered to cover the hole again I didn't know; it had probably been as it was for years, and was of no real significance any more. I suppose I was simply trying to divert my mind from poor Dame Jenny's plight, by filling my imagination with other problems – making a mystery of something that in reality was no mystery at all.

The cottage seemed a solitary place when I went in.

I found myself eagerly looking forward to the next day, when Jan was to bring the dog to Tregonnis, accompanied – hopefully – by Rupert.

But when morning came only Jan and Brutus arrived. The master, the youth told me had sent a message saying he'd probably call at the end of the week.

My heart sank.

Probably. Sterile comfort indeed considering how passionately I longed to see him. Under a veneer of brightness, however, I covered my disappointment, and enquired about Dame Jenny.

'She'm a bit better, Miss, so I've heard tell,' Jan replied. 'In bed o' course. Well, she would be wouldn' she, an old wumman like her, after such a turn – you'd've thought she'd've managed to avoid such things – her with all that grand knowledge she do have – '

I supposed he was referring to her reputed mystic powers, and was about to make some trite reply when the dog, a golden labrador, prevented me by getting up on his hind legs and giving an affectionate lick on my chin.

'He likes you a'ready. That he do,' Jan remarked. 'You've got a friend, that's for sure.'

And I had.

Quite soon he'd fitted into his new routine and seemed to know from the start he was there for my protection. His bark was fearsome to strangers, but few visited Tregonnis, unless it was a pedlar or someone from the farm, and on such occasions a word from me would silence him and bring him to heel. Occasionally, if I went for a stroll, I'd allow him to accompany me, but only for a short time. He was, after all, sole guardian of the cottage and its treasures during my absence, and Rupert would have been annoyed if he'd called and found neither of us there.

But he didn't call, and I became restless and resentful – tired of being bound to the country through duties I hadn't willingly undertaken. Mysteries of smuggling, secret rooms, legends, and having long hours alone to ponder and brood on the past and the uncertain future, frequently irritated me to a point almost beyond endurance. I would long then for the colourful steamy excitement of the Golden Bird – to be whirling round in my coloured skirts and shawls, dancing and singing – always singing – with faces transfixed before me, blurred discs of watchfulness through the smoky musty air.

More than once I impetuously packed my valise, ready to disappear leaving a note for Rupert Verne, saying:

> I'm sorry, being caretaker doesn't suit me. Thank you for all you've done for me, but as I've failed in becoming a great singer like you wanted, I'm going somewhere where I can be myself and let my voice do just what it feels like. I did love you, Mr Verne, but my sort of love isn't what you need.
>
> Yours respectfully,
> Josephine Lebrun.

Once I even went so far as to put on my bonnet and cape, and leave the note on the small table in the hall. Then Brutus's bark from the scullery where he slept, made me change my mind, and I went inside again. It wasn't fair to leave the dog alone. Supposing Jan for some reason didn't call in the morning? The poor thing would be left without food or company for goodness knows how long.

The thought of Rupert himself, too, from a niggle at the back of my mind, came to life again. He must *one* day call at Tregonnis, and I needed to be there when it happened – to make him realise how his neglect – and surely it *was* neglect, considering the passion of his kisses and meaningful glances of his eyes, the many many avowals of unspoken love – had hurt me! and angered, too. Oh yes, I was angry. Before perhaps I'd had no rightful cause to show it. But now I had. I would *not* be treated like any rich man's cheap little plaything to be flattered one moment, bullied the next, then pushed into oblivion just when he felt like it.

During my period of waiting for Rupert's possible visit, I rehearsed the scene several times – how I would greet him in a dignified fashion telling him of my decision to leave Tregonnis, of my intention to make my own career – even inventing another vague sponsor anxious to promote my voice. The latter would be a lie, of which Pierre no doubt would have disapproved. But for once I didn't care. I would be *me*! my words would be haughty, my gaze cold and remote. I even practised the lift of head and manner of addressing him before my looking glass. And I was careful these days always to appear my best in my most attractive clothes, and do my housework mostly at nights when I would not be caught on my knees in my working calico dress under a long apron.

Oh yes! I made what I imagined were all necessary preparations for the longed-for event. But, of course, when it happened, as is so often the case – everything was completely unexpected.

The morning had been windless but damp, with fine rain turning to fitful mist by afternoon. Twilight, later, hung a grey shroud over the horizon of moors and sky. Steamy rivulets of moisture hugged the windows of Tregonnis; every slight sound there was from outside seemed intensified – the drip, drip of wet leaves from bushes, crying of a gull and flap of wings as it rose into the air, the scuttering rustle of some wild creatures through the undergrowth – and something else – something sensed rather than heard, an uneasiness that seemed itself an entity, chilling my blood. A more practical person would have called it imagination, but Brutus was aware of it, and several times lifted his head as though alerted to danger. Twice a low growl came from his throat. He left the rug by the hearth and went to the door, then returned and lay down again, stretched out, head on paws, but with eyes watchful, tense.

I laid my needlwork aside, lit the oil lamp and went to the window to draw the sittingroom curtains. Intuitively I glanced out towards the west. It was almost dark, but as I paused there briefly a dot of light flashed for a second, then was gone. It could have been a shepherd's lantern perhaps, I told myself reasoningly, although it had appeared over-brilliant for that, and would not so quickly have been snuffed out. It was about to move when I saw it again, only a pinpoint on the moor, somewhere to my far right in the direction of my walks around Rosecarrion. The second flash was quickly followed by a sharp crack of sound like that of a shot being fired. Brutus sprang to his feet and came towards me.

'It's all right, down boy! down!' I said, and pulled the blinds together with a rattle. Then I returned to my chair. For a time the dog was restless, but when no further noise followed, he eventually settled. I crossed once or twice to the window again; everything was dark, muted grey, showing no sign of life or movement. Yet in my bones still I felt something was astir; and when I went to bed made sure that the pistol was beside me on the small table by my side.

I closed my eyes, hoping to get to sleep early and that no troubled dreams would disturb my rest. It was no use. Brutus, who slept in the hall, was uneasy, and at one point gave a mournful howl followed by a low growl and bark. I went to the top of the stairs and gave the command used by Jan to quieten him. For a time it seemed to work. All was silent except for the thickening steady drip of rain that had intensified during the past hour.

Then, suddenly, there was a wild yelling and barking from the animal, together with a frantic pounding of paws against the wooden door.

I jumped out of bed, flung a wrap round my shoulders, and ran downstairs.

'Quiet!' I called to the dog, 'What's the matter? Whatever's got into you – ?'

He was standing on his hind legs, paws against the wooden surface, and didn't obey me when I told him to, 'Come back and be a good boy'. He gave a further yelp, turned his head towards me, and I saw then his excitement was partly pleasure. The limpid eyes were alight, his tail was wagging wildly; his whole attitude was of supplication.

No animal could have begged more obviously, 'Open it, open the door'.

I paused for a moment, uncertain, apprehensive.

And then I heard it – a man's voice and a hammering against the wood – 'For God's sake let me in – it's me – Rupert.'

With my heart quickening and thumping painfully, I rushed to both bolts, drew them, and turned the key in the lock, and pulled the door wide.

Half staggering and breathing heavily, Rupert Verne plunged into the hall. He was wet and hatless. Rain from his dark hair ran down his face, mingling with the trickle of blood from one temple. I tried to steady him, but he waved me aside, and with the dog nosing about his legs and feet, blundered into the parlour. In the glow of the lamp his face appeared drawn and haggard, and I saw also that one arm had been wounded near the shoulder. When he tried to lift it, he winced in pain.

'Sit down,' I said, although I didn't need to; before the words were out he'd slumped on to the sofa. 'I'll get you a drink.'

Knowing where the old lady kept her special toddy, I went

to her secret cupboard in the kitchen, filled a wine glass full of the liquid and took it through to him. His breathing had eased; he gulped it down eagerly, sat for a moment without speaking, then laughed ruefully, and said, 'I must look a sorry sight.'

'Yes, you do,' I affirmed.

And it was true. It was not only the damp clothes and blood-stained neckscarf; mud and twigs clung to his black coat and breeches, lumps of soil tangled his hair; it was as though he'd been in an earthquake.

'What happened?' I asked. ' – No, wait. You must have a wash first. Those cuts are more than scratches. Can you get your coat off?'

'If not, you'll have to saw it away, won't you?' He was trying to make light of the business, but I knew he was in pain.

I didn't wait to give reply to such a stupid remark, but went through to the kitchen, where the range was still warm from baking, and had a kettle of water on it. I poured some into a bowl, and with a clean cloth hurried back to the parlour. In my absence Rupert had managed to remove his coat. The blood was already clotting near the shoulder, and when I'd wiped it clean I saw that the wound, though nasty, was probably from where a bullet had grazed it. Superficial, thank God, like the graze near one temple; but neglected either could have given serious trouble.

How long it took for him to appear clean and in respectable shape, I don't recall. I was surprised at his submissiveness to my help. It was not until the dabbing and washing and bandaging were over that I could relax and notice his expression.

There was a little smile about his stern mouth, his long eyes were slightly crinkled at the corners. It was as though he was mildly amused. *Amused* – when I'd been so frantic with anxiety, so wrought-up and tense on his behalf.

'Thank you,' he said. 'You missed your true vocation, Miss Lebrun. You would make an excellent nurse – or should I say, you already *are* one.'

'There's no need to pay me compliments,' I said abruptly. 'I'd just like to know – '

'What I've been up to? How and why I've arrived here in such a dastardly uncivilized manner? And what the devil I'm thinking about, placing a young woman in such a compromising situation?' he interrupted. 'Of course, naturally.' He regarded me reflectively then continued after a short pause, 'There was trouble tonight near the creek – '

'Smuggling, you mean!'

'Don't hurry me. Yes, smuggling. Brandy and lace. Unfortunately a certain excise officer who in the past had been – fairly co-operative shall we say – in turning a blind eye – had been replaced for some unknown reason by a particularly odious character who'd been on bad terms with me for quite a time. When the force arrived on the scene the small boats – French – were luckily away. But the cargo hadn't yet been completely cleared. My men were spotted after removing the last kegs from that old wreck you saw, to the mouth of a cave that's generally blocked by a slab. There's a tunnel there leading to the old chapel – '

'I *thought* something like that.'

Ignoring my statement he continued, 'Rosecarrion is a hive of tunnels. Very useful routes to dumping depots. You found one, when you located the old chapel so cunningly.'

'Why are you telling me all this?' I asked. 'And why – how did you arrive at the kitchen door of this cottage? I don't understand.'

He lazed back on the sofa with an enigmatic look on his face that discomforted me. It was as though he was assessing me properly for the first time, wondering whether or not he could trust me perhaps – or about something else – something deeply personal that brought the rich colour to my cheeks and set my heart racing.

'I don't think you're telling me the truth, Miss Lebrun. You understand far more than you admit. For instance – if you search my coat pocket you'll discover a shred of linen –

a lady's handkerchief, I believe – that I found on a thorn bush when I struggled up those abominable steps. You knew very well there was a passage hidden below all that rubble.' He smiled wrily. 'A pity you didn't realise I'd have to use it – maybe you could have cleaned it up a little.'

Enlightenment dawned on me.

'*Oh*! the *hole*.'

'Exactly. This cottage was used in the past as a dumping place for goods. But not for many years. I needed it for – other things.' He lowered his gaze. His voice dropped a little sadly, reminding me of what 'other things' probably implied – mostly the image of the lovely girl in the portrait.

'I see.'

He sighed. 'Maybe you will eventually, and I expect you're wondering why I took that foul passage tonight?'

'Well – why did you?'

'I became a fox, Josephine, so the revenue, like hounds, could hunt *me* instead of my two faithful men, which they did. The entrance to the passage is some distance from the cove, leading from a rock crevice, just wide enough to squeeze through. Conveniently for me, the clouds thickened at the most important moment, leaving the Preventative completely bemused. Hopefully, my accomplices had sufficient time to be properly away and replace the slab. If they didn't – '

'Yes?'

'Ah well, there's always a risk about this sort of thing but I'm not really worried now. What worried me was when I came upon blocked places in that foul passage. I had to scratch and burrow like an old mole; the air was fetid at times – nothing but dust and mud. Still – I've done it, and still live, thank God.'

I thanked God as well, in my heart.

'The trouble is,' he resumed, 'that old wreck won't help us any more. You may be sure the area will be well watched from now on.'

'A good thing too,' I said tartly, surprising even myself; I must have sounded exactly like Dame Jenny.

'And just what do you mean by that?' he asked in the hard determined way I knew so well.

I was confused and taken aback, realising I had actually no right to comment on what Mr Verne should or should not do. My cheeks burned as I replied, 'I'm sorry, I suppose it isn't my place to speak like that. I was merely thinking of your safety. I mean – '

'Yes, do go on.'

'Well – you could – you could get seriously hurt or worse, couldn't you – if anything like this happened again? Have you *got* to go on with smuggling?'

He raised his brows and shrugged.

'A man like myself has to have certain things in his life such as – excitement of a kind perhaps – challenge, and the means of retaining certain standards, of having the luxuries he's used to.'

'Like your treasure room?'

His face was expressionless when he answered, 'Something of the sort.' It was as though a veil had clouded his features, and I knew he was thinking of the girl in the portrait. I was suddenly impatient, and filled with jealousy.

I went to the door abruptly, turned and said in matter-of-fact tones, 'You must be hungry. I know *I* am, after all the disturbance – '

'For which I profoundly apologise.' His voice was filled with mockery.

'There's cold ham,' I told him, ignoring the sarcasm. 'I'll make sandwiches and find something for Brutus. Come along, boy.'

Without waiting for Rupert's reply, I left the parlour, with the dog obediently at my heels.

Two o'clock struck when the snack meal I'd managed to provide was over. A curious silence had arisen between Rupert and me, an awkwardness filled with unspoken questions, doubts, hesitancy, and longings on my part, which made me gauche and unable to speak or behave naturally.

'You'll be very late back at Kerrysmoor, won't you?' I said at last. 'I mean, without a horse or anything – ' I broke off stupidly. He got up from the chair, put a hand to the grazed cheek, which was no longer bleeding, and agreed with an ironic semblance of a short laugh. 'Certainly. My horse, I'm quite sure, is already back at the stables, in more respectable shape than I am. But a few miles' walk should freshen me up, and I know the quickest route there is.'

'Is it safe? Or would you rather – '

'Bide here till dawn?' The golden eyes gleamed with mockery. 'My dear girl! What man in his senses wouldn't? But under the circumstances it would be a little rash I think; in my own way I have principles, and I've no taste for testing them where you're concerned. A young woman of your type is – or *should* be – sacrosanct, in this particular instance. In other words – ' His jaw tightened, the light in his eyes smouldered with the rising heat of desire, ' – I *respect* you, Josephine, and if you go on looking at me like that, then heaven help both of us. I must be off, or dammit, darling, I'm only human – ' He made a gesture of leaving, but I was before him at the door.

'No. Don't go.' The plea broke from me heedlessly. 'There's no need. I don't care a fig about respectability or what's done or not done. Rupert – please – '

He sighed, shaking his head slowly, then suddenly gave in, and gathered me to him, cradling my head against his breast. Half sobbing, half laughing with joy, I clung to him in complete abandonment, while he kissed my forehead, my cheeks and lips, burying his mouth in my hair. The scent and strength of his male body was all around – both a torment and opiate soothing and exciting me to forgetfulness of the world, of everything but the knowledge that it had happened at last. We were alone together, free to belong in the richest and deepest way possible to man and woman.

'Love me, Rupert,' I pleaded, as he carried me to the sofa, 'Oh, please, please love me.'

Very gently but firmly, he laid me down, and removed my

wrap and nightshift. He was trembling. The scar near his shoulder showed briefly as he freed himself of constricting clothing. I touched it lightly, caressingly, but his lips were on mine again and the world was blotted out as our flesh became one, borne on a surging flood-tide of passion in which nothing registered but the wild fulfilment of mutual desire and need.

There was no doubting any more, no questioning or uncertainty. What had to be *was*, and had been destined assuredly as spring must follow winter, with summer's glory to follow.

When it was over we still lay entwined as emotional tumult died into sensuous sweet acceptance. My heart ached from an overburdening of joy. 'Until this moment,' I thought, 'I had no knowledge of what life could be. If I died now it would be with no regret, because heaven is here – beyond the limits of Time or mortality, and he is with me – '

'Darling – ' I heard Rupert murmuring, stirring yet again closer. 'Oh, love, my love.' And like a flower suddenly brought to full blossoming, my body once more reached towards him, and was possessed, as was my spirit, until peace came, and eventually we slept.

*

At the first streak of dawn before it was perfectly light, Rupert set off once more for Kerrysmoor, after a quick drink and a piece of cake I'd baked the previous day. He set off from the back of Tregonnis taking a short route I didn't know of, bordered by small stone-walled hills beneath the base of the moor. As his strong figure strode away to be lost in the half-light I wondered if Lady Verne would have missed his presence during the night, or even been aware of his absence. The mere thought of her existence momentarily chilled me. But when I went through to the kitchen doubt died in a rush of warm memory, and the knowledge that I was beloved.

All that morning I lived in a dream, untroubled by

practical issues. It was only when evening approached that it occurred to me no concrete plan had been discussed concerning a future meeting. He would soon come, I knew that, but waiting was going to be a strain. I must be careful *always* of my appearance – never appear overtired or slip-shod in the slightest way. My face must never be shiny from exertion or steamy from the washtub, nor my hair ungroomed. My aprons must be spotless, and my skin sweetly smelling from cologne for his delight. There would be no difficulty in appearing the young lady of Tregonnis rather than its servant or caretaker, there was so little to do domestically without Dame Jenny. For myself I would keep cooking to a minimum, and prevail on Jan to spend more time washing the floors free of Brutus's footmarks and any mud stains brought in from his walks. I had made it my business to be friendly with the youth from the beginning of our acquaintanceship, and I think in an admiring fashion he liked me. He was also very loyal to Rupert.

So the first day passed, then another, and another.

Against my better judgement and optimism a niggle of anxiety seized me.

'Have you seen the master recently?' I asked Jan when the fifth afternoon arrived, and there was still no sign of Rupert.

He shook his head. 'I haven't seen en, Miss, he hasn' showed up at all when I took butter an' such to the big house. But I've heard tell 'er ladyship wasn' well, so I suppose he've bin spendin' more time with 'er. Nat'ral that, edn' et?'

'Oh yes, of course,' I replied mutely, thinking with an irrational burst of pain and disappointment, 'but it's not true. She may *call* herself his wife, but it's here he belongs – with *me* at Tregonnis.'

I longed to burst out with the truth. Let not only Jan but the whole world know of our relationship. Love like ours should never be secret or hidden, but declared openly with honesty and pride.

Something of my inner struggle must have shown.

'Is everythin' all right, miss?' Jan asked. 'Nuthen wrong, is there?'

I pulled myself together quickly.

'No, nothing wrong at all,' I declared, hoping it was true. I was just wondering if – if her ladyship was likely to be ill for long.'

'Oh doan' worry 'bout 'er,' the boy said, with a laugh. 'She gets turns sometimes, an' then the Master has to be around, that's all.'

'What sort of turns?' I asked.

He shrugged, eyed me with curiosity for a moment, then replied, 'Just headaches. Megrims they call it at Kerrysmoor, the thing most fine high-up ladies suffer from, I do b'lieve.'

With that I had to be content; but fear, like a frail shadow, rose to haunt me, because I sensed more lay behind Jan's words than he was willing to admit, and that it very easily could concern me, and the night Rupert had spent at Tregonnis.

VIII

Another week passed following my conversation with Jan, before Rupert appeared.

It was a golden afternoon that day, and I was cutting a few of Dame Jenny's crimson roses for the boy to take to her when he went to Kerrysmoor the next morning. There was a slight breeze rippling the surface of the pool, and a sighing sound stirred the branches of an overhanging willow. Bees buzzed and a blackbird sang from a thorn tree. I was humming under my breath. That fact combined with Nature's murmuring was probably why I didn't at first hear footsteps approaching along the path. The sound didn't properly register until he spoke.

'Josephine – '

I looked round sharply, and he was there, standing only a few yards away. At first I couldn't speak. Surprise, combined with a welling up of sudden joy shocked me to silence. Then I gave a little cry and ran to him. He kissed me. But the kiss was a gentle one. It was as though since our last passionate meeting something had happened that had drained energy and initiative from him. I stood back, studying him anxiously. His face too, appeared drawn. A little of the fire had left his eyes, but tenderness was there – a kind of weary compassion.

'What's wrong?' I asked. 'Is anything the matter?'

'My wife's – ill, as you must have heard or I should have been here earlier.'

'I'm sorry,' I said politely. 'Is her sickness serious?'

'Yes.'

'Are you trying to tell me we shan't – you won't be able to visit me or something?'

He moved towards me again; his touch on my shoulder felt for a brief moment like that of a parent trying to break bad news to a child. Instinctively I pulled myself away, and facing him with my chin raised an inch or two higher, said, 'Please don't try and evade the truth, Rupert. I'm a woman, and quite capable of hearing it. If you regret what happened, you've only got to say. But – '

In an instant his tired calm deserted him, and his arm was round me, while with the other hand he tilted my face up to his. This time his lips were firm and warm on mine. Through my thin dress I could feel the thudding of his heart. Then he released me, and I was thankful to see his countenance flooded with a warmer colour, and that something of the old flame lit his eyes.

'Don't you dare ever speak like that again,' he said sternly, 'or I'll have to spank sense into you. *Regret*! how can there be regret for the best thing that ever happened to me.'

'Then what *is* it?'

'For a time, my love, it's better for both of us that we don't meet too frequently. Only for a time, remember. After that – ' he broke off hesitantly.

'Yes? Afterwards?'

'I think you know,' he replied ambiguously.

'I don't though,' I told him frankly. 'I *thought* I did – at least – perhaps I didn't think much about it – practically. But I *did* believe that in the end we'd be together,' I paused, continuing when he said nothing, 'Will we, Rupert?'

'My love, as soon as possible. In the meantime I'm quite sure you need something more to occupy you than being closeted alone here with only a great dog and occasional visit from Jan for company. So I've contacted my friend Luigi, and he's consented to give you further singing tuition, twice a week for so long as necessary to renew your confidence – '

I gasped.

'*Luigi*? But – I don't think I could. I don't *want* to any more. I simply couldn't face going through the kind of thing that happened at Exeter again. I know my voice is all right, of its kind – for singing at places like the Golden Bird. But not in opera. Truly, Rupert, fame isn't important to me any more. Surely you understand?'

'Yes, I understand what you feel at the moment; but Luigi still has great faith in your potential, so have I. You needn't necessarily make a career of your voice; that will be up to you; but the knowledge of being *able* to should count. Don't you understand, darling?'

I tried to, but it was difficult. Once more my life was in a whirl. From an over-quiet daily routine lit to expectancy each morning that the evening might possibly bring Rupert to my bed, I was suddenly confronted with a period of lessons under the tuition of the strict little Italian to whom I'd already brought disappointment and my own humiliation.

I protested strongly at first to Rupert's plan which meant that each Tuesday and Friday I would be taken to Truro in the chaise as before – and brought back again at a certain hour.

It was no use.

When I objected not only on personal grounds, but pointed out that the treasure room would be left unprotected, which was the primary reason that I'd stayed on following Dame Jenny's departure, he smiled reasoningly and assured me I needn't worry on such grounds. 'Beth Johns, a capable housemaid, will arrive with the chaise on the days of your departure,' he said, 'and be taken back again when you return. She's a sturdy character, quite capable of defending herself, if necessary, and she'll have Brutus don't forget.'

He paused. I was aggrieved, and when I didn't speak, he said, '*Please*, my love. For me.'

I wheeled round with a flurry of skirts and a flame of hot colour in my cheeks.

'Why for *you*? Is it your conscience pricking you or something? Why should my voice be suddenly so important again? Are you *frightened*, Rupert?'

His expression darkened. 'What the devil do you mean?' Both hands enclosed on my arms. I thought at first he was about to shake me, but he didn't.

I stared at him defiantly and answered with a lurch of my heart, 'What I said – *frightened* – of her, your wife? Is *she* at the bottom of this?'

He freed me then, and his voice was cold when he replied, 'That is my business, Josephine. Some things must remain private to me – even from you.'

Misery engulfed me. 'Yes, yes – I'm sorry. Oh, Rupert – '

I turned away. The next moment I felt his mouth brush the nape of my neck at the back. His voice was soft against my ear when he murmured, 'Be patient. I love you. But unless you accept the situation as it is, it's just no good, Josephine. Remember I have other things in my life as well.'

Hope stirred in me.

'You mean the smuggling? But I thought – '

'What you thought is neither here nor there. Just trust me and be co-operative.' He swung me round. 'Is that understood?'

I sighed. 'All right. If you insist. But I can promise you I shan't enjoy it – having to tra-la and solfa before that fussy little man.'

'Oh I don't think it will be too bad,' he said ambiguously, obviously relieved. 'And now, look at me, you witch! and smile, d'you hear?'

I did; I couldn't help it. Against that certain warm look in his strange eyes I seemed to have no defence.

So the issue was settled, and the following week lessons recommenced with Signor Luigi in Truro.

They weren't so onerous as I'd expected. He was unexpectedly pleasant to me, and assured me he'd never lost interest or faith in my voice.

'Your patron though – my good friend, Mr Verne – has

slightly different plans for its promotion,' he said affably, 'or shall we say its use.'

'Oh?'

'Opera, he told me, is not entirely to your fancy, at the moment, so we shall take a lighter approach in training – calculated for a more suitable role such as highly born ladies indulge in, at soireés and in drawing rooms.'

'*Drawing* rooms?' I gasped.

He smiled, stroking his little beard, with a calculating look in his bright eyes. 'You have all the potential it takes to become the rage and toast – the reigning queen of fashionable gatherings,' he stated. 'That is the line we shall follow from now on. Movements and grace will also play an important part. I can assure you when your coaching is completed, no duchess in the land will compare.'

'But I don't *want* to be a duchess, or a – a warbling socialite creature,' I exclaimed rashly. 'I'm not like that. I'm *me* – Josephine Lebrun. Rupert – I mean Mr Verne – is *wrong* in trying to make me into something different. Oh I don't think having lessons again is a good idea at all.'

'Maybe not at the moment,' the little man said acerbically, 'but you *will*. It's what you're here for, and I trust you're not going to be difficult. Under the circumstances such an attitude would be most unfair – to me.'

Realising there was no point in arguing I gave in with as good a grace as possible and decided piquantly that if I was destined to become a drawingroom party-piece and dainty triller of ballads, then I should dress in a manner befitting the character. I would write a note to Rupert telling him my wardrobe needed refurbishing, had I his permission to order a new cloak and bonnet, and if it was not asking too much two new gowns also from the costumier's in Truro, as I did not now care to appear in Signor Luigi's presence dressed in anything but the best. Yes, I would do that, and send the note by Jan, or the coachman. Either Rupert would have to reply, or call in person at Tregonnis to give an answer. The mischievous impulse stimulated and lifted my spirits considerably, and after making the decision I had the note ready for the man to take on the next day when I returned by chaise from Truro.

The following morning Jan was due to call at Kerrysmoor with some farm produce, and I waited hopefully for his return, and a message. It was twelve o'clock before the youth got back.

'The Master sent this for you,' he said, handing me a gilt-edged envelope. 'Tell Miss Lebrun to give et to the place marked in Truro, and everythin' should be all right, he said.'

'Very well, thank you, Jan.'

When he'd gone I looked at the name on the envelope. It was addressed to the most select costumiers in the City, and was unsealed. So obviously I had permission to read what was inside:

> Madam, I should be obliged if you would equip Miss Josephine Lebrun with any select feminine garments she fancies. I am sure your advice would be of great help to her as she is likely to be launched socially at a suitable time in the future. Expense in this case is of no consideration. If you let me know what is owed I will see you have the sum at the nearest possible date.
>
> Yours truly,
> Rupert Verne.

'Launched into society,' I thought. How very ridiculous when at the moment all that Rupert appeared to wish – except for my sessions with Luigi – was to keep me pushed away at Tregonnis. Still, I would certainly take advantage of his offer and acquire the most elegant and flattering gowns in the fashionable establishment – if only for *his* benefit, so that his desire would be intensified and he would be stimulated somehow to decide what future we could have together.

Madame Juliette's salon was situated in the vicinity of Lemon Street. It was richly carpeted, with tall mirrors placed conveniently at every angle for viewing the figure, and curtained wardrobes intriguingly parted to display clothing of a tempting variety – luxurious more than of a utility type. Flowery and be-feathered headgear rested daintily on tall stands; gilt furniture of a French style was arranged so that it allowed a wide space for clients to wander to and fro studying their reflections under cunningly contrived lighting. Tall-stemmed flowers in crystal vases added an exotic, yet delicate, atmosphere and the air was fragrant with subtle perfume. Everything, in fact, induced an expensive sense of luxury that was both stimulating and relaxing.

Feeling free to choose, and mildly mischievous, I wandered about for some time trying this and that, while Madame Juliette obsequiously 'modomed' and flattered me. As time passed a faint irritation sounded in her voice. I wasn't surprised – no high-born lady in the land could have appeared more demanding and critical that the creature I was pretending to be for that intriguing half-hour.

However, at last my choice was made: a deep lilac satin gown, having an over-mantle of olive green velvet trimmed with violet braid; and a cream heavy silk costume consisting of a short-waisted coatee and full skirt gathered from the hips to the back forming the suggestion of a bustle. The hem of the skirt was heavily embroidered in gold thread, and there were tiny gold buttons down the front of the coat. To go with it I discovered a cream boat-shaped hat to be worn saucily tilted forward; it was trimmed with osprey and had chiffon veiling behind.

Then there were accessories of fine kid gloves, and a feather boa – a gilt chain handbag also, and cream boots with pointed toes. Oh, I was very rash, stimulated not only by vanity but a touch of defiance to make Rupert once more aware of my presence in his life. I doubted that he could grudge the expense, although I was sure that her ladyship would, if she ever found out.

Lady Verne!

As usual, whenever the thought of her crossed my mind a vague shadow of resentment fell on me. Rupert might not love her – I was sure he didn't. But she was always there, in the background, his wife, and therefore the one with legal power. There were two of them really who stood as obstacles to my love, I thought that day when I left Madame Juliette's: Lady Alicia, and that girl in the portrait, the elusive beauty whose claim at Tregonnis remained a mystery, and haunted my imagination every time I caught her wistful stare from its heavy frame.

Two days following my second new singing session with Signor Luigi, Rupert called to tell me that my famous tutor was pleased with my voice and my acceptance of his new plans for me. The girl from Kerrysmoor who came for a few hours daily, had already left and I was chagrined that I was not wearing one of my new gowns for his attention.

'You mean *your* new plans,' I corrected him.

'Ah well! let us say *mutual*,' he agreed, smiling. 'You should be pleased – it's a guarantee, isn't it, that I intend our life together to be far closer after certain obstacles have been worked out.' He took my hand, drew me close and embraced me warmly.

'It would be more helpful if you could tell me how – explain just a little,' I pointed out. 'Signor Luigi speaks a lot about drawingrooms and social occasions, but I'm not really a drawingroom kind of person. Is that what *you're* looking for? Someone to entertain at your grand parties warbling away while some stuffy accompanist pounds ballads on a piano. Is that what *she* was – the girl in the portrait?'

The moment the question was out I could have cut my tongue out. Rupert's face darkened. In a strange way it seemed to close up – shutting me out. 'I'm sorry,' I added quickly, 'I didn't mean to – to pry, but – '

'You're too curious by half,' he said shortly, 'and I don't like it. Impertinence, even from you, is extremely distasteful. Remember that in the future, Josephine. When I wish to confide in you I will. Do you understand?'

'Very well,' I said. 'I'm sorry.'

He softened a little. 'Forget it. You're very young still, and have a lot to learn. Maybe – ' he shrugged, ' – we both have. It's so long since – ' He broke off aggravatingly and made to leave. 'Well, I must be off now, I've much to do. Take care of yourself – I felt I had to drop in and tell you how pleased I was about the lessons, and also, by the way, that you'd assembled a new wardrobe in Truro.'

He kissed me before he left. But more gently than usual; it was as though his mind was on other things. A little disappointed I turned away and went through the kitchen into the garden. The clippety-clop of his horse's hooves gradually died away into the distance. I felt alone, and resentful of the secret places in his heart and life that I could not share.

Sunlight was only fitful that day, but towards evening the clouds broke up leaving clear skies lit with dying gold over the moors. My spirits lifted. I would have gone for a stroll, but Jan had taken Brutus for a 'good ole gallop' as he put it, because the dog had been left on his own a good deal lately, and needed 'a bit o' fun like'.

The air was heady with the scents and soft murmurings of summertime. I walked down the garden path to the wilderness covering the passage used by Rupert on the night of his escape from the Revenue. Once more the weeds and briars had crawled across the entrance leaving only a glimmer of darkness through the tangled branches. I returned to the site of Dame Jenny's roses and broke one idly from its stem, holding it to my nose and drawing the sweetness into my lungs. Then I wandered to the pool, thinking dreamily and longingly of the treasured hours when Rupert and I had lain and loved together through that never-to-be-forgotten night.

Frail reflections and shadows of early evening already patterned the surface of the water. A kind of enchantment enfolded me, inducing me to sing in a low tone – a sweet-sad melody in a minor key that I'd heard in far-away childhood. I was aware of no other sound – of no other human being invading the solitude, so my senses froze when a ripple of strange laughter broke the peace. The song died on my lips.

At the same moment, as I started to turn my head, the touch of hands brushed the back of my neck, gradually tightening until I could hardly breathe. At first I didn't attempt to move, sensing that my resistance might mean danger. Then there was a further laugh, deeper this time, holding a subtle obscene triumph. I managed to strain round briefly to catch a glimpse of the intruder. What I saw shocked me – a pale malicious face staring from glassy mad eyes. A trickle of saliva coursed down the long chin from twisted lips.

I was terrified. The grip on my body seemed to have super-human strength.

'Don't move,' whispered a thick harsh voice, while thumbs pressed deeper into my neck. 'Like the other one, aren't you? Trollop – staring down from her great frame. And where did it get her – *where* – ?' The voice became a hiss. 'In the pool. Drowned like a rat.'

I was propelled round and pushed forwards so I thought I must surely tumble in. But the hard arms still held me. Shadows drifted and faded in the cool water. 'There she is – *there*!' the malignant tones continued. 'Watch her eyes where the fish swim. Holes now in an empty skull. And she was his once – his dream. He loved her. *Love*!' Wild laughter momentarily shrieked through the air. 'And she still is. So – leave here you fool – or you'll end up like her and the Three Maidens. The Three Maidens, do you *hear*?' I was shaken wildly and forced to face the creature again.

There was no smile now on the macabre lips. Only hate.

Then suddenly it was as though all force left the wild figure. The arms dropped from my shoulder and neck, and like some grotesque great bird from a nightmare, the shape in its black cloak turned and fled flapping crazily to the lane where it disappeared into the shadow of the trees. I sank on to the ground with my head bowed to ward off faintness. How long I stayed there I don't know. But presently I heard Jan's whistle from the fields followed by the happy barking of a dog. The youth and Brutus appeared minutes later. By then I had got up and was already in the kitchen.

'Why, missie,' the youth said, after one glance at my face, 'Whatever's the matter with ee? Anythin' wrong? You do look frit to death – '

I tried to speak, but it was difficult to be coherent. My throat hurt so. 'Someone – attacked me,' I managed to say at last. 'It was – I don't know – who. You'd better tell the Master – '

'But I can't do that, Miss Jo – I've heard tell he took himself off on business 'bout an hour 'go – Truro or somewhere, maybe Plymouth, I doan' know. But I could get a message to her ladyship – '

I lifted a hand in negation. '*No*.' Even in my own ears my voice was a mere rasp. 'Don't tell her, whatever you do. It's all right – ' I swallowed painfully. 'I've Brutus now. And – and the girl comes in the morning.'

He looked dubious. 'Ef the Master did know he'd get the p'lice mebbe – '

I shook my head. 'It's all over now. With the dog and the doors locked there'll be no danger. I shall – I shall be all right.'

He looked doubtful but in the end agreed. 'S'long as you keep Brutus with ee when th' girl edn' here,' he said. 'It's my fault p'raps f'r leavin' y' alone – although it wasn' f'r long. But if Master Verne knew, I'd get the push from Farmer Carne sure 'nuff.'

I managed to smile.

'Farmer Carne *won't* know,' I promised, 'and neither will Master Verne. You're a good lad, Jan, I wouldn't want to get you into trouble.' He scratched one ear thoughtfully. 'Thank 'ee, Miss. I hope I'm doin' right.'

'I'm sure you are. And it's best not to worry the Master anyway.'

'Yes. That's right. He does have plenty to worry him without any more shoved on him. I'll say goodnight to ee then.' And still shaking his head thoughtfully he left Tregonnis for the farm.

Later I wondered what his reference to Rupert's worries meant. But I was still too bewildered and upset to think clearly. I had Brutus sleeping by my bed that night, with the pistol on my side table, but it was a long time before I got any rest. I recalled the harsh voice's reference to 'the Three Maidens', and to the girl in the portrait, and when at last I slept my dreams were of a witch-like face glaring down on me, and of a fair face upturned – a floating image in the pool – the face of the girl in the portrait.

When I woke in the morning my neck was still swollen. The next day I was due for my lesson with Signor Luigi, but I knew there would be no point in going to Truro. Although I could speak, somewhat gruffly, I couldn't sing. When I tried nothing came from my throat but a rasping cough. My voice had gone. How permanently I didn't know. It was a terrible feeling thinking I might never sing again.

IX

For the next few days following the assault my neck was still swollen, and dark bruises showed at the throat. None of my dresses could be buttoned near the chin, so I swathed chiffon round the neck to hide the marks, fastened with a cameo brooch. The effect was not perfect, but to any casual observer would give, hopefully, no sign of injury. To the daily girl I simply made excuses of having caught 'some kind of a cold in my throat' and Jan did not give me away. When the chaise arrived to take me to Truro I asked the man if he would be kind enough to drive there and inform the maestro that I was unwell and not likely to be able to attend the theatre for a little while. At the same time I concocted an excuse for needing cough mixture from the apothecary's and told the man I'd be grateful if the mixture could be picked up and delivered to me at Tregonnis.

The coachman was dubious at first, but when I asked if Mr Verne was back at Kerrysmoor, if so I was sure he would give permission, I was told no, the Master was still away, having had to take a trip to Plymouth.

'And her ladyship?' I questioned, although the girl had already informed me she was in a mood.

He shook his head. 'She still isn't well, Miss.'

'Then *please* – my voice is so rough, and I can hardly swallow – '

Eventually the man agreed.

When the sound of horses' hooves and wheels rattling down the road had died away, I went back into the house, miserably wondering if the Plymouth business had anything to do with Rupert's contraband interests. Even with the girl and Brutus for company I was miserable and on edge, and still very shocked. At night I locked and bolted the doors early, and left Brutus free to roam the cottage – except for the Treasure Room, for fear his animal presence might dislodge any precious relic.

I slept badly; but one evening, about five days following the attack at the pool I was so exhausted I went upstairs early, and immediately on getting into bed fell into a heavy sleep.

It must have been about two o'clock when I woke suddenly, disturbed by a sound below – a crashing noise followed by a tinkle and several short bangs. I felt my whole body go rigid except for the wild thumping of my heart. For some moments I lay unmoving, waiting for Brutus's heavy snarl and growling.

There was nothing.

Everything, after a matter of only minutes, was completely deadly quiet. Had I been dreaming, I asked myself, and woken from some nightmare? Or was I perhaps no longer completely sane and balanced following my frightening experience? I knew somehow I had to pull myself together and venture downstairs to find out what had happened, and if Brutus was all right. So I pulled on a wrap and slippers, crept out of the bedroom and tip-toed to the top of the stairs. I paused, then, listening.

'Brutus,' I called in a croaky whisper, ' – Brutus, Brutus –'

There was no response.

Cautiously I went down.

The dog was lying completely still, as though unconscious or dead, near the front door; there was blood and a small amount of red meat lying nearby, and the pane of a small side window had been carefully cut away. I caught my breath with horror and rushed to the dog's side. He was still breathing, and appeared not to have been hurt, but a curious smell came from the meat. Obviously he had been poisoned in some way, or drugged.

Jan, I thought, I must get Jan. But at such an hour it would mean walking a distance to the farm and then rousing the whole household. In the meantime further vandalism might occur. I was still wondering what to do, when the animal stirred; one eye opened, then another. There was a feeble wag of the tail, and with relief I realised the dog was recovering. It was then I noticed the door of the Treasure Room. The lock had been somehow forced, and it was half open. Holding my candle shakily, I went in.

Glass lay shattered everywhere about the floor, with one or two figurines; but that was all. Torn from its frame and ripped into several pieces was the portrait of the girl. The lovely limpid eyes stared up at me through the wan flickering light. Her head was severed from the body at the throat, and by it was a piece of cardboard on which, scrawled in wild zig-zaggy writing, were the words: 'THE THREE MAIDENS. Now there are *Four*'.

A fit of trembling shook me from head to foot. Whoever had committed the destruction could be no other, I was sure, than the mad creature who'd assaulted me in the garden. But why? And *how* had Brutus been kept quiet then drugged, while the break-in was made? He was a trained guard, only obeying a well-known voice. Then it must be someone at Kerrysmoor. And that someone must be Lady Verne! Was it possible? She disliked me, yes. But she was ill, bedridden, and the malicious damage had been directed more towards the portrait than myself – except for the garden episode, and I certainly had not recognised her ladyship in the attacker.

Somehow I got through the morning. The loneliness was frightening – intense, and Jan did not call at the usual hour to take the dog for his walk. No one came – no one, until early in the afternoon when a handy-man from Kerrysmoor arrived on a horse with a message to say the girl who usually helped at Tregonnis on certain days was unavailable, and that under the circumstances, Master Verne thought it better for me to go to Truro for a few days. A room had been booked for me at The Crown coaching house, he'd be in touch with me sometime, there. The chaise would pick me up at four o'clock.

'I don't understand,' I said in my rusty voice. 'I have a cold in my throat, and – and why must I leave here so quickly? – Who'll look after the cottage?' My objection of course was quite stupid. I should have been grateful for the chance of avoiding another night alone at Tregonnis.

'That'll be all looked after, Miss,' the man said. 'There's a note here from Mr Verne. He's got back not long since. Perhaps you'd better read it.'

I took the envelope from him and tore it open:

> Josephine, please do what I wish – pack a few things and be ready for the chaise to pick you up by four. Things are happening here which are exceedingly unpleasant. I have sent instructions to The Crown to see that you are comfortably accommodated. I shall see you as soon as possible. When that will be I cannot say. Until then, yours as ever, Rupert.

I looked up at the man, bewildered, shocked, and taken aback by the brevity of the note which seemed to imply great anxiety on his part to get me out of the way – or was it out of his life?

'Why didn't Mr Verne come himself?' I asked. 'And does he – do *any* of you up at Kerrysmoor know what's been happening *here*? But of course not. How could you – ?' I broke off coughing.

We were standing at the gate of the garden. The man was holding his horse by the bridle, and the animal whinnied shrilly, as though sensing my distress.

'Is something wrong, Miss?'

I gave the semblance of a laugh, a derisive gruff sound.

'You'd better come and have a look.'

He tethered his mount to a sycamore, and followed me up the path into the house.

'Sakes almighty,' he exclaimed, 'how did this happen?'

'Last night – about two o'clock,' I explained. 'I was in bed and was woken up by a sound. No – not Brutus. *He* was – he must have been drugged. I came downstairs and found – *this*.'

The man simply gaped, patting the dog's head idly, as it gazed up at him mournfully, wagging his tail in a lazy way. 'He seems all right now,' he said at length. 'And that's something.'

'Oh yes, Brutus will soon be his old self I'm sure. But don't you think you should inform your Master what has occurred as soon as possible and have investigations started? The vet too. The vet should have a look at Brutus.'

'Yes, yes. Of course. I'll begone, and you may be sure someone'll be around – the police most likely to take charge of things. I can tell Master Verne you'll be ready then to go to Truro as he said?'

I nodded bleakly, and without further ado the man left kicking his mount to a swift pace down the lane, towards the main road.

In a daze I went upstairs to my bedroom and began mechanically to pack my small valise, feeling in an unreal dream that had the quality of an unending nightmare. I put a cape and bonnet ready on the bed, and when I looked at the clock saw I had an hour and a half to wait. But before then, I told myself, someone would arrive – Rupert? Oh surely, Rupert himself must come when he learned what a terrifying experience I'd been through.

Waiting can be agonising. From time to time I wandered through the cottage aimlessly, tidying this and that, talking to Brutus who seemed content to rest in the hall – thinking as each quarter of an hour passed, 'Why doesn't he come, or at least send *someone*? A fast horse has had plenty of time – ? Suppose some lurking madman or murderer appears again suddenly? All I have is Brutus who's still shocked, and the gun – the pistol. Where is it?' I searched my mind wildly for a moment, then remembered it was in a drawer in my bedroom. I went upstairs again, found it, and put it in a pocket of my gown. Then I returned to the parlour.

When, at half past three still no one had arrived, nervous exhaustion drove me to a quick decision. I would wait no longer. I *couldn't*. If Rupert cared for me at all – and I'd believed in him so deeply, so truly – he'd somehow have contrived to rescue me before this from Tregonnis, which had now become no more than a sinister prison. But he didn't love me. He never had – not sufficiently anyway. Whatever it was that was keeping us apart at such a dangerous time – whether some smuggling business, or her ladyship's 'megrims' (what a word, I thought contemptuously) any feeling he had for me was of merely secondary consideration to him. And I knew I could no longer bear it. I didn't want his charity, his help, or being pushed about from one place to another without any explanation, just because it suited him. I didn't want any drive to Truro in his rich chaise just to be closeted in some stuffy hostelry at his command. If I hadn't a real place in his heart, I wanted nothing of him at all. For a time he'd desired me – and managed to win me. But now it seemed it was over; he was being devious and polite, and maybe in his way trying to fit me into some kind of mutual future. On the other hand, perhaps not.

Either way it didn't matter. I was weary of fretting, and hoping and fighting the long terrifying hours without him.

I would make a clean break. I could still do it – I was young and strong, and one day, surely, when the bruises in my neck faded and healed, my voice would return. So I'd leave on my own and somehow make my way back to Falmouth. Taking a route along the coastal lanes below the moors I could be there, walking, in a matter of two days, perhaps even less. Furthermore, if I hurried, I could catch a private waggon that drove part of the way, leaving Tharne each evening at four-thirty. So I'd hurry, and start off immediately for the village before Rupert's chaise arrived.

Once my plan was made I allowed no other consideration to change it. The past was over and a new period in my life beginning. I must somehow forget Rupert – or at least blot him from my mind.

In this hard determined mood it was that some time later I was ensconced in Mr Jago's private waggon, with five other passengers jolting along the road southwards towards Falmouth. After numerous stopping places I left the vehicle at Penhallow and from there started walking cross country, avoiding Redlake, in the direction of my home town.

*

The air was sweet with the tang of heather, thyme, gorse, and a salty mild wind blown from the sea. I wore my lightest boots, and loosened my cape at the neck. Gulls occasionally wheeled overhead, and everywhere were the low rustling sounds of Nature's creatures about their secret ways.

Sometimes I left the lanes for farm footpaths, but mostly I kept to narrow roadways used from hamlet to hamlet, and frequented I supposed chiefly by gypsies, pedlars, or wanderers like myself wishing to avoid attention. As I had money in my reticule it was easy enough to call at a wayside tavern or cottage and find temporary resting place and something to eat. Directions of route were willingly provided, 'always bear left now,' I was told at one small kiddleywink, 'keepin' that theer old mine Wheal Flower on th' right. An' kip thy face an' gold hid, case some lurkin' vag'bond spies 'ee.'

I took the advice for some part of the way after leaving, but as the lane climbed upwards and vegetation became more sparse giving a clear view on every side, I removed the hood of my cape from my face, and let the fresh air brush my cheeks and loosen my hair. A pedlar passed driving a cart pulled by an old donkey; pots and pans rattled, together with the sound of creaking cart wheels. The man was a wizened, puckish-looking fellow, with a blue feather in his hat. The vehicle was loaded with a conglomeration of goods – bottles of lotions, ribbons, winking glass beads, cutlery, household goods, and haberdashery of all sorts, mostly secondhand, I guessed. He drew up the cart and introduced himself as Barnaby Goine.

'Give 'ee a lift, missus?' he asked with a lopsided grin showing a single broken tooth. 'Or wantin' a pretty ring are 'ee? – or mebbee a ribbon for thy pretty hair?'

I declined the offer of a lift, there appeared to be no room anyway, but bought a glass bauble I didn't want just to show goodwill, and presently with a word in the old nag's ear he was away again, and I continued walking, keeping always slightly to my left.

The sky began to fade into twilight and bringing a greenish glow to the landscape. As the stark dark shape of Wheal Flower faded ever further behind me, I began to feel tired. How many miles I'd walked since leaving Mr Jago's waggon, I didn't know. But at last, to my relief, from a high point of the lane I saw far ahead of me and below, the darkening silhouettes of buildings against the paler glimmer of sea, and knew I was approaching Falmouth.

I arrived, heavy-limbed from carrying my valise, about an hour later. Lights dotted the streets and waterside, and a lump of emotion seized me, whether for good or ill, no one could say.

I had come home.

Wearily I threaded my way down narrow cobbled byways leading to the harbour. I must have looked a sight indeed, when I reached The Golden Bird. But the landlord, astounded at first, welcomed me.

'So it's you,' he said, as I tried vainly to adjust my bonnet, 'Come in, my dear, come in. This place hasn't been the same since you left.' He took my case, and shouted for his wife. 'She's back, luv, our nightingale's back with us.'

He didn't know then that I couldn't sing.

X

Joe Burns and his wife, Maria, were heavily disappointed when I had to admit to them then my voice had gone. I invented a story that I'd been involved in a carriage accident, hence the scars on my neck, but that shock as well contributed to my sorry state. News travels quickly, and I didn't wish Rupert to hear in some roundabout way what had happened, or even, at the moment, of my whereabouts.

'I shall recover in time, I'm sure,' I told them, with more optimism than I felt. 'In the meantime, if I can stay here for a bit, I'd be very grateful. I have money. I can pay – '

'There's no need for payment – ' Joe said quickly, but his wife interrupted, 'Now wait a bit, Joe. If Josie's got it to spare – only a *very* little mind you, just a token as they say – she'd probably rather. She was always the independent sort, weren't you, love?'

'Yes,' I agreed honestly. 'I would rather give something.'

'Only until it's convenient to you then,' Joe agreed grudgingly, 'and when you c'n sing again the boot'll be on the other foot. There'll be a good salary coming along.'

So a minimum weekly sum was arranged. I had sufficient in my pocket to cover at least a month, or two. And when that was gone? If my voice never properly came back again? The thought was frightening. I knew the Burnses would never turn me adrift, but I wanted to feel secure in some way, to depend entirely on *no*-one – neither Joe, Maria, nor – Rupert.

Should I ever see him again? If he really wanted to find me would he recall the Golden Bird and walk in one night as he had the first time I ever saw him, tall hat in hand, his yellow eyes searching through the crowds and lamplight for a sight of me? I was pondering the question to myself when Maria put a suggestion to me one evening.

'You haven't told us the whole story, have you, girl?' she asked. 'About your singing, and what happened between you and that fine gentleman, Mr Verne – '

'I – '

She lifted a hand. 'No. I don't want to pry, but it seems to me not natural you should just be staying in the background all the time, or taking a walk round the streets when there's life here you could enjoy. After all singing isn't everything. You've still got your looks, and your legs is all right, aren't they?'

I gave a short laugh.

'My legs? Why – yes, I suppose so. They weren't broken or anything. But what makes you ask?'

She shrugged.

'You c'n dance as well as sing. There's a man, Johnny Bliss, that comes here every night now. Plays the fiddle real good. A smart one, Johnny. Been on the sea and lost a leg in a shindig with pirates. He'd play for you an' make a handsome turn of it. Why don't you try, girl? You're fretting 'bout something, and that's no good for the young. Joe'd pay you too, an' don't say you carry the wealth o' the world in your pocket. You dropped your reticule in the bedroom the other afternoon when you went wandering, and it'd spilled over the floor. I picked it up for 'ee. Not much there, Josie – well, you just think about it.'

I did, and although the prospect didn't appeal to me at first, after my first negative reaction I began to see possibilities. Perhaps at the back of my mind, too, was the sneaking idea that such a plan might enable Rupert and me to meet again.

'But I've no dancing clothes with me now,' I told Maria when she next broached the matter. 'I've only the clothes I came in, a few undergarments and a spare dress – it's much too sophisticated.'

'H'm. Yes. You're certainly quite a young madam to look at these days,' Maria said thoughtfully. 'But I've a Japanese shawl tucked away upstairs, and when you went there were slippers left behind, and a flowery skirt. They earrings, and a few flash beads – oh, we could fit you up all right.'

Eventually I agreed, and when I tried the bright garments on the following afternoon a little of the lost magic of former days returned. I longed and longed to sing as well as pirouetting only to Johnny Bliss's fiddle, but my voice, though clear enough by then for talking, was just a harsh croak when I attempted any melody. I found Johnny amusing. He was a wiry ginger-haired little man, half Cornish, half Irish, with a whimsical one-sided smile, and bright eyes filled with mischievous humour.

An hour before the bar opened we had, as he called it, 'a try-out', and for the first time in months I felt an uplift of spirits. There was no command to move gracefully or with dignity – no sharp reminder that I must control myself as befitting the part I was playing – no – 'Now return and make your entrance again' as there'd been time after time at Signor Luigi's. I was free – *free* to sway and gesture and kick my heels uninhibited by restrictions or etiquette. With my hair loose, and to Johnny's winks and elfin manner of playing and half dancing, I could be for however brief a time, myself. And it was invigorating.

Joe and Maria watching the rehearsal, were delighted. 'You must come on tonight, girl,' Joe said. 'Word will soon get around then. We'll be the best known tavern in all Falmouth.'

And so it was.

Keeping my thoughts firmly away from Rupert or Tregonnis, I was able to put all my conscious capacity for life and enjoyment into dancing. I became, as days passed, a popular feature at the inn, and by degrees even the lingering hope and possibility that Rupert might appear one night, died into a mere shadow.

Then, one evening, at the very end of the performance I

felt suddenly faint. No one noticed – not even Maria, who was helping Joe at the bar. I managed to retire after blowing a kiss to the blurred faces crowding the tap room, and somehow made my way upstairs. Once there I lay on my bed and waited for the unpleasant feeling to pass. My face and hands were dripping by then with cold sweat, and there was a sickening pain under the pressure of my corsets. Presently I felt better, but by then a suspicion was growing in my mind that I'd never even considered before.

Suppose I was with child?

Could it possibly be? But of course it could. When two people loved – or *had* loved as Rupert and I had – any sensible person would know better than to be shocked by the suggestion.

Elation, mingled with fear and a sense of unreality seized me. I couldn't visualise the future. I didn't try.

But that night I had a dream.

I was standing on a lonely hill – black as a moonless night under a cold sky. There was no wind, no sound at all; the air was icy cold – the ground hard and lifeless like that of a dead land. I tried to move, but at first my limbs were fixed and motionless; then slowly my head lifted, and the summit of the hill clarified into the shapes of three grotesque hooded figures, who slowly, menacingly, dragged themselves from the earth towards me.

Magnetised by horror, my unwilling feet moved upwards. Black arms, like the wings of great crows reached to the sky, then slowly, rhythmically descended, gaunt clawlike hands gropingly thrust to my neck. I caught a glimpse of hungry ravaged faces with twisted lips – teeth bared, approaching in a strange haunted rhythm. And in a flash recognition swept through me in blinding terror.

Lady Verne! – Lady Verne!

For a second I was rooted again to the foul earth. It seemed as though my feet were sucked into a sickening mire of evil. Then, suddenly, sight failed. I tottered backwards and fell – fell into the well of darkness swirling round me in a suffocating cloud.

I screamed then, screamed and screamed, until no longer even sound registered. I knew no more until I woke up, bathed in perspiration, with my heart pounding heavily against my ribs, and my whole body shaking.

As surroundings of my room at the inn came into focus, the door opened and Maria entered, her face full of concern in the flickering light of the candle.

'Sakes alive!' she exclaimed. 'Whatever's the matter, girl? Enough to waken the dead it was – that *noise*! – thought you were being murdered for sure. What was it, girl? What's the matter?' She bent down, studying me anxiously.

'I had a nightmare,' I answered. 'A dream. It was awful. I'm so sorry.'

She went to the ewer, poured some water into the basin, and returned with a cloth to wipe my forehead. 'There, there,' she murmured soothingly, 'You'll be all right presently. Just take it easy. Something you had to eat, maybe?'

I shook my head. 'It was the Three Maidens and her – her. It was – ' I broke off, knowing the fear was still on me, and that in any case Maria wouldn't know what I was talking about – I hardly knew myself.

'Three maidens? Who are they then? Now you tell me what it's all about. Seems to me you've bin seein' strange sights since you went off with that fine gentleman. I never did approve of it in the first place, and I said so to Joe. *Italians*!' she gave a sceptical short laugh. 'You wasn' bred for furriners and their carryings on, girl. Now you just rest quiet, and there'll be no more dancing, and remembering wicked goings on. If you're no better later I'll have the apothecary to see you.'

My head ached badly all day, and when night came I had a fever. Dr Prynne, Solomon Prynne, who was not only regarded as a fine medical man, but a clever 'wizard' as well, came to examine me and provided some pills and herbal remedies which he said would be of great assistance in easing the pain.

'Then, later, we shall have to see,' he said, rubbing his chin thoughtfully, and I started to laugh, thinking how much like a goat he looked, with his wispy beard and tufts of hair sticking upwards on either side of his wide forehead.

Maria looked at me aghast. 'It isn't funny, Josie,' she said. 'Dr Prynne's doing his best to help you. What the joke is I cannot for the life of me see.'

'No – no,' I apologised weakly. 'I'm sorry.'

The 'goat' patted my hand reassuringly, took a small glass from his case, poured something into it from a bottle, and bid me take it. I swallowed it chokingly, not caring at the moment what it did to me – whether I lived or died seemed suddenly quite unimportant.

Minutes later the two of them walked quietly from the room, Dr Prynne's boots making a squeaky creaking sound, just like the whinnying of the goat he so resembled.

On such a thought my senses began to relax, taking fear with it, until I drifted into peaceful slumber.

How long I slept I didn't realise. At times I roused, and recalled being fed from a spoon and given more of the pills and draught. Days must have passed in this semi-conscious state, or maybe weeks, I had no manner of judging. But one morning, magically, I felt better.

I remembered everything. Not all at once, but piece by piece, putting facts together like the pieces of a puzzle.

'How long have I been ill?' I asked Maria when she came in with my morning gruel.

'A week or two, but you're better now. Oh how pleased Joe will be too. It's been worrying for us, girl. But Dr Prynne – he said you'd be all right in the end. Some sort of shock, he said, and then that strange fever following! Later you'll have to tell us properly what's been happening. It's only fair, love.'

'Yes. Yes, I know. But – '

'Not yet. Oh, there's no hurry. You just take things easy and do a bit each day – not much mind you, but – '

'I've got money,' I said, as I'd told her before. 'Not a lot,

I suppose, perhaps not sufficient to repay what you've done for me. But I can work, can't I? – I could help in the tap-room perhaps – the bar; if I don't – '

'Tut-tut!' she exclaimed, 'no more silly talk. You're our nightingale – our own Golden Bird whether you c'n sing or not. Tomorrow's tomorrow, remember, and today's today. So we'll remember that shall we, and just get on with the present.'

And that is just what we did. By the time I'd recovered sufficiently to take proper walks about the harbour and help Joe and Maria run the inn, autumn was already turning the leaves of the trees to yellow, and evenings closed in bringing salty grey mists from the sea. I neither saw nor heard anything of Rupert, but one day, overcome by the sudden nauseous feeling for no reason whatever – or so I thought – a very tangible fact registered that was bound to affect my whole life.

What I'd guessed before was true.

I was going to have a child.

*

For two months I waited, saying nothing to anyone about my condition, being careful to hide any fits of nausea I felt, and not worrying unduly about the future; indeed, a strange kind of placidity enveloped me. Whatever trials, challenges, and maybe disappointment in life awaited me, at least my love for Rupert had not been entirely in vain; something of him already thrived within me – something no one could take away. Even my sleep became comparatively peaceful. Following the horror of the dreadful nightmare the scene changed. In my dreams I wandered through an unreal but generally pleasant vista of meadowlands and ethereal waving grasses, with a young boy, a child, holding my hand. When I woke I never recalled his face clearly, and seldom felt any fear or real anxiety, although just occasionally a sadness lingered, like the sadness of trying to recapture an old forgotten tune.

'That rich Mr Verne you used to know – ' Joe said to me one day, 'they say he's not there any more – '

My heart jerked for a second, stood still, and then raced on again. 'Gone away, do you mean?' I asked.

'Not exactly. But I've heard tell he goes up country a lot. Funny though – he called the other day – '

'Here? At the Golden Bird?' I gasped.

'That's right,' Joe answered, polishing a glass and not looking at me.

'But why didn't you say?'

'I wasn't here,' Joe told me with a shrug. 'Neither was Maria – she'd gone out to the market. It was that new boy we have who took the message.'

'For me?'

'He *asked* for you. According to the lad – what he said was – did a young lady called Miss Brown or something or other live here – one who sang and danced at nights?' and the boy said no, he hadn't heard o' one, there was only a guest, he said, a rich lookin' lady with a deep voice, not a singin' one at all. An' he doubted she could dance. She was kind o' proud, an' a bit buxom-like. He'd not heard her name, he said. Well, it was true, wasn't it?' Joe looked up and eyed me quizzically. 'You never *do* sing now, and you don't converse much either, and the lad'd only bin here two days.'

'I can't sing,' I said. 'My throat's still a bit raw. But I wish you'd told me before, Joe. How long ago was it?'

'A week or so,' he said. 'I didn't think it was that important. *Is* it?'

'It could be,' I replied evasively. 'It could be something to do with Signor Luigi, I suppose.'

'Oh. That Italiano. But he don't matter to you any more does he?'

'If – when – when I *do* recover properly,' I said, 'and I shall, I'm sure I shall – '

'Then you'll be here with *us*, won't you? Isn't that what was arranged? Once you was better you said, you'd be part of the Golden Bird like 'twas in the past.'

'Yes,' I said, feeling suddenly miserable. 'Of course.'

The matter was dropped there outwardly, but I knew the time was coming for a change. Either I had to tell Maria about the baby, or find a future somewhere else. But where? And what would I do? Somehow I had to make a living. 'Oh Rupert,' I thought, 'why didn't you stay here longer? Why didn't you wait to see Joe or Maria? And where are you? Why did you have to go away?'

The string of questions rang through my brain ceaselessly. But it was not until a week later that I found courage to face Maria with the truth.

'I have to leave, Maria dear,' I told her one evening before the taproom opened. 'Oh, I'm so sorry. I know I can never properly repay you for all you've done for me, but – I have to find Mr Verne.'

She stared at me for seconds before making any comment. I could feel her gaze searching my face. Then she said, 'I see. So it's him.'

'Him? What do you mean?'

'You know very well. Part of you's been with us since you landed here those months' ago, but not your heart, girl. Oh, you're fond of us, but being fond's a different kind o' thing to loving. And I reckon you love that rich gentleman, for all he's left you wantin' and longin'.'

'No, he didn't leave me. I left him,' I stated flatly. 'Because he didn't need me enough, and because of his wife. She hated me, and things happened that weren't – good. Strange, dreadful things. I think she was at the back of them all.'

Maria sighed.

'Then for heaven's sake why d'you want to return? 'Specially when he probably isn't there. I've told you what the lad said, how he was always taking off up country. What's the sense of going back then? You tell me that.'

'There isn't always sense in loving, I suppose,' I admitted, feeling the old knot of pain at my heart. 'It just happens and once it's there, there's no way of stopping it. You go on, and on, and try to think the world's the same place, but it isn't – it never could be. These few months I've tried to harden myself against it, I have *tried*. But, Maria, what's the point when – when – ' I stumbled over my words, hesitated, while she questioned, 'Go on, when what, girl?'

'When I'm going to have a baby,' I blurted out.

There was a long pause; my heart steadied gradually, relief at telling her made me suddenly more relaxed and content. When I looked at her face she was shaking her head, astonishment slowly giving place to acceptance of news that was distasteful to her.

'So that's it,' she said at last. 'The reason for it all – your silences and dizzy spells. I might've known.'

'No, how could you? You didn't expect it of me. Neither did I – I was always so – well, prim with the men, wasn't I, during the time I sang for you? But this is different, Maria,' I touched her hand tentatively. 'It's true, and real, and I couldn't fight against it – I *wouldn't* have anyway. From the first moment I saw him it started. How can I explain? I just can't. It was just – '

'A middle-aged man with gold in his pocket putting a spell on an innocent girl,' Maria interrupted tartly. 'Oh, I know the sort. But I wouldn't have expected it of him – not of Mr Verne.'

'You don't know him. And it wasn't like that at all. Rather the other way round. I don't expect you to understand. But please *try*.'

Maria clasped her hands over her ample breasts. 'I don't know what Joe'll say. He'll be shocked, 'specially as he has a weak spot for you and expected you'd carry on here later as you did before.'

'Perhaps I will – later, when everything's over, the baby, I mean,' I told her. 'If you'll have me, that is. It all depends on Rupert. But you see now, don't you, why I have to go?'

'*No*. You could have the child here. This is a decent tavern. The child'd have a good home. There'd be no stintin' or scrapin'. – Whether you sang or not, you'd be good for the Golden Bird; you could help – '

'Not if Rupert wants me,' I said firmly.

'But, Josie, just get things straight in that muddle head o' yours. As you said yourself, he's married. His wife's sick and difficult – what d'you think your appearing in your state is going to do for him? Tell me that. Expect a welcome, do you? Then it's high time you had another think.'

But I was beyond thinking.

'I must go to Rupert,' I said. 'There are things I have to find out, and explain. I have to know what's been happening to him. I *have* to.'

'And *where* will you go? That there cottage of his? Or Kerrysmoor itself?' Her voice had become hard, bitter.

'No, I shall go to Truro first, The Crown where Rupert meant me to be when I left Tregonnis. They'll help me there, I'm sure they will, and I shall at least have news. There's Signor Luigi, too. He's sure to have knowledge of Rupert's affairs and whereabouts.'

At last, after further argument and protestations, Maria had to accept my decision. When Joe heard later, he was saddened rather than shocked; his attitude was more reasonable than Maria's, perhaps because men in certain circumstances have the aptitude for seeing things in a different light.

It was arranged, therefore, that I should take the postchaise from Falmouth for Truro the following week, on the understanding that if matters were unsatisfactory and didn't work out for me I would return immediately to the Golden Bird. Oh, they were good folk, and insisted on returning most of the payment I'd forced on them to help pay for my board at the inn.

'You take it,' Joe said, forcing a wallet into my hand when I was about to start off for the square where the chaise waited. 'You'll need it sure enough, in that fancy place. Put it in your valise now, an' don't let any pryin' Johnny know you've got it. Funny folk travels about nowadays.'

Gratitude almost brought tears to my eyes. I felt

momentarily guilty at abandoning the two people who'd grown to care for me almost as a daughter during the time I was with them.

Was I doing the wise thing? I didn't know, or really care. Ten minutes' later, to the clatter of wheels and hollow sound of horses' hooves, only one thought registered in my mind. I had started on the journey that in one way or another must bring me news of Rupert Verne.

XI

Although quite a time had passed since Rupert had written the note ensuring his responsibility for me at the inn, the landlord received me politely, and I was given a pleasant but old-fashioned bedroom, looking over a kind of courtyard bordered by a granite wall and a few almost leafless trees. There was a framed oleograph of General Gordon hanging on one wall, and a picture depicting Queen Victoria's coronation on another. Two angels escorting a little child in a nightgown to Heaven hung immediately over the heavy oak four-poster bed. The furniture was dark mahogony, and a smell of camphor mingled with the faint tang of malt permeated the air. The china ewer and basin on the washstand were patterned with pink roses, and the curtains were heavy crimson plush, on each side of a blind that rattled when pulled by a cord.

A framed religious text stood on the chest of drawers; I had no doubt that it was considered a privilege to occupy such a room, but a weary sense of depression fell on me. I felt smothered at first, with an almost hysterical urge to escape and somehow find transport to Tregonnis immediately.

But I managed to curb my impatience and to eat the ample evening meal provided of roast beef, vegetables, and apple pie.

I didn't think I'd manage to sleep well in the stuffy surroundings, but I did, I was too exhausted to keep awake, and in the morning after a good breakfast of gruel and boiled ham, I made enquiries about Signor Luigi.

'Luigi?' the manageress asked me, arching her heavy

black brows over a hawk-like nose. 'You meant the proud little Italiano? – the music teacher?'

'Yes. I have to contact him.'

She was a stout woman with her dark hair piled high over a plump pink face. Gold rings dangled from her ears, jet beads and locket decorated her large bosom.

'He is a friend of Mr Verne's,' I explained, 'and was giving me singing lessons until – well, until my throat became bad – I had a fever you see, and had to stop them. But it's important I contact him now. Which is the quickest way to his home? I feel like walking, and – '

'Oh, but you won't find him there now,' the plump woman stated very definitely, 'He's gone.'

'*Gone?*'

She shrugged. There was something Spanish about her, nonchalant and slightly contemptuous, as though a famous maestro was of no consequence to the clientele of the hostelry.

'That's what I said,' she told me. 'You never know when those foreigners are likely to take off. He'll be back, of course, sometime; he often does it in the winter – prefers a bit of sun on the continent to the cold here. I don't blame him, being a free man, *if* he is. But then you never know, do you? He could have a wife or a woman tucked away in Italy.' She paused, eyeing me shrewdly, 'Was your business important with him, Miss – Miss – ?'

'Lebrun,' I answered. 'Josephine Lebrun.'

'Ah yes. I remember now.' She folded her arms and regarded me knowingly.

'And my business wasn't important,' I added, before she could get another question in. 'Not with Signor Luigi. The person I really have to contact is my – my – ' I searched for the right word and miraculously found it ' – my sponsor, whose name you have, Mr Verne. First of all, though, before going to Kerrysmoor, I have to call at Tregonnis.'

Her jaw dropped. 'Isn't that the place, the cottage where – where that dreadful thing happened?'

'What dreadful thing?' I asked sharply. 'What do you mean? What's happened?'

Her mouth tightened into a small button.

'Ah. That's what we'd all like to know. But if you go there you'll certainly have a shock, Miss – Miss Lebrun. As for Mr Verne – it's hardly likely you'll find him at Kerrysmoor. Not at the moment.'

'But *why*? You *must* explain.'

'Pardon me!' she said in ridiculously haughty tones. 'There's no must about it. I gave my solemn word to Master Verne to keep my mouth shut about things going on in that bad place – we all have. All of us here. Of course, there are all manners of rumours spreading, some may be true, some not. But if you take my advice you'll stay here for a time until Mr Verne makes it his business to contact you. When you didn't turn up before he was very put out, and called here twice. It was, if I may say so, a little thoughtless of you to go wandering about when you were under his protection. Still, that's not my affair. I have collateral, and assurances from him that any expenses incurred by you will be amply repaid. You are, in a way, under our protection. I hope you get my meaning, Miss Lebrun.'

Yes, I got her meaning, and I had not the slightest intention of complying with it.

At the first opportunity I decided to sneak out of the Crown and somehow make my way to Tregonnis.

The opportunity arrived that same afternoon. A November mist hung heavily over the streets of Truro, and with my valise packed, and wearing my brown cape over the warmest and most inconspicuous gown I had with me, I made my way softly down the stairs, tip-toed past the parlour where the landlady was having her beverage of tea, laced, I guessed, with something stronger.

A wave of foggy air greeted me as I stepped into the street. Any traffic there was, crawled. Figures were mere blurred shapes passing by. This was all to my advantage. No one would be likely to notice the indeterminate figure of a woman passing with chin sunk into dark clothing, just one chilly pedestrian among others making her way to some vague destination. I walked aimlessly for a time, simply taking any corner that appeared unexpectedly willy-nilly, uncaring of where it led. At one point I tried to hail a cab, but the jarvy was huddled into his coat and passed unheedingly, which perhaps was as well. I was getting short of funds, and realised that I'd probably need all I'd got for cheaper transport covering a longer distance. Tregonnis was a considerable distance from Truro – a fact that I'd not properly considered before.

At last I came to the outskirts of the city. The lights that had feebly illuminated the streets before, had flickered out one by one. All now was hushed and grey, and dark. Hedges, the occasional distorted shape of a building or shed came into looming blurred visibility then faded again, taken into coils of thick vapour. A damp river smell crept from low land to the road, and I had a brief glimpse of what could have been water lying beyond a clump of bushes. The next moment it had gone. I walked on mechanically for some way, chilled and a little frightened, knowing I had behaved unreasonably. It would have been wiser to have waited until the morning when the fog might have cleared. How would I reach Tregonnis in such weather? How would I find shelter of any kind to help me on my way?

I was debating whether to turn and somehow find my way back to the Crown when a beam of reddish light straggled through the mist some distance ahead of me. As I drew closer I realised it filtered from somewhere round a bend in the roadway, carrying with it a distant malty smell characteristic of a tavern or kiddleywink. Relief filled me. An inn of any kind must provide temporary warmth and shelter.

I quickened my steps, and was taking the corner when a broad shape lumbered against me, swaying and muttering obscenities. I almost fell, but managed to step aside and plunge on, with the reeking smell of spirits thick in my nostrils. The inn stood on my left. There was a sign of some sort swinging over the door, making a creaking sound that became peculiarly interrupted with the rise and fall of voices and raucous laughter from inside. Remembering to keep my reticule safely close in an inner pocket of my cape, I entered. The air inside was thick and cloying, steamy with male breath and beer. I hesitated before entering the tap room, and put my valise down for a moment to easy my aching arm. It was then that a burly figure emerged from the bar, obviously on the point of leaving. In the glow of the reddish oil lamp his face showed a rubicund and rustic kindliness that somehow suggested he could be a local man, probably a farmer, and that he was not inebriated.

'Well!' he exclaimed in a Cornish burr, 'a lady, on a night like this, an' alone. Where ee bin from, m'dear, and where ee be too? Tedn' a right place for ee in theer. Travellin'? Eh?'

In a rush, because I had no one else to confide in, and he appeared honest enough, I told him I had to get to Tregonnis that night somehow, that I could pay a certain amount for transport, and that if he knew of anyone willing to take me, or a waggon –

'It's very important,' I urged. 'I was wondering whether to stay here, if they could put me up, and then start off early when the light was better. But what I have in my – in my bag – isn't enough for a proper bedroom and food, and – and –' I broke off desperately, knowing I was making a poor exhibition of myself.

A large palm descended on my shoulder.

'Midear young wumman, this place edn' for the like of you, an' like as not theers no space 'tall for virtue this night. A man o' any kind c'n take care of isself, but *you*?' He gave a gruff laugh, 'Now tell you what, chile, I can't say I've heard tell o' this 'ere Tregonnis you do speak of, but I've me cart outside an' good stout mare. Goin' westwards I am, ef I can give ee a ride – alongside, I'll do et willin', an' no questions asked. No pay neither. Joseph Killiwarne I be, an' the

Killiwarne's is honest farmin' folk – '

Well, I accepted the offer gratefully, and minutes later I was once more setting off, with someone I'd never seen or heard of before, into the dark and thickening Cornish night. He'd said westwards, and Tregonnis was to the west, in the direction of the wild North Coast.

We'd been driving only a few minutes before he asked, 'Where's it near to? This Tre – Tre-whatsit? – you mentioned?'

'Kerrysmoor,' I told him. 'Mr – Mr Verne's place.'

'*Ah! Him.*'

'Do you know him by any chance?'

'Only by repute midear, as they say. 'Bin trouble like, I do b'lieve. Some wumman.'

My heart sank. I felt suddenly so very alone and lost again.

'Oh. I had heard but wasn't sure what the trouble was. But I – ' I thought up as reasonable an explanation as I could. 'I used to work there. And I've business to discuss.'

'I see. I see. Tedn' my affair midear. Whatever business you do have mus' be important to get you goin' theer on a night like this. Funny weather. I doan altogether like et. Could be a storm comin', one o' they freak kind you doan quite know what t'expect. Bein' used to the land an' its ways, I got a nose for this sort o' thing. Ais! – a storm brewin' for sure.' He paused, and when I said nothing, continued, 'Know Tharne, do ee?'

'Oh *yes*,' I exclaimed. 'Tharne isn't far from Tregonnis. If you could put me down there, I'd be perfectly all right.'

'Depend on th' fog,' the man said. 'We'll see. I've a nephew theer, callin' on him I am, before tekkin' off 'gain, f'r Penzance way.'

I didn't ask his nephew's name, or probe in any way about his business. Neither did I comment on the fact that it was unusual for any farmer to be making such a journey at so late an hour. It wasn't my affair. He could be involved in any lucrative sideline. What lay under cover at the back of his cart was his concern and his alone, whether of a legal or smuggling nature.

So we clattered on down unknown ways and turns stopping only occasionally to give the horse a rest, while Joe Killiwarne took a nip of whisky from a bottle, and forced a little on me.

Very gradually the fog lifted considerably, revealing, as the man had predicted, a sullen belt of black cloud, blanketing the night sky. Everything was very still, but occasionally the clouds parted to reveal a thin stream of watery moonlight emphasising the deep gloom of approaching rain.

When we reached Tharne he offered to take me on to Tregonnis after his business with his nephew was over. But I refused.

'It's only a short distance,' I told him, 'and once I reach the main road I can soon be there. I don't want to waste any time or hurry you. I'm very grateful for the lift.'

I offered him payment once more, but he wouldn't accept it, and following a few more polite and cursory remarks we parted, and I was on my way towards the cottage.

The light became eerie. The overhanging heavy sky seemed to lower as an insidious rustling wind scurried along the ground swirling what remaining mist there was in grey coils over the wet earth. A few dead leaves tapped my ankles; the surface of the nearby stream quivered into glassy brilliance for brief seconds when shafts of silver-green moonlight momentarily pierced the massed clouds before dying again into stygian blackness. I found my way more from habit than sight. Every moment I half expected to hear the clip-clop of hooves and heavy wheels of Joe Killiwarne's cart approaching. If I had, then I'd have taken an offer of a lift for the rest of the way to Tregonnis if it was still forthcoming. But there was no sound of human presence or activity – only a low rumble of thunder from the distance and intermittent flashes of lightning.

Soon spatters of rain intensified. The wind rose, and I

pulled the hood of my cape well down over my head, pushing my hair beneath. As the storm properly broke, realisation of my own folly swept over me. Who would have thought though, that from such an over-quiet misty afternoon and evening, such a deluge could arise? And why hadn't I waited until the morning before making my reckless journey to Tregonnis? Who or what did I expect to find there?

There was only one answer. Rupert. Rupert – Rupert – I almost called his name aloud. Surely something of him – some sign of his presence, or that he had been there – must await me at the cottage?

I pushed on, while the rain increased into torrential force. When I took the turn in the main lane leading round the base of Rosecarrion I was already soaked to the skin. The wind had become a savage elemental force whipping its fury against me, and as a tree crashed down ahead, my head rang with the mocking illusion of wild fiendish laughter – the triumphant screeching of the Three Maidens. Gasping for breath and trying to wipe the dripping water from my eyes, I clutched at the twisted trunk of a bush for support. The ground seemed to rock beneath my feet, and when I tried to move on I was helpless against the holocaust. How long it was before the storm gradually eased enabling me to continue, I had no idea. Thunder still rolled ominously through the air and my boots were ankle-deep in mud when at last I reached the gates of Tregonnis. Moonlight zig-zagged across the path, or where the path had once been.

I blinked, screwed my eyes up, and looked again, hardly believing what I saw. An acrid bitter smell rose from the boggy earth. Rocks and stones were strewn about everywhere, and the building was just a hump of debris – no more. The outhouse – where I'd thought I could shelter if there was no one there and the door was locked against me – was merely a blackened pile of fallen granite and timber. The cottage too, – there was nothing; just nothing but charred relics of what once had been a dwelling.

I rubbed my eyes, wondering if I was suffering from some strange hallucination, but the ravaged scene only appeared intensified. A feeling of weakness made me lean against a blackened stump of tree, and slowly the fit of trembling ceased. I knew I had to get away as soon as possible. Nothing remained there but desolation; I had either to find my way back to Tharne where some cottage might provide refuge until the morning – or take the turn along the main road to Kerrysmoor. Presumably someone was in residence there – if not Rupert or Lady Verne – servants who'd take me in. To wait longer in my wet and shivering state could be dangerous not only for myself, but for the child I was carrying.

So I forced myself from the gate, and with my head bowed into my cape, made my way down the lane to the road. The rain slowly ceased at last, leaving the black and savage landscape washed to luminous sinister clarity from the moon which was now fully risen. Cold! everything appeared cold and clearly cut – black and lemon silver-white, as though a cruel giant hand had swept Nature free of growth and future life. A dead land. No bird even cried or flapped its wings from the beaten undergrowth. There was no sound but a dripping and murmuring of water trickling in streams and rivulets from the moor.

At last in its darkened valley I saw the turreted shape of Kerrysmoor crouched beneath the hill. I stood for a few seconds to get my breath and gather more strength before taking the turn leading upwards to the house. As I walked up the avenue and joined the drive, I lifted my head and stared upwards, at the stretch of wild moorland rising from the back of the mansion, to its rugged summit where the vividly silhouetted shapes of the Three Maidens stood.

There they were – primeval, stark against the cold sky, emitting a malignant elemental force that to my heightened nerves heralded disaster. Long shadows streaked like clawing gigantic fingers down the slope. At the same time I heard an ominous rumble as though the earth itself was shuddering in response. Then, before I could force myself ahead, I saw it – a dot of black, with arms outspread to the moonlight. It wavered and jigged against the sky, before leaping and jumping downwards towards the house.

Terror held me rooted where I was. I thought at first I must be in a nightmare or had lost my senses, as my fixed gaze detected another – either human being or some distorted creature of the night scrambling and crawling up the moor for combat or greeting. And as I watched, the trembling of the earth intensified. Horrified, I saw the great stones – the Three Maidens – move convulsively from their beds and with the crashing and roaring of Nature come rolling, tumbling down the moor, accompanied by great boulders and an eruption of earth and stones that claimed the dots of figures, bringing them in their landslide of destruction to the valley.

Rivers ran; the far wall of Kerrysmoor collapsed. Above the thundering and screaming of rocks and debris, I seemed to hear a frail human crying for help.

Why I thought of Rupert I don't know. But suddenly, with terrifying certainty – a knowledge far beyond human sense or reasoning, I knew he was there – dying maybe, and needing me. I ran then, rushed with an energy I'd not known I possessed – stumbling, crawling, getting to my feet again, and going ahead, climbing over mounds of mud, forcing myself against the angry streams of stones, shale and wrenched undergrowth, to the great wall of erupted moor where any victims of the avalanche must be. Sometimes I had to sink breathless to the boggy ground, clearing my eyes of dust and mud. Once I glanced back and saw the creeping filth claiming the near wall and roof of Kerrysmoor – an immense tide of hungry destruction.

I went on again, pulling myself up by any projecting root of tree or rock available, and at last, beyond the barrier came to a pit already half-filled with still slipping boulders. I slid some yards down, and then saw them – the Three Maidens. One was half upright, the other two sucked to the ground, almost submerged by rubble. The largest lay over the dot of a victim – a human figure with gaping mouth in its distorted face, entangled in reddened debris. I could have vomited, but forced myself to look away.

And then I had the worst shock of all. Only a few yards ahead was the body of a man lying flat on his back, with a stream of blood coursing from his head. A rock lay over one leg which was twisted at a distorted angle from the knee. Despite the fitful wan scene which at times flared still from flashes of receding lightning blending with the moon's glow, the features were clear and could have been those of some legendary knight resurrected from his tomb. The rest of his form was caked with thick mud.

Rupert.

I knelt down, whispering and crying his name, pressing my face to his own cold wounded countenance. He didn't stir; only a flicker of an eye-lid gave an indication at all that he still lived.

Despair filled me. I had to get help somehow. But from where? The part of Kerrysmoor facing the moor was gone, submerged by the elemental upheaval. Tregonnis was empty and a ruin. The farm? But God alone knew what had happened to that, and it was some distance off. I searched the landscape wildly, then turned my eyes again to the victims, recalling that there were two. The other – a woman – was obviously dead, completely crushed by the great stones on top of her. Her eyes were blank, wild and staring; a claw-like hand, greenish-white, was clutched round the handle of a knife, reddened by blood. Lady Verne.

I put my hands to my eyes, struggling to keep control of my nerves, and then, after getting to my feet, started running, slipping, sliding, crawling, jumping, sometimes slithering in streams of earth, until I came to a mound of bricks, mortar and granite that had once been the whole back portion of Kerrysmoor.

Somehow I found my way to a winding lane of slush that had been the road. Driven by an urgency stronger than exhaustion, fear or limitation of my own strength I pressed on, and eventually saw a small crowd of rescuers plodding to the scene of the disaster.

'He's there – ' I managed to gasp before I collapsed, 'injured under a rock – the Three Maidens – and her, Lady Verne. Save him – save Rupert – '

I could continue no more. Suddenly the whole world seemed to fade into darkness; there was a roaring in my ears, and I fell, mercifully into unconsciousness.

*

When I came to myself I was lying on a sofa in the housekeeper's parlour at Kerrysmoor. A small group of locals were standing in the hall, near the door which opened to a path leading to a side drive. I could feel the sting of something warm in my throat, and saw Mrs Treen carrying a flask and glass to the table.

It took me some moments to recall what had happened, and when I remembered, I sat up and cried shrilly, 'Rupert? – Mr Verne – have you – have they found him?'

Mrs Treen took me by the shoulders and forced me to lie back. 'The Master's badly hurt,' she told me, 'but still alive, thank the good Lord.'

'*Hurt?* Of course. I know that. Where *is* he?'

'In the study. Washed and clean as possible,' she answered. 'The doctor will be here soon as somethin' can get going along the lane – no more than a mud track it is now, and as for the house – ' she threw up her hands – 'just half of it left, if that.'

'And her ladyship?' Even in such terrible circumstances I could not keep the bitterness out of my voice.

'She's – she's beyond what this world can do to her any more,' the woman answered. 'They've put her in the back parlour, poor thing. You saw her though, didn' you?'

I nodded, feeling a sudden shame at my own hardness. But the knife clenched in the thin hand, and the expression of the face – how could I feel pity for Lady Verne when it had obviously been her intention to harm Rupert?

All other thoughts were swept away as I remembered how still he'd lain in the moonlight – how ravaged as though dead.

'I'd like to see Mr Verne,' I said, 'please let me.'

The housekeeper shook her head. 'No one'll see Master Verne until the doctor's been. *No* one. He's in a coma of sorts, and anyway what right have you?'

'It's not a matter of *right*. It's – I *found* him. I was *there*.'

'Well, I hope you're not going to be difficult,' Mrs Treen said severely. 'I'm housekeeper here, and in charge. When the doctor comes we'll see. But everyone's had a shock remember – I'm not feeling too good myself. No one is. Fanny, that new housemaid swooned and had hysterics – and William, the footman, slipped in the rubble and broke his leg. So it's up to you, including all the rest, to act as normal as possible without argument. It's a mercy any of this place is left, but we've the kitchens, the dining room and the front parlour, and the main staircase is left – at the bottom; some bedrooms too. How many no one knows yet, nor how any roof or walls stayed. Cornish granite though – that's what my da always said, you can't beat Cornish granite for putting up a fight against storm – '

She babbled on as though she'd never stop talking; I guessed it was shock; no one else could get a word in until the doctor arrived, and then, when she'd taken him to where Rupert lay, she returned, and suddenly collapsed by the fire place, her skin turned a ghastly green colour, with her eyes closed. One of the rescuers, a man I knew by sight, who'd worked in the grounds, rushed to her aid, and heaved her into a chair. I grabbed the flask from the table, and he forced a drink on her; she revived, made a feeble effort to push him away, and muttered, 'Don't fuss me up. I'm all right. And look at you – all mud and dirty marks on the floor – '

He smiled grimly, and replace the brandy. Tiredness claimed me again. I slumped back on the sofa, and gradually warmth from the fire soothed me once more into a half state of consciousness. I was aware of movement, of comings and goings, the murmur of voices, but until the arrival of the doctor nothing seemed to matter. All I wanted was to rest and drift into forgetfulness.

The rest of the night passed like a jumbled half-dream. When morning came Mrs Treen had recovered sufficiently to give orders to the bewildered and shocked staff. Breakfast was served in the kitchen, and attempts made to clean up what remained at Kerrysmoor. Rupert, I learned, had had his leg straightened and dressed, and his wound attended to. The doctor had said that later he'd have to see a specialist from Truro about the leg, but so far as he himself could judge, no irretrievable damage had been done.

How wrong they were.

When at last I was allowed to see him, it appeared at first he was his old self. A bed had been made comfortable for him in the study, and he was lying half-propped up with the injured limb bandaged and stiff before him, a bandage over his temple. He smiled, as after a light knock, I entered. There was a glow in his yellow-gold eyes that told me all was well between us.

'Oh Rupert – ' I cried, running towards him, 'you're better – you'll be all right. I thought at first you were – you'd died.'

'*Died?*' He gave a short laugh which held also a wince of pain. 'It takes more than a thunderstorm to kill a hardened adventurer like me. Don't look so shocked, Melissa – '

I was puzzled. '*Melissa?*'

'That's your name, isn't it? You can't be called darling all the time.'

'I – I don't – '

'Come on, my love. No games. It seems to me – ' and he stared at me reflectively, with just a hint of teasing in his glance, 'since you sat for that portrait you've got slightly – shall we say, above yourself?' His voice was mocking, but warm and caring.

'Rupert – ' I began, puzzled. 'I'm *not* Melissa – I'm – oh don't you remember? Josephine, Josephine Lebrun – ?'

I broke off, trembling, waiting and fearing his answer.

He said nothing for a moment, then replied, 'Another little act? *Don't*, love, *please*. Not just now. I've had a fall, remember? My horse slipped, and this damned leg's giving me hell. Yes, sweetheart, you're a very good actress, and one day – ' He didn't finish, exhaustion overcame him, the lids fluttered down over his eyes, and I realised he was asleep.

Mrs Treen came to the door. 'You've been long enough,' she said acidly. 'You know what I told you, what the doctor said, you could have just a glance and pass a word or two if he spoke, but it seems to me you've had a good old chatter.'

I shook my head. 'No – he thought I was someone else, that's all.'

My voice must have betrayed the desolation I felt; her expression softened and changed.

'Oh?'

That one word was a question.

'Yes. Someone called Melissa.'

Was it my fancy, or did what little colour she had, suddenly fade from her face?

'Well,' she said after a pause, 'the Master's known many folk – gentlemen *and* ladies in his time. He's had a great shock remember, and that gash on his temple may've set him rambling a bit. Anyway, it's not *your* worry, girl, and seems to me I've done wrong to let you bother him at all. Now come along. You look whisht enough yourself. And I don't want invalids around me, there's enough to do getting what we can in order here. There'll be the funeral to arrange too.'

'*Funeral?*' I gasped.

The housekeeper's mouth went prim, almost condemning.

'Have you forgotten her ladyship? The Master won't be able to attend, if I'm any judge, but all who are fit should see they pay due respects.' She eyed me severely. 'Including *you*.

Between them the Master and Lady Verne have done a good deal on your behalf, girl.'

'*He* had,' I admitted sharply. 'But she always hated me.'

The next moment I knew I shouldn't have spoken so, and before she could reply I'd swept from the room and made my way to the hall and out of the door to what remained of the grounds that side, and the lane.

Destruction was everywhere. Though the mud had drifted and dried in patches on the road, trees and bushes were broken from the onslaught, rocks were strewn about, streams still trickled in rivulets of filth from the devastated area of moorland behind the house. The freshened clarity of cold paper-clear skies, only emphasised the desolation – a desolation magnified by despair and the loss of an illusion in my own heart.

It was Melissa Rupert loved.

Not me.

XII

During the weeks that followed I stayed on at Kerrysmoor to help Mrs Treen in the extra work involved by the landslide. At first I'd thought I'd be sent away, and had made tentative plans to return to the Golden Bird, but when the housekeeper made it clear I could be of use to her, I agreed willingly – not only on her account but because of Rupert. There was Dame Jenny, too, who had mercifully been spared, but had become a semi-invalid.

The considerable part of the house that remained was comparatively untouched, but the constant walking to and fro of workmen employed in building a back wall as ballast for the surviving wings of the mansion, and for levelling as effectively as possible the hundredweights of rubble left, meant continual extra cleaning and brushing up. There was as well the carrying up of trays to the bedroom where Rupert was taken following the first two days spent in the library, and to Dame Jenny. A specialist, who came from Truro, sent a nurse along for a week or two. She also had to be looked after, and Mrs Treen daily seemed to be showing more strain. The housemaid had left, and only a small staff remained, so I would not, in any case, have deserted her.

My brief meetings with Rupert were poignant and painful – not only physically to him, but because he struggled so hard to get well, and because he continued to think of me as Melissa. I corrected him once, but when he clearly thought I was joking, I knew he didn't recall there had ever been a girl in his life called Josephine Lebrun. Only that other – the girl in the portrait.

At Mrs Treen's request I had attended Lady Verne's

funeral held at St Clemo's Church in a nearby village. It was a grey day. My spine felt rigid and cold from strain and the chill wind blowing. Except for myself only two or three servants and a few natives attended. I was thankful when the sordid ceremony was over, and I was once more in the carriage driving back to Kerrysmoor.

One day when Jan called with eggs, I asked him about Tregonnis. 'What happened *there?* Was *that* a landslide, too?'

We were standing outside the house on the path. He looked round cautiously in every direction as if he wished no-one to hear his answer, then replied, 'Haven' they telled you then?'

I shook my head. 'There's been so much else going on, and whenever I brought the question up, Mrs Treen pretended not to hear and changed the subject. It was the same with the other servants – the two men.'

Jan shrugged. 'I do suppose they'd bin given orders earlier,' he said, 'when she was sick like.'

'Sick? Who?'

'*Her*. The dead woman – Master's wife, Lady Verne. She'd gone funny in the head, an' so I've heard was took up country to some place where they have mad folk. Then she got away – '

'Escaped, you mean?'

He nodded.

'That's right. An' it was her – *her* who set fire to Tregonnis. I heard from him, ole Johnny Trink – only nobody says, nat'ruly. An' if you ask me – ' his voice lowered, 'she'd gone real *murderous*. Seems unfair, doan' et? A man like Master, travelling up country just to see her all right – an' then her havin' a go at him like that.'

'I see,' I said slowly. 'So *that* was it.'

'What, miss?'

'The reason for him being away so much.'

'O' course. Only we wasn' supposed to know, or speak of it. Some do say though she was a witch. An' tell you the truth, missie, one night at full moon I did see her dancin' like in a queer way round they ole stones, the Three Maidens, just as though she was one o' them. All in black she was, wearin' a dark hood thing – an' I recognised her. Oh yes, I knowed it was her. Quite near I was, lookin' for a lost lamb. I told em 'bout it at th'farm. But they said as how I shouldn' go spreadin' tales, but keep me mouth shut – 'cos after all she was Master Verne' lady wife, and harm'd hit us if I said anythin' bad 'bout her.'

'I don't believe she had any power to hurt you, Jan,' I said in a sudden spurt of commonsense, 'and I don't believe the Three Maidens were anything but old stones, either.'

'No?'

'That's what I said.'

'But they was once young women what was enchanted 'cos they danced on a Sabbath. That's what I heard from my ole granny. Turned into stone they wuz, but stones havin' strange powers o' wickedness at the full moon.'

'Just a story, a legend,' I told him. 'They *have* a *kind* of magic, I suppose – I've felt it myself, but it's just the age of them and the way they stood there on top of the moor. Imagination itself is a very strange thing, Jan, you must remember that.'

'An' was it imagination then what saved the picture?' Jan enquired in a knowing kind of way.

My heart jerked.

'What picture? What do you mean?' Even as I asked the question, I guessed.

'The one the Master had hung at Tregonnis – the lady with the bright hair. He fair worshipped her, he did. An' et's funny edn' et? Although everythin' else was burned in the fire, her face wasn'. Just that one bit saved. Just her face.'

I went cold all over.

'Where is it now?'

'I dunno. I reckon Mrs Treen's got it somewhere. I heard the Master give it to her for safe keepin', away from his wife.

Just because of her madness you know, she had a real hate of it. So it was a *kind* of magic saved *that*, wasn't it? – a magic stronger than the witches' put together. An' I reckon that's religion, doan' you, miss? The *real* kind, meanin' the power of good over evil?'

'Perhaps you're right,' I admitted. 'Yes. And try to remember it.'

He nodded and started to walk away.

'Jan – ' I called.

He turned his head, 'Yes, miss?'

'Who was she? The lady in the portrait? And what was her name?'

'I never knowed her,' he said.

'But you called her beautiful. So – '

'My mam said so. Everyone knowed it, but no one talks of her 'cos the Master forbid it.'

I sighed, and he went on his way, leaving me feeling bereft, lonely and bewildered, by a mystery that seemed to me then beyond solving.

Once or twice later during the week I sounded Mrs Treen as tactfully as possible about the matter, but she refused point blank to give any information or even answer me except to say, 'I've told you before to mind your own business about things that don't concern you.'

Little she knew how very much I *was* concerned, although I was beginning to realise that quite soon I should have to confide in her about the child I carried. For some time I'd taken pains to conceal as effectively as possible the thickening of my figure by wearing a full apron-front to a full blue dress I'd been careful to bring along with me from the Golden Bird. Somehow it had survived all my adventures. Joe Burns' remark to me before leaving Falmouth, about his new employee's description of me as a plumpish, haughty-like young woman, following Rupert's enquiry, had made me aware that I must be increasingly vigilant over my shape. But the truth couldn't be hidden for ever, and I wondered what would happen when I told Mrs

Treen. She mightn't want me there anymore – probably wouldn't. And if I mentioned Rupert – but how could I when he was still ill and thought of me as Melissa?

When I wasn't working, the problem went round and round in my head, and I began to sleep badly.

'What's the matter with you these days?' the housekeeper asked one morning, when I couldn't eat my breakfast. A sudden nausea seized me. I got up and rushed from the room. She followed, and panting reached me as I stumbled into my bedroom. I stood over the basin at the washstand, vomited, but nothing came of the effort. I just felt faint and ill, and slumped on to the bed.

'Now you'd better be straight about this,' I heard her saying firmly, in a manner that was almost an accusation. 'You're expectin', aren't you?'

I nodded bleakly, and for a moment didn't speak. Then life returned to me, and courage from the relief of confession. 'Yes,' I said, lifting my head and facing her with a certain defiance. 'And please don't tell me I should be ashamed, because I'm not.'

'That's why you left Falmouth, I suppose,' she said primly, 'to come here and dump your – your – ' She struggled to get the odious word 'bastard' out, or possibly 'by-blow', but before she could do so I'd stopped her by interrupting:

'You needn't say it. I know very well what you think. It's no matter now. The baby will be loved and brought up properly, I'll see to that – somehow I'll see to it. I will, I *will* – '

'And how? Where? In the back streets of Falmouth?' she snorted contemptuously. 'You've been a fool, girl.'

'Maybe,' I agreed. 'In your opinion. Not mine. You see I *loved* the father. And when you love – '

'Then where is he? This seducer of young women who cares so much for his own appetite he leaves one like you to bring his bastard into the world without means or a name to face the world. *Love*! I'm surprised at *you* – you'd respect from a fine family, and a grand singing career mapped out for you, looks and – yes, I'll admit it – a certain presence – and yet you throw it all away because some lying, lusting male takes you like any – any – '

'*Stop*!' I cried. 'I won't listen. I'll – '

'You'll tell me his name, girl. An' if it's anyone known round here I'll see he pays for it.'

I almost laughed in her face. Anyone that was *known*! The whole picture was ludicrous. If I said, 'Well, for your satisfaction, it's the Master, Mr Rupert Verne', how would she have reacted? *Believed* me? Or accused me of lying and sent me packing there and then? Who could say? She might even have had a stroke and died. And anyway what good could have come of bringing Rupert's name into it when he already remembered nothing of me at all?

From that point I refused point-blank to discuss the matter further, except for immediate domestic plans. In the end the irate housekeeper soothed down, following a glass of a special concoction she kept to calm nerves and ward off an attack of the megrims. The result was that because she needed me just then, I could stay on, provided I managed to keep my condition quiet until necessity demanded otherwise. Then we'd have to have another 'think' she said.

There really wouldn't be any thinking to do, I decided later, when I was on my own. I'd return to the Golden Bird. Joe and Maria would take me in, and the baby could be born in comparative comfort. In the meantime, perhaps there'd be a miracle, and Rupert would remember.

Christmas came and went. I saw very little of Rupert, simply because he kept mostly to his own quarters upstairs, and partly due to my own embarrassment. He could not yet go riding, or even walking more than a quarter of a mile, and it was painful to me to have to witness so pronounced a limp in a man who before had been so active, hardy and athletic.

Whenever we met, by chance in the house or garden, he would regard me with a warm but puzzled look in his eyes.

Once he asked, 'Why do you avoid me, Melissa? You know I still care for you. Another thing – is it wise to leave Tregonnis so often? It could be dangerous for you under the circumstances. I had to do it you know – ' His voice trailed off as he wrinkled his brow trying to remember something I knew could be a vital link in the mystery that separated us.

'Had to do what, Rupert?' I asked.

'Marry Alicia,' he answered dully.

'Oh yes, of course,' I said.

'If it hadn't been for that damned war I'd never have left, and you'd have been all right. You wouldn't have – ' he put his hand to his head. 'Oh God, what am I saying? Leave me, Melissa, I'm all at sea. But I shall remember in time; heaven help me, I will.'

I tried to think he was right, although his confusion not only worried, but frightened me badly.

The doctor, who called every week, said only time would show how deep the injury to his brain was. There might be nothing permanent at all. His physical condition was remarkable considering what he'd been through – although again, the fractured leg might never completely recover.

When I asked Mrs Treen about Rupert's references to the war, she replied, 'Oh yes, the Master had served in the Crimea and been a very brave soldier. He'd been away a year, and during that time his elder brother, Lucas, had died, after playing ducks and drakes with the estate.'

Although such information didn't explain Melissa, it did give a possible clue for his reason in marrying Lady Alicia – provided of course she had means for assisting him in getting the estate into order again. I didn't like seeing him in any mercenary fight, but then Rupert was the kind of man who once he had set his mind on a thing there was little he wouldn't do to achieve it. If only he could have wanted me that much. Oh, if only something would happen to bring us together. Even now, though insisting he cared for me, he didn't see me as I was – but as Melissa, the girl in the portrait. And I didn't look like her – not a bit. No wonder he was confused and moody, looking at me lovingly one moment, the next suspiciously, as though resentful of my presence.

One day, when I was dusting and tidying the library, he limped in unexpectedly, and said, 'I like you in that dress, it suits you – the colour of your eyes.'

I went towards him and he pulled me to him for a second, kissed me, then inexplicably pushed me away.

'What's the matter?' I asked, 'Why did you – why don't you – don't you like me any more?'

His golden eyes narrowed and darkened, became slits of condemnation. '*Like*? What a word to use. Don't dare make such a tom-fool remark again.'

'Rupert – I – '

'And don't argue, for God's sake. You know we can never marry. But there's no point in rubbing it in. And another thing – '

'Yes?'

'Apart from the rest – the barrier – I'm a cripple.'

'I don't care what you are,' I told him recklessly. 'You say you love me, well I love you. And where's the barrier now? She's dead. Alicia's dead.'

'I don't know what you are talking about.'

The tone of his voice, set of his jaw and obvious dislike of talking with me at all, brought a lump to my throat.

'All right, Rupert – Mr Verne,' I said. 'I can see I'm annoying you. So I'll – I'll go – '

And I did.

I left him standing in angry posture, with his hands behind his back, morosely facing the fire. Depression weighed heavily on me. Just then I could see little hope for a happy outcome.

January followed into early February, sprinkling the earth with snowdrops. Christmas roses bloomed behind the house, and even signs of green pushed bravely through the ground where such destruction had been only a month or two ago. Most of the land had been levelled, though the gardens had been obliterated and would have to be replanned and made later, if Rupert wished. Workmen were still about, rebuilding the large wing under the moor, although on a smaller scale.

The man I'd loved so passionately and who before had appeared so dedicated to his estate now showed only a desultory interest, giving orders and directions when asked for, but in a bored way as though Kerrysmoor no longer vitally concerned him. I sympathised deeply with his concern and the shock he'd suffered, but his attitude of giving way so obviously to frustration, frequently irritated and almost goaded me into crying:

'Why don't you at least *try*? – why don't you *fight* and live again? You're alive and strong, and in time your leg will be normal – if it isn't, you'll still be able to get about and ride, and love me – *love*, Rupert! have you forgotten what it's like to hold me in your arms and kiss me, to take me in passion as you once did? I'm going to have a child – *yours*. Do you hear? – *do* you – ?'

Yes, often I was near to the outburst, but the words never left my lips. He wouldn't know what I was talking about, and I was gradually beginning to think that if he did, he wouldn't care.

If it hadn't been for the child day by day developing healthily within me, I'd have been unbearably lonely. The dark flame in Rupert's eyes sometimes – a haunted, brooding look on his haggard face – almost savage – made me believe his personality must be dual and that two beings lived beneath his forbidding exterior. One the man, stern but warm and kindly whom I knew so well, the other cold and aggressive, akin to the wild elements of moors and raging winds and sea that tore the coasts.

One afternoon when I was not needed at the house I decided to take a walk to Tregonnis. I needed fresh air and a change from the smothering doom-like atmosphere of Kerrysmoor. The weather was fresh, but not cold. I thought longingly of the spring that should soon come, trying to ignore the knowledge that it would probably mean my parting from Rupert and that part of my life forever.

As I walked down the lane to the road curving beneath Rosecarrion I had a queer feeling I was on a farewell visit – a goodbye to the many pleasant and exciting days I'd spent at the cottage, where my true involvement with Rupert had had its beginnings. And to Dame Jenny, the quaint old lady who'd once been such a vital part of my existence, but who now, since her stroke and the holocaust at Kerrysmoor had lain lifeless in her room, and did not often recognise me. There was also something else in my mind – a sense of Nemesis – of being drawn to the cottage by a purpose hidden from me, but of vital importance. When I rounded the bend of the hill, my pace quickened, I hurried on, light-footed, almost running, until I reached the place where once the gate had been, and where the charred remains of Kerrysmoor were still humped in a darkened lump.

Fresh undergrowth was beginning to sprout pale green in haphazard patches. I stood for a few moments staring at the scene where a few birds pecked among the stones. All was clear and very distinct under the pale blue sky. The fresh breeze which had met me on my way from Kerrysmoor, was now still, sheltered by the shape of the great hill. The only sound was the faint trickle of a stream from nearby, and I remembered there had been one curving past the pool. What a strange, fey-like atmosphere there'd been about the pool. I wondered if it was still there, and decided to look.

Holding my cape and skirt above my ankles, I picked my way carefully through stones and rubble to where the back of the cottage had stood and where Dame Jenny's roses once bloomed so profusely. Ahead of me I saw the silver glint of water through the charred branches of willow and rock. At the time of the fire it would probably have receded into the general rubble, but when I drew close I realised with a start of surprise, the ground had reverted to a semblance of its original shape, forming a shallow dip where once silver and gold fish had darted and lilies spread their fan-like leaves. There was little water left there now, but the frail spring sunlight gave it brilliance, and as I stared a flash of silver light made me suddenly blink and shut my eyes. When I opened them I noticed something lying at one side of the quivering water.

I went forward, and picked it up, gazing in bewilderment. It was a delicate box made of mother-of-pearl, and shaped exquisitely into the form of a heart. One of the lost treasures of Tregonnis? But no. I had never seen it in the locked room. Could it have belonged to her? Melissa?

Trembling slightly I examined it – it wasn't damaged at all, or even rusted. The lid fitted perfectly; a small quantity of soil clung to it, but that was all. Either it had lain hidden for a period of time, buried perhaps beneath a stone, or it had been impervious to erosion by water or the elements.

I opened the lid carefully. What I saw inside took my breath away. The velvet lining was damp and one corner faintly mildewed. But a perfectly carved profile of a man's head in ivory – a miniature without a frame – stared up at me – the unmistakable likeness of Rupert, at an earlier age. I fingered the shining surface, took a lawn handkerchief from the pocket of my skirt, and rubbed it free of moisture. Then I turned it over and saw engraved in fine script writing on the back, 'To Melissa, with love. Rupert.'

An aching sense of nostalgia tinged with – not jealousy – but painful envy, swept over me. So he *had* loved her. Melissa, indeed, must be beyond doubt, the girl in the portrait – the girl his tortured memory had turned to when he'd begged her to understand why he'd married Alicia. At that moment I didn't seem to fit in anywhere in his life, except as a means to forgetting, – a sort of passionate compensation for the one he'd either lost or renounced. And now, through the accident, I wasn't even that.

How long I stood gazing at the memento lying in my palm I never knew. I was about to replace it near the water when I changed my mind, and decided to take it with me to Kerrysmoor. Even if it belonged to the past, it was also Rupert's property – something that must once have meant a great deal to him. Perhaps in finding and returning it, I might gain a little gratitude and warmth. I would carefully choose what I considered a propitious moment to bring it out, at a time when he appeared free of bitterness and out of pain. Such occasions were rare, but each day now his leg appeared to be easing. He walked more, and seemed on the whole less self-centred. On the other hand I could show it to Mrs Treen and ask her advice. She might, under the circumstances, confide what she knew of Melissa.

I was so deep in thought over the problem that I didn't hear the tread of heavy footsteps over the uneven ground. The first intimation I had of anyone else's presence was the crackling of undergrowth and sound of a stone being dislodged.

Startled, I turned my head quickly and to my astonishment saw Rupert standing only a few yards away. He was staring at me intently, with no smile on his lips, no trace of warmth or pleasure at finding me there, only a grim curiosity holding, I fancied, a hint of censure. He was bare-headed, wearing a caped greatcoat. One hand rested on a gold-knobbed walking stick, as support, I supposed, for the maimed leg.

There was a pause of some seconds between us before he spoke.

'What are you doing here?'

'*Me*? – I – I've been for a walk. I wanted fresh air, and I – I found this – ' I held up the box for him to see. He glanced at it, frowning – a frown that gradually gave place to bewilderment.

'Where? Where did it come from?'

'It was on the ground, near the pool,' I told him. 'It could have lain in the water, but I'm not sure. It must have been yours once, and you – you gave it, I suppose, to Melissa.'

'Melissa?' The way he spoke her name told me nothing.

'Yes.' I opened the box and pushed it towards him. 'Read it,' I continued. 'Look at the back.'

As though in a daze he propped his stick against the withered trunk of a willow, and accepted the memento with both hands. I watched his face anxiously, as he studied it, trying to follow any changing expression betraying inner emotion. There was none. Then, slowly he raised his head, and stared hard into my eyes, as though searching my very soul.

'I thought *you* were Melissa,' he said at last. 'I thought – oh God in heaven! What's happening to me? And who are *you*? Tell me, for the sake of any sanity I have left.'

'You don't remember what happened, do you?' I said, keeping my voice as gentle as possible. 'Nothing except that you once loved someone very much – '

'I know I had a fall,' he said, 'from my horse. It was when I returned from the Crimea – the war. Yes, I remember that, but afterwards – You're right of course, everything's a jumble. Even Melissa – if she ever existed.'

'I'm sure she did exist, Rupert,' I told him calmly. 'She was the girl in the portrait – the one that used to hang in your treasure room here, at the cottage, Tregonnis, before it was burned down.'

He eased himself on to a tumbled granite slab and sat there with his head in his hands, the bad leg stretched out straight before him. For that brief interim all the desire and longing in me for him turned to compassion – a deep need to comfort, and reassure. I suppose love has many sides to it, and I'd never quite experienced this overwhelming forgetfulness of self before.

I stretched out a hand. 'Rupert – ' I said.

He looked up enquiringly. 'Yes? What else have you to explain? You call me Rupert instead of Mr Verne or the Master. What *am* I to you? All these weeks – I recall it now – you've been Melissa. Now, suddenly, I'm confronted by a lie, some fantastic story, about Melissa dying.'

'No,' I corrected him firmly. 'I never said Melissa died.

You did. At least that's what you believe, obviously. You must have known her – loved her, a long time ago. Look at the miniature again, your head. You were a young man, Rupert, and Melissa must have been young too. Doesn't that tell you anything?'

He got to his feet, and reached for his stick. 'No. And this conversation leads nowhere, proves nothing, except I've lost my mind.' He regarded me closely, with a rising angry despair on his face, and when I said nothing, he continued, 'So shall we end this ridiculous conversation? I've no heart for play-acting. Here – ' he thrust the box at me – 'take this thing. It's of no use to me. Put it back where you found it or wear it close to your heart. I don't care. I care for nothing at all. You understand?'

The cruel words inflamed and hurt me. As he turned in an effort to find his way back to the lane, I rushed after him and clutched his coat. 'No, I *don't* understand,' I shouted, 'I know it's miserable for you losing your memory and being in pain, but what about *me*?' I broke off breathlessly for a moment. 'As you don't recall anything about me I'll tell you. I'm Josephine. Josephine Lebrun, and before this awful landslide we were lovers. It was after you heard me singing at the Golden Bird in Falmouth, you brought me here and sent me to have lessons from Signor Luigi in Truro. Then we fell in love. And – and I'm going to have your baby. Can you take *that* in? It's true. A *child*. *Yours*.'

He spun round. His eyes were blazing. I noticed that his hand trembled on the stick. Whether he believed me or not I couldn't tell. The expression on his grim face told me nothing.

Fear, the sudden knowledge that my speech might have shocked and in some way harmed him, made me draw away, step backwards, and as I did so one of my feet, the heel of a boot, caught something – some projection entangled in the furze. I lost my balance, tried to retrieve it, but failed and pitched to the ground, tumbling over the broken prone statue that had once overlooked the pool, and rolled.

As I hit the water I heard Rupert's cry of, 'No, oh *no*. Melissa?' then – 'Josie – *Josie* – '

I clutched through the strangling weeds and water, struggling blindly for support as muddy slime clouded my eyes. There was no danger of drowning once I could get a foothold. The pool was shallow. But it seemed some dark deadly power was sucking all energy from my heavy body.

In those few instants I was aware of only one thing – the necessity somehow to protect the young life I carried, the fruit of our love, Rupert's and mine. I gasped for air, forced myself up, reached for the bank, and fell again, face down. Somehow I pushed my head up, and it was then I felt a strong hand gripping an arm, pulling me firmly to safety.

I lay with my chest heaving, heart pumping against my ribs while Rupert wiped my face and dripping hair. 'Oh Josie – Josie – ' I heard him saying as though from a dream, 'I'm so sorry. Darling, darling – don't fret, be still. It's all over now. I *remember*. It was when you fell – And the baby – the shock of it all – '

I tried to speak, but he silenced me.

'Hush. Don't say anything. We'll talk later. My poor love, the first thing to do is get you back. Lie still now, that's a command, d'you hear? I'll get the man. He's waiting in the lane with the carriage. He'll help us.'

I smiled, though the gesture must have been a travesty, with mud still all over me.

'I must look awful,' I said feebly.

And then he too, gave the lopsided half-grin I knew so well – the first I'd seen for months.

'You do, my love. Quite a mess. A wonder I can bring myself to kiss you.'

But he did, and a minute later was escorting me over the brown earth to the lane. He hardly limped at all, and when he ushered me into the waiting carriage, his eyes were alight. It was only when we reached Kerrysmoor that reality seemed to register with either of us. I knew then that there was still a deal of explanation to follow, but whatever it might reveal, everything was well with Rupert and myself.

XIII

Mrs Treen was shocked when she saw the two of us enter the hall at Kerrysmoor.

'My dear soul!' she exclaimed, throwing up her hands, 'What a sight you do look – oh, not *you*, Master – but *her*, the girl. What mischief's been going on? I think I've a right to know seeing that you're supposed to be kept quiet, sir, and not be bothered by any flibbertigibbet maid who doesn't seem capable of knowing her place or where she's allowed to be and where not. I tell you, Master – it's getting me down these days – one shock after another. I do my best to run the house in a normal fashion. But how can I, I ask you? What with fires and landslides, and her ladyship going queer and dying – and now this Josephine – this French miss appearing like a drowned rat – look at the floor, all spattered up again. And that funny old Dame Jenny upstairs – full of omens she is again. It's too much – just too much – '

Rupert let the spate of words tumble out, making no attempt to stop her. When at last, with a great sigh it was done, and Mrs Treen, after a gasp, drew out a handkerchief and rubbed her nose and eyes, he said soothingly:

'I can understand. It's been very difficult for you. But things will be easier for you from now on, so calm yourself. Relax woman.' He took her arm and urged her quietly but forcibly to the parlour. 'Now sit down, and have something to liven you up.' He went to the cabinet, brought out three glasses and a decanter, and proceeded to pour three drinks. When I'd had mine which I quickly swallowed, he said, 'You'd better go and change into dry clothes, Josephine. Leave me with Mrs Treen to do a little explaining. And when you come down, see that the end of your chin and nose are clean. You *do* look rather – spectacular. It might be advisable to have a bath.'

'Thank you so much for you advice, sir,' I said, with a mockery equal to his own. 'I'll bear it in mind.'

I gave the semblance of a curtsey, then rushed from the room, and up the stairs, but not before I heard Mrs Treen saying in outraged tones, 'To think of it! – the *impertinence*.'

I didn't hear whether Rupert replied or not, neither did I really care. Happiness was bubbling up in me, in spite of my wet clothes, dripping hair, and bruises and scratches which were starting to smart.

However, when I looked into my mirror a little of my elation vanished. I was indeed a sight, and could have been some bedraggled beggar-woman or gypsy from the slums of Falmouth's dockland. Yet Rupert hadn't seemed to mind. Was it because he loved me so much or because he didn't really care? It was odd how one mood could so quickly follow upon another. But maybe exhaustion combined with my condition accounted for the creeping heaviness that gradually overcame my body.

I felt my stomach tentatively, wondering if any harm could have been done by my fall into the pool. No pain registered there, so I guessed I was all right, and proceeded to undress, for washing and perfuming myself. It was important to me, oh terribly important that when Rupert saw me I should be looking my best and most desirous – even though I might have to be uncomfortable in corsets, and somehow disguise my increasing plumpness. He'd been pleased about the baby, which had shocked his mind alive, yes. But men were queer creatures when it came to a woman's looks, and not always reasonable about cause and effect.

Although my news concerning the child combined with the shock of seeing me tumble, had so miraculously restored his past, I couldn't be sure yet to what extent or how permanent it would be. There might be blanks which would return and thrust him back into the torment of doubt. This mustn't happen. He knew me again now as Josie, and must never for a moment be allowed to forget the fact. I must so dazzle and delight him, that all the rest – the unhappiness and perhaps tragedies he'd had to endure – would fade into shadow and eventual forgetfulness.

Of course, I was being extremely optimistic, but the joys of loving can be irrational, and when I made my way some time later along the landing towards the stairs, my heart was beating wildly; even through the film of rice powder on my cheeks, I was aware my skin must have a radiant glow. I was wearing the best dress I had – soft blue silk, trimmed with small blue velvet bows and a white lace collar and cuffs. I had no time to dry my hair properly or arrange it in an elegant fashion, but left my dark front curls to fall to my shoulders, and caught the back portion of hair up, with a blue ribbon.

I had to pass the door of Dame Jenny's room near the head of the stairs, and paused for a moment thinking I heard a thin high call. I looked in quietly. She was lying in a huge four-poster bed under a pink silk canopy with hangings to match. She could hardly move, poor old thing, but was clad in her usual fancy manner, with her bright small eyes peeping inquisitively under a frilly lace cap like a perky robin. Her bed-jacket also was ornate and fluffy, twinkling with necklaces and jewels. It must take considerable time for Mrs Treen or the girl to have her looking like that every day, I thought as I approached the bed, and the whole room must take a deal of dusting. It contained a number of ornaments, and a crystal bird swinging in a gilt cage near the window, occasionally broke with a twittering sound, into brief song.

The old lady was obviously pleased to see me. A little smile twitched her lips. She made a very slight beckoning movement of her head. I bent down towards her. A spray of rosemary lay on the quilt near her withered hand. From vague words and whispering I gathered that she meant me to have it, and remembered that she had once told me how rosemary placed under a maid's pillow at a certain time of the moon ensured happiness in love. I took it, and her smile widened. Before I had time to brush her cheek with my lips, her eyes closed, and she was asleep.

I left the room, quietly closing the door behind me, and went downstairs. Outside the parlour I waited and listened. All was quiet, so very cautiously I tapped the door, and heard Rupert's voice saying, 'Come in.'

I entered. He was alone, standing by the fireplace. I hadn't realised until then how – despite my buoyancy and exhilaration at the mere thought of contact again – apprehension and anxiety still lingered. Just inside the door I paused, wondering if I'd be disappointed, recalling other times in the past when his mood had suddenly changed from one of loving endearments to the chilly politeness of a stranger. He didn't appear unduly tired. His expression was reflective and thoughtful, until a flame from a glowing log caught his eyes lighting them to blazing gold.

'Come here, Josephine,' he said, stretching an arm towards me. 'You look quite – ravishing.'

'I hope my face is clean,' I remarked stupidly, trying for the moment to keep the conversation in a light tone, I felt so nervous. 'It got a good scrub.'

I smoothed a curl from one temple, and striving to appear dignified took two steps in his direction. Then, suddenly determination crumbled, my poise was shattered, and I ran the rest of the way straight into his arms.

When the first passionate embrace was over, but still holding me close, he led me to the sofa, laid me down gently, and half seated on the edge, bent over and once more kissed me, uttering the endearments I'd ached to hear for so long a time. He paused briefly at intervals to smooth the hair from my forehead, his hands tracing the outline of my face – from temples, over cheeks and jaw, then travelling tenderly over curve of breasts. And all the while I was whispering, 'I love you so. Oh, Rupert – I do love you – '

'And I – ' he whispered, 'for ever and ever – ' A hand rested gently on the swelling curve of my stomach beneath the blue silk, and it was as though sensing the touch of love the unborn baby stirred in response.

'When will it be?' he asked presently. 'The birth?'

'Some time in April,' I told him, 'the spring.'

He stared at me thoughtfully before saying, 'Poor little devil! With a cripple for a father!'

'You're *not* a cripple,' I said indignantly, 'and you don't know it will be a boy. We could easily have a daughter.'

'Of course. And what would we call her?'

On impulse I said, 'Melissa, if you like; I wouldn't *mind*. Truly.'

'Ah! – Melissa. I'll have to explain about her, I suppose.'

'Only when you want to,' I answered. 'She doesn't – she doesn't seem so important any more.'

'Oh but she *is* important – very,' he said. 'She was the beginning of it all – many years ago, when we were both children. In her way she was the loveliest creature I'd ever known – until now.'

He was gazing at me so intently I looked away. A hand sought mine and pressed it. I could feel the warm pulse beating – almost as quickly as my own heart. I almost asked, Who *was* she? Is she alive still somewhere? Or did she die? But I bit my lips to keep the words back, leaving him to admit of his own accord.

'Yes, as you said earlier, I loved her. She was the daughter of our housekeeper at the time, in my father's day, so you could say we grew up together. My mother had died when I was very young, and Mrs Pendrake in most ways took her place in my life. When we were older – I was in my twenties, I determined to marry Melissa who returned my – passion. It was a young passion, but nonetheless sincere and overwhelming. But in the end – '

'Yes, Rupert?' I urged, 'what happened? Wouldn't your father agree? Was that it?'

'My father by then was dead,' he said, in colder tones. 'I

doubt he knew about the affair. We'd been wise and kept our affection as secret as possible. It was only after his death that Lucas, my elder brother let out the truth – maliciously, mockingly, because unfortunately he was that type of man. Lascivious – brutal in his fashion.'

There was a pause, after which I said, 'Please go on.'

'Following the funeral, and after the will was read,' Rupert continued, 'when I told him of my decision to marry Melissa, he informed me casually, but with a particularly nasty triumphant note in his voice that I couldn't because she was my own half sister – the daughter of my father – his bastard, by Mrs Pendrake. I shall never forget his words. "My dear fellow, I'm so infernally sorry. She's certainly a tasty little piece. But incest is not regarded favourably by the law, as you must know. A shame. But never mind, when you've grown up some more, you're sure to find some eligible filly to satisfy your sexual and romantic needs". I lunged out and only missed him by a quarter of an inch; and he laughed, blast him, laughed and walked away, swaggering as though he'd played an extremely clever trick – and won.'

'Was it true, though? About Melissa?'

'Being my half-sister? Oh, yes. When I confronted her, Mrs Pendrake admitted it.' He closed his eyes for a second as though to blot out that faraway scene. When he opened them again he was staring straight ahead expressionlessly. I waited for him to take up the story. 'There was proof enough in many ways,' he went on at last, 'There was no question at all that Lucas had lied. He'd known the truth since he was a youth. I think he rather revelled in it, it gave him a subtle sort of hold – or maybe equality's a better word – over my father. Neither had a scrap of conscience concerning women. They were, shall we say – of the same ilk.'

There was contempt in his voice, 'Well, the upshot of it was that Lucas inherited the greater part of the estate, and from the first moment proceeded to enjoy it. At the same time Mrs Pendrake went sick and died, she was never robust – leaving Melissa alone and unprovided for. Now the secret of her birth had become common knowledge round the immediate district, it seemed wiser under the circumstances – for her to live elsewhere, a little further out of Lucas's orbit; my father had left a certain sum to me, with a portion of land, – the cottage Tregonnis. The Crimean war was still raging; I felt I had to be there, not only because of duty, but because of the pain caused by my broken relationship with Melissa. I had to get away, somehow try to forget, for her sake as well as mine. So I arranged for her to live there with a companion – the daughter of a farmer from Penjust way. She seemed a reliable girl, better educated than most of her class. When I told Lucas he sneeringly agreed. He may have had his eye on Melissa in a certain way, but he certainly didn't *like* her; despite her looks, which he'd have ravished without a qualm given a chance, – her 'prudishness' as he termed it, got on his nerves, and irritated him. So to Tregonnis Melissa and the girl went.'

There was a long pause.

'Go on, Rupert, tell me,' I said at last. 'What happened?'

'I was away for a year,' he said. 'During that time the young woman, the farmer's daughter, got married, leaving Melissa alone and unprotected. Oh, she had her weaving and spinning, kept a few fowls and goats. And the few natives round about respected her. But Lucas, seeing his chance of revenging himself on a girl who'd spurned him, proceeded to do it in his usual blackguardedly way. He called one evening and raped her. Yes. That's what the heir and owner of Kerrysmoor did, with the result that later she found herself with child.'

His voice was bitter. Even now after so long, the knuckles of one hand showed white on his clenched fist. The jaws tightened in his lean face. I didn't speak. Trite words like – 'how dreadful' or 'Rupert, how simply terrible', would have been a travesty, and of no use at all. Gradually his tension eased, and he said in matter-of-fact tones, 'It was too much for her of course. What exactly happened no one exactly knew; Lucas was thrown from a horse one day after a mad gallop over the moors and was killed. I returned when I heard, and it was then I discovered that Melissa, too, was dead, drowned in the pool at the back of Tregonnis. Whether by her own hand, mischance or deliberately murdered will never be known. I suggest the latter, because I knew Lucas so well. Anyway – ' he took a deep breath, ' – that's the history, in brief.'

'And the portrait?'

'I'd had that painted by a good friend of mine earlier – an artist from London who came to Kerrysmoor occasionally for a visit. Later, following Melissa's death, I had it framed and hung in that small room among certain other precious relics. The place became through the years almost sacred to me – a shrine. Anything of particular beauty I could purchase, I bought and had installed there. Oh, yes, I must admit it, my love, I adored Melissa with a youthful infatuation that only seemed to increase with time – until I met you.'

'Maybe you still do, in a – in a dream-like kind of way,' I suggested wistfully, with faint pain gnawing me.

'As one admires anything that is beautiful and true,' he agreed. 'Apple blossom against a pale blue summer sky – the golden fire of summer sunset tipping the hills and passing clouds with flame – great art, and chords of forgotten music played on distant violins – oh – Josie, Josie – don't make me sound a sentimental fool. I'm an adventurer and smuggler, remember? An unscrupulous character who's defrauded the law and married a mad woman – not that I knew that at the time – to gain my own ends and get the estate on its feet again. Lucas had played merry hell with Kerrysmoor, and there were debts to face I'd never have met if it hadn't been for a bit of sharp practice on my part. When Alicia came along, highly born, apparently rich and besotted with me, I'd no scruples in using her. I'd no personal illusions – I knew what I was doing, or *thought* I did. As it happened, she wasn't quite so rich as I'd believed, and the greater part of what she'd had was spent for her own comforts and apartment in the best wing.

'From the beginning our marriage was a travesty, one founded on my own bitterness and fanatical heartache, and her insatiable craving for a husband. I knew nothing of her family's taint – of the inherent insanity which eventually flared up and made her destroy Tregonnis. Jealousy! It can be a very evil thing. She would have destroyed *you* if she could; that's why I arranged for you to stay at the Crown in Truro. But you didn't trust me, did you? You merely decided I was throwing my weight about showing who was master.'

'No.' I told him. 'Not exactly. It looked rather as though you were trying to get me out of the way.'

'So I was. With Alicia escaped and on the warpath, it was the only sensible thing to do. Good heavens, Josie, she might have *killed* you. She had a knife, did you know that?'

'Yes,' I said, and I related then the sordid frightening episode when I'd been attacked in the garden of the cottage.

He sighed. 'You should have let them know at the farm. They'd have somehow managed to contact me, or the servants at Kerrysmoor.'

I didn't tell him I'd told Jan, but that he was too scared to spread the news in case he was blamed for gossiping about her ladyship. Instead, I merely remarked, 'Can't we try and forget about it all now? Oh, Rupert, shouldn't we just be thankful to be alive, and together – and – and – '

'Yes?'

'Couldn't we – couldn't you give up the other thing – the smuggling?'

'For the time being, with this wretched leg, I have to,' he answered. 'But the house is going to cost a good deal getting into order, and when we're married – '

'*When?*' I remarked pertly, 'I never said I *would* marry you, did I? How could I, you've not asked me yet.'

He paused before taking my chin in his hand and turning

my face up to his. Then, before kissing me, he said whimsically with mock politeness, 'Dear Miss Lebrun, I should be most honoured if you would consent to becoming my wife.' His voice was restrained and formal, but laughter lit his golden eyes, laughter and all the love I'd hoped to find some day from this one man in the world to whom I knew I could be totally committed.

'Of course,' I said. 'Oh, Rupert – Rupert – I do love you so.'

'And I you – forever.'

From outside came the high sweet trilling of a bird. One day maybe I would also sing again. Whether or not was unimportant to me just then. We had our whole life together ahead, and spring seemed everywhere.

*

Our son was born on a day when the lanes and hedgerows foamed with wild cherry blossom and gorse flamed gold over the high moors. From the distance a cuckoo called; the newly laid gardens of Kerrysmoor were already starred with primroses, and the thrusting speared heads of bluebells. We called the baby Pierre Rupert – which I guessed would naturally become shortened to Piers. He was a lusty, laughing, strong-willed child, whose greenish eyes soon changed to sparkling amber. Dame Jenny, who had made a miraculous half-recovery from her stroke, insisted on placing one of her well-known lucky herbs under his pillow for the first week of his life. 'T' guard 'en against witches an' pellars and the evil doings of smugglin',' she said. There was no need for the latter precaution; due to the intricate and numerous underground tunnelling of the moor behind the house, the ground had completely caved in, and been levelled not only by Rupert's men, but by Nature.

'Still, maybe it's for the best,' Rupert said a little ruefully, 'With this damned leg of mine, and you to control, my wilful love, I shall have enough to do without further adventure.'

Which proved to be perfectly true.